David Brown served in the British Army for almost forty years and between 1969 and 1976 spent a good deal of time in Northern Ireland serving with a top infantry regiment as both a platoon sergeant and later as a platoon commander. He left the infantry for the elite Army Physical Training Corp and received a commission, eventually reaching the rank of Major, having been awarded both a military BEM and an MBE.

In loving memory of Carole Anne Baggaley, 1944 to 2020, the special person who kept me sane for so many years and gave me the will to go on.

David Brown

THE DARKNESS

AUSTIN MACAULEY PUBLISHERS

LONDON • CAMBRIDGE • NEW YORK • SHARJAH

A CIP catalogue record for this title is available from the British Library.

ISBN 9781035813513 (Paperback)
ISBN 9781035813940 (ePub e-book)

www.austinmacauley.com

First Published 2023
Austin Macauley Publishers Ltd®
1 Canada Square
Canary Wharf
London
E14 5AA

My thanks to Lynda Sweet, who spent so much time proofreading and amending my grammar.

Also, thanks to my publisher, Austin Macauley, for believing in my scribblings.

Table of Contents

Prologue

It has been said, 'One man's terrorist is another man's freedom fighter'. In my opinion, it should be, 'One man's terrorist is everyone's murderer'.

Terrorists don't care who dies in the name of their cause.

Politicians, poets and storytellers could dress it up with all sorts of justifications and patriotic prose, which means nothing to those who have been killed or the survivors who have to live without their loved ones.

Those faceless men and women who planted bombs and shot people who dared to stand against them, do not consider themselves answerable to the normal rule of law. They don't recognise any law other than their own, which they enforced with beatings, knee-capping and executions.

Many brave men and women had been taken by these killers in the night and brutally murdered, their bodies never found. Still to this day, those killers had never revealed the location of their victims' remains.

Why should they, when a weak government gave them immunity to prosecution for the most heinous crimes that they committed. Not so for the security forces who had been hounded on the most spurious of accusations. Double standards and totally misguided politicians with no grasp of the situation in Northern Ireland.

Only a few politicians of worth had any idea what it was like for the security forces dealing with the violence day after day and certainly the current political parties behaved as if they had lost touch with the reality of dealing with a terrorist war and its aftermath.

To be fair, the difficulty for those politicians who drew the short straw and served in Northern Ireland, dealing with the hard-line stance by all sides both north and south of the border was such that even one of the many Irish saints would have given up on any hope of reconciliation.

The people as always suffered the most, especially in 1971 and 1972, which were probably the most violent of the war. I say war rather than troubles as it was a war. The use of the word troubles made it sound as if it was just an annoying neighbour who parked his car on your drive.

I had made it clear in the story that the security forces did make mistakes but remember, the overall strategy was approved by the government of that time. Those in charge were having to deal with a situation that was unprecedented in our country's history since the English civil war.

How to deal with it was a catch twenty-two and that was the terrorists' greatest asset. However, the terrorists failed to take into account the ordinary British soldiers and RUC ability to take them on, no matter what shackles were placed on them.

Officers, both army and RUC led by example, fighting to keep a balanced response whenever it was needed but always hampered by political and conventional law restraints.

Now we could see the evil of the IRA raising its head again and this is when all good people of whatever religion or political persuasion should stand together, united against the stirring up of old, bigoted hatred by a few evil people and their misguided supporters.

Bomber's story sees things from a soldier's point of view during the period 1971 to 1974. This period was one of savage violence with many old concepts of anti-terrorist warfare being debunked, while new methods to combat terrorism evolved.

A terrorist war is a horrible business and unlike the old movies, the bad guys don't wear black hats and the good guys white hats. The good guys had to get down in the dirt to root out the evil, even if it meant taking the fight to the enemy in ways beyond the norm. They don't expect thanks but they do expect the politicians to show a little understanding of what was involved in dealing with such an evil cancer.

Finally, I will mention the bomb disposal teams who, day after day, answered the call to deal with IRA/PIRA bombs with little more than a screw driver at that time. Their courage and skill saved many lives, sometimes sadly at the cost of their own. I salute all of them, both past and present.

Chapter 1
1972, No Time to Wonder

Bomber woke to the sound of his stepfather's voice telling him there was a phone call for him. Still drowsy with sleep, Bomber picked up the phone. The voice on the other end snapped, "I need you back here now. We have a problem! Go to Marshalls airport. Show them your ID. There's a plane waiting." The phone went dead.

'Shit,' thought Bomber. *'Why me at this moment in time?'*

Bomber could have walked from his parents' house to the small airport run by Marshalls of Cambridge but he took a taxi as he wanted to leave a message for someone on the other side of the city.

At the airport, the security man checked Bomber's identity card and then directed him to a hangar to the left of the main building. In the hangar, he found an Army Air Corp Warrant Officer standing by a de Havilland Beaver. The Beaver was a rugged 'go anywhere' single engine, propeller driven plane that could land and take off on a ploughed field if it needed to.

The warrant officer pilot introduced himself as Bob and said, "Stow your bag in that open side bin and we will be off."

The plane took off in less than a football pitch length and headed west. Bob had already told him that he had to make one more stop before crossing the Irish Sea. The weather forecast was good with a tail wind so they should make good time, he told Bomber.

'Good time,' thought Bomber. *'If this thing can do more than a hundred and sixty knots, I'll buy Bob a crate of beer.'*

He hoped the message he had left with the college porter had been received. He had made it clear he had no choice but to leave but still it nagged in his mind that he could not deliver the message personally.

Bomber watched the patchwork countryside below as it slid by, which was the sort of thing one missed when flying up high in a commercial airliner.

'I guess this is what makes the Beaver such a good observation aircraft,' he mused.

He must have dozed off for a while as suddenly they were descending and preparing to land at RAF Cosford where they took on more fuel and one passenger. He too was in civvies but it was clear he was army, probably SAS from Hereford.

Having met a number of Hereford lads before, Bomber could detect the signs. The air of confidence and the way they moved marked them out as somewhat above the average, beside the fact they always looked as fit as hell.

As they waited for the refuelling to finish, the new passenger stuck out his hand and said, "Bill, not seen you before on this run; new, are you?"

Bomber was not sure what to make of this, so just gripped the offered hand and said, "David, been recalled early from leave. First time travelling this way so something must have kicked off."

Bill nodded, then said, "Don't I know you from somewhere?"

"I don't think so," replied Bomber.

"Oh, I'm sure we must have met! I never forget a face. You're not Regiment so it must have been on a course or a mixed op." Bill stared at Bomber as if trying to see into his mind.

"Well, right now, I can't think where it could have been," answered Bomber

The conversation ended at a signal from Bob to climb aboard. They lapsed into silence as the Beaver raced along the runway and took off, gaining height quickly. Then Bob pointed the plane westwards and out over the Irish Sea.

Bomber hoped that Jenny had received his note explaining why he couldn't meet her for lunch. He felt a great sadness come over him and he had the silly idea of asking the pilot to take him back to Cambridge.

'You've blown it again,' the voice in his head taunted him. *'She's the best thing to happen to you and as usual, you put the army first.'*

'It's my job, I have to go or I would be AWOL.' (Absent without leave)

'Just another excuse to avoid getting too close to someone,' the voice mocked. *'Think of all the other nice girls you have met and then done exactly the same thing.'*

Bomber dismissed the voice and concentrated on the mountains of Wales below, then it was out over the Irish Sea. The ships and boats he could see below looked like toys on the emerald sea. Everything was tranquil but in the back of his mind, he knew the aircraft carried him towards another day of violence and death in a beautiful country that throughout history seemed doomed to suffer the turmoil of religion, war, famine and death.

As they approached the coast of Northern Ireland, a dark bank of clouds was building up and moving in from the west. As they descended to land, the rain started; a driving rain but not hard enough to cleanse the country. Only blood it seemed would do that.

As the Beaver taxied to a halt, Bomber could see Sgt Paul Small and Andy there to meet them. They were standing by a beat up looking black Ford saloon car. Paul ushered them into the car, telling them time was wasting. Paul drove while Andy sat in the front passenger seat cradling his SMG (Sub machine gun). The way Bill greeted him, it was clear they were old pals.

"Good to see you back in business, Andy," said Bill.

"It's good to be back in harness. The Brig is a good man to work for, lots of action," replied Andy.

'So Bill is on the team,' thought Bomber.

"What's happening Paul, why have we been recalled early?" asked Bill.

Paul looked up in the rear-view mirror with a smile on his face and said, "Oh, the shit's really hit the fan, thanks to Bomber here. The Brig is beside himself with joy as he has been given a free hand to sort it."

Bill stared at Bomber who knew Bill wanted to ask questions but was too well disciplined to do so.

'Great,' thought Bomber, 'that's all I need, to be the cause of the trouble and probably the sucker who will be honoured with trying to clean it up but I'm not going south again.'

'Oh yes, now when have I heard that before,' the voice in his head mocked.

They gathered in the Brig's smaller briefing room, just the six of them. The Brig sat quietly while the Colonel did the talking. He told them all about the consequences of Bomber's last foray south of the border when he had been forced to shoot two PIRA thugs.

Not that Bomber regretted doing it. If he hadn't, two others would have died. The meeting that had taken place at a remote farm had resulted in a split in Sinn Fein. Now, there was a Provisional Sinn Fein and an Official Sinn Fein, both with members in the Southern Irish Parliament.

The split was not amicable. However, it was suspected that several senior figures in the Republic's government supported the IRA and PIRA, if not openly then covertly, using their influence to help make both factions untouchable south of the border.

The Official Sinn Fein, who were the political arm of the IRA, still followed the Marxist view that had originally cemented them together while the Provisional Sinn Fein, representing PIRA, followed the traditional Nationalistic line whatever that meant. Either way they were still both hell bent on reuniting Ireland against the wishes of the majority by any means, especially violent intimidation.

The Brig's informants had indicated that both factions were determined to strike hard in Northern Ireland without delay. Having received weapons and training from Libya and more financial support from Irish Americans, they were keen to flex their muscles.

Bomber, with his Recce Platoon lads had been given a large stretch of border to watch. While Bill, the Brigadier's SAS liaison and jack of all trades Sgt would coordinate SAS cut off teams to back up each of Bomber's OPs. Bomber was still not sure if this was a Brigade job or the Brig's own operation. If it was the latter, it was an impressive show of his power.

Once the briefing was over, the Brig who had been silent throughout the meeting called Bomber to him.

The Brig seemed thoughtful and fiddled with his packet of mints, then told Bomber to sit down.

"How are you, David?"

"Fine sir."

"One of my contacts over the border has told me that PIRA are hopping mad over you topping two of their most valuable men. Questions have also been asked by Sinn Fein in Leinster House, the Irish Parliament about British Army hit squads operating in the south."

He paused before taking out a mint and popping it into his mouth, then in an absentminded fashion offered one to Bomber who shook his head and waited for what he suspected was the really bad news. The Brig sucked the mint, then crunched it before continuing.

"O'Brian has fingered you for it. Apparently, he recognised you during the car chase and has made a point of telling everyone he will settle with you, come hell or high water. You weren't named in the questions but they did say a serving

British soldier was seen in the vicinity. Of course, our government has pooh-poohed it but there have been a few people sniffing around to see what we have been up to but I've taken care of them."

Bomber looked at Paul who had stayed in the room when the others left but Paul wasn't giving anything away and just faced front.

The Brig continued, "Your CO wants you posted out of harm's way, as he puts it. Rightly or wrongly, I have advised against it as here you will be surrounded by armed friends. Elsewhere, you will be vulnerable with people unaware of the situation. That is partly why I called you back."

He stopped talking and fiddled with the packet of mints, putting them first into one pocket then the other.

"Your thoughts, David?" the Brig asked, looking directly at Bomber.

"I'm not going anywhere, sir. If O'Brian and his dogs want to come after me, fine. I rate my chance better here than in England where I'm sure the police would object to me going around tooled up."

"Yes, quite but if you do have to go back, I can help on that score."

"It's the politicians I am worried about. You know how they like to offer up a sacrificial goat when the finger pointing starts." Bomber felt himself getting angry and breathed deeply to regain control.

"You haven't any worries on that score. Outside of this room, no one knows that it was you and that's the way it will stay."

A gentle knock at the door interrupted them. Bill entered and handed a paper to the Brig who studied it, then folded it and stuffed it into his jacket pocket.

"Well, we will leave it there for now but call me or the Colonel at any time if you need to."

He then walked past Bomber and out of the room with Bill following.

Bomber turned to Paul who sat looking at him with a half-smile on his face.

"What?" Bomber asked, a little too sharply.

"I know what you are thinking but I'm not letting you do it on your own. Andy and I want in. Bill also said he can arrange some extra back up without anyone asking questions."

"It's no good if I don't know where that bastard O'Brian is hiding out."

"Oh, I think the Brig will find that out for us," Paul said, grinning.

A day later back at the border, Bomber watched a car drive from County Monaghan in the south across the border. The grey Ford Consul with Northern Irish plates drove carefully past the hidden OP. Bomber could clearly see the four men in the car through his binoculars and they looked grim. The intel was they were heavily armed and were going to attack the RUC station in Newtown Hamilton.

Bomber listened to Dusty pass the information over the radio to the SAS cut off groups and HQ.

"They have acknowledged, boss," Dusty whispered.

Bomber nodded and waited. It was less than two minutes before the action started. The sound of gunfire shattered the peaceful country air and Bomber thought he recognised the heavy chatter of an AK47.

It was immediately answered by the wicked whiplash crack of multiple Heckler Koch MP5 sub machine guns and the heavier thump of SLRs. Bomber timed it, one minute twenty seconds to when the last shot was fired. *'I wonder how many men died in that time,'* he thought.

Dusty listened intently as the radio traffic started to flow and he scribbled in his notebook.

"They got them boss, three dead one wounded. One of the cut-off team has also been wounded. Chopper coming in to pick up the casualties."

Without taking his attention away from his line of vision, Bomber acknowledged Dusty with a nod and a grunt. Stretched out before him lay a picture of tranquillity that was the Armagh countryside, matched by County Monaghan south of the border. A complete contrast to the violence and death that had taken place a short distance away.

Bomber's mind wouldn't let him enjoy the view. *'So who else is there coming this way and who supplied them with AK47s? They must have some back up if they were going to attack a police station or were they hoping surprise would make it easy for just the four of them?'*

All of Bomber's Recce Platoon were deployed in the five OPs along this stretch of the border. Reporting anything that crossed the border, truck, car or donkey, it was all passed to the cut-off teams made up of heavily armed SAS. As always, it was difficult to identify who the terrorists were until they had been stopped and that was when the shooting usually started.

Dusty nudged Bomber, jerking him back to reality and pointed to the two cars that had pulled up at the border.

"Garda," said Harris handing the binoculars to Bomber.

Several Garda Officers were now standing by their cars parked at the border. One of them was scanning the area with binoculars. The others watched the helicopter that was coming in for the two wounded men less than half a mile away.

After a few moments of talking, they got into their cars and drove back south.

Bomber shifted uneasily in the damp hedgerow and camouflage netting that made up their hide. He needed the toilet but couldn't motivate himself to go through the rigmarole required to do a furtive shit into a plastic bag. So he just sighed and clenched his cheeks.

The day was slowly drawing to a close, several of the OPs had reported vehicles crossing which the cut offs intercepted but without any results. Once the news was out that vehicles were being intercepted, the terrorists would move to another part of the border or just wait it out.

Dusk was just beginning to make its presence felt when a heavy firefight erupted about a mile north of Bomber's location.

"Contact report from six two alpha, boss. They are under heavy attack," Dusty said into Bomber's ear as if he couldn't hear over the noise of the gun fire.

"Their cut-off group is responding and so is ours. What do you want us to do, boss?"

Without vehicles, there was little point in trying to hot foot it across country to six two alpha. Two cut-off teams were about sixteen heavily armed SAS men who could be there in a flash. Six two alpha would just have to hold on until they arrived.

Harris nudged Bomber, "We've got company, boss and they seem to know we are here."

Bomber saw that three cars had pulled up just short of the border. Men got out, some holding weapons in clear view not worried about being seen. Bomber told Dusty not to call it in straight away as he didn't want their cut-off team being diverted back from six two alpha fire fight.

Studying them through the binoculars, Bomber thought there was some sort of argument going on. After a further minute of arm waving, they all got back into the cars and drove back south. There hadn't been any point in trying to engage them as they were out of effective range of the SLRs and the orders strictly forbade them taking on targets south of the border. That didn't stop Bomber once again wishing he had more trained snipers. Zika, his best shot was with six two alpha.

As Bomber listened, he could tell the firing was getting less from six two alpha's position with just the odd burst of automatic fire.

"All of six two alpha are okay, boss. The SAS boys are reporting several attackers killed or wounded," Dusty reported. Then in a quieter voice he said, "It appears the attackers left their vehicles and started walking straight to six two alpha's position, probably without knowing they were there."

"Okay Dusty, call this in." Bomber handed him his notebook containing their own contact report.

"Seems some want to fight and some want to go home. Crazy day," muttered Bomber to himself.

Bomber decided he needed some thinking juice, so turning to Harris he said, "I think we deserve a brew and as you are the best tea maker I know—"

The sentence wasn't finished before Harris said, "Yes, boss."

Crawling backwards into the depths of the OP he said, "I'm on it, tea for four coming up."

Bomber mulled over the events. *'Their own ambush worked perfectly. Six two alpha situation was different, so did the terrorists know they were there? Or after the first ambush, were they trying to flush out any OP? Was the Garda patrol checking the coast was clear or trying to suss out Bomber's OP position for the attackers?'*

'Strange the Garda turned up, just took a look and then left just before the gunman turned up. On the other hand, they could have been a plain clothes Garda team hunting the terrorists.'

Bomber's thoughts were broken when he heard Dusty acknowledging a radio message.

"We are being pulled out at first light, boss."

Bomber made a mental note that if they did this again, he wanted the Ferret armoured cars close so that they could bring the Browning machine gun into action should it be needed.

"Here boss, get your laughing tackle round this while it's still hot." Harris thrust a mug of tea into Bomber's hand.

"No biscuits?" Bomber asked without looking at Harris.

"Fuck me! I should have been a bloody butler, not a soldier." Harris crawled backwards again and returned with a half packet of Jammy Dodgers, everyone's favourite.

Sipping the tea, Bomber felt tired and his mind wandered back to his short leave. *'I wonder what Jenny is doing? Is she wondering what I'm doing? Or has she given up on me as a waste of her time?'*

He recalled how he had seen her to her digs in Cambridge that evening and then the confrontation with the man who had been following them.

After seeing Jenny into her college digs, Bomber had turned and stepped out heading for the Round Church and back towards the Baron of Beef pub. The shadow tailing him kept pace. At one point, he thought the shadow had stopped following him but a quick check and he could see the suited and booted man still on his tail.

At the back of the church, he stood in the shadows and waited. The man came into sight. Bomber thought he looked a bit tubby. He stopped and looked left then right, seemingly confused that the street was empty. Then he walked to where Bomber was standing, hidden in the shadows.

As he drew level, Bomber drove his left leg out and into the side of Tubby's right knee. He went half down and Bomber hit him hard in the ribs. He grunted and turned, then hit Bomber back in the body with a blow that because of his off-balance position, lacked any body weight behind it but the force of it still knocked the stuffing out of Bomber. He realised that the shadow wasn't fat but solid muscle and was now ready for a fight.

'He's bigger and harder than you sucker, so now what?' the voice in his head chimed.

Bomber wanted to tell the voice to go to hell but instead he pulled out the Beretta and levelled it at the man's face.

"Okay, who are you and why have you been tailing me and the girl all evening?"

The man stopped and looked at the gun, then at Bomber. He seemed to relax, shrugged his shoulders and said, "I'm employed to make sure no harm comes to her."

"Who by?"

"Her father, Arthur Morrison. If you will allow me, I will give you my business card." He gestured to his coat pocket.

Bomber thought this guy too polite and not afraid of him or the gun, which made him very dangerous. Now he could hear voices coming closer, so he lowered the Beretta to his side to hide it out of sight. "Go ahead," he said.

Tubby removed a card from his pocket and held it out.

"Put it on the wall and then step back."

The man did so and Bomber took the card, squinting in the poor light. Smith and Drew Private Security was printed on the card with a Cambridge address and phone number.

"Okay," said Bomber, "I'm going to put the gun away if you promise not to break me in half." Bomber grinned, hoping Tubby would be put at ease.

"That's a deal. I have no desire to tangle with you in the street, so perhaps I can buy you a drink. We can just beat last orders." He was smiling when he spoke but Bomber wasn't sure if it was a smile meaning 'truce' or 'the minute the gun's gone, I'll pulverise you', something Bomber was sure he could do very easily.

Bomber agreed and they went into the Baron of Beef pub. The barman seemed to know Tubby and jerked his head to a side door. The two of them went into a small room with tables and chairs arranged along the walls.

The room lacked any decoration except a large, nicotine stained oil painting of the River Cam and the backs of the colleges. In the room were half a dozen other men and one woman. The barman appeared and placed two large whiskies on to the table Tubby had chosen.

"I'm Charlie Smith," said Tubby. Charlie indicated with his glass a couple sitting drinking at a table in a corner. "The scruffy one over there is Dean Drew and the woman is our secretary. We specialise in personal security to people who can afford it."

"Does Jenny know her dad has you shadowing her?"

"No and he and I would be very grateful if you didn't tell her. It's clear she knows you and likes you but who are you?"

"You can call me David, I'm in the army and we met in Northern Ireland when she had a spot of bother. Her father doesn't know me."

Charlie nodded, "I thought you were army, I was Army Physical Training Corp. Specialised in boxing and unarmed combat amongst other things."

"That explains the physique. The way I hit you would have put a normal man down but I don't think you even felt it," said Bomber.

"Oh, I felt it but should have been more prepared for it. It's just the sort of trick I taught on the Close Quarter Combat courses at the Northern School of Army Physical Training in York."

"That's exactly where I learnt how to do it," Bomber said.

He looked at his watch. It was well past chucking out time but no one was leaving. Charlie explained that the landlord allowed his special regulars to drink on in this room away from the public. No money exchanged hands but the drinks were put on a tab.

Technically, they were his private guests in a private room.

After another whisky, Bomber said he had to go but Charlie wanted him to meet his business partner, Dean Drew who was an ex-police Sergeant. Dean was the opposite in looks to Charlie. Tall, probably six foot three, beanpole thin and a face that would have done credit to a hunting hawk.

So another round of drinks came and Bomber felt obliged to tell the two that if anyone from over the water came for Jenny, they would need to be tooled up.

They both grinned and said they were and had special police firearms licences that Bomber had never heard of.

"I suppose yours is a special Home Office licence?" Dean said, raising his eyebrows and grinning.

"Oh, very special!" answered Bomber who raised his own eyebrows in return and the three of them burst out laughing.

Bomber made it home via a taxi and sank onto his bed, diving into a deep, trouble-free sleep thanks to the large quantity of whisky he had consumed.

Back to reality, Bomber heard Harris say, "Tea not to your liking then, boss?"

Bomber looked down at his half empty mug and saw the Jammy Dodger floating in it. *'What a waste,'* thought Bomber, *'That'll teach me to daydream.'* He answered Harris. "It was fine. I was just lost in thought."

The next morning, the vehicles came to lift them out. Bomber felt cold, damp and tired, having had to relieve himself in the early hours, much to the discomfort of the others.

The drive back to Lisburn went without incident, which was a good thing as everyone struggled to stay alert after the long night in the OP.

The debriefing room was packed. It held not only Bomber but each of his OP commanders and the SAS cut-off commanders. The Colonel quickly rounded up the debriefing by congratulating everyone on a job well done. The general debrief over, the commanders were dismissed to go and get fed in the cook house.

Bomber, Bill and Paul Small were taken to the Brig's smaller office cum briefing room with its long table. The Colonel had sent for coffee and when Andy delivered it, he was told to stay.

Once everyone had coffee, the Brig started by saying the SAS lad that had been wounded was fine, nothing serious. By that, Bomber guessed he would survive physically but whether he would be mentally okay was another question.

Being shot and surviving was bound to change a soldier, no matter how hardened he had become.

'Stop being a big girl's blouse,' the voice in his head said. *'They are ten times tougher than you, you pussy.'*

'Piss off!' Bomber countered, then looked round wondering if he had said it aloud but no one was paying him any attention.

"Now," said the Brig, raising his voice. "I've been on to my contacts about the attacks on the OP and the other group. It seems they were to attack two more RUC stations, each one in conjunction with a car bomb at the stations before the attack went in."

"However, with the ambush of the first team, one of the other teams changed plans to their cost, running into six two alpha, either by accident or design." He took a sip of his coffee then picked up his mints, fiddled with them without getting one out and then appeared to forget about them.

"As for the weapons, they were definitely supplied from Libya and they came in on a ship six weeks ago to the South. Reportedly, they also included some heavy machine guns, RPGs and Semtex explosives, so things are beginning to get very serious indeed."

Bill interrupted by asking, "Do we know if the stuff came in with the knowledge of the Government in the south?"

"They deny that the ship even stopped at Libya before it arrived in the south. We know at the moment they are turning a blind eye to events and that some MPs are secretly involved."

"As Bomber put in his report, it's possible that some of the Garda are also involved in assisting both the IRA and PIRA in the border area or at least turning a blind eye. On the other hand, we could give them the benefit of the doubt and assume they could have been hunting them."

The Brig stopped talking and picked up a paper from the table, looked at it and frowned before putting it down again.

"I have various other operations planned that will involve all of you. However, they have to go on hold for the moment. Against my advice, in the early hours of tomorrow morning, you will all be busy implementing an operation that will divide this country completely."

"We will lose all support from the Catholic community and create a new generation of terrorists because we are about to lock up fathers, sons and brothers."

The Brig sounded angry and shook his head as he finished speaking.

He then continued, "Of course, I have not told you any of this and you will look suitably surprised when briefed on this operation."

The Brig looked at Bomber. "I've not forgotten about O'Brian but he has to wait. He was not amongst those killed yesterday, more's the pity. So just make sure you stay alert and keep your Recce boys close."

"Yes, sir," replied Bomber, wondering when he would ever get the chance to deal with the threat of O'Brian.

"Okay, I or the Colonel will be in touch in the next few days."

Everyone stood and left the room. Outside, Bill turned to Bomber.

"It's just clicked with me where we have met before." Bomber looked blank but Bill went on. "Brecon Training Camp Senior NCO's Tactics course. I remember interrogating you after the escape and evasion exercise. Stubborn bastard, weren't you?"

Bomber laughed. "Seemed easier to be bloody minded than talk." With that, they broke up and Bomber walked over to his team waiting in the Lanny that would take them back to Ballykinler. During the drive, he pondered on just what he would be doing in the early hours of the morning.

Chapter 2
Internment

It was four o'clock in the morning. The woman sat on the sofa hugging a cushion to her chest and crying. She was in her early twenties and attractive, despite the tears and having had three children who were asleep upstairs. Her husband, of similar age had been handcuffed and taken out to the waiting Pig armoured car. They had carried out a search but had found nothing to incriminate the man so Bomber left, feeling they had made a big mistake.

All over the North of Ireland, some three hundred and forty men were being lifted and taken to be incarcerated without trial. Lumped together, Bomber considered that the innocent ones would now be mixed together with the few hard liners and out of bitterness from being taken from their families, would become useful recruits for either the IRA or PIRA.

Bomber sat in the Pig not wanting to take part in handing over the man to the RUC at the Crumlin Road jail. The drive back to Ballykinler was strangely silent, the lads not indulging in any banter and Bomber decided to speak to the whole platoon when they were back in barracks.

Bomber's pep talk didn't seem to lighten the mood and when he reported to the ops officer, Captain Bass, he told him that the lads were in a sombre frame of mind. It was clear that dragging people from their homes, on nothing more than someone deciding to put their name on a list, was not the lads' idea of soldiering.

Captain Bass nodded and handed a report to Bomber which told of one soldier being shot dead on one of the lifts and that rioting was now taking place in many Catholic areas.

"Make sure everyone gets fed and has some rest. I think we will be deployed to Belfast shortly."

Bomber nodded and made his way to the platoon office where he briefed Sgt Ian Mason, his number two who in turn briefed all the other NCOs.

Sitting in the office, Bomber looked out of the window at Armalite throwing a ball for Regis, the German Shepard dog he had rescued. '*Well, at least Regis is happy,*' he thought.

"Anything you should tell me about your leave?" asked Ian, standing in the doorway looking at Bomber. "It's just the lads are beginning to wonder if you have a second job."

"Close the door and have a chair."

Bomber then told him about O'Brian and the threats he had made against him and Captain Bass but did not mention about his trip south.

"Speak to the lads and tell them that if they see O'Brian, he has to be treated as very hostile and not to take chances. He's no longer one of us but the enemy, PIRA to be exact." Bomber's words echoed in his head and he wanted to add '*shoot on sight*' but didn't.

Ian nodded, still standing and looking at Bomber and said, "And what else?"

Bomber thought '*what the hell!*' and said, "You can tell the lads I get tasked occasionally to do the odd job for the sneaky beakies, nothing too serious."

Ian snorted and half smiled before saying, "Okay," and leaving the office.

The platoon was back in the old stomping grounds of the Ardoyne working out of Flax Street Mill. The Catholics had barricaded themselves in, blocking roads and reacting violently to any sight of the RUC or security forces. 'A' company was responsible for containing them, suffering a constant barrage of petrol bombs, nail bombs and shootings.

The list of lads in the Regiment getting injured was growing. The lads had already shot two men, one a gunman, the other a nail bomber but still the violence flowed.

Even the fire brigade had been attacked when they tried to put out the houses that were on fire in the Ardoyne. The last of the Prods that lived within the Ardoyne had fled, some setting fire to their houses as they left in order to deny the Caths the chance of occupying them.

'*Jesus Christ*,' thought Bomber, '*what a state of affairs! Bloody politicians couldn't organise a piss up in a brewery! What the hell made them think internment was a good idea!*'

The Recce Platoon was being used a little like the fire brigade. For instance, "Go to such and such street, a bus has been hijacked," knowing by the time they got there, it would be on fire and 'rent a mob' would be ready to confront them with rocks and petrol bombs. They had stopped wasting fire extinguishers on burning vehicles and instead worked on getting round the flanks of the rioters and dispersing them with baton rounds.

Three times they had come under fire from un-identified gunmen but no injuries had been sustained and they had not returned fire. It was frustrating and hectic with little time for any real sleep or eating meals. Tempers were fraying and there was a feeling it was all coming to a head without really knowing what that climax would be.

Then it happened in the district of Ballymurphy that all hell was let loose. Captain Bass briefed Bomber that the Para Regiment unit there had come under attack and had opened fire on the attackers. At the time of briefing, there were at least nine civilians dead.

It was not known if any were IRA or PIRA members but everyone had their own version of events and what they thought was the truth. The repercussions of this event were felt over the whole of Northern Ireland and beyond. Bomber read all the official reports that came to the Ops room and all the reports in the papers.

None seemed to completely agree on what happened and who was to blame. It was typical of urban warfare, the difficulties of identifying where a shot came from or who fired it. Soldiers under fire in a built-up area seeing a likely target are bound to open fire.

Bullets are indiscriminate and may miss the intended target but travel on through doors, through windows and through the innocent! It happens and often this is the IRA, PIRA intention that the innocent get caught up in the cross fire. It makes damning reading of the security forces in the papers and on the TV.

Four days later, the pace had slowed. Bomber's regiment had managed to contain the riots in the Ardoyne but they had shot three rioters in the process. In all, some twenty-two people had been killed of which at least two were known PIRA. Two soldiers had been killed and many more injured. Now it seemed the mob and the terrorists needed a break from the riots to regroup.

As Belfast became calm, the Recce Platoon was ordered back out into the country side, deployed on KPs and OPs. The Brigade Commander felt these had been neglected and were vulnerable when so much effort was being directed into the cities.

It was with some surprise that Bomber found that they were to deploy to an area of Armagh where it was not normal for them to carry out check points.

Bomber guessed with so many units deployed in Belfast; they, the Recce Platoon, had to cover a greater area.

Bomber, with half of the platoon covered the road between Markethill and Armagh while Ian Mason and the other half covered Keady to Armagh. The object was to establish road check points there, allowing the word to get around. These would then be avoided by the baddies who would then use the Middletown road to get to Armagh.

This road would be covered by covert teams from the SAS who, working on cross border intelligence, were to ambush any PIRA or IRA members coming in from the south. From the briefing, Bomber knew this was one of the Brigadier's operations and would have been built on solid intelligence. So with this in mind, he warned everyone this was to be treated as hot.

As they sat on the grass by the vehicles in Ballykinler waiting for the order to go, Dusty started showing off his knowledge of Armagh to anyone who would listen.

"Of course, those of us who know how to read can tell you that Armagh means high place and on that high place is a large church. It's also where the Catholic Archbishops of all Ireland have their seat. Whatever that means?"

"Shut up about the bloody church and tell us what you know about the fucking PIRA South Armagh Brigade." Harris threw at him. "I want to know who's going to be shooting at me not shagging well blessing me."

"Well now, let me see, most of the so-called Brigade is probably about thirty to forty strong with many operating from south of the border. Hence us going to do road check points there. They probably have many more volunteers who live in the north who can be called on for minor stuff. These numbers will likely have increased now we have internment."

Dusty was interrupted by Ian Mason shouting, "Mount up and let's go."

Bomber had worked out a back-road route to the check point locations, avoiding the normal routes to reduce the chance of any road side or culvert bombs. Once in location, they adopted a high-profile stance with the Ferret armoured cars in full view as cut-offs. Hidden close by, he placed two men to prevent anyone sneaking up on the Ferrets from across the fields.

Zika, his one and only sniper, he positioned on the roof of a Pig loaned to them by the MT Platoon (Motor Transport) in case they had to transport any prisoners. The height advantage of the Pig allowed Zika to see over the cars and hedges, providing a clear field of fire.

They were to stay in position for eight hours, very unusual for road blocks, which were normally twenty to thirty minutes before moving to another location unless told to pull out before that. The traffic soon began to build up as the delays on checking vehicles and the occupants brought the traffic to a snail's pace.

Every ten minutes or so, Bomber would order vehicles to be let through, so this kept the number of cars manageable and reduced the amount by which they pissed off the locals. Carefully, they checked number plates for any that had been flagged up on their list as they drove through. This way they kept the traffic jams manageable as well.

They had been checking vehicles for just over an hour when it happened. Bomber had warned everyone that it was a possibility. They were surrounded by fields and hedgerows, so plenty of places for someone to conceal themselves and take a shot. When it happened, it still came as a surprise.

The shot struck the side armour of the Pig and glanced off, hitting Harris in the back of his flak jacket. Harris spun sideways and fell down on the tarmac, where he lay swearing fit to bust. Everyone had taken cover and scanned for the shooter.

Bomber moved to Harris. "Can you move?"

"I feel okay boss, everything seems to be working and I don't think I'm bleeding," replied Harris.

"Roll over, let me look." As Bomber said this, a shot struck the Pig again just above his head, making him swear.

Harris rolled over and Bomber could see the round had ricocheted off the Pig and torn into his flak jacket side on, tearing through the layers of material but not penetrating to the flesh.

"You're okay, crawl to the back of the Pig," said Bomber.

Now shots were cracking overhead as the shooter started enjoying himself, then Zika fired just one shot.

"Got him, boss! Two fifty, hedgerow corner, ten yards left."

"Can you see anyone else?" Bomber wanted to make sure he was a loner before he sent a team for the body.

"No one that I can see but there are people gathering on a lane one hundred and fifty to the right, maybe twenty of them."

Bomber sent Cpl Jacob and three others to get the gunman and his weapon, having instructed Cpl Wells to cover them with his Ferret's Browning machine gun.

Bomber had stopped all the traffic from moving, just in case the shooting was aimed at distracting them from someone trying to get through the road block. Suddenly, a shout from one of the sentries alerted Bomber to a car trying to pull out of the queue and turn round. It didn't get far. The Ferret blocked it in and one of the sentries pulled the driver out.

Dusty was going full tilt on the radio sending the contact report, then a situation brief. Bomber let him get on with fielding HQ's questions. He could talk later. Cpl Jacobs and his men returned breathless, carrying the lifeless form of a young man between them.

Jacobs put a Garand semi-automatic rifle in the back of the Pig next to the body of the man who, until a minute ago had a wonderful life ahead of him. Now, he was just another victim of senseless violence, with no future but that of rotting in the ground long before his three score and ten were completed.

"I've unloaded it, boss," said Cpl Jacobs, pointing to the rifle. "Zika's shot went straight through the top of his head. He didn't know what had hit him."

Bomber looked at Jacobs whose face was pale and he looked grim.

"Tell the lads who carried the body back, well done. Be aware we have a crowd building not too far away."

"Ambulance on its way, boss," Dusty spoke with his face looking through the driver's side hatch on the Pig.

Just then Armalite appeared, leading a man dressed in black. As they came closer, Bomber could see he was a priest.

The priest looked angry and continually tried to shake off Armalite's grip on his arm. As they stopped in front of Bomber, the priest burst out in a loud voice clearly designed to carry to those in the cars waiting to get through.

"By what right—" he started to say but Bomber stopped him by putting his hand up in front of the priest's face and said:

"Father, you are needed to say some words but not those. Please come with me."

With that, Bomber showed him the body in the Pig, carefully pulling down the blanket that was covering the mutilated head.

"Dear God in Heaven!" the priest exclaimed and then turned his head away. When he had recovered, he started to pray. Armalite told Bomber how the car had tried to pull out. He also said there were two other priests and a driver in the car.

"Okay, go back and use the Ferret's radio to do a 'P check' on all three. Search the vehicle as well but be polite, I'll deal with this one."

The priest had finished praying and when he came back, he stood staring at Bomber in an odd way.

"Are you a Catholic soldier?" he asked.

"No Father but I believe in God and I don't think He gives one hoot which foot I kick with," replied Bomber.

To Bomber's surprise, the priest laughed and replied, "I think you have it right there, son. If only everyone could see that." He paused and held out his hand saying, "Thank you for allowing me to pray for that poor soul in there."

Bomber nodded and shook his offered hand. "Now tell me Father, who are you and why did your car try to pull out from the queue?"

"I'm Father Dowey, Senior Chaplin to the Bishop of Armagh. We foolishly decided we would try another route to avoid the wait."

Bomber turned at the sound of a car driving up slowly behind Armalite, who was jogging towards Bomber.

"They all check out boss, nothing in the car except some wine in the boot."

Bomber acknowledged and turned to Father Dowey saying, "Please continue Father but I need a favour from you on your way home, if you would be so kind?"

Bomber watched the car drive on. At the first lane after the Ferret armoured car, it turned left and drove to where the crowd was gathering. It stopped and Dowey got out. Bomber could see he was talking and gesturing with his arms towards the road block.

After a few minutes, the crowd started drifting away. When they had all gone, he saw Dowey turn and look in Bomber's direction. Bomber raised his arm in salute and thanks.

Twenty minutes later, the armoured ambulance turned up, escorted by a half section of RMPs. They quickly got the body into a body bag and loaded it into the ambulance. The S/Sgt in charge of the RMPs came and spoke to Bomber, making notes and asking a few questions. Then he had a look at the Pig, where the scars of the bullet strikes were. He also asked to see Harris, checking the bullet tear in his jacket.

"Lucky, that could have been nasty," he said to Harris. It was then that Bomber recognised him from somewhere but couldn't think where or what his name was.

The RMP put his notebook away and turned to Bomber.

"Rather you than me here C/Sgt. There's been a shootout just to the north of your location, two cars ambushed by the SAS boys. I expect the word is out now and they will be coming out of Armagh to vent their anger on you."

"Thanks for the tip off!" said Bomber. His curiosity got the better of him as he then asked the RMP, "Have we met before?"

The RMP laughed and said, "A long time ago when I was a Cpl in Aden. You and your mad Irish boys threatened to shoot my Staff Sergeant!"

"Jesus, I knew I recognised you but not from there. It never occurred to me as it was so long ago."

The RMP laughed again saying, "We all learnt a lot there, pity the politicians didn't. Got to go, take care."

"And you," responded Bomber.

Bomber looked up and saw Dusty staring at him through the open-door hatch, his mouth wide open. Bomber knew Dusty wanted to ask him questions about what he´d just heard.

"Better close your mouth or the hatch Dusty, before something flies in," he said.

Dusty looked embarrassed to have been caught listening and busied himself with the radio.

'Shit,' thought Bomber, '*that will be all round the platoon by the evening.*'

"Dusty," Bomber shouted. Dusty poked his face back out of the hatch. "Anything from Sgt Mason's location?"

"No boss but I'll check."

Bomber stood by the side of the Pig and spoke to Zika on the roof. "Good shot, forgot to thank you with the priest and stuff going on."

"No problem, boss, just aimed at the rifle flashes," answered. Zika.

"Still a great shot. Any activity you can see from up there, let me know."

"Will do, it's looking pretty quiet now the priest has got the crowd to leave. I wonder what he said to them?" questioned Zika.

"Whatever it was, I'm glad it worked. There´s been too much violence and death today for my liking," Bomber replied and meant it.

Dusty waved Bomber over to the hatch. "Six one said they heard a lot of firing an hour ago but it was very faint."

Bomber nodded and decided to allow all the vehicles to drive through the road block as the lads needed a break from stopping and searching.

Half an hour later, Dusty informed Bomber they were to pull out and return to Ballykinler. Six one had also been told to return.

'So,' thought Bomber, *'the Brigadier's plan must have worked. The baddies, alerted to two of the routes into Armagh being blocked, tried the third and went right into the arms of the SAS lads.'*

'Not sure they will fall for the same trick again but you never know. Guess our shooter was a bonus but it could have easily gone the other way for Harris or any of us.'

Chapter 3
Slippery Bastard

Ballykinler camp seemed like a ghost town with everyone but the Recce Platoon deployed in Belfast. It had been ten days since the Armagh road block job and Bomber had to admit he was getting a little bored with the constant routine of KP checks and patrols.

He had been summoned to the ops room and as he got closer, he could see two cars parked near the HQ building. Andy and two others were standing by the larger of the two cars talking.

Andy waved as Bomber got closer. Bomber could see that one of them was a woman. She was dressed in jeans, wearing a shirt with a loose-fitting jacket to cover the shoulder holster Bomber guessed was under it.

She was about five foot six tall and gave the impression of being fit and strong. She confirmed this when Andy introduced her as Chris and she shook Bomber's hand, crushing it with a strength that an all-in wrestler would have been proud of.

'Shit,' thought Bomber, *'I hate people who think they can impress by turning one's hand into jelly and broken bones.'*

The other man, dressed in a suit that had seen better days, was at least forty years old and looked a real hard case. Andy introduced him as Smithy. He did not shake hands but kept his gloved hands by his side. He was at least six feet tall, muscular and had a face that had seen far too much of the wrong end of a pair of boxing gloves.

Andy was excited and it was clear he wanted to show off the new toy they were looking at.

"It a beauty, feel here," he said, running his hand over the windows of the bigger of the two cars. "Armoured glass and toughened steel bodywork that will stop a point five round plus run flat tyres. Everything you can think of, it's got!"

He was beaming from ear to ear. "And you know what's more, Smithy lets me drive it now and again." He was almost jigging up and down now and could hardly contain himself. "Oh and there's a four and a half litre engine with a self-sealing fuel tank. This beast can do over a ton but turn on a sixpence."

"Very impressive, Andy and I'm pleased for you. When's the wedding?" asked Bomber.

Andy laughed. "Sorry, was I getting carried away? Anyway, the Brig and Paul are inside, we are going hunting."

Bomber nodded and walked into the HQ building. *'We,'* he thought, *'sounds as if I'm part of a pack now.'*

As he went, he heard Chris say, "So that's him, not much to look at, is he?" Bomber thought he detected an Irish accent but wasn't sure. He couldn't hear what Andy said in reply.

The Brig was in the ops briefing room with Paul and Captain Bass who must have driven back from Belfast last night.

The Brig beamed a welcome, stood up and shook Bomber's hand saying, "Jolly good to see you David; excellent result on the South Armagh Brigade job." Then he rubbed his hands as if he was cleansing them in some antiseptic solution before saying, "Only one problem with that. The man I was really after may have got away or maybe he wasn't even with the buggers we clobbered. Either way, the result is another setback to PIRA."

Bomber was sure he already knew the answer to who got away but the pause told him he had to ask the question.

"Who was it that got away, sir?"

The Brig lowered himself onto his chair and lifted a packet of mints from the desk top and began to fiddle with them before replying.

"Your old friend, O'Brian. He should have been with those we ambushed but we know two got away but as those left behind were dead, we couldn't ask them who it was. However, the RUC are checking fingerprints in the cars for me, so I might get an answer as to who the missing ones are."

The Brig took a mint out of the packet, put it in his mouth and crunched. "We believe he is now in the north, recruiting volunteers to go south to be trained. I have a list of possible locations that he is working around. I want you, with Sgt Small, Andy and Sgt Picket to go looking for him."

Bomber noticed that Paul smiled when the name Picket was mentioned by the Brig. "Who's Picket, Sir?" Bomber asked innocently.

"She is one of our new combat intelligence operators." The Brigadier stared at Bomber. "Not anti-female on the front line, are we David?"

"Not at all, sir. Just one question, did you select her or was she foisted on you?" Bomber knew he was close to being giving a serious reprimand but after the last encounter with a devious female on the team, he felt he had a right to ask.

The Brig didn't seem to mind the question. In fact, he smiled and replied, "I selected her myself, seems her robust ways and sharp mind were a little too much for her last unit."

'Okay,' thought Bomber, 'another misfit that works for the Brig! Now I'm in good company.'

The Brig went on, "Starting today, what's left of it, I want you out there looking for O'Brian before he recruits and trains anymore would-be terrorists. I know he plans to have the best of them shipped to Libya for training. I have given a list of known locations and contacts to Captain Bass. You can work out a plan and co-ordinate it with him."

The Brig got to his feet saying, "I have to go to London to see my masters but Captain Bass will liaise with the Colonel until I get back. Good hunting and if possible, bring him in alive. I would like to talk to him."

With that he left, striding out as if he was an athlete warming up for a hurdles race. As he got to the door, he stopped and waved Bomber over to him. Bomber complied.

"Jenny Morrison," he said speaking quietly, "not a good idea David, could be very dangerous for her as well as you." Bomber felt stunned but before he could say anything, the Brig had gone.

Bomber felt deflated, then in a split second, angry. He churned it over in his mind, 'Charlie must have informed her father, guess he had to, then the father must have spoken to the Brig. Shit, I really like her but the Brig is right, or is he?'

As Bomber walked back into the room, Paul slapped him on the back saying, "Good to see you again. I'll get the other two in and we can start planning."

"Before you do that, tell me about Picket."

Captain Bass interrupted, "I'm going to have some coffee and sandwiches sent over from the cookhouse as it's close to lunch time so we can get the planning done without having to take a break."

"Thanks sir, what about Sgt Mason and the platoon?" Bomber asked. "I would like a patrol not too far away from us when we are out and some OP work if we can do it?"

"I'll brief him and we will do that. The Brig said you are to have whatever you needed and the CO has agreed," said Captain Bass.

Paul sat and looked at Bomber, then began. "Sgt Pickett, Christine likes to be called Chris. Age twenty-five, joined the WRAC (Women's Royal Army Corp) aged eighteen and was picked up by the intel boys as a high flyer. She's smart, thinks outside the box all the time and that's why the group she worked for couldn't handle her."

"Wouldn't conform to her boss's ways. Close quarter skills are some of the best I've seen and she excelled at unarmed combat. Very fast, maybe even faster than you. Can shoot the eye out of a fly at ten paces. Only one problem, she is a little too keen to get out on the ground and prove to everyone that she is as good in the field as well as in the office."

"And the accent, where's that from?" Bomber asked.

"She was born in Belfast of a Prod family. They all left for Liverpool when she was nine years old. Her family are still in Liverpool and she thinks of herself as a Liverpudlian."

"Tell me some more about Andy."

"Andy was SAS, had a run in with an officer on an operation. He refused an order which turned out to be the right thing to do or they would have been killed. But the shit still hit the fan. The officer was backed and Andy took the shit. After that, Andy put his ticket in and now works for the Brig as a civilian contractor."

Bomber sat quietly thinking, *'Team of four. Paul, I know and trust, Andy I know but not done any ops with him, except to have him along for the ride but ex SAS, that's good. Chris, anxious to prove herself and I have no idea how she will react if we run into real trouble. We are going to need more on this than just four of us.'*

"I'll get them in then, shall I?" Paul asked.

"Perhaps wait until the lunch arrives. I think we should rough out a plan that Captain Bass agrees to before we get them in. Then we can present it and see how they react."

By the time the sandwiches had arrived, they had agreed as to how the operation should be conducted. Captain Bass hashed it around into a working plan. With some suggestions from Paul, finally Bass agreed the plan.

Bomber felt more confident that Bass had shaped the plan as he respected his judgment probably more than anyone else when it came to putting a workable plan together. Still, a lot would be off the cuff when they were on the ground reacting to what unfolded.

The Brig's list included known associates' addresses, pubs and clubs, some thirty locations that they could not hope to cover but the majority were in three towns, Portadown, Dungannon and Cookstown. That was where Bass and Bomber had decided to concentrate the team's efforts.

So it was back to watching and waiting, eliminating faces from wanted lists. They all knew that this operation could throw up more than just O'Brian and the opportunity should not be squandered to net as many terrorists as possible but without giving away the main target.

Captain Bass had approved the use of half the Recce Platoon to help them cover those places on the list. All the Recce lads knew O'Brian and now considered him a traitor to be captured or killed. They didn't see him as a traitor to any political cause or country but to the Regiment and themselves. That was his big sin and that's what made them all determined to track him down.

They had been checking addresses during the daylight hours for three days in Dungannon and now they were staking out Donaghy's Bar on Williams Street. The rain had started again. It had been drizzling on and off all day, annoying for the two in the car as it caused the windows to steam up, making it obvious someone was in the car.

In the dark and with the rain, it was easier to be one of the un-noticed outside. Bomber knew O'Brian would send in scouts, local lads who knew the area and the people in it before turning up himself.

Bomber was standing with Chris in a shop doorway. Chris was dressed as one would expect a local lass would for a night out. They looked like a courting couple while watching the entrance to the pub but they could only linger for about twenty minutes before moving on or they would stand out like a sore thumb and then someone unpleasant would be sent to check on them.

"What about him?" Chris said as a man in his early thirties approached the bar. Bomber looked and studied the man for a minute before answering.

"No, too tall but the face is familiar."

Chris pulled out a small booklet and flicked through the pocket-sized mug shots, "Him?"

Bomber looked and thought, *'The girl's good.'* He thought, *'That could be O'Malley, John Ryan, a known PIRA man.'*

"Might be O'Malley," he replied, "but he normally hangs out in Portadown. Come on, let's walk." Bomber pulled the hood of his jacket up and put his arm around her shoulder. She in turn put her arm around his waist and they strolled slowly along the pavement on the opposite side of the road to the pub.

As they drew level with the pub, a car drew up and two young men got out and the car drove off. One of the lads, tall and skinny, stayed outside looking up and down the street while the other went inside.

Bomber stopped and pretended to kiss and hug Chris while she watched over his shoulder.

"The other one's back out and talking to the skinny one," Chris whispered. "Wait, he's gone back in."

They walked on slowly to the corner and started the hugging again. "He's back out. They're looking at us."

"Okay, I want you to shout at me and slap my face, then walk off around the corner and wait there."

Chris pushed herself away from Bomber.

"You dirty bastard," Chris shouted, catching Bomber a little off guard by the volume of her voice. Her slap was not half-hearted. The stars and giddiness only lasted a second and Bomber took a step back as she shouted at him again. "What sort of girl do you think I am, you shit?"

With that, she turned and flounced off.

Bomber stood and rubbed his face while half watching the two men. They were both laughing and one jeered at Bomber.

"Yer not get your leg over tonight then," the tall skinny one shouted.

Bomber held his hands out to his sides and shrugged then walked off following Chris, the laughter still ringing in his ears.

He caught up with Chris just around the corner. They ran round the block, back to the car which they'd left parked in a side street, just a hundred yards from the pub.

Andy was standing on the opposite side of the street to the car where he had a view of the pub. Paul was at the corner doing the same. When he saw Bomber and Chris return, he came to them saying in a low voice. "Good show; while you were going round the block, a car cruised by. Three men inside, they never saw us."

Then a low hiss from Andy made them all step back into the shadows as a car drove past on Williams Street.

"That's the same one," Paul said.

The car pulled up outside the pub and two men got out. The stockier one of the two had stopped and looked up and down the street and Bomber took a sharp intake of breath as despite the new facial hair, he recognised O'Brian.

Chris spoke, "So that's him, is it?"

"Yes, that's him. A little stockier perhaps and sporting a beard but it's him alright," replied Bomber.

Calling Andy over, he asked, "When you did the recce on the back area of the pub, did you see any possible escape routes?"

"Not any obvious ones but as I said then, I don't think he would pick a location that didn't have one."

Bomber went and sat inside the car. Opening the glove compartment, he switched on the radio hidden inside. "Hello six two this is six zero alpha, we have contact, target inside with ID twelve, over."

ID twelve was the number on the photo book showing O'Malley.

"Six two roger moving now, out," came the reply.

Bomber waved the others over. "Okay. Paul, you and Andy will take care of the two outside. Chris and I are going into Sloane Street at the back. Just in case, six two will be here in five minutes. Once they have entered the pub, you two come round the back just in case we need help."

Paul and Andy acknowledged and Bomber saw Andy remove a small black cosh from his pocket, slipping the strap over his wrist. He then slid the cosh up his sleeve. Andy saw that Bomber had noticed and smiling said, "Saves breaking the knuckles on their thick heads."

Paul and Andy walked towards the pub acting like they had already had more than enough to drink. Once they could hear the vehicles of six two, they would clobber the two men standing guard outside the pub to prevent them warning those inside.

Chris and Bomber quickly moved back the way they had come in order to cross over the junction to Sloane Street. If there was a back exit to the bar, this would be where anyone using it would appear.

There they stood in the shadows and waited. Bomber took deep breaths to calm himself, noticing that Chris seemed relaxed and confident. Opposite them was a large brick building with double wooden doors closed and locked. To one side was a large dirty picture window with a notice taped in one corner saying Murphy's repair shop was closed.

They heard the Ferret and Land Rover pull up at the pub and the sound of shouting. Then nothing, Bomber pulled the Motorola radio out of his inside pocket to check it was on when it broke into life.

"Boss," it was Andy, "got ID twelve but the target plus one have gone out the back. We can't find him."

"Okay, get the car. Meet us at the back."

Chris indicated that she had heard and had her pistol in her hand. The car pulled up in record time and Paul and Andy jumped out, pistols ready.

'Where the devil is he?' wondered Bomber. Then the dirty picture window of the building exploded as bullets ripped through the glass, narrowly missing Bomber and Chris. Bomber ducked and ran to the side wall of the building out of the line of fire.

Chris had stood firm, pumping rounds back at the window from her nine-millimetre Browning, only stopping when she had to change mags. Bomber waved her over to the side of the window.

"Chris, stay here. Paul, you and Andy cover each end of the street," said Bomber as he knocked out the last of the glass from the window. He was climbing through when Chris caught his arm.

"I'm coming with you."

"Like hell you are, if he gets me and doubles back, I need you here to kill the bastard." Bomber shrugged off her hand, then fell through the window onto the floor, cutting his knuckles on broken glass as he did so.

He ignored the pain and ran through the building in the dim glow of a security light, cursing as he cracked his shins on some sort of machinery. *'Slow down and think,'* the voice in his head warned him. Stopping, he listened; then a sound, steps, someone going up some stairs. Bomber edged forward, the Beretta in his hand. He didn't remember when he had taken it out but it was cocked and ready.

Then the sound of a door being opened and closed. Bomber stared. His eyes had adjusted to the gloom and could now make out a stairway going up to what looked like a glass fronted office. Then a flicker of movement and Bomber raced to the stairs taking them two at a time, not worrying about how much noise he made.

Opening the door he went in on all fours, two shots smashed through the glass of the door at chest height. Bomber held his fire and moved round a pile of cardboard boxes.

'What's that?' the voice in his head said, then answered, 'It's a window opening, he's climbing out the back of the building. Where the hell does that lead to?'

Bomber was up and running. He could feel the cold air coming through the window. Then he looked out. Below him was about a twenty-foot drop to a narrow alley where he saw a shadow moving along it towards the street which ran at ninety degrees to Sloane Street.

Bomber was wondering how O'Brian hadn't broken his legs jumping down, then he saw the old iron drain pipe at the side of the window. Grasping it, he swung out and shimmied down. A fleeting memory of doing the same from his bedroom window as a child flashed through his mind. Then he was down in the alley, running after the shadow. The shadow was almost at the end of the alley when Bomber called out.

"Army. Stop or I'll shoot."

The shadow stopped. Bomber moved closer, all his instincts telling him to shoot now but the orders were clear and he held his fire. Then the shadow spun round, firing wildly. Bomber ignored the shots hitting the wall to his side. He stood still and squeezed the trigger twice.

The shadow staggered backwards and dropped to the ground. Bomber felt his heart pounding as he moved to the figure, keeping his Beretta aimed at the body. As he got closer, he had a cold feeling creeping through his body, gripping his pounding heart.

He knew before he looked at the face; it wasn't O'Brian. As he knelt by the gunman, he sensed rather than heard a car driving by and looked up just in time to see O'Brian's face peering at him from the rear passenger seat.

"Shit, shit you bastard," Bomber screamed in rage and jumped out into the street, firing at the back of the speeding car. The Beretta clicked on empty just as Paul came running up from the corner of Sloane Street.

"Get the car, get the car, the bastard's getting away," Bomber shouted. His fury was clear for all to hear.

Paul was already on his radio and a few seconds later, Andy pulled up with Chris in the front passenger seat. The two of them jumped in the back. Paul used the radio to update six two on the body in the alley.

"Go Andy, put your foot down, he's got a good head start," Bomber shouted in his frustration.

Andy raced the car to the end of the street, took a left then onto the main road going south. They all knew they had lost O'Brian but they searched for over an hour anyway.

"Jesus, how the hell did we miss him?" Bomber thumped the door panel in frustration.

"He must have had an alternative way out. He couldn't have got past six two and the other guy was just a diversion to keep us occupied," Chris replied.

"Yes, I know. They know the layout of the places they use better than us, which means they can plan several escape routes should they need them," said Bomber.

Back in Ballykinler, Captain Bass chaired the debriefing. The team plus Sgt Ian Mason, Cpl Wells and Cpl Jacobs were all present.

"Okay, let's start with the positives, we have one wanted man in custody, two minions and one dead PIRA gunman who was also on the wanted list. The two minions who you brought in," he indicated Ian Mason, "will be charged with assault by the RUC." He paused and took a sip of coffee. "Now how do we think O'Brian got away? Sgt Mason, you lead on this."

Ian cleared his throat and put down his coffee mug. "We went in fast and secured the bar, I'm pretty sure O'Brian wasn't in the bar or the back room which we occupied in seconds. Cpl Wells did the upstairs and it was empty."

"Well we know he went in, so where did he go?" Bass asked the room.

Cpl Jacobs spoke. "There's a side door, sir that went into a sort of dividing yard with a door into the next building but it was locked solid."

"Right C/Sgt, what happened outside?" Bomber related the events, getting confirmation from Chris and the others.

"Well, the dead man was wanted for the murder of two RUC officers and was believed to be hiding in the south. So something important brought him north with O'Brian," said Bass.

The debriefing rambled on, the tactics used were dissected and reassembled. Then everyone went for food and sleep.

Bomber found sleep eluded him to start with and when he finally fell asleep, he was plagued by the dream that had haunted him for years. It never changed and he woke sweating and feeling sick.

Chapter 4
The Pugilist

Bomber and the team were in the area known as the murder triangle. They had been watching houses and pubs in Banbridge and were now on their way to Portadown to visit a pub called Brankins. They pulled up in Obins Street and observed the comings and goings.

After a few minutes, they drove around the area to get the lie of the land. In Portadown, the two communities had a clear divide marked by a large area of waste ground which had once been part of the railway. The Caths occupied the area over on Obins Street side and the Prods the other.

Darkness had descended and lights had come on in the shops, houses and bars, giving the buildings a softer tone. The darkness also made it easier for them to become invisible while they watched.

The plan was for Andy and Chris to go into the bar, have a drink, scan the place and then come out, walking away from the pub and car. Bomber and Paul would watch and make sure they were not followed. Then once they were out of sight of the pub, they would pick them up in the car.

Bomber and Paul watched as the pair entered the pub arm in arm. "What do you think of her so far?" Paul asked.

"Chris has done well, followed orders and acts the part required of her." Bomber rubbed his cheek in memory of the slap. "Packs a punch too!"

Paul laughed, then adjusted the rear-view mirror to ensure that no one could approach unobserved. Bomber continued, "She stayed cool when the shooting started. She will be even better if she takes more care of herself when the bullets are flying."

"Ha," Paul laughed, "that's the kettle calling the pot black!"

"What do you mean by that?" Bomber asked in genuine surprise.

"On your own, chasing a target through a dark building and an alley way!" exclaimed Paul. "Knowing he was armed, you crazy devil."

Bomber reflected on that, perhaps he was right and made a mental note to take more care and have some back up in future.

Twenty minutes crept by, then they saw Chris and Andy come out of the bar hand in hand, walking along the street away from the car. A minute later, a man in a leather jacket came out of the bar, he looked left then right, turned and followed the couple.

Matching their pace, the man stayed on Andy and Chris. Bomber got out of the car and followed, his right hand in his coat pocket gripping the Beretta. The couple turned the corner, the man increased his pace, paused at the corner then followed. Bomber did the same, staying about fifty paces behind the man who was so engrossed with the pair that he hadn't once looked behind him.

Bomber knew Paul was following in the car and it wouldn't be long before he drove past and parked somewhere ahead. Bomber quickened his pace to close the gap.

Andy and Chris must have realised they were being followed as they paused in a shop doorway where they embraced and kissed. The man following stopped and turned away only to come face to face with Bomber who shoved him in the chest with the Beretta and said, "Keep walking, one wrong move and you're dead!" The man nodded before turning back towards Andy and Chris who were now watching.

Paul pulled up beside Bomber who grabbed the collar of the man's jacket and yanked it half way down his back so his arms were trapped. Andy and Chris arrived and Andy bundled the man into the rear seat. Bomber got in next to him so he was sandwiched between himself and Andy.

Chris got in the front and Paul drove off until they were on the outskirts of the town. Pulling off the main road onto a country lane, Paul found a place to stop.

"He's clean," said Andy, having frisked the man.

He looked frightened but not cowed. He was about thirty years old, Bomber guessed, stocky with thinning hair and a ruddy complexion. Putting his face very close to their unhappy passenger, Bomber said. "Let me tell you how this works, I ask you a question, you answer. If you don't answer, then my friend here," Bomber nodded to Andy, "will inflict some pain."

Andy grinned the sort of grin only a sadistic maniac could produce and Bomber felt the man shudder.

"Now, what's your name?"

"Joseph O'Connell and I work for you fuckers!"

An hour later sitting beside Lough Neagh, Joseph O'Connell told them his story. He had turned informant after his brother, who was on the periphery of PIRA was shot dead by the IRA in a local feud.

"I work part time in Brankins Bar as a general dogsbody and I pick up lots of useful gossip. When these two came in, I thought they were PIRA scouts. There's something going down tonight but I don't know what it is. Security is tight and they have a room upstairs that the PIRA boys use."

Bomber's mind was working overtime. "When are you due back in the bar?"

"Eight, that's when it gets busy."

Bomber looked at his watch, an hour and a half to go. Could he get the Recce Platoon organised in time? Did anyone see them snatch O'Connell? Could he risk letting him go and informing on them to PIRA? He obviously hated the IRA but might be working with PIRA and playing a double game with the security forces.

"Watch him, Andy. Paul, Chris come with me," Bomber ordered.

Bomber walked away from the car and stood by the water's edge. The other two joined him. They stood in silence for a moment then Paul spoke.

"I don't think we can release him to go back to the pub, too much of a risk," said Paul. Bomber was looking at the dark water of the lough, listening to Paul and Chris discussing the options. Finally, he interrupted.

"We have one section within ten minutes of us. The others will all have to come from Ballykinler and we only have one hour fifteen minutes."

Chris spoke up. "I think Andy and I should go back in for a couple of drinks and then come out when we have spotted the target. Then everyone can move in fast."

"I don't like that," Paul said. "If Chris and Andy go in and are spotted as strangers, O'Brian may call the meeting off or have Chris and Andy taken out the back and topped." Paul spoke with conviction, Chris agreeing it was a possibility but she still thought it worth the risk.

Bomber was weighing up the options and the risks of which there were plenty.

"Okay, there are risks but this is what we will do." They all listened as Bomber outlined the plan.

The car was parked in a side street off Obins Street, a short distance from the bar. Andy and Chris went into the bar. Bomber knew he was taking a chance as he had also allowed O'Connell to go in to work and he had arranged a set of signals between him and Andy and Chris when targets came in.

Bomber had warned O'Connell if he betrayed them, he would hunt him down and kill him. O'Connell looked as if he believed him. Bomber and Paul got out of sight as best they could on the corner of Parkside.

Cpl Wells, with his section was parked off the main road in King Street meaning he could be with them in a couple of minutes. Back up was on its way from Ballykinler but would take another hour at least and had to stay further out to avoid arousing suspicion.

The rain started and Bomber pulled his jacket collar up. *'Just what we needed, a bloody soaking,'* he thought. He looked over the street trying to make out Paul but failed. For a big man, he melted into the background with ease.

Andy and Chris emerged from the bar, then hugged and kissed four times, the signal that four targets were in the bar. Andy made to walk off with Chris but she pulled his arm and dragged him back towards the bar but Andy resisted and they walked away.

The Dicker (lookout) was trying to shelter from the rain in the doorway. He laughed at them, then shrugged his shoulders and went in out of the rain.

Bomber was just about to give his orders over the radio when a car drove slowly along the street with two men inside. It stopped outside the bar and the men got out, walking quickly away without locking the car.

The light went on in Bomber's head and he shouted, "Paul, get after those two and call Wells to help you. I'm going to get everyone out of the bar. It's a car bomb!"

Paul, while talking into his radio, sprinted after the two men who were disappearing quickly.

Bomber shouted at Andy and Chris to run. Bomber had only gone about four paces when the car exploded. It felt like a tidal wave of fury had hit Bomber. The air was sucked from his lungs as he was thrown backwards along the pavement. The force of him hitting the concrete made him gasp in pain, then it was as if rain was falling but instead of water, it was debris. Bomber struggled to sit up.

His mind was telling him to move but his body was telling him to lay still and have a rest as it was too painful to get up.

He could see Andy and Chris staggering out of a doorway towards him. Andy was mouthing words but Bomber could not hear what he was saying until he and Chris lifted Bomber to his feet.

"Shit, shit," Andy was shouting. "The bastards, no warning; if we hadn´t got into that doorway, we would have been dead."

"Where's Paul?" Chris asked.

Bomber pulled the radio from his jacket pocket. "Paul, where are you?" His voice sounded a long way off.

Paul responded, "Half way down Park Road. Six two's after one of them, the other got away across the park."

"Stay there. We're coming."

Bomber looked at the bar. The windows and door had gone, having been blown inwards by the blast adding to the carnage inside. The car was a twisted, smouldering wreck. People were staggering out into the street, dazed and bleeding, holding each other up. Then the crying and screaming started.

Bomber felt sick and angry that he had not been able to stop it. *'Jesus,'* he thought, *'I hope Joseph is okay.'* Bomber knew they couldn't stay and help as they would be picked up by the police and out of action for hours, maybe even turned on by the people from the surrounding houses who were beginning to gather to help the injured.

As they drove to pick up Paul, they could hear sirens as the fire brigade and ambulances raced to the scene.

"How did you know it was a car bomb?" Chris asked, picking blast debris from her hair and jacket.

"Two men park a car outside a pub, don't go into the pub, don't lock the doors and leg it fast. Can't be anything else!"

Paul was standing by the park and Andy pulled over to allow Paul to jump in.

"Sorry," he said, "the bastard was fast and by the time I got here, he was nowhere to be seen."

"Where to now?" Andy asked.

Bomber felt drained and looking at the others, he knew they were fighting back the horror of the bomb. *'We all need a stiffener,'* thought Bomber.

"Take us somewhere we can get a drink in relative safety. If we hang around here, we will be picked up by the security forces," Bomber answered. "Chris, call Wells and the others, tell them to go back to base."

Andy spoke up, "I know a safe pub, been there before with Bill." He then drove in silence to the outskirts of Lurgan, pulling into the car park of a busy pub. The place was packed and it was clear everyone was drinking in hard time. Paul pushed his way easily to the bar, everyone standing aside for him.

Then a cry went up, "He's here!"

Bomber put his hand in his pocket and gripped the Beretta noticing that Andy and Chris did the same as they looked around.

Suddenly, two middle-aged men came out of the crowd. The fatter of the two put out his hand to Paul and said. "Thank God you made it. It's the best crowd we have had for years and money is changing hands in the thousands. So come on, we have to get started."

With that, they led the way out into the back yard of the pub where an improvised boxing ring had been rigged. The crowd was jammed tight, right up to the ring. When they saw Paul, a great cheer went up.

"Fuck me," said Andy. "It's a bare-knuckle pub fight and they think Paul is the opponent."

"Right, we are out of here," said Bomber, trying to turn round but was trapped by the press of the crowd.

"Wait," said Paul, "there's money in this."

"Are you mad?" Bomber snapped. "Have you seen the gorilla in the ring swinging his arms around?"

Paul ignored Bomber. "Right, how much money have you all got? Andy, find the guy taking the bets and put it all on me to win." As Paul said it, he pushed a large wad into Andy's hand.

"Come on, cough up," Andy nudged Bomber who emptied his pockets of the twenty-six pounds he had. Andy grabbed it and took thirty pounds from Chris.

Paul gave his jacket to Bomber who could feel the comforting weight of the pistol in the pocket, Bomber thinking that Paul should take it with him into the ring! Paul climbed into the ring and when he stripped his shirt off, a hush went over the crowd.

Bomber knew Paul was a big man, you couldn't fail to notice that but his physique would have put Charles Atlas to shame and there were scars that could clearly be seen. Paul walked over to the fat man in the ring and whispered into his ear. Fat man seem startled at first but quickly pulled himself together.

Bomber wedged himself by the corner post where there was a bucket of water with a sponge, a large towel and a stool.

The fat man raised his hands and the crowd became quiet. "Gentlemen, there is a change in the programme. The opponent tonight against our six counties bare knuckle champion is the Manchester Mauler, undefeated in thirty fights, so let's give him a great Luuuurgan wellllllllcome." The crowd whistled and jeered and again Bomber wished they were somewhere else.

"Now, let's hear it for our own champion, Pat O'Leary." The crowd went wild and Bomber had the feeling this whole thing was definitely not a good idea. There must have been five hundred people crammed into the yard with more in the bar.

Paul was now standing in the corner and Bomber shouted in his ear, "I hope you know what you are doing. This lot could tear us to bits."

"Don't worry, I'll make him look good for a bit then lay him out," Paul was grinning when he said it.

'Fuck me,' thought Bomber in amazement, *'He's in his element and really wants to do this!'*

Chris had pushed her way through the crowd and stood by Bomber. Her face was a white mask, no expression but Bomber could tell by her eyes she was more than just anxious.

Andy had found his way back and took the sponge, wet it and wiped Paul's face and shoulder. "Got the bet on," he said "The guys given me three to one, the sucker." Bomber wished he had Andy's confidence in the outcome.

The fat man called the two opponents together in the ring where there was a white line painted on the floor and the two fighters toed it. Pat was a big man, not as tall as Paul but big in width and depth of body. He was solid like a huge oak tree but with a scarred and battered face. Legs of ham masquerading as arms and hands were attached to the huge body.

Paul was taller with muscles that rippled when he moved, his long arms bulged with muscles. Bomber thought of Paul as a tiger facing King Kong. *'This is the stuff movies are made of,'* he thought *'not happening now to us. Shit, what if it all goes wrong?'*

The fat man was acting as the referee, he raised his hand then dropped it. Pat swung his huge fists at Paul's body. Had they connected, they would probably have broken Paul's ribs but he had stepped back and countered with a left and right that landed squarely on Pat's chin.

Pat made no effort to get out of the way and just soaked up the punches. Several minutes of swapping punches, then Paul went down to a round house punch that Bomber felt he could have avoided.

The referee stepped in and Paul staggered to the corner where Andy sponged him down. "I've got one minute to toe the line, I'll let him knock me down one more time and then I'll finish it."

True to his word, Paul toed the line within the minute, then they were at it again. Punches that would have killed any normal man were exchanged but then it all went wrong. Whether it was an accident or deliberate, Bomber was not sure. When they were in close, Pat's head came up under Paul's chin and Paul went down on one knee.

Andy was in the ring like lighting and Bomber followed as they helped Paul back to the corner. Fat man said, "Forty-five seconds," as they assisted Paul to the corner. The crowd was cheering and jeering and Bomber could see more money changing hands.

They sponged down Paul, who opened his eyes and winked at Bomber and said, "Watch this!"

Paul staggered out and made a show of toeing the line. At first, he clumsily blocked Pat's punches, throwing weak jabs to keep Pat away as if trying to recover. Then after a minute of this, he went to work on Pat; hard punches to the body with the occasional head shot.

At first, Pat soaked it up but little by little he was feeling the effects of the heavy body punches. The body shots landing on Pat sounded like someone slapping a side of beef with a wet towel. It could clearly be heard throughout the yard even over the noise of the crowd.

Pat's hands were no longer held up protecting his head but were dropping, his mouth was open sucking in air and he staggered round the ring but he wouldn't give up. Bomber had to admire his courage which was all that was holding him up and keeping him going.

The crowd became silent. They could sense the end was near for Pat and the upper cut that finished it could be heard clearly by all. Pat slumped to his knees and his head was down. For a split second he knelt there, then fell face down on the hard floor of the yard.

The crowd was silent, no one moved except Paul who grabbed the bucket of water from Andy and went over to Pat and started sponging his face.

Suddenly, there were cheers as Pat heaved himself up and the fat man walked over and grabbed Paul's arm and raised it. Pat's seconds had got him to the corner. Paul walked over and Pat stood up on wobbly legs and Paul raised Pat's arm. There was more cheering and money was thrown into the ring like confetti for the loser.

Paul stood in front of the three of them grinning, while Andy sponged him down then dried him with the towel.

Bomber was in awe looking at Paul. "Bloody hell Paul, where did you learn to do that and don't tell me you haven't done it before."

"I'll tell you over a drink once we have our winnings."

Paul was putting his shirt back on when three men came over, the bookie and his two minders. Bomber wondered if they were going to have to fight to get their winnings. He needn't have worried. The bookie was delighted that Paul had won since he had made a killing as everyone more or less had bet on Pat.

Their one hundred and seventy pounds had multiplied by three and the large wad of cash went into Andy's hand for him to count. Fat man arrived and paid Paul his appearance fee of three hundred pounds saying he could get Paul as many fights as he liked taking on all comers. Paul declined saying he had to get back to Manchester.

"Not bad for a nights work," Paul said, downing a second pint with ease. "Andy, get me another, mate. I think I'm dehydrated."

Bomber and Chris nursed a small whisky as they figured that at least two of them should stay sober and alert.

As they all drove back to Lisburn, Bomber said, "I don't think we should mention this to anyone, especially the Brigadier. However, how are we to explain the cuts and bruises on you, Paul?"

"Oh, we can just say it was as a result of the bomb blast!" Paul laughed. "The Brig knows I was a fairground fighter for a year or so and believe it or not, I was called the Manchester Mauler. Took on all comers and never lost and some of those were semi-professional boxers."

Bomber shook his head and laughed but Chris was angry, the pent-up fury flying from her lips.

"What the fuck are you all laughing for? We could have blown our cover. We are supposed to be looking for terrorists, not acting like schoolboys in a playground."

"Oh come on, Chrissy," said Paul. "It was just some fun, letting off steam after a shitty night and we were safe in there. It's a hard-line Prod pub. The RUC use it all the time."

"Good reason for the PIRA to blow it up then with us in it and don't fucking well call me Chrissy. You know I hate it."

"Sorry Chris," said Paul as he blew her a kiss.

"Are you going to put up with this, Bomber? You are supposed to be in charge of these idiots." Chris had turned her full fury towards Bomber who suppressed a smile.

Bomber knew Chris had been afraid in the pub, not for herself but for Paul but she couldn't voice it.

"You're right Chris, the whole thing was deplorable," Bomber said in a mock stern voice. "Brawling in the back yard of a pub, Paul! And you Andy, encouraging gambling when we are on duty. I'm ashamed of both of you!"

The three of them broke down laughing and realising she had been a bit over the top, Chris joined in saying, "You are all hopeless cases. I give up!"

"Seriously," Bomber added "We were pushing it so let's keep it low profile from now on. No more public shows!"

Everyone agreed and the rest of the drive went by in companionable silence.

In the briefing room, the Brig and the Colonel sat and listened to the account of the pub bombing.

The Brig continually fiddled with his packet of mints while looking at Bomber who felt himself getting a little irritated by this. So when the Colonel paused with his questions, Bomber spoke out.

"Is there something you wish to ask or tell us, sir?" Bomber said, looking at the Brigadier.

The Brig carried on playing with the packet for a second or two then said, "O'Brian was there in the pub in the back room. He walked out of the back unhurt after the bomb went off."

Bomber was stunned. Chris and Andy looked at each other, then Chris spoke. "We never saw him and if he came in while we were there, I would have spotted him whatever he was wearing."

Andy nodded in agreement. "He must have been in there before we went in. Joss never indicated anything to say he was there so he must have come in through the back."

"Yes but you should have stayed and watched to see who came out," the Colonel said. "It could have made a difference."

Paul spoke up, sounding a little stung by this. "We would have been picked up by the security forces or the local IRA if we had hung around doing nothing."

Bomber had a thousand things going on in his mind but the little voice kept saying, '*Forget that stuff and get after the bastard.*' "Brigadier, I think you know where he is, so why don't we stop all this and get after him?"

A smile creased the Brigadier's mouth but it never made his eyes when he looked at Bomber. "He's gone south but my contacts have informed me that he is going on to organise a bombing campaign in England." Bomber went to speak, wanting to get after O'Brian but the Brigadier held up his hand.

"Once he's in England, it's in other people's hands. If he comes back here, you will get another chance to nab him."

Bomber wasn't letting go that easily. "But he's not in England yet, we could get him south of the border." Then the light went on. "Or are you tailing him to see who he contacts in England?"

The Brigadier and the Colonel looked at each other and this time, the Brigadier smiled for real. "That could be the case but you will not voice that outside of this room, that's an order."

Bomber relaxed a little, answering, "Yes sir, of course not. Do we know if anyone was killed in the bombing?"

"Three that we know of but many have serious injuries," the Colonel said. "Bad business and the IRA and PIRA will want revenge."

The Brigadier spoke without looking up from the papers he had on his desk. "It could be the local UFF (Ulster Freedom Fighters) or one of the other Prod groups knew of the meeting and decided to take out the pub in the hope of getting O'Brian and the rest. On the other hand, it could just have been a random 'Kill the Caths' bombing.

"I will endeavour to find out and hopefully we can bring the culprits to justice, so for now everyone back to normal duties. And Paul, no more bare-knuckle fighting. Don't want you getting back into bad habits." The Brigadier said this without looking up from the papers he was studying on his desk. The Colonel looked at them and smiled.

Everyone knew they were dismissed.

Outside Bomber said, "How the hell did he know about the fight?"

"Oh, he knows me and he has eyes everywhere. I expect he has an informer in every pub in Northern Ireland and a good few south of the border. That's how he must have known about O'Brian," Paul said, shrugging his shoulders and walking towards the mess.

Bomber followed, deciding that this time he was going to have more than one small whisky. Turning to Chris he said, "Come on Sgt P, it's our turn to have a drink or two and these buggers are paying!"

"Why me?" squawked Andy. "It was Paul who was doing the fighting and got an extra three hundred quid."

"You have a good point, Andy. Paul my man, the drinks are on you!" Bomber shouted above Paul's mock protests.

"Okay, okay. I'm paying." Then Paul put his arm round Chris's shoulder and said, "Thanks for worrying about me. Now let's go and party."

Chapter 5
Manure, Machine Guns and Bombs

Bomber was sitting in the front seat of the Land Rover, desperately trying to come up with some way of being more proactive out on the endless patrols but without solid intelligence, it seemed hopeless. He felt weary. The patrolling of country lanes, doing stop and search was a bit like, 'How can we piss off the locals by constantly stopping them from having a normal day.'

"Tractor coming, Boss," Armalite called from his position in the hedgerow.

"Okay, let's stop it and see where he's going."

The Ferret blocked the road and the tractor ground to a halt. The driver looked nervous, seeming to hang on to the steering wheel as if it was his lifeline.

'What's the matter with him?' muttered the little voice in Bomber's head. *'He sees the army out and about every day.'*

The tractor had a trailer hitched to it which was full of fresh manure and the smell was overpowering.

"Where are you going?" asked Armalite.

"Back to the farm," the driver replied, half smiling but avoiding eye contact.

"Your farm, is it?" asked Armalite, knowing full well that the driver was not the farmer. The owner was a large, florid faced man who loved his dairy cows probably more than his wife. He had probably never washed his wife down as lovingly as he did his cows.

"No, I just work there as a farm hand," he replied while again turning his face away after speaking.

Bomber got out of the Land Rover and walked round the tractor and trailer. The manure steamed in the morning sun.

Bomber called Harris over. "Why would he be taking manure back to the farm? Surely he collected it from the cow sheds at the farm to spread on one of the fields. So why is he taking it back?"

"Beats me, boss, unless he is trying to hide something under that stinking mess."

Bomber nodded in agreement, giving Harris a mischievous smile.

Harris looked horrified "Oh no, not me boss, these combats were clean on this morning."

Indicating a gate leading into a grassy field, Bomber said, "Okay, get him to take it into that field, then he can tip the trailer up and we can have a look."

Harris looked suitably relieved and ordered the driver to take the tractor and loaded trailer into the field.

A look of panic spread over the driver's face and he protested that they were stopping him going about his lawful work. Armalite stopped his complaining and encouraged him to comply by poking him with his rifle. The driver got the message. Once the tractor was positioned in the field, Harris had the driver tip the trailer load of manure out onto the field.

As the manure slid out, Bomber could see a bundle wrapped in plastic in the load. Harris made the man wade in and retrieve three bundles. Bomber took out his wicked looking knife from his map pocket on the side of his trousers and sliced open the bundles. Two contained cigarettes. The larger bundle contained two boxes, each containing six bottles of brandy.

"Look, I'm only the driver," the man blurted out. "I just do what I'm told!"

He stared at Bomber who smiled and said. "You have nothing to fear from us, relax."

Bomber walked back to the Land Rover and told Dusty to call it in and to request RUC support as tobacco and spirit smuggling was a police matter.

Twenty minutes later, an armoured RUC Land Rover turned up with four armed officers who took over the job of dealing with the smuggled goods, which may have been for local use or intended as a means of fund raising for the IRA or PIRA.

Handcuffed and still protesting, the tractor driver was put into the RUC vehicle as Bomber and his section drove away to continue their patrol.

"Well at least that has made the day a little more interesting," Bomber said to Harris who was concentrating on guiding the Land Rover along the narrow road.

"Do you think the stuff was for the IRA or just a bit of private smuggling, boss?" Harris asked as he braked so as not to run over several ducks in the road.

"IRA or PIRA would be my first guess. By all accounts, they are moving into a number of rackets to raise money. Most of their players don't have jobs or are wanted by the security forces so can't go looking for brew money. Hence, they have to give them something to live on."

The patrol worked its way back to Ballykinler along the coast road, doing several vehicle stops and searches without any positive results. The shadow of the Mourne Mountains made a brooding backdrop and despite the sun breaking through the clouds, Bomber felt his mood getting darker the closer they got to barracks.

They had just passed the outskirts of Newcastle when Armalite, who was standing up in the back of the Land Rover looking out of the hatch, started banging on the roof.

"Pull up and debus," Bomber ordered Harris who was driving.

The vehicles stopped on the grass verge with the Ferret covering the rear. Harris took cover behind the Land Rover and Dusty stayed at the back of the vehicle to answer the radio.

"What is it, Armalite?" Bomber asked.

"Can't see it from here but standing up in the back of the Lanny, I could see a parked car on the verge just around the bend."

"Okay, you and I will go ahead on foot and have a look," said Bomber.

Satisfied that those left behind were alert and covering the road both ways, Bomber and Armalite moved forward until they could see round the bend. Green hedgerows flanked the road and on the left, there were fields with cattle grazing unaware of the armed men on the road. On the right, more fields met the Irish Sea which washed the shore line with its grey-green waters.

Bomber studied the car through the binoculars. It was a dark brown Ford. Bomber scribbled the registration number down in his notebook. He handed the binoculars to Armalite who sprinted across the road to study the car from a different angle.

"It's got a flat tyre and the driver's window is open," called Armalite. "Can't see anyone in or around the car."

Bomber waved Armalite back to him. Kneeling on the grass verge, Bomber tried looking at the fields and hedgerows further behind the car. If it's a car bomb, then there must be someone around to detonate it. Finally, Bomber made up his mind as to what he should do.

Turning to Armalite, he told him to find a spot where he could look through the hedgerow and try to see if there was anyone lying in wait to blow the car. Armalite took the binoculars and wriggled his way into the hedgerow.

At the Land Rover, Bomber radioed in the details and asked for a vehicle check. Within two minutes, it came back the vehicle had been reported stolen two days before. Bomber asked for the bomb squad to come out but was told none were available as all hell was letting loose in Belfast.

When Bomber asked for a backup section, he was again told no one was available. His patience wearing thin, Bomber asked what they wanted him to do. The operator replied, "Use your own judgement."

'Great,' thought Bomber, 'there's not enough of us to do a secure road block on the road either side of the vehicle. We don't have a Carl Gustav to blast a practice round through the car. So what to do?'

Bomber ordered the Ferret armoured car to move to the bend, then he briefed Cpl Wells, whose eyes widened with excitement. As the Ferret driver and Wells closed the armoured hatches, Bomber went to Armalite who was still studying the fields.

"Anything?" Bomber asked.

"Only possibility that I can see is to the left of that gate two hundred yards up the hill, which would be about right for a wire detonated bomb." Armalite handed the binoculars to Bomber who studied the spot.

'Could be,' thought Bomber. 'Looks like a hole in the hedgerow with a view to the road.' Bomber rolled over and looked at the Ferret with its Browning machine gun pointing at the car while he pondered the options. 'What to do first, go for the suspect bomber or hit the car?'

Armalite shook Bomber by his arm. "Someone's on the move, boss."

Then they heard a motor bike starting up and driving away. "Shit," said Bomber and waved at the Ferret to open fire. He knew Cpl Wells was watching through the periscope and would react.

Bomber clearly heard the double cocking of the Browning machine gun by Wells. The burst of fire from the Browning would have been heard in both Newcastle and Ballykinler. But it was nothing compared to the explosion that tore the car apart and sent bits of metal high into the sky. Bomber was lying in the shallow ditch slightly behind and to the left of the Ferret. The shock wave from the explosion pulled at his helmet and sucked the breath from his lungs.

He heard a heavy thud to his left where the remains of a car seat landed. Other smaller objects continued to rain down, making them all hug the ground.

"That was close!" said Armalite as he shook his head, trying to clear it.

Wells had opened the commander's hatch and was looking out at Bomber, a huge grin splitting his face.

"How's that for a result, boss?" he shouted.

"Pretty dam good, nice shooting," replied Bomber, with his ears still ringing. He went back to the Land Rover and reported in. A different voice to the operator came on the radio at HQ demanding to know what the machine gun fire was and where the explosion had taken place.

'Here we go, you just told them what had happened,' muttered the voice in Bomber's head. *'Told you to use your own judgement then slope shoulders when they think there will be trouble!'*

Bomber chuckled to himself and said, "What did you expect, using the Browning to blow up a car bomb and make a hole in the road. Someone is bound to complain!"

"What's that, boss?" asked Dusty.

Bomber realised he had spoken out loud. Looking at Dusty, he smiled and said, "Take over the radio and let me know when or if they are sending anyone out to us. Oh and tell them the bomber has got away on a motor bike heading west."

Bomber led the way, jogging over the field towards the gate with Armalite on his right and Harris on his left. Bomber was sweating and panting by the time they had reached the gate. They spread out, hunting for the spot where the bomber would have been waiting.

"Over here, boss." It was Harris. "Someone has been lying here in wait. Several cigarette ends and the grass is flattened but no wire that I can see."

"Looks like it was a motor bike." This time it was Armalite looking at the ground where tyre marks could clearly be seen in the muddy ground.

They collected the cigarette ends and put them in a bag and even though they searched, they could not find any wires. *'So it must have been a radio remote job,'* thought Bomber. Back at the vehicles, Dusty showed Bomber the messages he had recorded on his pad. There were several questions: Why had he not asked for the bomb squad?

Why had he not called for backup?

Who authorised the use of the Browning machine gun?

Dusty explained, "I told them that they had said to use your own judgement, boss but I think it's someone at that end who has fucked up."

"And trying to pass the buck?" Bomber muttered.

"That's how I see it too, boss," Dusty answered.

It was two hours before an RUC patrol and a warrant officer and Cpl from the bomb squad arrived. The warrant officer spent twenty minutes poking through the tangled remains of the car. Then he approached Bomber holding up a small mangled and burnt box about the size of a cigarette pack.

"This is what would have received the signal to set off the explosives if your Cpl hadn't blasted the car to pieces first."

"So what would be the range of something like that?" asked Bomber.

"Oh, depends on the terrain but line of sight, say a maximum of five hundred yards but there are more powerful transmitters that that can do it from a lot further away than that."

Bomber nodded, realising that from now on they would have to extend the potential area for any suspect road side bomb by more than double, making the task even harder.

"Is there any way we can jam the signal?" Bomber asked.

"Yes there is but we are still waiting for the equipment to be approved. Then someone's got to authorise the funds to buy it," replied the warrant officer.

"So could be a long time coming then?" said Bomber wryly.

"Well, I think people are beginning to understand that the problem isn't going to go away and are at last pulling their fingers out. So could be sooner than you think."

They were interrupted by the sight of the recovery truck arriving. The Warrant Office went to supervise the loading of the remains of the car which would have a good going over by the experts in some police garage.

Once back in Ballykinler, Bomber submitted his report direct to Captain Bass in an effort to avoid the ops room duty officer and a long series of questions about his actions resulting in the car blowing up.

In his summary, he justified the action by stating that if they had not destroyed the bomb on their terms, the bomber would have done it on his terms, possibly injuring or killing innocent people driving past. Bass was more than happy with Bomber's explanation and told him not to worry. If Bass said that, then Bomber was happy to believe him.

Chapter 6
Death Watch

Bomber was sitting with his mouth open, wondering how he had drawn the short straw for this one. The duty officer was actually smiling and enjoying himself giving this task to Bomber's team. Everyone in the room had smiles on their faces enjoying Bomber's discomfort, the great Recce Platoon guarding corpses.

They were to RV with a hearse carrying the body of an important IRA man shot in Anderson Town who later died in hospital.

"You are to escort it to the city morgue and see that the body is placed securely in there. Once that is done, you will place guards inside and outside the morgue until relieved."

"Any idea when that will be, sir?" Bomber asked.

"Well, its Friday already and the coroner won't look at the body until Monday. So you will have to stay there until someone else is available."

'Fucking great!' thought Bomber *'Just the way I like to spend a weekend. The boys will love this one!'*

"Any other questions, C/Sgt?" the duty officer asked, trying to hide the smile on his face.

"No sir, I'll brief the lads and get going."

Bomber had no takers for who was to stay inside the morgue for the weekend on their own with coolers full of bodies.

"For God's sake," said Bomber, getting totally pissed off with trained soldiers armed to the teeth being afraid to spend the weekend with a few dead bodies.

"We will draw lots for it. Armalite, where are the cards?"

Armalite produced a pack of cards from one of the Lanny's ammo boxes. "Okay, lowest two cards get to stay inside." Having shuffled the cards, he dealt one out to each of them.

Everyone took a card and turned them over placing them on the tail gate of the Lanny. There were cheers when Harris and Dusty turned over a three and a five.

"Okay that's that settled, get the gear loaded and let's go and collect the zombie," Bomber ordered as Armalite collected the cards, grinning fit to burst.

"Wait a minute boss, you didn't pick a card," Harris quickly interjected.

Bomber gave a look of what he hoped was pure innocence. "I can't be inside. I have to take overall control of the defence of the place and that can only be done from the outside."

"Shit," said Harris and flicked his card at Armalite who caught it and burst out laughing as Harris climbed into the Land Rover muttering about the living dead.

The night was strangely quiet. Normally after an IRA or PIRA man had been killed or arrested, there would be rioting, a bomb or two and at least a few pot shots at the security forces.

"Most strange," Bomber said to Armalite. "You'd have thought we would have had some aggro by now but nothing."

"You're right, boss. We haven't even had a visit from some knob head from the IRA to see if the place is guarded."

The night passed slowly, the only thing to break the monotony being a black saloon car driving slowly past the mortuary at three in the morning. Bomber could see two men in the vehicle. The passenger stared directly at Bomber who was standing by the side of the Land Rover.

Bomber nodded to Armalite who tapped on the side of the Ferret. The driver responded by starting up the engine, ready to charge forward and ram the car if necessary. The car stayed on the road and carried on but Bomber called it in with the registration number.

After a few minutes, HQ called back and said not to worry about it. "What sort of answer is that!" exclaimed Armalite.

"Someone checking up on us by the sounds of it," answered Bomber, "but if it comes back, let's block him front and rear with the Ferret and Lanny and see who they are, just to let them know we mean business."

Armalite briefed Cpl Wells who was sitting in the Ferret turret. Bomber could see the steam coming out of the hatch from a hot cup of coffee.

Picking up his own flask, he poured a tepid cup of tea but it tasted just as it would at four hours old so he threw the dregs on the floor in disgust.

"Armalite, knock on the door and tell Harris to refresh the flasks."

"Okay boss, seems like there are some perks at being locked up with the stiffs. A warm kitchen for a start!"

Dusty and Harris had changed their tune about being with the bodies when they saw that they didn't have to share the room with them but could stay on in a warm kitchen. Bomber's only stipulation was that one of them had to be awake at all times and that they were to make brews for those outside, which they had done at regular intervals.

The dawn was struggling to make an impression when Sgt Ian Mason arrived with his section to relieve them. The hand over took ten minutes, the only unpleasant part was showing Ian that the body was still in place in the cooler. Not that anyone had expected Dusty and Harris to have cut the body up and flushed it down the toilet but it was a requirement of the handover that the oncoming commander saw the body.

Back in Flax Street Mill, they ran the gauntlet of comments from the other platoons. Top of the list was, 'Here come the death watch boys!' and 'Any trouble with the prisoner, lads?' Ignoring the comments, Bomber went to his bunk, undressed and slept until six that evening.

Later after a good supper, they went back to the mortuary to take over from Ian's team. Harris and Armalite had cadged extra brew kit and biscuits to take with them.

Ian had nothing to report and the body was still safely tucked up in the cooler. Bomber went through the ritual of seeing the body. He could just be asleep, thought Bomber but resisted the urge to give him a poke. Armalite and Wilkes now swopped with Dusty and Harris as the insiders.

As the darkness enveloped them, a light but persistent rain set in and a cold wind began to make life outside just a little more unpleasant. Bomber could hear Harris grousing about having to be outside. All his protests of twenty-four hours ago about being with the living dead forgotten.

Time seemed to have stood still and Bomber had to force himself to stop looking at his watch as the hours dragged by. Dusty was switching through the radio channels, picking up bits of information from different units.

"Riot in Anderson Town, petrol and nail bombs. No shootings yet," Dusty reeled the stuff off like some TV presenter with an audience of millions.

"Suspect car bomb near the city centre, bomb disposal team there. Bet they use the Carl Gustav on it, they love that thing now they know how to fire it!"

"Quiet," said Harris. "Car coming, boss."

Bomber heard the car coming towards them and signalled Wells to start the Ferret.

As the car got closer, it swung into the small car park of the mortuary and stopped. Without waiting to be told, the Ferret drove forward and blocked the exit. Harris and Bomber rushed the car, shouting to the driver to keep his hands on the steering wheel.

Instead of doing that, he put his right hand inside his jacket. Bomber heard the Browning machine gun being doubled cocked by Wells. Harris cocked his SLR, shouting at the driver to put both hands on the steering wheel.

Something must have finally clicked in the driver's head because he slowly removed his hand from the inside of his jacket and placed it with his left hand on the wheel.

Harris was pumped up and yanked open the driver's door, trying to pull the driver out but the seat belt stopped him. Harris just got more frustrated and pulled harder.

Bomber opened the passenger door, reached in and released the seat belt. The driver was protesting loudly, saying he was army but it had no effect on Harris who dragged the unfortunate from the car onto the ground and started smacking him around the head with his open hand screaming, "I nearly fucking killed you, you shit. All because you wouldn't do as you were told."

Then he smacked him some more. Harris was a solidly built man who played rugby for the regiment so every smack he delivered must have felt like a leg of ham landing from a great height on the unfortunate's head.

"Okay, that's enough," ordered Bomber who had now come around the car to Harris.

"The bastard. Boss, I was squeezing the trigger when he put his hand inside his jacket."

"I know, I was doing the same and I bet you he has a Browning in a holster there."

The unfortunate was now sitting up holding an I.D. card which Harris snatched from him.

"I was trying to show you this," he said in an injured voice, holding his head with the other hand as if that excused his actions.

Bomber looked at him, then helped him to his feet guiding him back to the car and the seat where he slumped, looking somewhat confused. "Is this how you treat everyone?" he asked Bomber.

"Only those who don't do as they are told," Bomber snapped back but then relaxed a little as the adrenalin flowed a little slower.

"I suggest next time soldiers tell you to keep your hands on the steering wheel, you do just that," added Bomber. "You were a hair's breath away from hell, my friend. Now, what are you doing here at this time of the morning?"

"I was sent to check you guys were on the job," he replied, rubbing the back of his head where one of Harris's more powerful blows must have landed.

"Well, next time anyone sends you to check up on us, do it carefully because we don't like cars prowling around with dodgy looking people in them."

Bomber noted the name on the I.D. card in his report book and asked him his rank.

"Sgt," he replied without any real conviction.

"Well, I'm not going to ask you your unit as I don't believe you will tell me the truth anyway. So take this and go." Bomber handed him his I.D. and stepped back from the car, signalling the Ferret to back up.

The unfortunate started the car and left the car park, quickly accelerating away.

"Okay everyone, back in position."

"What outfit do you think he was from, boss?" Harris asked.

"Well he wasn't a Sgt, far too polite so was probably from Brigade HQ or one of the Mickey Mouse Int units."

"I really did nearly shoot the fucking knob head," Harris spoke softly and for the first time Bomber noticed that Harris was shaking as the adrenalin left his system.

"I know and I was with you. He should have complied but I can bet you he won't be so cocky next time. I think you scared the shit out of him!"

Bomber got onto the radio to report the incident and to cover their backsides, he reported the roughing up part, stating that the whole situation was instigated by the reckless action of the unfortunate. Bomber wanted to say that whoever the knob head was who sent him out in the first place should have briefed him properly but held back, common sense winning for once.

Bomber got a terse 'Wait out' from HQ, then after a few moments the radio came to life and he was surprised to recognise the CO's voice asking him to repeat the report.

The CO sounded quite cheery when he signed off and Bomber wondered if the CO was saving himself for when Bomber returned to base to give him a rifting.

When relieved by Ian Mason later in the morning, Bomber led his section back to the Mill. On arrival, he was expecting to be summoned to the ops room but nothing was said, so Bomber decided to keep his head down and go straight to bed hoping that when he woke up, some other platoon would have the job of guarding the corpse.

The next morning, much to their relief Bomber and his team were on immediate standby with Ian Mason's section on fifteen minutes notice.

The morning was quiet and they had just eaten lunch when the air was ripped apart by a horrendous explosion. It was so loud Bomber thought it was very close to the Mill but a clerk from the ops room ran up to Bomber and thrust a piece of paper into his hand.

The clerk gasped, "Big bomb, city centre, the CO wants you there fast and then to give him a sitrep."

Bomber looked at the paper which just said Donegall Street.

Harris drove fast using pavements when a road was blocked and cursing drivers who were too slow to get out of the way.

As they approached, Bomber could see smoke rising above the buildings. Just before Donegall Street, they came to a stop. Leaving the Lanny and Ferret, Bomber went forward with Dusty and Armalite. Dusty had shouldered an A41 radio and they jogged the short distance into the bomb site.

Bomber stopped, his mind not immediately registering what he was seeing. It was a slaughter house. Bodies of men, women and children lay scattered on the road and pavements. Shattered bodies, dismembered bodies. Then Bomber heard the screams. Later, he would realise his mind had probably shut out the sound at first while he made some sense of the scene from hell in front of him.

"Fucking hell!" said Harris as he knelt down and started wrapping a field dressing round the arm of a school girl to stop the blood pumping. The girl made no sound but just stared while Harris talked to her, trying to reassure her that help was on its way.

"Dusty, have we got comms?" Bomber asked in a hushed voice.

"Yes, Boss," said Dusty, handing the mic to Bomber.

Bomber looked at Dusty and could see tears running down his face.

He reported in a major incident with between one hundred to two hundred civilian casualties.

Bomber felt his temper rising when HQ asked him to reassess the numbers as if they didn't believe him.

He confirmed the numbers and said they needed every medic and ambulance possible without delay.

Now Bomber could hear voices calling, some for help, some for God and some just simply crying. Then other soldiers, the medics and police officers started to bring some order to the chaos, bringing comfort to the shocked, treatment to the injured and body bags for the dead.

Bomber looked for Harris and Dusty who had left the radio at his feet. Both were giving first aid to what appeared to have been a party of school girls.

"Boss, can I have your field dressings?" Dusty shouted at him from where he was sitting holding a young girl covered in blood.

Bomber ripped off the dressings where they were taped to his webbing and tossed them to Dusty.

The radio was squawking and Bomber reluctantly listened. It was HQ wanting a reassessment and if there was an incident commander there.

Bomber confirmed his earlier report and scanned the street picking out an RUC officer who seemed to be directing the response. Next to him was a Parachute Regiment officer in his distinctive maroon beret, directing soldiers as they appeared.

Passing the information to HQ, he was told to pull out and return to the Mill. Before they left, they each carried a girl to where the ambulances were parked and handed them to the medics. Bomber saw the regiment's medic, Sgt Mike Smith loading walking wounded into his armoured ambulance. Stretcher cases were hurriedly loaded into civilian ambulances that left at speed with sirens howling.

Bomber looked again at the carnage and felt an uncontrollable rage rising within him. Who would do such a thing to innocent people? It wasn't as if they were security forces but just mums with their kids going shopping, men doing deliveries or meeting wives or girlfriends. Bloody hell, there was even a large group of school girls in their uniforms!

No one spoke on the drive back but as they parked up, Harris exploded hitting the side of the Lanny with his fists, the fibre armour vibrating with each blow. Armalite went to hold him but Bomber told him to let him be.

They sat on the floor of the garage in a circle. "We should have stayed, boss," Dusty choked out.

"We should be out there hunting the bastards who did it," sobbed Harris, who had exhausted himself using the Lanny as a punch bag.

Bomber responded in an effort to ease their anger and pain. "There was little we could do without masses of first aid kit plus the incident commander had the response organised. As for the bastards who did it, they will be caught and justice will be swift."

At that moment, a clerk from the ops room turned up, "You are wanted in the—Jesus Christ!" he stood staring at them.

"What?" Bomber asked.

"You're all covered in blood!" exclaimed the shocked clerk. Bomber looked at Harris and Dusty. Harris had blood on his face and hands. His combats were stained dark with it and Dusty was no better. Looking down at his own combats, he could see blood had soaked his jacket and trousers when he had carried the girl to the ambulance.

His hands were caked with it but he knew it wasn't his but that of some small girl whose life would never be the same again, that's if she survived the journey to hospital.

The voice in his head was goading him, *'What are you doing here? Get out there, find the bastards. Kill them or don't you care anymore?'*

But Bomber did care, inside he was seething, thirsting for justice for those killed and injured but now was not the time.

Keeping his thoughts to himself, Bomber tried to close his mind to the nagging voice in his head. The clerk kept as much distance as he could from Bomber as they walked to the ops room. The voice in Bomber's head kept up the chant all the way and he feared for his sanity, having witnessed at first hand such an atrocity.

In the ops room, the CO and company commander with Capt. Bass were poring over a map. They all looked up when Bomber came in.

"Sorry to drag you in before you have even had a cup of tea, C/Sgt. Good lord!" The CO had stopped talking and stared at Bomber.

"Are you hurt?" he asked.

"No sir, it's a school girl's blood not mine."

"We thought you were slightly over estimating the casualties at first but the reports coming in put the dead and wounded at least one hundred and sixty. So you have our apologies. Sorry for doubting you."

The CO paused and looked at the map of Belfast, then turning his gaze back to Bomber he said, "I'm afraid I need you and all your lads back on the streets. However, you have time to change and have a cup of tea if you are quick."

They were part of a large number of troops who were deployed putting road check points in a cordon around the city centre. The saying 'horses and stable doors' sprang to mind as Bomber deployed his platoon to cover four different junctions.

"What day is it?" Bomber said out loud.

"Monday," answered Dusty.

"No, the date, what's the date?"

"Oh, let me see now," pondered Dusty.

"It's the twentieth of March," Harris offered from his position squatting by the side of the Lanny.

'Twentieth of fucking March,' thought Bomber. *'I wonder if they will have a memorial service every year for this. I certainly won't forget it.'*

Bomber watched as Armalite turned another car back the way it came. The orders were clear, no one in except emergency services until further notice.

Bomber didn't move from his position in the Lanny when another explosion was heard several blocks to the north of them.

He heard Harris swearing and made a mental note to keep a close eye on him.

Dusty, who was monitoring the radios said, "No casualties reported."

"Must have had a telephone warning, time to evacuate the area," said Armalite who had moved back to the Lanny.

"That's it. They didn't get a telephone warning for the first one that's why there were so many casualties." Dusty seemed almost relived by the thought.

"Or," said Bomber "the RUC had been given the wrong location or not enough time to clear the area. Or it was a deliberate set up to kill as many as possible."

"Do you really think the IRA are sick enough to do that, boss?" asked Harris.

"Yes but it was more likely to be the PIRA. They are the sickest of the bunch."

Everyone sank into silence and watched more cars turning away from their road block.

"Christ!" said Harris who was really getting jumpy. He stood and walked up and down in response to another explosion further north than the last one.

"Well, they are really getting into the swing of it today," said Armalite trying to sound upbeat.

"It's in the Para's area boss, no casualties," Dusty said. Then he fiddled with the dials on the C42 radio. Bomber guessed he was trying to eavesdrop on the Brigade net.

"I heard you've got friends in the Para's from Palace Barracks, boss," Armalite spoke casually as if trying to pass the time.

"Yes, a couple from my hometown, we were in the cadets together and they went to junior Paras in Aldershot and I went to IJLB in Oswestry. They are both Sgts now."

If the rest of that day was long and frustrating, then the night was doubly so. The only relief was when the CQMS visited and served up some stew and sandwiches. The CQMS was a tall, lean man with a narrow, pinched face. He was from the west coast of Scotland so what he was doing in a southern regiment was anyone's guess.

Normally a man of few words, he seemed eager to bring Bomber up to date on the result of the bombings. "Aye, it was mass murder alright," he said with a high-pitched burr in his voice. "The bastards had no thought for whom they would kill. Prods, Caths, police or soldiers, they didnae care. Mike Smith was telling me they are still trying to match body parts to victims. Two RUC officers who were near the bomb, clearing people away, well they were vaporised, nae a thing left of them!"

He paused to regain his thoughts.

"At least seven dead, others not expected to survive. A hundred and fifty or more casualties. Terrible, terrible what these people will do just to sate their own lust for power."

He hung his head and sighed and Bomber saw his shoulders sag and thought he was going to cry but he continued.

"I have been a strict teetotaller all my adult life but I tell you, I had the devil in me after delivering medical supplies to the scene. It was go on a mad hunt for the bastards that did it or empty a bottle of scotch." His voice had risen as he spoke and everyone was now looking towards him.

"What did you do?" asked Bomber, placing a hand on his arm.

He sighed and looked at Bomber, "What I always do at times like this. I said to hell with the devil and buried myself in work and made sure you all got some food and tea." At that, he straightened up and marched back to his truck, waving his escort to mount up, then without another word he drove off to his next stop.

It was then that Dusty, who was sitting by his beloved radios said something that Bomber thought was quite profound.

"There's a man that one day will either go bonkers with a gun in a riot or find a quiet corner and top himself."

"Why do you say that?" questioned Bomber.

"No release for all that tension and anger. He doesn't get pissed or go out on an operation to find the baddies, so he is sinking into a pit of frustration that he can't climb out of."

Bomber looked over the top of the metal divide in the Lanny that held the radios and spoke in a low voice. "You could be right, Dusty but keep that to yourself and I'll mention it in passing to the Med Sgt who can pass it on to the MO (Medical Officer)."

Dusty nodded and said, "I wish he hadn't mentioned the whisky. I could do with some right now."

"I know," replied Bomber. "A good piss up and some girls to liven up the party would be an excellent idea."

"I'll drink to that," Harris said, raising his mug of tea and Bomber and Dusty laughed which was all the relief they would get that night.

When they were finally ordered back to the Mill, Bomber felt they had nothing left to give, so he ordered everyone to get a good breakfast and to sleep. Everything else could wait.

Two days later, a large car bomb exploded in the car park at Great Victoria Street Station next to the Europa Hotel. First report indicated sixty plus casualties bringing the total deaths and casualties of innocent civilians to well over two hundred and fifty in three days.

The voice in Bomber's head kept repeating, *'Go after the bastards, find them and kill them!'*

Chapter 7
Blackmail and Deceit

"You are wanted in the briefing room, C/Sgt," Cpl Jones said in a tired voice. Jones was one of the senior clerks and Bomber guessed he had been on duty for over twenty-four hours with all the action happening in Belfast.

It was easy to forget that the operations room was on the go twenty-four hours a day dealing with everything that happened and soldiers like Jones did all the hard graft for the ops officer, who in turn had to make life and death decisions constantly.

Bomber turned off the kettle which sat on a small table in the room that passed for a combined officers' and SNCO's mess. Following Jones, he asked, "What's happening?"

Jones shrugged his shoulders and simply replied, "I'm just a messenger, no one tells me fuck all these days. Jones get so and so, Jones make the tea, Jones why haven't you answered the phone. I really want to tell them it's because I'm fucking well making the tea and fetching someone while marking up maps of the latest bomb explosions and terrorist sighting's for the CO."

"I take it you've had a tough shift," responded Bomber.

"Seems about the norm at the moment. The ops officer's been run ragged. He's been on the go for thirty-six hours now. How he's stayed awake I don't know, bloody machine he is!"

Bomber opened the briefing room door and went in. Sitting at the map table were two men in civilian clothes. The older of the two looked up, smiled and said, "C/Sgt, pull up a chair and take the weight off your feet."

Bomber picked up one of the folding chairs that was stacked against the wall and wrestled it open, while reflecting on the greeting. Far too bloody jolly, this is trouble. Sitting opposite the two men, he studied them.

The older man was well groomed, a little overweight but not flabby and probably in his early forties, dark hair gelled down but going thin on top. The younger one, Bomber judged to be about thirty. He was lean and had shifty eyes that never seemed to stay still.

"I'm Major Beckley and this is Captain Winston. We need you for an important job."

"What sort of job, sir?" Bomber asked with that lead weight feeling in his gut already.

"What I am about to tell you is not to be repeated outside of this room for the sake of security and is a job that I am assured suits your talents."

The voice in his head was competing with the alarm bells and saying, *'Where have you heard that before? Time to run away now while you have the chance.'*

The Major continued while Shifty Eyes stared intently at Bomber, who was doing his best to stay calm.

"We have a name for the Donegall Street bombing and we know where he is. Unfortunately, he is south of the border and that's why we need you."

'Fuck you,' thought Bomber, *'I'm not going south again for anyone.'*

"I think I should stop you there, sir," said Bomber firmly. "I told the Brigadier that I would not be going south again. I've done my share of that stuff. Let someone else stick their neck out. Where is the Brigadier by the way?" Bomber added, thinking it strange he'd sent these two for such a job.

The Major looked down at the notebook in front of him, then glanced at Shifty Eyes. "The Brigadier is in hospital, heart attack. That's why I'm here and before you ask, Colonel Wilson is in England."

In the silence that followed, Bomber realised that the two men who could protect him were out of the picture and he was on his own. He had now guessed that these two weren't anything to do with the Brigadier.

"Now," the Major said firmly, "I was not asking you if you wanted to do this but it's an order from the top."

Bomber butted in, "That would be an illegal order sir, which I do not have to obey."

To Bomber's surprise, they both smiled and Bomber knew they were going to sucker punch him right there and then.

"Maybe you are right but it is well documented you have done this before and committed," He paused, flicking through the pages of his notebook as if trying to find the right page. Then he went on, "murder in some people's eyes, totally unauthorised off your own bat as it were. Not that we are judging you, in fact we applaud you."

Shifty was smiling, his eyes darting from Bomber to the Major in some sort of lunatic's eye dance and Bomber had an urge to poke his fingers in those eyes.

"Now, you wouldn't want to be thrown to the legal system without any back up, would you?" The menace in the Major's voice was unmistakable.

Bomber felt his temper rising and he had a desire to launch himself over the table and smash both of them to a pulp. His hand felt the handle of his knife in his trouser map pocket and wondered how easy it would be to pull it out and slice their throats open. Bomber paused and counted to ten in his head, breathing deeply.

"Well, would you?" Shifty Eyes asked, interrupting his meditation.

Bomber had collected his thoughts and remembering the Brig's words, 'There are no documents linking us with any operations south,' calmed him down.

"Well sir, you could, of course, fabricate some documents but there is no way the General is going to allow you or anyone else to make any of this public." Bomber wanted to add, 'So go fuck yourself.'

The smile had left the face of Shifty Eyes and the Major looked at Bomber who stared back. Eventually the Major dropped his gaze, cleared his throat and said, "I think we have got off on the wrong foot here, C/Sgt. I hear what you are saying but I think we need to come to some agreement. We need you to do this for us and for the victims or the perpetrators will go unpunished for their hideous crime."

'Christ,' thought Bomber, 'Trying emotional blackmail now, what sort of prat does he think I am?'

"Even if I was willing, just how do you think I can go south undetected and either arrest or do whatever to whomever you have down for this bombing?"

"Very much as you have done in the past, C/Sgt. We will of course help you with the planning and have the final say in approving the plan."

'You are weakening,' the voice mocked. 'No chance of that,' Bomber thought, 'wouldn't trust these two as far as I could throw them.'

Just then the door opened and Captain Bass stepped in. "I'm sorry to interrupt but I need the C/Sgt urgently, just for a few moments Major."

The Major looked put out by the interruption just as he assumed he had won Bomber over.

"Very well but don't be long, time is of the essence."

Bomber followed Bass out of the room and as they were walking towards the mess room, Bass asked in a stage whisper, "Not agreed to anything C/Sgt, have you?"

"Not with them sir, don't trust them an inch." Bomber looked at Bass. His shoulders were drooping and his face looked haggard.

"Good," he said, pushing open the mess room door.

Inside were Colonel Wilson and Paul, drinking coffee.

"Hello sir, I thought you were supposed to be in London?" Bomber said with a relieved grin on his face.

The Colonel stood and shook hands but looked grim. "Someone's trying to send me on a wild goose chase to get me out of the way while the Brigadier's laid up. He's okay by the way, should be out of hospital in a few days."

"So what's going on, sir?" Bomber asked as he shook hands with Paul.

They all sat and Bomber and Bass helped themselves to coffee.

"Power struggle!" the Colonel said in a clipped voice. "New initiative by the new Brigade Commander with an Int group who have no moral or as I see it, legal guidelines whatsoever."

"So what's their game sir, trying to get me to go south?"

"Oh, now we have a lead on who the bomber is and where he is, they want a big coup to prove they should be in charge. However, the bomber is just a kid. He was told to drive and park the car in a certain street, which he couldn't do as the street was blocked off."

"Instead he panicked, knowing the bomb was due to go off, so he dumped it in Lower Donegall Street. That's why there were so many casualties as the phone warning gave a different location. The real culprit who ordered it and fucked up was Seamus O'Neill, the PIRA Belfast commander."

The Colonel paused, sipped some coffee and Bomber waited. "Our Brigadier found out through his contacts and when he informed the Brigade Commander, he passed it to that lot in the briefing room."

"How do I deal with them, sir?" asked Bomber. "They are trying to blackmail me into going south."

"Right at this minute, your CO is in the briefing room telling them he is refusing to make you available. They might take that up with Brigade but your CO is highly thought of by the commander and he is unlikely to overrule him."

"Their plan, if you had gone along with them, would have been to get you to do the dirty work and if you succeeded, they would take the credit. If you failed, they would say you are the Brigadier's man. As for blackmailing you, they have nothing and no one to support anything, purely guess work."

"I feel better already, although I am concerned that the bomber is living it up in the south and we are doing nothing."

"If you want to do something then I'm happy to listen but he is small fry. It's O'Neill we want, who is also hiding in the south. However, even our gung-ho new Brigadier is wary about anyone going south after the last hue and cry by the Irish and English MPs."

"However, this Brigade Commander is very 'let's get them no matter what' and the General backs him all the way, so even a small fry can be turned into a big fish. Now if it was done quietly without anyone getting killed, I could be persuaded to put it to the Brigadier."

"It would depend on where the target is holed up. Once I know that, Captain Bass, Paul and I could come up with a plan that might work," said Bomber.

'What happened to never going south again, you prat?' Bomber tried to close his mind to the voice but it persisted. *'Death wish, is it? Guilt over the bombing and being a survivor when so many better than you are dead or dying?'*

"You okay, David?" asked Paul who had his hand on Bomber's shoulder. "You've gone a bit white and you were shaking your head."

"I'm okay thanks, just thinking of the carnage in Donegall Street and what the hell am I thinking of, even considering going south again."

"You don't have to go," said Paul.

"I know but what the hell, if we give them a safe haven, how many more will they murder?" answered Bomber angrily.

Chapter 8
Engaged

Sitting in the passenger seat of the VW camper van, Bomber felt confident about getting through Irish customs without any trouble. His Australian passport and Chris's Southern Irish one looked the business. Bill had produced them in double quick time when the plan was approved; he had also given them lots of tips on how to stay under the radar.

The guy at passport control was fat and looked bored as he casually flicked through passports. Only two more vehicles to go and they would be through. The ferry crossing had been calm and uneventful despite the number of passengers who seemed determined to drink the bar dry. Partying at any time of the day seemed to be the norm on the ferry.

Then it happened, the customs officers changed. Mr Bored went off and a bright, young looking female took over. She pored over the passports of the occupant of the two vehicles in front.

"Just what we bloody well need. An overzealous passport checker," Bomber grumbled, hoping theirs were as good as they looked.

"Don't worry, let me do the talking, the passports are genuine so don't worry," said Chris.

'*Sure, the passports are genuine but we aren't,*' thought Bomber who had decided that he was not cut out for this stuff. Sneaking about in the trees and bushes in the hills and country side was okay but parading in full view, well it takes nerve and he felt he was running out of that.

Chris pulled forward and handed over the passport. Smiling sweetly, she cooed, "This is my fiancé. We're going to see family before we get married," she said, giggling.

"That's lovely," said the girl with a face that looked like she was sucking a lemon. "Do you have a return ticket?"

"Oh yes, we have to be back to work in London in ten days," Chris replied, handing over the return ferry tickets.

The girl ignored the tickets, leaving them on the small shelf of her cubicle and continued to study Bomber's passport. "Where were you born, James?" she asked, looking at Bomber.

"Sidney, Australia."

"And your middle name?"

"Bradley, after my grandfather," replied Bomber, feeling his mouth go dry.

The girl handed back the passports, smiled at Chris, said "Good luck," and winked.

Chris laughed and said, "Thanks," as they drove off.

"Thank fuck for that. I thought she was going to ask me about my family tree at one point!" exclaimed Bomber in relief.

"No," Chris said confidently, "She just wanted to get the measure of the man I was going to saddle myself with."

"Wonderful," muttered Bomber.

They drove away from the ferry terminal sticking to the speed limit and for once, the sun shone out of a blue sky studded with small, fluffy white clouds. Using the minor roads where possible they wandered northwards, checking that they weren't being followed.

When it got dark, they pulled off the road and Bomber fired up the small gas stove in the camper van, emptying cans of beef stew into a pan.

"We seem to be going to a lot of trouble for a low-ranking PIRA man," Chris spoke softly and Bomber had to turn his head to hear her over the noise of the stove. He thought about his answer while he stirred the stew.

Speaking just as softly, Bomber explained to Chris, "As I understand it, the point of this op is that they are seen to answer for their crimes and until the South's government acts against the IRA and PIRA on their side of the border, we have to do something, no matter how covert."

"Hopefully this sort of atrocity will help them change their attitude," Chris replied without any conviction.

"Not while they have Sinn Fein MPs in their government. Anyway, I thought you were dead keen on this when I outlined the plan."

"Oh I am. It's what I signed up for with the Brigadier. Take the fight to the enemy, not wait for them to kill more people." Chris had lightened up now, a smile on her face. "It's you I'm worried about. You seem subdued now we are here."

"Well, the truth is I would rather be hiding in the bushes spying out the land and going really covert. This out in the open stuff scares me but I have to admit, it also gives me an edge. I now notice everything because the bloods pumping and I'm thinking all the time."

Chris lapsed into silence. Bomber filled two bowls with stew and they ate in silence.

Then Chris asked, "Were you scared on the other ops south?"

Bomber stopped chewing. "Scared maybe, some of the time but mostly I was too busy to worry. Before and after are the worst times. It's then you have time to consider the dangers. Being scared is natural but it's knowing how to control the fear that's important. Controlled fear can give you an edge as it keeps you alert and stops you doing stupid things."

Chris reflected for a moment and then said, "Paul and Andy have been used for some hairy stuff recently but I seemed to have been in the ops room handling comms or intel (communications and intelligence). So this feels like I am now being really useful again but at the same time, it doesn't feel real yet."

Bomber studied her, good looking, athletic and intelligent. He wondered what drove her to this sort of work.

"Why are you looking at me that way?"

"Just thinking how lucky I am to have such a good partner on this job. I would have hated sharing the van with Andy farting and swearing. As for Paul, he would have taken up all the room," replied Bomber.

Chris laughed and said, "Especially if Andy had been on the curry again. He can stink like a rotting rat up a drain pipe."

They unpacked their sleeping bags. Bomber spread his on the front seat and Chris used the bench seat in the back.

"What about the hardware?" Chris asked. "I would feel better if it was closer to hand."

Bomber agreed and lifted the floor panel under the bit of carpeting by the stove. What looked like the top of a twelve-volt battery was revealed. Turning the two terminals half a turn anti clockwise, he was able lift off the top of the dummy battery.

Wrapped in a cloth were two pistols, his beloved Beretta and a short barrelled thirty-eight revolver for Chris. He picked up the two spare clips for the Beretta and a box of rounds for the thirty-eight.

"Do you want the whole box or just a few rounds for that thug's gun?" asked Bomber.

"Thug's gun," Chris said with some scorn in her voice. "I'll have you know this is an American police special and a lot better than that antique thing you have."

"Agreed, the Beretta is a bit old but very reliable and easy to conceal and has enough stopping power for close quarter work."

Bomber checked the Beretta, cocked it and then took a roll of masking tape and tore a piece off, taping the Beretta under the dash board where he could reach it if he was driving or in the passenger seat. The clips he taped just to the side of the gun.

Chris took the roll of tape from Bomber and reaching up, she pulled back a part of the ceiling padding. She taped the gun to the roof and spare rounds that were wrapped in a handkerchief and then replaced the padding. Satisfied with her work, she stretched out on her sleeping bag and within seconds was asleep.

"Looks like I have first watch then," Bomber muttered to himself and put the kettle on the stove for a brew. *'It's times like this,'* he pondered, *'when it's easy to switch off and not bother with keeping watch but that's not a mistake I intend to make. Getting killed or caught is not on the agenda for Ma Brown's little boy.'*

Chapter 9
Time Spent on Reconnaissance Is Seldom Wasted

Chris was driving and Bomber was studying the map on his lap. They had spent the day working their way back eastwards towards Drogheda coming in south of the river Boyne. Chris was complaining that if they had to make a quick getaway, they would be better off running.

Bomber had to admit that with a top speed of just under fifty miles an hour with a tail wind downhill, the camper was not ideal but who would expect them to use such a vehicle.

"Stay on this road and it should take us across the river," Bomber instructed. Their plan now was to drive around the town, familiarising themselves with its layout so that should they have to, they could bug out quickly without having to look at a map.

If they were stopped and asked what they were doing, they would say they were looking for a place to park up for the night. An hour later, they had had enough; the main landmarks were etched into their minds, the round fortress like building on the hill, the old gate of the town wall with its round towers and the tall spires of two of the churches, pointing like fingers to heaven as if saying 'This way for redemption'.

Bomber thought that the town had a slightly run-down appearance, like an old man who had worn the same suit for too many years but couldn't bear to take it off.

As Chris drove east on the north side of the river, she started reeling off facts to Bomber. "There used to be a busy docks here which made the town really prosperous. Of course that old bugger Cromwell came over in 1649 and smashed his way into the town killing all the garrison, who were royalist and a good deal of the locals as well." She paused at a junction as if undecided which way to go. "For Christ's sake James, cheer up and smile."

It took Bomber a second to realise he was James. "Sorry, just trying to memorise everything we have seen."

"That all very well but it's not good for our cover you looking like you are going to a funeral, yours!"

Bomber straightened up in his seat and smiled, "How's that, my darling? I'm really looking forward to the wedding!"

"Bollocks!" Chris replied, a broad grin on her face. "Paul said you were serious and worried about things too much but hey, who knows we are here? We've got the camper, plenty of money in our pockets and time to enjoy ourselves a little. So why don't we park and walk into the centre and have some food and a drink?"

Bomber looked at his watch. It was close to six, the evening was drawing in and he was feeling hungry and they did have a meeting to keep. "Okay, sounds like a plan." They found a quiet street with plenty of parking space.

Drawing the curtains, they removed the pistols from their hiding places. Bomber slid his into the inside pocket of his new leather zip jacket and then watched Chris lift her skirt to reveal a pocket sown into her knickers that were like tight fitting shorts.

Seeing Bomber looking, she blushed slightly and said, "I had them made especially and with the right dress on, no one can tell there is a real surprise there."

Locking the van, they walked towards the town centre. They could see the spire of a large church which Bomber knew was St Peter's, the main religious building for Drogheda. They strolled casually up St Peter's Street to the very end. Chris behaved like a loving girlfriend should, clinging to Bomber's arm and pretending to whisper sweet nothings in his ear.

Bomber kept his arm round her and replied by pointing out one-way streets and dead ends where they couldn't take the van.

Finally, they spotted the place they wanted at the end of the street, Clarkes and Sons. It was a traditional looking pub from the outside and very traditional inside with a highly polished bar, bare wood floor and rickety tables and chairs plus a chalk board advertising hot food served from one to nine in the evening. Bomber ordered two pints of Guinness with pie and mash for them both.

Finding a corner seat where they could see everyone coming in while they sat talking, the Guinness went down a treat.

"The two at the bar could be dodgy," Chris spoke while smiling and looking at Bomber.

"No, the fat one just tore up a betting slip. Bad day at the bookies so they are in here to drown their sorrows."

"What about the other two at the table by the door?" asked Chris.

"Well, the older one is so pissed he can hardly stay on the chair. The other one I can't make out, he is hardly drinking but I guess he is young enough to be the other one's son and is looking after him." Bomber offered.

"Naw, I think it's a drunken boss and possibly his minder," Chris countered.

The game was stopped as the pie and mash arrived. Huge plates with the biggest meat pie Bomber had ever seen complete with a mountain of mashed potato and gravy. The size of the meals was matched by the large woman who plonked the plates on the table.

Before either of them could say thanks, the woman turned and shouted in a foghorn voice, "Michael, will you take Seamus home before he passes out and pisses himself again?"

"Sweet Jesus! Mary, he's going to sack me if I take him home to the dragon before ten o'clock." The man stood holding his hands out to the side.

"You're an idiot, Michael! Put him in the car and drive him around until then. I'm not having him puking on the floor. Now get him out!" The last words flew from Mary's lips with such force that Michael jumped to his feet and heaved the man up. Hooking his arm around the old man's waist he headed for the door, the old guy's feet dragging along behind.

The barman opened the door and Michael staggered out with his burden. As those two went out, two others came in. They looked like builders, boots with smudges of cement, dirty jeans and checked shirts of the type worn by workmen. They ordered pints and food, then sat at a table some distance away, talking quietly.

"What about those two?" Chris whispered in his ear.

"I wouldn't like to tangle with either of them," Bomber said, pushing his empty plate away and patting his stomach saying, "What's for pudding?"

"If you eat anything else, you'll never get off the chair," Chris laughed, her laughter drawing a look from the two sitting at the other table.

"I'm going to the toilet." Bomber stood and headed for the door with a sign saying proudly, 'Big Boys-This Way'.

Instead of having a pee, Bomber stood behind one of the cubicles and waited. He didn't have to wait long before the door opened and the taller of the two workmen came in. Bomber stepped out in front of him.

The man stopped and looked at Bomber. "All clear," said Bomber and Bill's face cracked into a smile as he grabbed and shook Bomber's hand.

Speaking softly, Bill briefed Bomber on the target at the same time handing him a set of keys. Then Bill went to the stained sink and stood washing his hands while Bomber left the toilet and returned to Chris. She had ordered two more pints of Guinness which sat on the table untouched while Bomber whispered to her the gist of Bill's report.

They sipped the smooth, dark liquid and exchanged small talk. Anyone watching would think they were a typical young courting couple.

Bill, having returned to his table raised his almost empty glass to Andy who sighed and went to the bar for a refill.

Bomber and Chris strolled hand in hand along the street Bill had indicated, passing the battered builders' van with Brady's Builders stencilled on the side in faded letters. Two cars further along was a dirty five hundred weight beige coloured van.

Checking the street was clear, Bomber inserted the key into the driver's door and turned it. The door creaked open and Bomber got in. Reaching over, he unlocked the passenger door for Chris who got in.

In the back of the van was a shovel, bucket, large hammer and some empty sacks plus an odour not dissimilar to mouldy cheese.

"Jesus, you would think we could do better than this for a backup vehicle and what is that smell?"

"Andy's socks at a guess. It may be tatty and smelly but it's got some oomph under the bonnet from the sound of the engine," Bomber replied, laughing. "It will blend in well with what we are doing."

Arriving back at the camper van, Chris got out and climbed in then started the engine. A quick wave and Bomber drove off with Chris following behind.

They drove out on the Ballymakenny Road, finally turning off on a side road to a secluded layby where they parked up. Bomber locked the van and joined Chris in the camper.

"Well, it looks like the address we have been given is a dead end," Bomber said as he put the kettle on. "Bill and Andy have been working on a house close by and Bill said no one has been there for the last three days. Not even a car parked outside."

"That's a shit, so what do we do now?" Chris asked.

"I think we will have a drive there tomorrow and once past the house, we can widen our search looking for likely houses nearby. It could be that they just got the house number or street wrong. If there is anyone in the house, Bill will leave his coat hanging in the porch of the house they are working on."

"What about the guy they are working for, Brady or whoever?"

"Bill said he's not a problem. Once he has given them their jobs for the day, he buggers off to the pub."

"Right," Chris exclaimed, "I'll take first watch tonight and wake you at two."

Bomber finished his tea but before settling down, stepped out for a leak. Looking up, he could see the sky had clouded over and guessed the fine spell of weather was over.

The drumming of rain on the camper's roof woke Bomber who turned over and closed his eyes again but a hand shook his shoulder and a voice said, "You're on, all quiet."

'Shit,' thought Bomber, 'It can't be two already.' Looking at his watch, he could see it was half past two. Chris had given him an extra half hour.

Bomber put the kettle on and stared out into the darkness. The rain was coming down like stair rods and the monotonous drumming on the roof was having a stupefying effect on Bomber. To shake it off, he reflected on how he had ended up once more on the wrong side of the border.

No one had really talked him into it but as he mulled over the plan to Bass and Paul, he felt himself getting more enthusiastic for the task. Especially as Bass, in his normal efficient manner, put the detail into the plan. While they were discussing this, the consequences of getting caught or killed never entered his head but now those consequences were very real and the British Government would certainly wash their hands of them as a rogue element should they get caught?

After a breakfast of bacon and eggs, they locked the camper and took the Dreadnought as they had nicknamed the other van. Chris was driving and Bomber had the map on his lap.

"Take it nice and easy and we can get the lay of the land as we drive," Bomber instructed Chris.

"Will do, I'm glad the rain's stopped. Makes life a little easier." Chris sounded overly cheerful to Bomber. Was she nervous or just happy to be on the move?

They entered the small estate of well cared for detached and semi-detached houses, situated on the north side of town. Chris, being careful to keep the speed below the limit, cruised past the houses. Only one or two had cars parked in their drives and Bomber guessed most of the owners must be at work.

After a few minutes, they came to the house Bill and Andy were working on. It had a tarpaulin over one end of the roof, scaffolding at the gable end and a variety of things stacked in what was once the front garden but now had bricks, tiles, sand and bags of cement in piles.

Andy was in the garden shovelling cement and sand into a mixer. He stopped shovelling and walked to the porch where he hung his jacket next to Bill's.

"What does that mean?" Chris asked.

"Trouble, that's what!"

"Okay, that's our target's house." With a nod of his head, Bomber indicated a semi-detached property with a neatly kept front garden. Parked outside was an empty dark blue Ford Escort car.

"Drive to the end and park so we can watch the house," instructed Bomber.

Chris did so, parking neatly between two cars and then turning the engine off.

Bomber climbed into the back of the van and sat watching out of the small window in the rear door.

Fishing out his monocular, a powerful single lens version of the binoculars, he focused on the house. As he did so, the front door to the house opened and two men came out. One, tallish with black hair, glasses and wearing an overcoat was talking to the other shorter, stocky man dressed in jeans and a denim jacket. The latter had his head down and was listening intently.

Bomber gave a sharp intake of breath as he suddenly realised who he was looking at. The taller one he was sure was O'Neill and the other was his sworn enemy, O'Brian, a man who had vowed to kill him. Once one of the regiment's own but now a hard-line PIRA man.

It took a second to realise Chris was talking to him confirming who the two were. Bomber shook himself and instructed Chris to be ready to follow their car but not to start the engine yet.

The two were now in the car with O'Brian in the driving seat, still with his head down. O'Neill was in the front passenger seat. Bomber could see he was banging his fist up and down on the dashboard. O'Brian was not looking at O'Neill who was reputed to have a very violent temper and was so hard line, even his own equals in the PIRA feared him. Bomber swivelled the monocular to the house and he could see Bill on the scaffolding looking towards the car.

"They're moving," came from Chris who had slid down in her seat so she would not be seen by anyone driving past. "We could take them now and save the world a lot of pain."

As much as he would have loved to put a bullet into each of them, Bomber had already dismissed the idea of a gun fight in a residential area. "No, we need to follow them very carefully and find out where they are holed up."

"Okay but we may never get a chance like this again," Chris grumbled at Bomber as she eased the Dreadnought out and followed at a distance. Bomber reluctantly agreed but trying to take them now was too risky. A running gun battle on public roads south of the border was not a good idea.

They followed the Escort northwest. There was enough traffic for Chris to keep the car screened from O'Brian even if he was looking for a tail. Bomber wondered what O'Neill had been blowing his top over. Certainly O'Brian seemed to be soaking it up and not replying, so it must have been serious.

"They're turning off left." Chris's voice pulled Bomber back to the present.

"Where are we?" Bomber asked, looking for the map that had fallen on the floor.

"The sign said Tullyallen." Chris eased the Dreadnought left behind a small truck.

Bomber caught sight of a road sign as they turned onto 'Townley Hall Road'.

They were now in open countryside with very few houses. Finally, the Escort took another left pulling up outside a stone-built house that would not have looked out of place as an English vicarage.

"Don't turn left, drive on and pull up by those trees on the left." Chris did as she was asked, bringing the van to a gentle halt. Bomber was out of the Dreadnought and running to the trees, monocular in hand, then pushing through undergrowth and brambles until he found a place where he could see the back and one side of the house.

Bomber trained the monocular onto the French windows and could see the outline of people inside. He tensed as he saw a hand raised then striking out at a smaller figure which fell sideways to the floor. Then the curtains were drawn blocking his view.

Bomber made his way back to the Dreadnought which Chris had now turned around.

"Christ look at you, blood everywhere!" Chris exclaimed as she started wiping his face with a piece of rag from the glove compartment.

Bomber looked into the mirror. He had several scratches on his left cheek. The backs of his hands were also scratched and bleeding from the tough thorns of the brambles. Cleaning himself up, he told Chris what he had just witnessed.

"Who do you think got smacked?"

"Well it wasn't O'Brian, someone smaller and by the way he moved, younger."

"Our target?" asked Chris.

"Most likely, if the story is true about him parking the car in a different place to where he was told. Now O'Neill's getting in the neck for it and is taking it out on the target."

"Do you think they will kill him?"

"Nothing would surprise me if O'Neill is pissed off enough."

"So, what's the plan, O'Brainy one?"

"Same as before. Watch and wait."

After an hour, Bomber realised that they couldn't stay put without drawing attention to themselves. While they were screened from the house, anyone going to the house or leaving would be bound to see them and become suspicious.

Bomber looked at his watch three hours before dusk. "Okay, let's go back to the camper. We need our gear."

"What are you going to do?" Chris quizzed, as she drove off back the way they had come.

"Need to get a message to Bill and Andy. Any suggestions how to do it without blowing their cover?"

Chris had a simple answer to making contact with them. She just drove the Dreadnought up to the house they were working on, got out and called out to them, asking the way to a fictitious address. Andy wandered over and they talked while Andy pointed down the street.

They all met up later on the Tullyallen road and put together a plan. Not much of a plan, Bomber had to admit but they had little hard intelligence to go on. Now they were staking out the house and waiting. *'Don't rush,'* the voice in his head said. *'You know how easy it is for plans to go horribly wrong if you rush.'*

Bomber shivered. He and Chris had been sitting in the trees near the house for four hours with Bill and Andy a short distance behind them. He wore a thick roll neck black sweater over his shirt and a dark green oiled cotton jacket. Black jeans and walking boots completed his outfit.

Chris was also suitably dressed for sitting in the wood during darkness. They had driven in from a different direction to the one they had used to follow O'Neill and O'Brian in order to avoid alerting any watchers at the house.

Bomber decided to ignore the advice of the voice in his head and to get moving. Nudging Chris, they moved forward towards the house. The lights had been off for almost two hours, long enough for the occupants to be in a deep sleep and Bomber had had enough of sitting still.

At the edge of the trees, facing the house were fifty yards of pasture then the garden fence which was little more than a three-foot-high wooden shield to keep the sheep out.

The sky had clouded over during the afternoon which made the night as dark as pitch. Bomber and Chris walked slowly towards the fence. Bomber had wanted Bill with him but Chris had argued her case that it was her job to watch his back and that she was better at picking locks than Bill who had admitted that he was a little rusty as a locksmith.

Quietly and carefully they made their way to the front of the house. *'Shit,'* thought Bomber, *'the car has gone.'*

Chris had also noticed it was missing and whispered in Bomber's ear. "Do you think they have taken the target with them?"

Bomber shrugged and they moved on. Certainly, he had not heard the car go while they were in the trees, when somebody switched the lights off in the house earlier.

Finally, they had circled the house and were now at the kitchen door. Bomber gently tried the door but as he expected, it was locked. He stood back and Chris took out a small wrap from her pocket. From the wrap, she extracted a metal tool which she fitted into the lock. Bomber heard a soft, 'Yes' escape her lips and then he heard the lock open. Putting the wrap away, she pulled out the thirty-eight special, then turned the handle. The door opened easily on oiled hinges.

Bomber felt himself breathe again and eased his grip on the Beretta. Chris led the way into the dark house, stopping every two of three steps to listen. Like all old houses, it had its own way of making noises.

Creaking wood as it cooled after the heating had been turned off, windows that whistled as the wind blew, the ticking of a clock. All had to be identified and eliminated from the intruder's mind before identifying the noise that would give away the position of another human being.

Slowly and carefully, they checked each room. The kitchen clean, neat and tidy. The hallway with coats hanging on the rack. Two warm jackets and an overcoat could mean two of three people in the house. The lounge, empty with a dying fire in the grate, two mugs sitting on a coffee table in front of a sagging sofa.

'Three coats, two mugs. So is it two or three people in the house?' The thought ran through Bomber's mind.

Chris touched his arm, making him jump. She gave a thumbs up to indicate that Bill and Andy were in the kitchen and following them.

Bomber nodded and pointed upwards, then moved to the hallway and the stairs. The stairs were wide with an ornate wooden balustrade, strangely out of keeping with the rest of the house. Bomber ascended slowly, keeping close to the wall and placing his feet tight to the side to reduce the chance of a creaking riser.

Feeling his throat go dry, he tightened his grip on the Beretta. Chris waited until he was at the top before she made her way up. Bomber knelt and studied the five doorways on the landing, three on the left and two on the right. One door on the right was open and he guessed that was the bathroom.

Heading to the first door on the left, he knelt down and gently opened it. He could see what looked like someone in bed with the covers pulled over but could not hear any sound.

Then it happened. The landing light went on! Bomber poked his head round the door frame just enough to see that coming out of the last room on the left was a man of about thirty years, wearing a vest and pants, one hand scratching at his nuts, the other his hair. He was almost at the bathroom when he realised there was someone pointing a nasty looking gun at him.

"On the floor, now!" snapped Chris.

The man's mouth dropped open and for a split second, Bomber thought he was going to comply. Instead, he turned and ran, shouting, "Sean, Sean help. Get the guns, quick!"

Before he had taken more than three steps, Chris was on him like a leopard taking down a deer. With a sweep of her arm, she cracked him hard on the back of his head with the thirty eight's butt. The man dropped like a felled tree and Chris, nimble as a gymnast rolled into the open bathroom doorway, gun trained on the closed door opposite.

Bill and Andy appeared at the top of the stairs and hunkered down, guns trained at the still closed door. Bill nodded to Bomber, then moved quickly to get to the other side of the second door, shoulder rolling to get past it, coming up with his gun on the door.

Bomber risked a glance at the bed. Behind him the bundle had not moved. He mouthed to Chris to call out as she had the best Irish accent in the group.

"You in the room, come out, hands in the air. No one will hurt you," Chris called in a firm but not unfriendly manner.

In reply, the door almost disintegrated as a shotgun with heavy gauge shot tore through the wood.

Silence then a noise, a sash window opening, Bomber guessed. Bill was already through the door and two shots rang out almost at the same time as another blast from the shotgun erupted.

"Bill, you okay?" called Chris.

Andy was already moving down the landing to enter the room when Bill called out, "Okay, room clear." On hearing that, Andy kicked open the last door on the right and went in.

"Room clear," Andy called.

Bomber gave a sigh of relief then turned his full attention to the bed. Flicking the light switch, a bare bulb hanging from the ceiling bathed the room in a bright light so strong, it hurt Bomber's eyes. Apart from the bed, there was a free-standing double door wardrobe, a small table with a cross on it and a bed side table. The floor was bare except for a small rug by the bed.

The bundle on the bed still had not moved. Bomber pulled back the cover to reveal a figure in T Shirt and pants curled up on its side. His hands, for it was a man, a young man, thin with long, dark hair, were clamped to his stomach.

Bomber looked at his face and saw the left side was swollen and his eye was closed by the swelling.

His lips were drawn back in a silent scream and blood stained the bed sheets and his chest, where it had erupted from his mouth. Bomber took off a glove and felt for a pulse, the skin was as cold as ice and there was not even a flicker of life.

Andy stepped in front of Bomber and lifted the man's T shirt, dark bruising could be seen on the abdomen and chest.

"They gave him a serious beating. Must have ruptured something vital and he was bleeding internally. Then they dumped him here, not knowing they had already condemned him to a slow and painful death," Andy spoke with a hint of sympathy. "Poor bastard didn't stand a chance."

Bomber nodded, punishment beatings were common both with the IRA and the Provos. It took an experienced man to know just how much punishment to inflict and more importantly, where to hit and how hard. Whoever had done this was not such a person or it had been done in a rage.

Bomber went through the pocket of the jacket on the floor next to a pair of scruffy grey trousers and found a wallet. Extracting a driver's licence, he pocketed it and dropped the jacket back on the floor.

Bomber and Andy went out onto the landing, Chris was looking down at the man she had struck. Bill was saying, "He's dead. Just leave him, if you hadn't done it, I would have shot him." Bill had her by the arm and started leading her to the stairs.

"Shit," Chris said with force, "We could have done with him to get some answers to the questions we have. Instead I smash his skull in, shit!"

"Andy, take the photos of their faces and check them and the rooms for any ID. I'll look for a hoover to clean where we have been and then we will get out of here," Bomber ordered.

Andy pulled a small compact from his jacket pocket and took the pictures that could be used later to identify the men. Bomber had found the vacuum cleaner in the kitchen and cleaned the bedrooms and landing, ready to start on the stairs.

"Okay, once I've done this, it's lights off and out of here."

Bomber was already half way down the stairs when Bill said, "Wait, why don't we stay here and get the other two when they come back?"

Bomber looked at Bill and could see a stain getting darker on his left leg. *'The adrenalin must be flowing fast through Bill,'* thought Bomber, *'if he hasn't noticed he's been hit.'*

Bill looked down at where Bomber was staring, "It's a scratch just a pellet grazed my leg."

In the kitchen, they examined Bill's leg. The pellet had entered deep into the thigh muscle and the small hole seeped a steady flow of blood. Chris used a kitchen towel to make a pad and then bound it with strips of another towel.

"Right, Bill has suggested we stay to see if the other two return and then we take them. It's an idea I like as we could get O'Brian off my back and nail that bastard O'Neill for the bombing. However, I'm against it for the following reasons."

"One, Bill needs that leg seeing to before blood poisoning sets in. Two, we have strict orders not to get caught, no one will help us if we do and you can bet your boots we would not live long in an Irish prison." Bomber paused and looked at each in turn before continuing.

"Thirdly we have completed our mission, the dead boy upstairs meets the description of the target. I believe they gave him a punishment beating for parking the car bomb in the wrong street but being heavy handed prats, they went too far and he has died as a result."

"Now the other two would be a big bonus but with three dead men upstairs, already hanging around is too risky. We don't know if or when the others might turn up. It could be more than just those two who turn up and then we have a gunfight on our hands for which we are not equipped. No, it's time to head north, agreed?"

Bomber looked at Bill who was sitting on a chair nursing his leg.

Bill nodded, "Yes, fuck it, you're right."

Andy and Chris nodded their agreement.

"So what we will do is double check we have not left any evidence." Bill held up the two empty cases from his automatic pistol that he had used on the third man and Chris pocketed the bits of bloody towel she had used on Bill's leg. Andy emptied the hoover contents into a bin bag which they would take with them. Fingerprints wouldn't be a problem as they all wore gloves.

"Good, when we leave the house, Chris will relock the door with her magic spanner then we drive back to the camper van. Andy will dump the builders' van and drive the Dreadnought with Bill, following us north. We will use the planned route back avoiding the main roads and cross at an unmanned crossing. All happy?"

They grunted their agreement and moved out, Bill refusing any help to walk back to the vehicles.

As they neared the trees, Bomber looked back at the house. It was in complete darkness and he thought that was where they were, in darkness, lost in a never-ending spiral of tit for tat deaths and he felt the darkness pressing down on him like the lid of a coffin.

Chapter 10
Shock Tactics

Bomber was driving with Chris checking the route plan as they headed north for the border. "Need to take a left in about half a mile."

Bomber glanced in the rear-view mirror. The Dreadnaught was about a hundred yards behind where Bomber could see it clearly as the weak sun rose in the east, bathing the countryside in light.

"Do you think Bill's leg will be okay?" Chris asked in a subdued voice.

"Yes, the pellet was heavy duty but it's not like a high velocity bullet that tumbles and tears its way through the flesh. What about you and the guy you clobbered?"

Chris was silent for a moment then sighed, "I was going to shoot him when he started shouting, then when he turned his back to run, I didn't think, I just rushed in and whacked him on the head. Didn't mean to kill him. What would you have done?"

"Oh, I would have shot him, front or back, no difference. If he had got to the bedroom, he would have come out shooting. What you did was brave, a little reckless maybe, so in future shoot first and think after. Hesitating can get you or others killed."

Chris was quiet, head down then looking up she said, "Next left," and Bomber took it.

"Will you be telling the Brig I cocked up?" asked Chris anxiously.

Bomber glanced at her and could see she was serious. "You never cocked up. You were bloody good. You'll learn from this and go on to be even better which is what will be needed as I feel this war will drag on and on and get even nastier than it is."

Bomber could see she was surprised by his words. Then she asked, "Why don't you join the Brig's team? I have heard him and the Colonel talk about you.

They think you are the perfect man for this sort of terrorist war. He would take you on in a flash and you could get promoted as well."

Bomber was silent, then blurted out what he had been feeling since leaving the dark house with its dead men. "To be honest, I'm thinking of chucking it all in. I've been involved in so much in the last two years I'm not sure how much more I can take."

Chris reached out and touched his arm. "Bill said you probably were thinking like that but that you're like him, hating it but addicted to it. You can leave but it won't leave you!"

"Bill said that?" asked Bomber in surprise.

"Yes, he's been there and back again, as he said in worse shit holes than this."

Bomber laughed. "Okay, we'd better pull over and check on the man."

"I'll get a brew on for everyone while you check on him."

Bill looked drawn in the face but in remarkably good spirits as he and Andy joined them in the camper for the brew. His leg had stopped bleeding and he gingerly lifted it up on the bench which served as Chris's bed.

"So," said Bill "I reckon we are half an hour from the border and there is no guarantee there will not be either a Garda patrol this side or RUC on the other." Bill let the statement hang in the air.

Bomber nodded. "We stick to the plan and the cover stories, we're on pre wedding visits and you guys are going north for work."

"If that doesn't work?" It was Andy who raised the question that was on everyone's mind and even though they all already knew the answer, there was an awkward silence until Bomber said.

"We use whatever force necessary to get north of the border. The RUC, no problem, we just explain and wait for the Colonel or Brig to confirm it with them."

In pensive mood, the others silently nodded and sipped their tea. Bomber was aware that none of them wanted a shootout with the Garda no matter what. They all had some sympathy with the Garda, caught between upholding the law and guided by politicians who probably supported the IRA, even if it was covert support.

They set off again heading north, crossing the border on a narrow country road into Armagh County without a patrol of any sort in sight but Bomber knew they could have been spotted by a covert army group. Maybe even one of his recce teams but then he dismissed the thought as they would normally be further east on the border.

Fifteen minutes later, they drove round a bend to suddenly be confronted by four masked men. Two held rifles and stood about twenty-five yards away on either side of the road, aiming the weapons at the vehicles. Two others brandished handguns and these two started waving for Bomber to stop. Bomber slowed right down to give himself time to think.

"Tool up," he said urgently to Chris, "and when we get level, you shoot the one on the left. I'll do the one on the right then I'll floor it, so just keep shooting at the rifle man."

Bomber pulled the Beretta from its place under the dash and drove left handed. He could see Chris had the thirty-eight nestled in her lap. Glancing in the rear-view mirror, he noticed that Andy had closed up behind them.

As Bomber got nearer to the two men with hand guns, he slowed almost to a halt and they approached on both sides of the camper, guns pointing straight at them. Bomber was in no doubt, if they realised they were not locals, their lives would be worth nothing.

He had a fleeting vision of their bodies lying in a ditch with a bullet through the back of each of their heads. The one on Bomber's side started shouting at them.

"You are now in free County Armagh and—" That was as far as he got as Bomber shot him twice. Chris pumped two rounds into the other man, then Bomber floored it, racing through the gears into third, aiming the camper at the nearest rifleman who, taken by surprise stumbled backwards away from the camper van that was spewing death at him.

The other rifleman stood his ground firing aimed shots at the camper. Bomber ducked as two shots shattered the windshield, spraying them in glass. He could hear Chris swearing and shooting at the rifleman but he had guts and kept firing at the camper. The sound of rifle rounds hitting the old camper in quick succession told Bomber that the rifle was a semi-automatic.

"Got the bastard," cried Chris. Bomber looked in the wing mirror and saw the rifleman was down on one knee. He had dropped the rifle and was holding his leg, big mistake. As Andy and Bill drove past, they fired at both riflemen.

Bomber did not see the result of their shooting as he was driving hard, taking the bend so fast the camper threatened to slide off the road but Bomber managed to hold it. The Dreadnought was close on their heels and Bomber could hear the engine screaming as Andy pushed it to the limit in each gear.

"That was close! If I hadn't been leaning out of the window, I would be dead or dying." Chris had to shout over the noise of the wind rushing through the shattered windshield. Bomber glanced sideways at where Chris was poking her fingers into a hole in the back of the bench seat laughing as she did so.

"Too fucking close," replied Bomber. "The bastards are trying to make this their patch. So where are the patrols that should be closing them down?"

Three miles later, the camper gave up the ghost with a bang. "That sounds like one of the big ends just went through the engine casing," Chris said in a glum voice. "They must have put a round into something vital and we've lost all the engine oil."

Bomber hadn't a clue what had caused the breakdown but knew it was bloody inconvenient.

The Dreadnought pulled in behind them and Bomber walked over to them. Andy got out and spoke to Bomber. "The left-hand rifleman got away, went through the hedge at a high rate of knots. I finished the other one."

"Right, let's hope he hasn't got some mates close by and raises a posse to come after us. The camper's finished so we will get into the back of the Dreadnought. Question is, what to do with the camper? Torch it or just clean it down?"

"Take too long to clean it so best torch it and we can get moving," Bill spoke through the open window in a tone that indicated he wanted to get a move on.

Bomber could see Bill was grey in the face and despite his denials, Bomber could tell that the leg was giving him more trouble than he was letting on.

They left the poor old camper a blazing inferno, having removed anything that could identify them, bundling it all into the back of the Dreadnought. Then Chris had stuffed a rag into the petrol filler before putting a match to it. Now they were going flat out heading for home.

Twenty minutes later, they were stopped at an army check point. Bomber asked to see the road block commander who turned out to be a Green Jacket Sgt he knew by sight from Rent a Company. A nickname they had given themselves as they were always being loaned out to bolster up other units.

Bomber briefed him on who they were and about the PIRA or IRA gunman that had tried to stop them. The Sgt told them to stay put while he used the radio to check in. Two riflemen kept them covered not wishing to be the victims of a double bluff by some English-speaking terrorists.

A minute later, the Sgt waved them through and once back in the security of HQ Lisburn, they took Bill straight to the medical centre. This time he accepted a shoulder for support. The medical Cpl took one look and called for the MO. Between them, they took Bill into an examination room, closing the door on them in a way which indicated they were not invited.

Bomber led the way as they headed for the Brig's office. As they approached, the door opened and Paul ushered them in. Bomber figured he must have seen them coming on the monitor. In the room, the Brigadier sat in his normal chair while the Colonel stood to one side, pouring coffee into mugs. "Best give that coffee a little boost," said the Brigadier in a firm voice. "I have no use for it anymore."

Bomber noticed he smiled when he spoke but still looked forlorn. They took the coffees and sat down. Enjoying the warm glow as the whisky laden coffee entered his stomach, Bomber studied the Brigadier as he asked questions. His hair was shot through with more grey and his shoulders were not braced back and straight as in the past.

'He's aged ten years,' thought Bomber. *'He must have been pretty ill, he should be somewhere in the sun resting not dealing with all this crap.'*

When the Brigadier had bled them dry of everything that had happened, he dismissed them. Attracting Bomber's attention with a wave of his hand, he said, "David, I would like a word."

Bomber sat down thinking he was in for a lecture for not waiting to try for O'Neill and O'Brian. There was just the four of them, the Brigadier, the Colonel and Paul who had a funny sort of smile on his face.

Suddenly the Brigadier stood up, squared his shoulders and said, "Well let's have a real drink, shall we?" Paul produced fresh mugs and a bottle of malt from behind some box files.

Bomber looked on in amazement at the complete change in the Brigadier, gone was the lack lustre man of a few moments ago. Replaced by a sharp eyed, straight backed man Bomber had known before.

"You're not really ill then, Brigadier?" Bomber asked.

"Had a little twinge in the ticker, played it up, wanted to find out who was after my job, my network and which snakes I should let my mongoose attack! Now I know but I want them to think I am on my last legs, draw them out a little more. Give them enough rope and they will hang themselves." He was smiling and so too were the Colonel and Paul.

"Only we four know the truth, so mum's the word, David."

"Yes sir, of course," answered Bomber but he thought, *'God, it's like a bloody suicidal circus being a sneaky beaky.'*

"You never said what you thought of our little trip south, sir. Did I do the right thing pulling out or not?" Bomber asked.

"Yes, yes, forgive me for not saying so. Absolutely the right decision. Tell me, how did our girl do?"

Before Bomber could reply, a phone rang, Paul answered and everyone waited until he put the receiver down. "That was the doc, they have removed the pellet from Bill's leg and he will be fine in a week or two."

"Splendid," said the Colonel. "Top man that, time he got a promotion, what!"

"Indeed he should," echoed the Brigadier.

Bomber felt relieved, then realised that they were waiting for him to say how Chris had done.

"She's good, no she is better than good, a natural if that makes sense. Stays calm, reacts quickly when it's needed and stays cool under fire. Smart too, I was glad she was part of the team."

"So she has lived up to expectations. That's good, thinking of giving her a team of her own now things are getting busy." The Brigadier paused and sipped his malt looking at Bomber over the top of his glass.

"Now what about you, David? Can I not persuade you to work for me full time?"

Bomber's words to Chris came to his mind and hers to him.

'What the fuck do I really want to do? Help catch the bad guys and risk becoming just like them or what?' he thought.

"I don't know sir, I really don't, part of me wants to be in the forefront of getting these bastards and yet—"

"That's alright, David," the Brigadier interrupted but spoke kindly. "No need to worry about it but the job's there anytime you want it. Now go and get some rest, Paul's fixed a room for you in the mess."

As they walked to the mess, Paul told Bomber it was all kicking off in the HQ. The new Brigade Commander was seen as the bee's knees in antiterrorist tactics due to his experience in many far-flung defunct colonies.

Their own Brigadier didn't agree that the same tactics would work in a modern society with all the complications of government and media on the scene. His policy was only good intelligence and well-trained police and soldiers could do the job until either the enemy was destroyed or a political solution was found.

Now new military groups were being formed at the Brigade Headquarters acting almost independently and worse, they were trying to poach each other's intelligence sources, putting the sources in even greater danger than they already were.

The MRF were active again, much against the Brig's wishes. Paul finished by saying, "It's like a fucking gang bang in a brewery. All acting as if they are pissed and no one knows who's fucking who! Everything we worked for over the last year has gone to rat shit." Paul was angry and Bomber had never heard him speak with so much venom in his voice.

Bomber showered and changed into the cleanest clothes he had salvaged from the camper. Fortunately, the rules were relaxed on dress in the mess due to all the requirements of the different elements working in the HQ.

At dinner, he had a chance to speak to Chris and Andy, chewing over the details and wondering what old man Brady was thinking about his missing builders. Bomber asked how Andy knew so much about the building trade. Andy told them he got it all from his dad who had a small building outfit in Bradford and as a kid, he would help out during the school holidays.

The talk eventually got round to the new power struggle in the HQ with the new groups forming. No one liked the idea of the MRF group especially as Bomber told them of a previous encounter he had had with them. After some more chat, Chris suggested they went to see Bill after dinner.

Dinner was a quiet affair, everyone keeping their thoughts to themselves as there were other people present who would not know who they were or what they had been doing.

At the medical centre, the duty medic said Bill was asleep and would not be up and about for a few more days. So they wandered back to the mess bar and had a couple of drinks. There was not much conversation with each of them nursing their drinks, seemingly deep in their own thoughts. Bomber finished his drink quickly as he wanted to get a good night's sleep before re-joining his recce boys the next day.

Sleep came easily to Bomber as he was exhausted but in the early hours, his old dream was back to haunt him.

A loud banging on his bunk door woke Bomber from a troubled sleep. Looking at his watch, he could see it was already six thirty. Jumping up, he took two strides to the door and wrenched it open, ready to tell who ever it was to Foxtrot Oscar when he saw Bill's grinning face looking at him. Bill was leaning on some elbow crutches, one of which he had used to batter the door with.

"Well, stop gawping and invite me in to sit down." With that, he pushed his way past and crashed onto the bed lifting up his injured leg.

"We came to see you last night but the medic said you would be in bed for a few more days."

"Oh bollocks to that, if I can't go out on the ground then I'll help in the planning of ops with Paul and the Brig. Got any whisky?"

The last bit caught Bomber by surprise, "Er, no and it's too early for the bar."

"Just as well, wouldn't do to turn up pissed for work but I intend to hang a few on tonight. Care to join me?" invited Bill.

"I would but I have to get back to Ballykinler today, been away from the platoon for too long," responded Bomber.

Bill raised his eyebrows, sighed and said, "You are allowed to relax after one of the Brig's little jobs, you know. He would recommend it."

"Maybe but I would rather keep busy then I don't have to think about what we've been up to."

Bill stared at Bomber. "I know what you mean but if you don't get it out of your system now, it will nag at you until you do. Anyway, time you stopped fucking about doing two jobs and concentrate on what you are really good at."

"What do you mean by that?"

"I mean you are born to work for the Brig catching the bad guys," said Bill.

"I don't seem to catch them, just kill them," Bomber said in a subdued voice.

Bill almost exploded and sat up on the bed. "Oh for fucks sake! This is a war, a dirty war. We don't pretend to be civil policemen and the terrorists don't act like your average criminal. They are murdering bastards blowing up women, children and the like. They kill policemen and soldiers just to make a political point. They even kill their own, so don't go all soft. War is war and we have to be better than the fucking IRA, routing them out and if we can't arrest them, then we kill them!"

A round of applause came from the doorway and Bomber turned to see Andy, Chris and Paul standing in the doorway. "You said it, Bill," cried Chris.

Bomber felt embarrassed standing there in his underpants so grabbed his trousers saying, "For crying out loud, is there no privacy in this place?"

Andy laughed "Fancy that, you and Chris almost married and still shy!"

Bomber couldn't help but join in the laughter. "Okay, okay, give me ten minutes and I'll meet you downstairs for breakfast."

Breakfast was a hilarious affair with Bill telling outrageous stories which, even if they were only half true would have been bordering on suicidal but somehow he made them sound funny. Before he left, Bomber quietly asked Bill what he thought about the MRF group.

"Well, my advice is to stay well away. Some of my regiment boys have been approached but as the MRF is made up of mostly volunteers, the majority have said no."

"What is the role for this lot?" asked Bomber. Bill knew of Bomber's previous encounter and took a minute before he answered.

"I hope it's not as before but I think they will get down and dirty. The new Brigade Commander has taken the gloves off, so who knows what will happen. One thing you can bet on is if anything goes tits up, the politicians will deny any knowledge of the group as they would have of us."

Bomber nodded and felt as if a weight was pressing him down. Then his tormentor kicked in, *'Who are you to criticise? Let's look at what you have done shall we?'*

'Be quiet,' countered Bomber, *'I'm a soldier and follow the rules of combat!'* The voice in his head laughed.

Bomber shook Bill's hand and left for Ballykinler.

Chapter 11
Retaliation

It had been two weeks since Bomber had said goodbye to Bill and the team in Lisburn and he had settled back into life with the platoon in Ballykinler. Despite the endless routine of KP patrols and stop and searches, Bomber didn't mind as he felt comfortable with the lads doing what they were good at.

He felt at home sharing the days in the rain and the nights lying in some hedgerow watching and waiting. Family, was that what it was? Did he crave some sort of cocoon of a group of brothers of some sort? Then the voice in his head chipped in.

'Family, what would you understand about family? You are too wrapped up in trying to be something between a hundred percent no holds barred soldier and an undercover idiot.'

'Is that true?' Bomber thought, *'Do I not have anything else?'* Then once again, he realised he didn't.

In Belfast and the rest of the province, the IRA and PIRA continued its bombing campaign, hitting defenceless civilian targets far more than the security forces. Then on the seventh of May, all hell broke loose in the Springmarten area. Gunfights broke out between the UDA and the two IRA factions. The security forces, caught in the middle, ended up shooting at both sides.

Bomber found himself and his recce teams on the periphery, acting as cut offs for any one slipping out of the area. They were stopping cars with frightened people in, fathers trying to get wives and children to safety, cars with tough looking youths who had decided that being in a three-way gun fight was not as much fun as the movies made out. Now they were eager to visit a distant cousin who lived out of town.

After two days, the shooting stopped and Bomber heard from Captain Bass that seven gunmen were confirmed dead. How many wounded he did not know. Several days later, while doing an escort for a bomb disposal team, they heard a massive explosion.

Back at the Mill, Bomber checked in with Captain Bass who brought him up to date on the explosion. A bomb had exploded outside of Kelly's bar, a place used by the local Caths. Casualties were estimated at sixty to seventy with one confirmed dead.

"Fucking UDA claimed responsibility, no warning," Bass shook his head as he spoke. "After the Springmaten gun battle, this could be the start of a mega retaliation by the Prods and you can bet your boots the IRA will counter with something just as hideous."

"Not what we need," replied Bomber, really just wanting to get something to eat and sleep for ten hours. Despite his tiredness, the thought of the security forces being drawn into a full-scale three-way battle was not lost on him. At the moment, the UDA had left the security forces alone but it would only take one small incident to change that and everything would suddenly become extremely complicated.

"Patrols, patrols and more patrols and not a shot fired or even a fucking toe rag with a nail bomb. Do you think they have had enough, boss?" asked Harris.

They were stationary on the edge of Andersontown near Finaghy Road North, watching for suspect vehicles on the list, which seemed to Bomber to get longer each day.

"No, I think they are up to something. Just what, where and when, I don't know but let's enjoy the peace and quiet while we can without getting careless."

Dusty, who was listening to the radio traffic, butted into the conversation. "We're to go to the junction of Crumlin Road and Brompton Park. It's a shooting, boss."

"Okay, let's go but we will debus a hundred yards before and go in on foot in case it's a set up."

They didn't have far to go before they could see a body on the pavement. Debussing, they approached cautiously while the Ferret drove in front and blocked Brompton Park, its deadly Browning machine gun pointing towards everyone's favourite, the Ardoyne.

Bomber approached the body with care, although he didn't expect it to be booby trapped, something he had encountered in the Middle East but he was aware that a sniper could be lining him up as he approached.

Bomber could see blood on the pavement around the man's head. He was lying face down, arms spread at the sides of his body. He was wearing work clothes and boots and it was clear that he had been shot in the back of the head at close quarter. Part of the top of his skull was missing and Bomber could see part of his brain.

"Ambulance on its way, boss. I've called it in and a patrol from B Company is on its way," Dusty told him.

Bomber was just about to tell him to forget the ambulance and get the meat wagon, when Bomber heard a low groan from the body. *'Can't be?'* thought Bomber, kneeling down and feeling the man's wrist for a pulse.

'It's there, I can feel it,' thought Bomber. "Dusty," he shouted, "Tell them to get a move on, he's alive." Something glinted to the side of the body. Bomber reached out and using his pen, picked up an empty round case ejected from the shooter's pistol.

Looking at it, Bomber could tell it was a nine-millimetre case. He slid it off the pen and into his pocket ready to hand over to the RUC who could check it for fingerprints. They would also check the markings to see if they matched any others in their possession.

Bomber could hear Dusty talking on the radio when Armalite shouted a warning. Bomber looked up and he could see a group of youths approaching the Ferret. As they got in range, a barrage of rocks crashed down, skidding along the road and bouncing off the Ferret. Bomber ordered Harris to park the Lanny to shield the wounded man on the pavement from the rocks.

The Ferret was taking a pounding from the thrown rocks but what damage they thought they could do to the thick steel armour of the Ferret was beyond Bomber's reasoning. Some of the yobs were now targeting the Lanny. Bomber was about to order Harris to fire a couple of baton rounds into the mob when the patrol from B Company arrived and pushed the mob back.

A squeal of tyres and brakes made Bomber look round to see it was the unit's armoured ambulance coming to a stop. Mike Smith, the medical Sgt, ran over with two others carrying a stretcher. They quickly loaded the man into the armoured ambulance and without even as much as a 'Nice to see you having fun,' they raced off towards the hospital.

The B Company lads had 'rent a mob' under control so Bomber headed back to the Mill to report in. Captain Bass debriefed him and put the empty case into an evidence bag.

"Any news on the victim, sir?" asked Bomber.

"He's in the operating theatre but I would be surprised if he survives having had a nine milli round through the back of his head." Bass paused and picked up a piece of paper. "We have this information from his wallet. He's a Cath from the Ardoyne, forty years of age and works as a bookies clerk. No known connections to either IRA or PIRA and goes by the name of Michael Brady. That's it so far."

"Well, somebody didn't like him. Wasn't working for us, was he?" Bomber asked.

"Not that I know of but he could have been working for one of the Int groups but no one has put their hand up yet. Must have been quick, maybe someone he knew just walked up behind him and 'bang' in the back of the head, no warning, just bang."

"Guess so, must have been someone shorter than him," Bomber replied.

"What makes you say that?" Bass asked, looking puzzled.

"The shot went up going through the top of his skull. Someone as tall as him would have had the gun horizontal and the bullet would have come out of his forehead," Bomber explained.

"I see, a shorter one would have had the barrel pointing up a taller one down perhaps. I'll mention it to the RUC Sgt when he arrives."

"Okay sir, I'll let the lads know that he is in the operating theatre."

Bass nodded and went back to the large map fixed to the wall and pinned yet another red flag to it where the shooting had taken place.

Bomber left and as he walked the corridor to the mess, he wondered about how cheap life had become, friend one day, dead enemy the next.

'Time for a well-deserved cuppa,' Bomber thought and turned on the well-used mess kettle.

"Heard the news?" Bomber carried on making tea before turning to look at Ian, his Sgt.

"What news?"

"The regiment's being pulled out," said Ian.

"Out of Belfast?" Bomber said casually.

"No, for fuck's sake, out of the province and back to Blighty!"

Despite knowing that the tour was coming to an end, Bomber felt shocked and must have looked it.

"You're spilling your tea and your mouth is wide open," Ian said with a smile on his face.

"Where are we going?" Bomber stuttered.

"Tidworth. Never been there myself but it's one of these new open camps. Which should be fun when it comes to security."

Bomber sat in one of the two beat-up armchairs that masqueraded as furniture in the mess. He was half listening to Ian while pondering if this was his chance to get out of the violent spiral he was in or if he should ask the Brig to take him on and stay?

The next seven day's activities gave Bomber no time to consider his options. It was a whirlwind of activity getting equipment ready for hand over, briefing the new unit's Recce Platoon SNCOs and showing them the area while still maintaining regular patrols.

This was the new unit's first time in Northern Ireland and they were eager to get to grip with the tasks. Bomber wondered if they were just a little too eager or was he just feeling jealous, handing over the job to new blood.

Before Bomber knew it, they were on a Royal Fleet Auxiliary LSL (Landing Ship Logistics) heading for Liverpool. The crossing was rough and bodies lay everywhere, the lucky ones having a bucket or sick bag. The others took turns in the heads vomiting into the toilet bowls and sinks.

Some, like Bomber who had managed to keep the contents of his insides under control crowded into the Petty Officers' ward room and sipped tea or tried to sleep sitting up wedged tight against each other to avoid being thrown on the floor. One of the Petty Officers admitted to Bomber that it was the worst crossing he had experienced and he had been doing it on a regular basis for the last two years.

The drive south to Tidworth in convoy was slow and tedious and the lads were grumbling about carrying weapons without having any ammunition for them. After more than two years in Northern Ireland, it all seemed an alien concept but worse was to come.

Settling into the barracks in Tidworth Garrison was something that made even the most laid back of the lads nervous. The bombing of the Para's barracks in Aldershot the previous February was fresh in their minds. The politicians' somewhat cavalier attitude to protecting the soldiers and their families in England was laughable.

The guard who had to protect the barracks and armouries were armed with pick axe handles. The married quarters were totally open to bombings or shootings. In the case of an attack, the guard commander was supposed to call the civilian and military police. Response time was quoted as twelve minutes.

Bomber and everyone in the Regiment wondered how many unarmed people a terrorist, armed with an automatic weapon could kill and still have ample time to get away in twelve minutes. As one Cpl of the guard said to Bomber after reading his orders, "They are having a laugh, C/Sgt. It's got to be a joke! There's best part of a thousand weapons in those armouries and not a piece of barbed wire or one gun between us and them!"

Ignoring orders, Bomber carried his Berretta everywhere hidden inside his combat jacket when in uniform. When in civvies, he hid it in a homemade ankle holster knowing he would rather be alive and in trouble than unarmed and dead.

"Some guy with a package for you in the company office boss, wouldn't give it to me with the platoon's mail," Cpl Wells informed Bomber while handing out mail to the lads.

Bomber went the short distance to the company office. He knew he hadn't ordered anything, so who and what was waiting for him?

As Bomber went into the company office, the duty clerk intercepted him. Cpl Mould was a skinny six-footer who could be relied on to know what was happening even before the company commander announced it. He waved Bomber towards his cupboard sized office that had a hatch which opened into the CSM office. The hatch was closed.

Next he put his fingers to his lips, then took an army issue towel from the drawer in his desk and placed it over the intercom system on the desk. Bomber pushed the door closed, "Okay, so that's how you find out what's going on before anyone else," Bomber said gently.

He didn't wish to alienate Mould as he was always keen to keep Bomber informed. "I guess a little bit of fiddling with the bulbs in the consoles in the CSM's and the commander's offices and they have no idea that you can listen in."

Bomber kept his voice low and a half-smile on his face so as not to alarm Mould.

"That's it but I wanted to warn you that the guy in with the CSM is military police and he is very anti something about you. I heard him say that he is going to take the matter to a higher authority and get the order revoked."

Mould stopped talking and looked at Bomber, hoping that Bomber was going to enlighten him on what it could possibly be.

"Well, I wonder what that could possibly be." Bomber pondered for a second then looked at Mould and said, "In the shit or not in the shit, Cpl Mould that is the question."

"With your track record C/Sgt, my money is on 'in the shit'. Oh, no disrespect intended," Mould added quickly.

"None taken, now listen in on that machine of yours just in case I need a witness later."

"You can count on me, C/Sgt."

Bomber grunted and left the office walking the few steps to the CSM door on which he knocked and waited for the CSM to bid him enter.

"Come in," barked the CSM.

Bomber went in and said, "You wanted to see me, sir?"

The CSM nodded to the figure sitting in the chair opposite him. Bomber looked at the man who was well over six foot and was dressed in a dark grey suit, white shirt, military police tie and highly polished black lace up shoes. An overly large shaven head added to the look of a man who was conscious that he could intimidate people just by his size and appearance.

"This is WO1 Roberts of the military police, Bomber." The CSM spoke in a way that suggested he was not impressed with his visitor. The fact he had addressed Bomber by his nickname and not by rank also gave Bomber the impression the CSM was pissed off with his guest.

Bomber turned to the WO1 and said in a neutral voice. "What can I do for you, sir?"

The man looked as if he was in pain as he spoke. "It's more what I have been ordered to do for you, C/Sgt. Although I cannot understand why and I will be taking the matter up with my Colonel when he is back in barracks tomorrow. This is most irregular." He patted the package as if it was an obedient dog lying there.

"I have been ordered to give you this and take you through the orders for use and storage of the contents of this package." He pushed a package across the desk towards Bomber. Stuck on the top of the package was a brown envelope with Bomber's name typed on it.

Bomber opened the envelope and took out the note which read, *'Dear David, I have obtained for you a special dispensation to carry the enclosed pistol for your defence. The licence you should keep with you in case you are stopped by the police.'*

It was signed by the Brig and Bomber chuckled at the Polo mint in the envelope.

Bomber then opened the package and slowly took out the pistol, it was a Ruger Bearcat encased in a soft pigskin spring clip shoulder holster. It was a .22 calibre with a walnut grip and a four-inch barrel.

Bomber spun the chamber and checked that the loads were empty. Bomber realised both men were looking at him but he didn't care. He was in awe of the workmanship of the beautiful but deadly shape of the weapon. No safety catch as the weapon had to be manually cocked with the thumb before it would fire. Bomber looked in the package where a box of high velocity, long rifle rounds sat waiting for him to open and slip six of the rounds into the chambers.

The WO1 stood, scraping his chair back on the wooden floor. He towered over Bomber and reached out to take the gun. Whether it was just to look at it or to take it away, Bomber wasn't sure but he flipped the gun from his right hand to his left, then slid it into his combat trouser pocket.

Stepping forward, the WO1 crowded Bomber but before he could speak, Bomber said without looking up. "Before you go speaking to your Colonel, sir, I should tell you that the people who have authorised me to carry this weapon are extremely powerful people. Not the sort you should go out of your way to upset if you value your career."

Retreating a step, the WO1 said, "Are you threatening me, C/Sgt?" He had lowered his voice and head towards Bomber and all of his words had a bite to them.

"No sir, just advising you. I have worked for them and I can assure you they don't take kindly to people who try to obstruct them." Bomber opened the box of ammunition, removed the pistol from his pocket and proceeded to slip the rounds into the chamber.

"Now I have to caution you that you cannot do that. The weapon has to be stored in the company armoury and the ammunition in a security locker," said the WO1.

Bomber finished loading the weapon, then opened the licence. Pasted inside was a passport sized photograph of Bomber with his name and rank and British Army below it. On the other side written in legal jargon, it stated the holder of the licence was allowed to carry a concealed weapon for self-defence at any time. Bomber was relieved to see it did not state what type of gun was allowed under the licence.

Bomber closed the licence and looked at the WO1. "Well, your instructions seem to be at odds with what is stated in the licence. According to this," Bomber held up the licence, "I can carry it loaded and concealed at all times."

It was obvious the man was struggling to keep his cool. "You haven't heard the last of this, C/Sgt." Then without another word, he stepped round Bomber and left without even a goodbye to the CSM who didn't seem too bothered. Bomber was disinclined to call out what about the orders for use of the pistol.

The CSM smiled at Bomber and then said, "Cpl Mould, I know you can hear me, so two coffees now!"

Bomber sat in the vacant chair and Mould brought in the coffees. As he put them down, the CSM said, "Mention one word of this Cpl and I will have you busted down to Pte and on jankers for the rest of your life."

Mould looked at the CSM and said in a subdued voice, "You can rely on me, sir," before leaving the room.

"I know he listens in but tell me a clerk that doesn't," said the CSM. "He gets his info from his opposite number in the headquarters and then tells me. It's how I stay ahead of what's going on." He paused and took a sip of his coffee, pulled a face and said, "How about bringing me up to date on all this?"

Bomber told the CSM of O'Brian and a little about working for the Brig but not about going south.

The CSM nodded when Bomber had finished, then he stood and put his hand out for Bomber to shake saying, "Thanks for telling me. I'll keep Mum but you should tell the company commander and for fuck's sake, be careful."

Bomber left the company office and headed straight for the unit headquarters offices where he found his mentor, Capt. Bass. He started to brief Bass who held up his hand to stop him. "I already know," he said quietly while un-zipping his combat jacket to reveal a semi-automatic pistol in a shoulder holster.

"This is very unusual, C/Sgt and we must be careful who knows and discrete when carrying the pistols. Your company commander knows, the CO of course knows and the second in command but they are the only ones other than the

CSM. If the press get wind that we are walking around carrying, then the public will think all soldiers are doing it."

Later in the privacy of his room, Bomber examined the pistol, cleaned it, reloaded it and tried on the shoulder holster. It felt snug and comfortable, then he noticed there were some loops on the strap above the holster. Into these, he fitted twelve spare rounds, then he hung the holster on the back of the chair.

Wondering why the Brig had sent him a .22 calibre pistol instead of the larger, more normal nine-millimetre semiautomatic, he pulled out his book on small arms of the world where he found the page referring to the gun.

Sturm, Ruger and Company Revolvers were made in America and introduced in 1958. It went on to describe the Bearcat as a classic, compact revolver with a four-point two-inch barrel. A competent marksman could expect to obtain an average of a two-and-a-half-inch group at twenty yards.

'That's impressive,' thought Bomber, *'Two and a half inches at twenty yards with a hand gun, hmm.'*

Bomber realised what was puzzling him was the small calibre's lack of stopping power. *'Why would the Brig send him that, knowing he still had the Beretta?'*

'Stop fussing,' the voice in his head said. *'Friday tomorrow, go to the indoor range and try it out, then you can get absolutely legless at the mess party later that evening with the whole weekend to recover in.'*

"Okay," Bomber replied and went to bed, blissfully unaware of what the next forty-eight hours would bring.

Most of the unit were getting ready for the big return party to be held that Friday night, to celebrate the completion of the tour in Northern Ireland. Rumour control had it that they would not be redeployed back there for at least a year. The various messes had each organised parties with bands, comedians and other entertainment.

The Privates had a big bash laid on in the NAAFI. Only the guard would be missing out but at least they would not have to put their hands in their pockets to pay for it.

Bomber stole an hour to go to the indoor range, having located Cpl Johnson who ran the range. Johnson was a complete gun and hunting nut and was known to have a large collection of handguns and hunting rifles. Anything you wanted to know about small arms, he knew.

Inside the range, Bomber removed the Bearcat. "Wow," cooed Johnson. "Where did you get that beauty?"

"You know the Bearcat then?" questioned Bomber.

"I've got one, extremely accurate. I can hit rats on my uncle's farm at twenty paces with ease."

"Really," Bomber said raising his eyebrows. He knew Johnson was an outstanding shot but twenty paces with ease, pull the other one!

"I can see you don't believe me, so let me show you," said Johnson.

He took the Bearcat, checked the load then casually turned and fired at the paper target at the end of the range, shooting until all six shots had been fired. He then emptied the chamber of the empty cases. Pulling on a cord, he brought the target back to him. Bomber could already see a tight group of six holes in the centre of the target.

Johnson inserted a fresh target and sent it back. Bomber reloaded the pistol and tried to imitate Johnson's relaxed style. When the target came back, Bomber could see his grouping was not as tight as Johnson's but he was impressed that all six shots were on the target, especially as it was the first time he had fired the weapon.

"Not bad for the first time," said Johnson. "It's a perfectly balanced gun. Virtually no recoil, so it stays on target. A little practice and you will be able to shoot the eye out of a terrorist at twenty yards."

"Yes, maybe but the thing that worries me is its stopping power as it´s only a .22 calibre."

"Now don't worry yourself about that, let me show you." With that, Johnson picked up a plank of two-inch-thick pine wood. Then he went to the end of the range and set the plank upright.

"Okay, just put a couple of shots into the plank," said Johnson grinning.

Bomber complied, then unloaded the pistol while Johnson retrieved the plank. He pointed to the entrance holes exactly the size of the .22 rounds. When he turned the plank round, the holes were big enough to insert his thumb.

Johnson explained, "These long rifle rounds have a high velocity and when they hit, the lead is compressed to several times its diameter, punching through the flesh and muscle. Bone tends to deflect it which causes more damage." Johnson looked as if he was about to have an orgasm as he talked. "No need to worry about stopping someone with this baby if you hit them in the right spot."

They chatted about guns while Bomber cleaned the Bearcat. Johnson told Bomber he was taking leave next week to go on a hunting trip in America with another group of gun nuts. Bomber thought, *'Well not me, I've had enough hunting, thanks.'*

Chapter 12
Party Time

Bomber was woken by one of the camp guard shaking him. "Wake up, C/Sgt! The regiment is deploying." Bomber could hear the words but didn't want to open his eyes. Now the guard was shouting. Reluctantly, Bomber forced his eyes to open and looked at the soldier who was still shaking him.

"Okay, okay, I'm awake. What's happening?"

"Orders! We are going back to Northern Ireland and we leave in two hours."

As the guard left his bunk, Bomber could hear others being woken. Looking at his watch, Bomber realised he had only been in bed for four hours. He had left the party at four in the morning and it was still going strong then. As Bomber stood up, the room swayed and the pounding in his head was making him feel as if the whole of the drums platoon were in there practicing for a parade.

Staggering to the sink in his room and rinsing his face in cold water while all the time fighting back the urge to be sick, Bomber decided he was never going to party again. *'Ha-ha!'* the voice in his head pounded.

After a quick shave during which he nicked himself twice, he threw on his combats, carefully putting the Bearcat in the shoulder holster and the Beretta into his combat jacket pocket. Thrusting armfuls of clothing into his holdall, he zipped it up and headed out to the Recce Platoon lines.

Half of the lads were there loading the vehicles or hurrying from the armoury with their weapons. Then Ian, his Sgt turned up in a Land Rover piled high with ammunition which he started handing out.

"Got your rifle, boss." Bomber turned and Armalite shoved his SLR into his hands.

"How come you are so bright and cheery? I bet you were totally legless last night," Bomber groaned.

"I was, boss but as you know, I've had lots of practice at drinking and quick recoveries. Anyway, since I've had Regis to look after I don't drink as much."

"Where's Regis now?" Bomber asked, wishing the ground would stop swaying.

"The Drum Major's wife is looking after him. They get on well together," Armalite laughed. "The Drum Major said she loves Regis more than him!"

"Knowing the Drum Major, I think that could be perfectly true," replied Bomber.

Ian pushed a mug towards Bomber who could hear whatever was in it fizzing in the water far too loudly for his delicate condition. He put his hand over the top of the mug, hoping to muffle the sound and ease his thumping head.

"Got the tablets from the medical centre; set you right in no time," Ian said with a chuckle. "Bloody good night; haven't enjoyed myself so much for years!"

"Yes, it was just what we needed but we could have done without this deployment straight after it. What the hell is going on?"

"We might find out now. Here comes Captain Bass," Ian spoke in a low voice as the Captain strode up, looking fresh and full of life.

Bomber groaned and swore to God he would never touch another drop of alcohol as long as he lived if he'd just make the pounding in his head stop.

Captain Bass briefed them on what was happening. They were to take part in Operation Motorman but what that part would be they wouldn't know until later.

Ian had been right; the pills had acted quickly, settling Bomber's stomach and reducing the pounding in his head to a tolerable level.

The journey back to Liverpool had seemed to take forever and Bomber could not believe it was just a few short days since they were going from Liverpool to Tidworth. At the docks, they loaded onto the same LSL as before. The sea gods must have taken pity on them this time as they sailed across the Irish Sea on a completely calm sea and now they were assembled at the Belfast Bus Company depot to be briefed on why they had returned.

The Catholic community areas under the control of the IRA had barricaded the roads leading into those communities and declared them as no-go areas. Riots extended out from those areas while looting, hijacking of vehicles, punishment beatings, bombings and shootings were common place. To drive past one of the areas was to risk being shot, bombed or stoned.

The Brigade was to take back the areas and restore control. Each of the regiment's companies had been given an area to retake. One area, Andersontown was considered particularly difficult to deal with due to its size and would be left until the other areas were under control.

Bomber and his platoon found themselves sleeping on the floor of a cloakroom in St Peter's school just on the fringe of Andersontown. Needless to say with all the violence, school attendance had been suspended.

The Recce Platoon was being used for escort duties, rescuing of hijacked vehicles and manning observation points. The lads had been bombarded with rocks, petrol and nail bombs. Being shot at was happening all the time but was opportunist stuff when they drove past any of the trouble spots.

Anyone with a gun considered them fair game and took a shot but so far none of the gunmen had been spotted in time to engage with return fire. *'Sooner or later, one of you will get careless and then we will have you!'* thought Bomber.

Bomber had lost Dusty to hospital after a nail bomb exploded close to them. He was recovering after several pieces of shrapnel had been removed from his leg. He had sent a message to Bomber via one of the medics which read, 'Don't replace me with any oik from one of the companies. I'll be back in a few days!'

Bomber smiled when he read it, not that there was any chance of a replacement as the companies had their own casualties and the numbers were mounting.

"You are wanted in the ops room, C/Sgt." The clerk interrupted Bomber eating a sandwich. Regular meals were just a distant memory. They had been on the go constantly, surviving on a quick bite and cuppa whenever they could and a couple of hours sleep before being redeployed.

Bomber followed the clerk to the classroom, which had been converted to an ops room. Inside, he found Captain Bass with two officers dressed in combats complete with nine-millimetre Browning pistols strapped to their waists. One was a Major, the other a Captain and they looked nervous.

"Ah C/Sgt, there you are." Bass sounded fresh and cheerful despite having been on the go for the last twenty-four hours. "Major Bright has been tasked with locating an illegal radio which is operating in Andersontown and you, with your section are to provide him with protection."

Bass was then distracted by a report of one of many bomb explosions. "We need to get at least three good fixes on the signal; more would be better if possible." Bomber realised the Major was talking to him and pulled his attention back from the squawking radio.

"I was thinking of doing it from the high ground above Andersontown, perhaps from the Upper Springfield road?" the Major said, pointing to a spot on a map he held in his hand.

"Well, the Springfield and White Rock roads have not been cleared. There are a few barricades and normally a few yobs guarding them but we can give it a go, sir," replied Bomber.

"That's very good of you, C/Sgt," said the Major in an almost gentle, school masterly way.

Bomber looked hard at the officer. Was he taking the piss or was he genuinely grateful? He noticed for the first time that the combat clothing looked brand new. They both had Royal Engineer cap badges in their berets which also looked new. Something about the way they stood and talked marked them out as something different.

"Okay, what vehicle have you got, sir?" asked Bomber.

Bass interrupted, "Before you go C/Sgt, the bomb explosions were in Claudy, which is a few miles south east of Londonderry. At least, eight people were killed, two dozen injured, no warning."

"Okay, sir," responded Bomber.

"I'll show you our vehicle," said the Major, heading for the door. In the playground, parked next to one of the Ferret armoured cars was a Land Rover with a tough looking L/Cpl sitting in the driver's seat smoking. The driver did look like a real soldier and Bomber noted he was a Trucky (Royal Corp of Transport.)

On their approach, he stood up and ground out the cigarette butt on the floor.

The Major showed Bomber the array of radio equipment in the back of the vehicle.

"Brian, sorry I mean Captain Smith, will operate the equipment and I will log everything on this chart."

"Okay sir, this is how we will proceed." Bomber explained how they would attempt to complete the task.

They had driven out into the country side in a wide loop to gain the high road above Andersontown. The Black Mountain that loomed over them made for a forbidding backdrop. Every half mile or so, the Major would stop his Land Rover and he and the Captain would then play with the radios. Each time they stopped, Bomber and the lads would deploy in all round defence.

They had just rounded a bend when they saw a fuel tanker blocking the road. It had been jack-knifed across the road. To the right of the tanker on the downhill side stood a large house. In its day, it must have been a grand sight but now it had an air of tiredness as if the deaths of the people of Belfast had dragged it down.

Jumping out of the Lanny, Bomber could see legs moving about on the other side of the tanker. Without more than a hand signal, Bomber, Harris and Armalite raced towards the tanker. The Ferret followed, the Browning machine gun swivelling left and right ready to blast any gunmen hiding nearby.

Bomber could see they had removed the fuel tank filler cap and a piece of rag was stuffed in it and was slowly burning. Harris reached it first and snatched it out.

"Fucking idiots, don't they know its diesel in the tank? It would take forever to burn that!"

"Yes but the main tanker is petrol. Look at the hazard marker," shouted Armalite. The legs were disappearing fast, some running away on the road while two sets headed for the house. Bomber and Harris followed while Armalite stayed with the Ferret.

Bomber reached the door just after it was slammed shut and then heard the lock turn. Unlike Bomber, Harris didn't stop. He was running full pelt at the door and Bomber only just managed to step aside in time. The door didn't stand a chance. It crashed open, the lock disintegrating under his weight and momentum.

They were in an old-fashioned scullery with a Belfast sink under the only window. An open door led into a hallway. Opposite the scullery, another door had just closed. Throwing the door open, he dashed in rifle ready and Harris followed.

Bomber stopped in amazement! Sitting at a long table were six priests. The table was laid for lunch and a middle-aged woman was standing serving soup from a bowl.

The priests were silent, staring at Bomber and Harris. The woman ignored Bomber and continued to serve the soup, moving from one priest to the other. Bomber detected movement under the table as had Harris and like a striking cobra, he dragged a squealing teenage boy out from under the table. The boy was tall, thin and had a spotty face.

Bomber looked under the table and saw the face of an even younger boy staring back. His eyes were wide and he was trembling. Bomber waved him out and he came out on all fours; Bomber hauled him to his feet. He was several years younger but looked very like the older boy.

The eldest of the priests at the table stood and Bomber pushed the young would-be arsonist towards him. The other stood still as Harris had a firm grip of his arm.

"I'm sorry to have burst in on you like this, Father," Bomber addressed the older priest, "but these young lads have a hijacked petrol tanker outside and were trying to set it ablaze."

Bomber paused as one of the sitting priests gasped, "Holy Mary, mother of God, which would have incinerated the lot of us!"

"Indeed it would have, Father and a good few of the houses below no doubt," Bomber added.

"Now I'm going to get the tanker removed, so I'm going to leave these two in your care. I trust you will ensure they don't bother us again."

"You can be sure of that, soldier," said a large priest who wouldn't have been out of place in the front row of a rugby team. He stood up and took hold of the boy who Harris was holding. Bomber nodded to Harris who released the lad.

The priest delivered a clout to the back of the boy's head and shook him saying, "How many times do you need telling to stay out of trouble Michael, you an altar boy and all? Dragging your young brother into this as well, you are supposed to protect him, you idiot. I should give you a good thrashing but it would be wasted, I've no doubt." A further clout was delivered with a little less force but Michael let out a cry and his brother started blubbing while the older priest told him not to cry.

"We will leave you to it, Fathers."

Bomber left the way they came in and Harris followed, complaining that the smell of food had made him realise just how hungry he was.

Outside all was quiet. Cpl Wells had called for recovery to collect the tanker and had been told it could take anything up to an hour for it to arrive.

The Major had been playing with his radio equipment and Bomber asked him how it was going.

"One or two more readings and we will have it pinpointed to the very spot," he said in a way that told Bomber he was unaware of the danger he had been in. Bomber was pleased to see his driver had taken cover and was watching back down the road with his rifle at the ready.

Forty minutes later a pickup truck arrived, escorted by Ian Mason and his section. Two men in overalls walked over to the tanker. Having checked round the outside, one of them climbed into the cab. After a few minutes, he had the engine started and under the direction of the other man, they got it facing the correct way on the road.

Bomber took the chance to have a quick word with Ian whom he hadn't seen for the last twenty-four hours.

Ian told him most of the lads were done in. Three days with little sleep and not much in the way of cooked food was beginning to wear them down.

Bomber watched as the little convoy set off down the road and then turned his attention to getting the Major his other readings.

They had travelled perhaps another four hundred yards when the Major asked to stop. Just as the lads were getting into position, the shooting started. Several rounds pinged off the Ferret's armour, then rounds hit Bomber's Land Rover. Everyone had taken cover in the roadside ditch.

"Can anyone see the shooter?" Bomber yelled as another shot cracked over his head. There was no answer and Bomber looked along the ditch and got angry. "Get your fucking heads up and observe the front for the shooter, you lazy buggers!"

Grinning, Armalite, Harris and the Trucky poked their heads up and watched.

"Not sure, boss but there's a transit van between those two houses and it could be coming from that," Harris shouted back.

Bomber pulled his monocular from his pocket and studied the van. 'Got you, you cunning bastard,' Bomber thought. He had spotted a tiny puff from the side panel of the van each time a shot was fired. A hole had been cut in the panel just big enough for the shooter to see out of and fire through.

"Section, rifles only," ordered Bomber who didn't want Wells opening up with the Browning machine gun, "Three hundred, white van and side of van by the logo. Rifle man, watch and shoot."

There it was, puff and a shot hit the dirt three feet from Bomber. At that instance, four rifles cracked sending four 7.62 pieces of death at the van. Bomber immediately calling, "Cease fire!" before the lads shot the van to pieces.

Bomber couldn't see if there were bullet holes in the van as it was too far away but they had been waiting ten minutes now and there was no return fire. 'Had they hit the rifleman? Was he just waiting for them to get up so he could take another shot? Let's find out,' thought Bomber. Telling the others to stay put, Bomber got to his feet. *'Nothing,'* thought Bomber. *'That's lucky, hopefully the bastard's dead.'*

Bomber made his way to the Major's Land Rover. Both he and the Captain were sitting on the ground behind it, pistols in hand.

"I think it is all clear now, sirs. We have either killed the shooter or scared him off so we can get on with the rest of the readings."

"I think we have enough to go on now C/Sgt, so no need to do anymore. We can return to our base now." The Major sounded shaken, then gingerly handed his pistol to Bomber and said, "Do you think you could unload our guns for us? I'm afraid we are not too familiar with them."

Bomber took both pistols and ejected the magazines, then cocked the pistols to remove the round in each chamber before handing them back. Now Bomber was really puzzled as to who they were.

Bomber spoke to the Trucky who was driving them, telling him they would be escorted back but where to? That was the question.

"Oh, they are from the GPO main building in town, C/Sgt. They normally spend their time listening to radio and telephone calls."

"So they are not Royal Engineers then?" queried Bomber.

"Don't think so, just technicians of some sort. Probably civvies dressed up to protect their identity."

Skirting the main trouble areas, they made it back to the GPO building, receiving a couple of stonings on the way. Then it was back to the school, only for Bomber to be told to get all of his available men over to the restaurant on the other side of the road to the school as they had had a bomb warning.

Bomber found Cpl Jacobs getting the last of the people out of the restaurant and into their cars and away. The manager was standing in one corner of the car park with his staff, sheltering behind a wall.

Bomber asked the manager, "How did you receive the warning?"

"It was a muffled voice on the phone telling me that there was a bomb and it was set to explode at eight thirty, so I started getting everyone out and called you lot."

Bomber looked at his watch. It was quarter to eight. They had less than forty-five minutes to search the place. Eleven of them could do it easily in that time.

Bomber instructed the manager to stay out and he replied he was sending his staff home but he would wait in the car park. Bomber went in and found the lads at the hot buffet stuffing their faces.

Bomber exploded, "What the fuck do you think you are doing! We have less than forty minutes to clear this place."

Everyone stopped eating and stared at Bomber.

"It's okay, boss, there's no bomb," Armalite said quietly.

"And how the fucking hell would you know that?" Bomber felt his anger turning to rage.

"Well," said Cpl Jacob, not looking directly at Bomber, "it seems someone made the call so we could get our first hot food in days."

Bomber was dazed and didn't speak. He just picked up a plate and loaded it with food and ate. When the lads saw this, there was a collective sigh of relief and everyone carried on eating. The food tasted wonderful and Bomber lost all his anger as he stuffed another beautifully roasted potato in his mouth.

Bomber felt his belly balloon out after gorging himself for fifteen minutes without stopping. Standing up he said, "Right you crafty buggers, if anyone pulls a stunt like this again, I'll have you in front of the CO. Now, I want this place searched, so get to it and leave the booze alone!"

The lads scattered and gave the place a thorough going over.

With five minutes to spare, they came out of the restaurant, much to the relief of the manager who insisted they came in and had something to eat. When Bomber refused as they were still on duty, he begged him to let the lads take as much food as they wanted back to the school for the rest of the team as it would all go to waste.

Bomber relented and, loaded up, they returned bearing joints of beef, roast chickens and lots of other goodies which they handed out to those who had not been involved.

Bomber took a bag of roasted chicken legs into the ops room and handed them to the radio operator and clerks. Captain Bass picked up a spare one and munched on it. As he did, he spoke quietly to Bomber.

"Lads been playing party tricks, have they C/Sgt?"

"It seems that way, sir but it won't happen again."

"Well, we have a field kitchen arriving in the morning, so from now on hot meals shouldn't be a problem at any time of the day or night."

Bass paused and having finished the chicken leg, tossed the bone across the room to land squarely in the waste bin.

"Good shot, sir," Bomber said without smiling.

"Okay, it's gone quiet at the moment so make sure the lads get whatever sleep they can."

"Will do, sir."

When Bomber arrived at the cloakroom, the boys had already got their heads down. As he pulled off his boots, Ian, his Sgt, came in with his section. They looked exhausted and slumped down onto their sleeping bags.

"Fuck me with a revolving fir tree," said Ian "If we have to be sent to rescue another vehicle that's been hijacked, I wish they would check to find out if it's already been torched."

"I know it's a problem and half the time 'rent a mob' is waiting to have a go with petrol and nail bombs when we arrive," replied Bomber.

"It's just a matter of time before they line us up for something worse," Ian shot back. "But right now, I don't care. All I want to do is sleep!"

As Bomber drifted off to sleep, he wondered why he didn't feel guilty about cheating the restaurant owner out of a pleasant evening with his customers and a night's takings.

'You must be becoming hardened to it all and not giving a shit about anyone,' said the voice in his head. Then sleep claimed him.

Chapter 13
Revelation

Bomber was surprised to see Chris and Andy standing by a car in the school car park when he arrived back from escorting a bomb disposal team to deal with a car bomb.

There was another guy in leathers leaning on a motorbike a few feet away, smoking a cigarette. His helmet, hanging from the handle bars, rocked gently in the freshening breeze that warned of more rain to come.

Chris gave Bomber a hug and Andy pumped his hand up and down while slapping him on the shoulder with the other one.

"Good to see you man!" said Andy, grinning as always.

"Nice to see you again, James!" quipped Chris.

"If this is about the wedding—?" Bomber laughed as he said it but noticed Armalite and Harris giving him a sideways look.

Andy laughed fit to burst but Chris blushed and poked Bomber in the ribs hard enough to make him gasp.

The bike man flicked his cigarette onto the floor and scowled.

"This is my team or part of it, two more are on stake out," Chris said. "Andy is my number two and Lofty Thorn is the guy on the bike. He's known as Prickly but no one calls him that to his face unless they want a fight."

"I'm pleased you have your own team, you deserve it but what brings you here?" asked Bomber.

Chris took Bomber by his arm and walked a few paces away. Lowering her voice, she said, "Paul's disappeared."

"What! Where? How?" Bomber was gibbering and he knew it.

"He and two others were staking out a pub near the Springfield when he suddenly got out of the car and sent the other two back to Lisburn. No explanation, no phone call or anything, that was two nights ago."

Bomber's mind was racing. "Paul may have seen someone and maybe followed them but didn't want the others to know for some reason."

"But why hasn't he checked in!" Chris almost cried the words out.

Bomber knew Chris had more than a soft spot for Paul and he felt the turmoil rising inside him but forced himself to take deep breaths to control his emotions.

"Now," Bomber said facing Chris, "if there is one person who can take care of himself, it's Paul. He's armed and well trained and harder than a concrete wall. Plus he's smart, so whatever has happened, I believe Paul is safe and in control."

Chris nodded. "The Brig said very much the same thing but he wants to see you tonight. Oh and by the way, our stakeout is for O'Brian."

'Shit,' thought Bomber, 'I wonder if Paul saw him and is on his trail?'

The voice in his head answered, 'Don't be a prat. He would have called that in. This must be something he couldn't call in and has had to go solo.'

'You're right, that's it, must be,' thought Bomber.

He was jerked back to reality by Andy touching his arm and saying, "Come back to us, Bomber. You had the thousand-yard stare."

"Sorry, just thinking. So what am I supposed to do now? Go to Lisburn to see the Brig?"

"Yes," said Andy, "so go get your civvies on."

"Wait, I want to take two of my lads with me," Bomber said.

"What, no way!" said Chris. "We have to keep this quiet."

Bomber went to the ops room and spoke to Captain Bass who nodded his agreement saying the Brigadier had already been on the phone to him.

Armalite and Harris sat either side of Bomber in the back of the car. Chris had taken some persuading but Bomber argued that if they didn't need them, no problem but if they did, they were ready.

The three of them had changed their combats for another uniform of jeans, trainers, t-shirts and a mix of jackets that covered their shoulder holsters and pistols. Andy kept the car at the speed limit and Lofty on his bike shadowed them.

Bomber leaned forward and spoke to Chris and Andy. "Tell me about Lofty."

Chris spoke softly so Bomber had to lean even closer to hear. "Lofty, rank Cpl, was in another of the Brig's teams. Came from the Paras originally but has been with the Brig since before sixty-nine. Not much of a talker and in his mind, you are nobody until he says you are."

"What does he know about me?" Bomber asked. He didn't want anyone connecting him with the past.

"Nothing," said Andy. "Except," he stopped and glanced at Chris.

Chris coloured slightly and said, "He was mouthing off about outsiders being involved in our work when we came to collect you. I told him you had done more than he and his now defunct team could have done in a lifetime. Sorry."

Bomber sat back and said nothing, knowing Andy was watching him in the rear-view mirror.

Armalite and Harris glanced at him but then looked front. Armalite whispered, "If O'Brian is involved, boss, we will get him, no worries!"

'O'Brian!' thought Bomber. *'The slippery murdering bastard is not the reason Paul has gone missing. It's got to be something else. But what? Personal or something more sinister? Christ, Paul you could have given us a hint.'*

Bomber sat in front of the Brigadier's desk. They were alone, no whisky laden coffee was served and for once, Bomber didn't want any. The Brig fiddled with a half-eaten packet of Polo mints, his hands never staying still.

"You may know," started the Brigadier, "that Paul has worked for me since nineteen sixty-six. What you may not know is he is the son of a retired General. Bit of a black sheep, fell out with the family by refusing to go to Sandhurst as an officer cadet. Family disowned him; not spoken to each other since."

"His mother, who is in fact a cousin of mine, asked me to take care of him. That and the fact he is a brilliant operative both in the field and at analysing intelligence reports is why he works for me."

"In nineteen sixty-eight, he got engaged to a Catholic girl, Mary Rafferty. She was a freelance reporter, did a lot of stuff for American newspapers at the start of the troubles in sixty-nine. She was very anti-violence and the IRA. So one day in late nineteen sixty-nine, when Paul was working, three armed masked men dragged her from her office in full view of the public and drove off."

"Her body was found twenty-four hours later just outside Belfast. She had been savagely beaten and then executed and murdered for standing up to evil."

The Brigadier paused and wiped his face with a large white handkerchief. "She was a lovely girl, intelligent, beautiful and fun loving. Paul worshipped her. The police drew a blank. Paul asked me for leave and even knowing what he was going to do, I gave it to him. Don't think I had a choice really. He would have gone anyway."

The Brig continued, "Well with the resources at his disposal and my contacts, we soon found out who the culprits were. They had fled to America to wait for the hue and cry to die down. Paul tracked two of them down in New York; he beat both of them to death having first extracted as much information as he could. The third man has eluded us. We know his identity but he went completely off the radar, maybe in Libya."

Again the Brigadier paused, wiping his face with the handkerchief. "I believe Paul spotted the third man and has gone after him. I need you, David to find him. Here is a list of possible places he is either holed up in or might have stashed the third man. I can't risk using any of my usual people or involving the RUC. Will you do this for Paul, for me?" The Brigadier finished, leaned forward on his desk and looked at Bomber.

He had seen the Brigadier concerned before but not worried. It was clear he thought Paul might go completely off the rails. In Bomber's mind's eye, he could see Paul standing in the improvised boxing ring in the back yard of the pub, exchanging blows with another man mountain and knew how deadly he was in a fight.

That evening Bomber had admired his courage, skill and even his compassion for the loser. What he would do to someone who had brutally murdered the woman he loved, Bomber didn't want to think about.

"Of course I will, sir. I have two of my recce lads here. I will ask them to volunteer."

"This is all off the record, David so please make that clear to them. I will do everything I can to help but it must be kept low key for all our sakes."

Bomber sat in the car watching the derelict building on the outskirts of Highfield on the west of Belfast. Armalite was in the rear passenger seat and Harris was standing by a tree watching for anyone getting inquisitive about the car. The rain had stopped but there was a promise of more to come in the sky.

After the meeting with the Brigadier, Bomber had simply said to them both, "I need two volunteers for some unofficial work."

Armalite didn't hesitate but just said, "I'm one, boss."

Harris had paused and then said, "My dad said never ever volunteer but he never had much fun in his life. So I'm number two."

The first place they checked was a small cottage on the Lisburn road. It was furnished in a Spartan style but with no sign of recent visitors, although in the back garden there was a vegetable patch and half a dozen chickens in a pen. So someone minded the place.

The second on the list was a newsagent with a flat above. As the shop was occupied, they couldn't go in and check the flat, which from the outside looked empty. Bomber decided they would come back once the shop was closed.

Now they were checking the third location which they had been watching for twenty minutes without any sign of life coming from the building. It must have been some sort of vehicle repair shop in its time but was now empty and sad looking.

"Okay, let's check it out," Bomber said. He and Armalite both got out of the car and walked towards the chain link gates. Harris stayed where he was, watching and guarding the car.

The gates were padlocked but that was a waste of a good padlock as the fencing was virtually non-existent either side. Bomber casually walked around the outside of the building, shadowed by Armalite who had his nine-millimetre Browning pistol held casually by his side.

Either side of the building and at the rear was a good deal of waste ground that had become overgrown with bushes and small trees, making it ideal if they had to stakeout the place, should they need to stay for a longer period of time.

From the road, the building had looked as if it was about to fall down but now Bomber could see it was weather proof and the dirty windows were intact. *'Strange, the local kids would have come here normally and smashed the windows by now. Perhaps it belongs to someone they don't want to upset,'* Bomber thought.

At the rear of the building was a solid looking door but as Bomber had suspected, it was locked tight. Peering through the window to the side of the door he could see what had been an office of some description. A dusty desk, two chairs and a metal filing cabinet stood in the room.

"We need to get in," Bomber whispered to Armalite.

"Leave it to me, boss." Armalite produced a steel ruler of the type Bomber had used in metal work at school. "Borrowed it from the school," he muttered as he slid it up between the sash window where the two sections met. Forcing it in, he then slid it sideways releasing the catch.

Climbing in, Bomber could smell the musty odour of an unused room that hadn't had any fresh air in a long time. Armalite stepped past Bomber and carefully opened the door which led into the main building.

"All clear, boss," Armalite whispered from the side of the doorway.

They were in a large workshop used for repairing vehicles, at the far end of which was a set of large double doors for vehicle access. Both sides of the doors were two sets of dirty windows and in the opposite corner to the office was another room. Bomber and Armalite stood either side of the door leading into the other room. For some reason, Bomber's heart was beating harder than normal.

'*What's the matter with me?*' thought Bomber.

'*You're scared,*' said the voice in his head.

'*Yes I'm scared but why?*' questioned Bomber.

The voice in his head replied, '*Frightened of what you might discover Paul has been up to?*'

Armalite opened the door and Bomber peered into the room. It was empty except for a bench, some clothes pegs on the wall above it and a toilet cubicle with the door missing. The toilet bowl looked intact, as did the sink with a dripping tap.

Armalite was studying a door which Bomber presumed led outside. "Look at this, boss. Someone's been in and out of here recently."

Bomber looked. Fresh footprints could be seen on the dirty floor, some coming in and others going out.

"What size shoes would you say made those, Armalite?"

Armalite put his right foot alongside the footprints. "Well, I'm a ten and these are much bigger. From what I've seen of Paul Small, he would be a twelve or more."

'*Yes,*' thought Bomber, '*these were made by a big man or a midget wearing clown's shoes. We could be on the right trail but I saw no sign that Paul or anybody else had been camping out here.*'

Bomber tried the door. It was locked tight and there wasn't a key in the lock.

They went back into the main workshop. Bomber stared around, wondering if they were missing something. Again it was Armalite who spotted the signs. In the centre of the floor was a pit covered with heavy wooden sleepers. The sort of pit a vehicle would have been driven over once the sleepers were removed so that a mechanic could work on the underside of the vehicle.

Armalite pointed to the marks on the floor that were clearly fresh. "These sleepers have been moved, maybe in the last day or two, boss."

"Okay, let's check it out."

They lifted four of the sleepers to one side and peered into the dark hole. Nothing! *'Shit,'* thought Bomber, then he stiffened. *'What's that at the end? A bundle of something?'*

Bomber removed his penlight from his pocket and shone the beam onto the dark bundle.

"Fuck me!" exclaimed Armalite. "It's a body!" The body moved, rolling over. "Christ," said Armalite "It's alive!"

Bomber went down the steps. Keeping his light on the body, he could see it was a man, maybe thirty years old, dressed in a dirty suit. The man was bound hand and foot with tape over his mouth. As Bomber got closer, he could see the wild, staring eyes. No, terrified eyes and from the smell, he had soiled himself.

Bomber reached down and eased the tape from his mouth, which then moved but Bomber could not understand what the man was trying to say. Then he got it. "Water!"

Bomber sat the man up but didn't untie him. Armalite had found an old cracked mug by the sink in the toilet and filled it with water. Now he held it to the man's lips. He sucked at it greedily.

When he had drained the cup, he had a fit of coughing and Bomber stood back in case he puked.

"Untie me and get me the hell out of here before that maniac comes back," the man pleaded.

Then he added, "I can pay you a lot of money, ten fucking grand, just get me out of here!"

"Now why would we do that?" asked Bomber.

The man's mouth fell open as he realised that Bomber and Armalite were not what or who he thought they were.

"Jesus fucking Christ, will this nightmare never end?" the man cried.

"The same nightmare that Mary Rafferty had to endure no doubt," said Bomber.

The man let out a long groan of despair. "I've told him everything. You have got to believe me! Take me in, yes, hand me to the RUC and I will confess all." Then he started crying, sobs that racked his whole body.

Bomber felt no sympathy, more a loathing for the man and for what he, Bomber, intended to do.

The man sat bound to the chair in the office, the tape back over his mouth. Bomber had got the full story out of the man and in truth, he didn't take much persuading. Now Bomber sat on the desk wondering what Paul would do next. It was dark now and Harris had taken the car and parked it out of sight and was lurking in the shadows outside.

It was close to ten o'clock when Bomber heard the sleepers being moved. Neither of them had heard the other door open but Bomber wasn't surprised, knowing that Paul could move as quietly as a cat. The noise of the sleepers scraping on the floor was what had alerted them. Armalite moved to one corner of the room, Browning pistol at the ready.

Bomber carefully opened the office door. He knew it was Paul by the silhouette of his body against the pale light from the windows.

"He's in here, Paul!" Bomber said quietly. He saw Paul freeze, then straighten up. In the semi darkness, he looked like a giant and Bomber felt himself tremble, not knowing how Paul would react.

Paul didn't turn but just said, "This is private business David, so you'd better leave," Paul's voice was not threatening or forced, it was as if all emotion had gone from him.

"Paul, we are not here to interfere, just as back up. The Brig and Chris were worried about you."

"We?" asked Paul.

"Couple of my lads; none of the Brig's outfit know we are here or what you are doing."

Paul sat in the chair that Armalite had vacated before going to stand nervously in the corner. Paul could have that effect on people, even those armed with a semi-automatic pistol.

Paul had not shaved for several days and he had bags under both eyes but otherwise, he seemed fine physically. Mentally, Bomber was not sure.

"You know the story?" Paul asked.

"I do but Armalite and Harris don't. They are here because I told them a friend needed help. That was all they needed to know."

Paul nodded and said nothing.

There was a sound of water dripping on the floor and Bomber realised that the man had pissed himself.

"What do you suggest I do with him?" Paul asked in a neutral voice, not raising his head.

"Well, if it was me and I had extracted all the information I could from him, I would gut shoot him and leave him here to die slowly and painfully."

The man started to struggle on the chair, making whimpering noises.

"However, it depends what you have done since he told you who ordered the killing of Mary?" Bomber was guessing now about what might have happened.

"Shit head here told me who and where he was. I found him at the address he gave me. Ironically, the bastard's shacked up with this guy's wife. Would you believe it? I thought I would kill him but to be honest, all the hate seems to have drained from me. I know Mary would have told me, 'No!' So I just phoned it in to the RUC. Then waited until they turned up and took him away."

"So what now?" Bomber spoke gently, hoping for a reasoned answer.

Paul shrugged his shoulders. "Maybe I could get a lift back to Lisburn with you. We could stop on the way and phone the RUC telling them there's a wanted IRA man in here. I have a code word I can use so they know it's not a trap."

"I like the sound of that," answered Bomber. "Armalite, chuck this piece of shit back in the pit but don't put the sleepers back."

The man started struggling again but Armalite smacked him on the back of the head, which put a stop to his struggling. Armalite dragged the man and chair through the door to the pit and tipped him down, chair and all.

The drive back was a quiet one with everyone deep in their own thoughts, Bomber thought Paul was asleep but you could never tell with Paul.

Chapter 14
Forty-Nine Is Not a Lucky Number

The Recce Platoon had spent three days driving round the streets of Belfast, keeping them clear of 'rent a crowd' so that the companies could close in on the no go areas without interference from gangs of youths armed with rocks, petrol and nail bombs.

The noose, as Captain Bass called it, was tightening and the clearing of the barricades was going well. The recce sections just drove at speed around the cordon to prevent the companies from being out-flanked. This meant they were constantly the target for petrol, nail bombs and the odd shooter. Slowly but surely, the companies cleared and secured the areas allocated to them.

Today though was different with two separate escorts for a bomb disposal team going to suspect car bombs, both of which proved to be false alarms but had to be treated as real, just in case a sniper was waiting to have a crack at the bomb disposal team.

After returning to the school, they were sent straight back out to look for a post office van which had been hijacked on the Andersontown Road, which marked the southern boundary of the Andersontown estate. As they knew they would, they found the van burning nicely.

Ignoring it and the small group of yobs waiting to stone them, Bomber ordered Harris to drive on. The van was a blazing inferno and the fire brigade were not going to turn up, so there was no need to wait there as a target for 'rent a mob'.

As they approached the junction with Finaghy Road North, it seemed as if the poor old Lanny was disintegrating around them. Harris had already slammed on the brakes and Bomber shoulder rolled out of his door into the gutter only to find Harris already there.

'How the hell did he get there before me?' flitted through Bomber's mind. A round pinging off the wheel rim and then clanging against the door brought Bomber's mind back to the critical situation they were in. Gun fire seemed to be coming from both the junction to their front and the right-hand side from within the estate.

As far as Bomber could work out, there was a semi-automatic rifle pumping rounds at them from the estate while other badly aimed bursts of fire, possibly from a sub machine gun were bouncing off the pavement and road around them. It appeared to be coming from a partly built construction the other side of the junction.

"Fuck, that was close!" snapped Harris. "The bastards are getting better but where the hell are they?"

The shelter of the kerb and the wheels of the Land Rover were scarcely enough to protect them and Bomber knew before long they would both catch a round or two. The VPK (Vehicle Protection Kit) which cladded the Land Rover was okay against nail and petrol bombs but wasn't bullet proof.

The Ferret, which was travelling some way behind the Lanny, now pulled into view and parked alongside the Lanny to protect it from the rifle fire. Cpl Wells, inside the Ferret with the hatch of the turret closed, had a very restricted view and was struggling to locate the targets.

Every time Bomber raised his head to locate the gunmen, a burst of fire came his way, like hail in a thunder storm, making him hug what little shelter the kerb offered.

Suddenly, Armalite was standing on the back of the Ferret directing Cpl Wells where to aim the Browning machine gun. This confirmed to Bomber where he thought the fire was coming from. The rifleman now intensified his fire at Armalite, who ignored it and continued directing the fire onto the other target.

"Christ," shouted Harris, "Armalite is going to get killed if he stays up there on the Ferret!"

Bomber knew he was right and at the top of his lungs, he screamed at Armalite to get down and follow him.

"Harris, stay here and try to spot the rifle man to the right. We'll take care of the others."

As soon as Armalite appeared by the left side of the Lanny, Bomber ran towards the construction site. Both he and Armalite zigzagged their way towards the building. As Armalite took cover and fired at the gunman in the construction,

Bomber raced forward. Wells kept up a steady covering fire at the building and then swung the machine gun in the direction of the rifle fire.

In front of the building site, some trees and bushes untended for years grew in a tangle of long grass. Armalite had stopped, so Bomber sprinted forward then dived into cover, ready to fire at the building. A startled cry came from Bomber's left and two small heads popped up. The frightened faces said it all to Bomber; the two boys could not have been more than nine or ten.

'Bloody hell!' thought Bomber, *'Poor little sods! One minute playing cowboys and Indians, then caught in the middle of a real gunfight where one bullet could smash their bodies to pulp and snuff out the promise of a wonderful life.'*

"Stay down lads," Bomber ordered, trying to sound calm. "Don't move until all the shooting has stopped, then go home."

The two heads nodded in unison, then dropped down out of sight in the long grass. Bomber could hear Armalite shouting for him. Gathering himself, Bomber sprinted the last twenty yards to the building, lungs bursting and heart pounding moments until he threw himself against the wall.

As he waited the second or two for Armalite to arrive, Bomber wished he had a couple of grenades to lob through the open doorway before they went in.

Bit by bit, one covering the other, they cleared the half-built rooms. As they worked their way through the building, Bomber realised that they were in a half-built church by the shape of it. He raced up a short flight of stairs and at the top, he stopped and waved Armalite up.

An opening that was going to be a window, possibly to be adorned with a scene of peace and love, looked straight out onto the junction and Bomber could see the Ferret and Lanny clearly.

The Ferret had its Browning machine gun pointing towards the direction that the rifle fire had been coming from.

"Look at these, boss," said Armalite, pointing to a scattered pile of empty cases.

Picking one up, Bomber guessed they were .45 cases. *'So, probably a Thompson Sub machine gun,'* thought Bomber. *'No wonder his shooting was all over the place, firing with a Thompson over such a long distance.'*

"I think the shooter has done a runner, boss," Armalite said in a low voice. "We can see just about everything from here."

Bomber looked down into the shell with its few half-built internal walls. "I think you are right. I'll just take a few more of these empty cases and then we can hot foot it back to the vehicles doing it the same as we came, covering each other."

At the Lanny, Harris was back in the driver's seat shielded by the bulk of the Ferret's thick armour. Bomber looked at the Makrolon shielding of the Land Rover. It had more holes than a sieve and the faint smell of CS gas could be detected.

Opening one of the storage boxes, he could see a round had punched its way through the metal box, two layers of the Makrolon and then torn a gash in one of the CS grenades.

Harris tried the ignition. The Lanny coughed and then started. "Yes," exclaimed Harris. "We have lift off!" Then the engine died. Cursing, Harris reached down and switched the petrol tap to the other fuel tank.

Bomber backed up Cpl Wells' contact report over the radio to HQ, who started asking all sorts of questions. Bomber answered most and then said that they now had to extradite themselves and that he would make a full report on arrival back at base.

With a cry of delight, Harris got the Lanny started again and with the Ferret flanking them, they chugged their way back to the school. It was slow going as the right rear tyre was shot out and by the time they made the school, they were running more or less on the wheel rim.

In the school car park, they had a chance to assess the damage. The Lanny's shell looked like an Airtex vest while the Ferret had numerous scars on the right-hand side armour and the turret.

"Still don't know how Armalite didn't cop one standing on the Ferret like that," Harris said.

Bomber spoke to Cpl Wells while Harris and Armalite counted the bullet holes in the Lanny. "Thanks, your covering fire got us out of that. Well done!"

"Well, I thought if this doesn't require the use of automatic fire, nothing does. So fuck the orders for only single rounds being fired," Wells said with feeling.

"We got away with it before so let's—" but before Bomber could finish a voice said:

"Not this time C/Sgt, you won't."

Bomber turned and looked at the stern face of the QM (Quarter Master). Their history was a bit rocky and Bomber felt the anger rise up but before he could say anything, the Regiment's Second in Command (2i/c) turned up and said, "Thank you Quarter Master. I will deal with this." The QM shrugged, turned and walked away.

"Now C/Sgt, let's have a look at your vehicle." The 2i/c was a large man who moved like a bear on the prowl. "Well, they certainly took a dislike to you and your boys; must be fifty holes at least."

"Look at the Ferret, sir," piped up Cpl Wells, not wishing to be left out of the appraisal.

"I will, Cpl. Show me." The 2i/c whistled a tune vaguely imitating the regimental march as he examined the bullet scars on the armoured car.

When he finished, he said, "Very good, carry on C/Sgt. When you have finished, come to the briefing room and we will take your statement, say twenty minutes."

"Yes sir," replied Bomber and the 2i/c strode off.

A small crowd of the HQ lounge lizards had gathered, wanting to look at the bullet holes and question the lads.

"Okay," said Bomber, "let's get things sorted. Cpl Wells, I need an ammunition expenditure report for all weapons. Harris, get that wheel changed on the Lanny and Armalite, you crazy bugger, get that CS grenade disposed of."

"Oh, it's forty-nine and twenty-six, boss," said Armalite.

"What is?" Bomber asked.

"Bullet holes in the Lanny and strikes on the Ferret," Armalite said with a grin on his face. "And none on us!"

Bomber studied the ammunition expenditure report as he walked to the briefing room. He and Armalite had fired eleven rounds in total between them. Harris zero and the Browning machine gun was listed at one hundred and eighty-eight.

Cpl Wells had confided that it was a lot more but he had made up the difference from what he called range surplus. Bomber thought it best not to ask about that for the moment.

"If they say it sounded more than that, tell them they heard the echo bouncing off the buildings," said Wells.

Bomber knew Wells was worried about the number of rounds fired on automatic, as he too could be facing a court martial for using automatic fire and contravening the yellow card orders.

In the briefing room was the Adjutant and Captain Bass who were sitting at a table and invited Bomber to join them.

"In your own words C/Sgt, tell us what happened," said Bass.

Bomber told them how it had unfolded and the Adjutant recorded Bomber's words.

"Would you say you were pinned down by superior fire power?" Bass asked.

"Yes sir, as both Harris and I were not in a position to fire until the Ferret appeared and put down covering fire directed by Pte Brown (Armalite). We were pinned down by fire from our right flank and to our front."

"If it wasn't for Pte Brown's actions in standing on the Ferret and directing Cpl Wells onto the targets, it could have all ended differently. In doing so, he exposed himself to considerable danger and became the target of the rifle man," Bomber answered.

"Did you see where the fire was coming from, C/Sgt?" asked Bass.

"The sub machine gun fire was coming from the part constructed building at the road junction and Cpl Wells told me the rifle fire was coming from a van in the estate. The firing stopped after he put a ten-round burst into the van."

"That would tie in with your previous report of a van being used," interrupted the Adjutant.

"It could well be the same van, sir," replied Bomber.

Bomber began to feel weary of the questions and longed for a cup of tea and sleep but the questions kept coming. Bomber found himself answering on automatic, not really thinking about the answers.

Finally Bass said, "Well that's it for now, C/Sgt. We will pass the report to the CO and Brigade HQ."

"So what happens now, sir?"

"Nothing for the moment, normal duties until Brigade HQ gives a pat on the back or—" Bass left the sentence unfinished, gave a shrug of his shoulders and left.

"Don't worry, C/Sgt. I have a feeling this will work out just fine. Your machine gun fire stopped three very bad riots and sent several gunmen scurrying away. Everyone's talking about it at Brigade HQ," said the Adjutant, grinning as he left the room.

Bomber was left wondering why the Adjutant's words had not made him feel any better. This was the first time a heavy machine gun had been used against gunmen in the province and it was bound to result in questions being asked at a higher level. Normally, the soldiers' needs took second place to what the politicians feared most, public opinion.

After a shower, some hot food and a short rest, Bomber was feeling better until he was summoned to the briefing room again. Waiting for him was the CO, Bass and the Adjutant. The RSM and the Provo Sgt were hovering in the corridor and Bomber thought that was a bad sign. Are they waiting to march me away to the jail?

Bomber halted in front of the CO and saluted.

"At ease, C/Sgt," said the CO. "The Brigade Commander has been on the phone to me and contra to what some people want to happen to you for the machine gun incident, he is delighted. His words were something like, 'Good show that will teach the buggers we mean business'!"

The CO paused and Bomber noticed all three were smiling. "He also said that you should get a pat on the back and your escort Pte Brown (Armalite) should receive a military award for his bravery. As you know, until now only civil awards have been made, BEM's and such. Now this will force the politicians to recognise we are in a war and not just some minor civil unrest."

"Oh, and the company commander of B company sends his thanks. Apparently he was dealing with a major riot, bombers and gunmen but they all packed up and went home when they realised it was the army using a heavy machine gun."

There were chuckles all round and Bomber felt as if a huge weight had been lifted from his shoulders.

"Seems we are also going to get a change in the yellow card orders to cover us in these situations," said the CO who paused, then carried on, "Good result all round I think, C/Sgt!" Just at that moment, a knock on the door made them all turn and in came the RSM with a piece of paper in his hand which he handed to the CO who studied it.

Looking up at Bomber, he said, "B Company have found a van which appears to be the one you said the fire was coming from. Plenty of bullet holes in it and full of blood on the inside with a small hole cut in the side panel, just as you said. Some empty cases were recovered too. I think our day just gets better and better!"

The CO was smiling and after a few more words, Bomber was dismissed. In the corridor, the Provo Sgt, 'Mad Mac Reagan', slapped Bomber on the back and congratulated him on getting out of the ambush and the aftermath.

As Bomber sat drinking a mug of tea, he pondered the situation. He knew the post office van and the ambush were a set up by the terrorists but how to counter those situations was the problem. Just then Ian, his long-suffering Sgt, came in looking tired. Bomber got up and said, "Like a brew, Ian?"

"Yes please. I've got a mouth like the bottom of a parrot's cage."

Once he had finished his tea, he told Bomber how he, with his section had been on the flyover looking along Finaghy Road North where they could see the action and two men running out of the building under construction. But when he asked for permission to open fire, it was refused.

"Damn well nearly disobeyed and let the Browning have a go but by then you were in the building and the shooting had stopped," said Ian.

"Armalite saved the day. If he hadn't jumped onto the back of the Ferret and directed Wells onto the targets, we may well have been fucking toast," Bomber said with real feeling.

"Having seen both vehicles I can't believe you all got away without being hit. The mechanic checking your Lanny over said every hose in the engine compartment had a hole in it," responded Ian.

Later that evening, Bomber was called to the ops room where the duty officer instructed him to deploy all the sections he had in order to place a cordon round the restaurant just across the road from the school.

"Suspect bomb, place is being emptied now, have just forty minutes left to boom time," said the duty officer.

Bomber marched out to the platoon's cloakroom feeling very angry. Pulling this stunt once was excusable but twice was totally unacceptable. Ian got everyone on parade and Bomber confronted them. "Okay, which one of you did it? Who made the call? Come on speak up, you idiots!"

Bomber was faced with a sea of uncomprehending faces.

"What's this about, boss?" asked Harris.

"Bomb in the restaurant again. If any of you—"

Harris butted in, "It's not us, boss, honest!"

Bomber studied the blank faces. "Shit, okay. I want a two-hundred-yard cordon setting up and no one is to go near the place until the bomb squad gives the okay."

They had the cordon in place and the road blocks set up when the bomb squad arrived. Bomber was checking with the bomb disposal officer, a Captain, asking him if he wanted two of his recce lads to escort him in case of an ambush. The

Captain agreed to Bomber's suggestion and had just set off with two of Bomber's lads leading the way, when the restaurant disintegrated with an ear shattering roar.

Wood, bricks and glass came raining down causing everyone to duck for cover. Bomber looked round the side of the Ferret he was sheltering behind and saw the Captain and the two escorts walking back unscathed.

"I make that explosion thirty minutes early. What about you, C/Sgt?" The Captain spoke casually as if he had just missed a bus.

Bomber looked at his watch. "I would say you were right, sir. Seems as if they were hoping you would be in there."

"You could be right, you could be right!" the Captain said without emotion. "Well, hopefully I will have time for a cuppa before the next call out." With that, he climbed into his Lanny and the escort drove him away.

Bomber turned to the sound of laughter and looked at Jones, one of the two lads who accompanied the Captain when the explosion occurred. He was doubled over laughing and pointing.

Bomber looked in the direction he was indicating only to see his Lanny windscreen was thick with what looked like blood and intestines in the failing light.

Harris was scraping it off and also laughing, "What's so funny, you bloody monkeys?" Bomber asked.

"It's Spag Bol, boss," Harris replied. In front of the Lanny was a battered looking large pot that must have contained the offending food.

"The old Lanny's certainly seen it all today, boss," Armalite said.

"You can say that again. Today must be our extra lucky day," responded Bomber.

"A lucky day is a day sitting by a river bank fishing and drinking an ice-cold beer, boss. Not counting forty-nine bullet holes in our Lanny!" Harris said, smacking his lips as if he could taste the cold beer.

They remained in place until the Fire Service gave the all clear. Bomber had spoken to the restaurant manager who remembered him from the last bomb call.

"What will you do now?" Bomber asked.

"See what compensation is available and rebuild, can't let the bastards beat us, can we? I had the Catholic ladies 'Support Africa's Children' group in for a charity dinner. Their biggest supporter is a local lumber merchant. He's a Prod married to a Cath who is the Chairwoman of the group, crazy fucking life eh."

"The IRA don't care who they blow up as long as they cause death, destruction and get the publicity." He looked around at the wreckage at what had once been his pride and joy, then at the press and TV who had arrived. "Have you ever thought how ineffectual this would all be if it was never reported on the TV, radio or the press?" he said.

Bomber realised the man just needed to talk but what he had said was right. Without the publicity, the IRA and PIRA would not be getting the misguided support they currently enjoyed.

Eventually, his wife turned up. Jumping out of her car, she hugged her husband and cried. Once he had assured her he was unhurt, she marched him to the car and took him home. His own car was buried under the rubble.

Chapter 15
Clear Up

They had been watching from the high ground above Anderstown for six hours, reporting the movements of 'rent a mob' of which there were two. They were also watching for any cars or vans driving around up to no good. The brooding mass of the Black Mountain behind them made a dramatic setting for what was unfolding below.

B Company supported by A Company and a team of RE (Royal Engineers) in an armoured JCB, nicknamed Scooby Doo, were clearing away barricades while the foot soldiers tightened the cordon into an ever-decreasing circle on the last part of the estate to hold out as a no-go area.

The two 'rent a mobs' were being marshalled by several men with masks on and Bomber carefully noted down the clothes they were wearing while estimating the height and build of the men. Hopefully later this information would help the company commander to identify the culprits and arrest them.

Bomber thought how easy it would be for a sniper to take those men out and save a lot of trouble but that was not acceptable. Right or wrong, they had to try and preserve life no matter who it was.

'Rent a mob' had been confronting the advancing troops with rocks and bottles but now the organisers seemed to have realised that they were going to be squeezed and rounded up, so tactics were changing. Every one of Bomber's team could see that the mob were armed with petrol and nail bombs, so Bomber ordered Dusty, who had returned that morning, to send a report over the radio.

Dusty sat in the rear of the Lanny and relayed the message. He should have been on light duties back at the school but he had whined on long and hard at Bomber who finally relented, letting him come out to play.

Bomber knew he would get a bollocking from the MO (Medical Officer) if he found out but he understood Dusty wanting to get back with the team.

"Boss," called Harris, "It looks to me as if the two mobs are joining forces to get that platoon." He pointed to the left-hand group of soldiers forcing their way through a minor barricade into a dead-end street.

"Could be a set up."

Bomber told Dusty to inform HQ and the company on the radio and was relieved to see the platoon stop. 'Rent a mob' had intensified its attempt to lure the platoon on but they stayed put while the company commander attempted to outflank them on the right. That was when the shooting started. The heavy crack of rifle fire was echoed by the lighter crack of pistols being used.

Bomber listened as Dusty reeled off the reports from the platoons. He estimated that there were two riflemen who had engaged the lead platoon, while the flanking platoon was being shot at by one or two men armed with pistols.

Now Bomber could hear the distinctive fire of the SLR armed soldiers. Not a cacophony of shots but spaced single shots and Bomber knew that either the platoon commander or section commanders were directing individual riflemen onto the targets in a disciplined manner.

"Boss, gunmen running through the gardens at the back of those houses." It was Harris again who had the binoculars held tight to his eyes.

Bomber looked through his monocular and could clearly see two men running, one carrying what looked like a rifle and the other a pistol.

"Permission to fire?" called Armalite.

"And me!" came from Cpl Wells in the hatch of the Ferret with its Browning machine gun pointing towards the gunmen. Wells had a huge grin on his face, knowing Bomber would not let him after the last time.

"It's too far Armalite, it must be five or six hundred yards if it's an inch." Bomber was aware that the SLR's open sights only went up to six hundred yards and you would have to be a very special marksman to hit a moving man at that range over open sights.

"Dusty, call it in," Bomber instructed. Now he could see the gunmen had taken cover by a wooden shed at the back of one of the gardens where they would be able to fire along an alleyway at any soldiers passing. Realising he only had a few seconds to act, Bomber turned again to Dusty and said urgently, "On the radio! Tell the platoon to stop! We are going to engage those gunmen."

"Okay boss," replied Dusty and sent the message.

"Amalite, now's your chance to show how good you are. Fire when you're ready."

'Even if he can't hit them, it will scare the shit out of them and make them give up the ambush,' thought Bomber.

Bang! Armalite fired; the round must have struck close as they could see one of the men jump up, then drop back down as Armalite fired twice more. They sounded louder than the first shot, making Bomber flinch while he tried to focus the monocular.

He guessed the rounds had hit the shed very close to the gunmen as they were now running straight for the house, entering by the back door. Bomber took the radio mic from Dusty, giving the details of the house direct to the platoon commander while Harris watched to make sure the men didn't leave by the front door.

In less than a minute, the house was surrounded by the lead platoon. Bomber could visualise the scene in his mind, the platoon commander giving his orders with teams going in the front door and the back door at the same time, weapons ready and shouting, 'Army, drop your weapons or we fire!'

In any other situation in the world, it would be a grenade through the window and then rushing in firing as you went but this wasn't any other situation, this was Northern Ireland part of the United Kingdom. There could be innocent people in the house, someone's mother or grandmother, children who knows?

However, we did know there were two gunmen. Would they put their weapons down and move away from any innocents? Or would they use them as a shield and fire at the soldiers as they came in?

After a few moments, Bomber was relieved to see the soldiers come out with the two gunmen and the weapons. He said a silent prayer and sent a mental, *'Well done lads!'*

Two hours later, it was all over. Anderstown was quiet with foot patrols and armoured Pigs back in control of the streets. The Scooby Doo was clearing the last of the barricade debris, loading it into the back of a ten-ton truck to be taken where it couldn't be used again. Not that that would bother the local mob who would just hijack a few more cars to use next time.

Bomber felt his stomach rumble. It had been a long day and breakfast was so long ago, he couldn't remember what he had eaten. Dusty produced a brew and some biscuits and they took turns at the back of the Lanny to drink the nectar. *'Christ, how would we function without a cuppa?'* thought Bomber. The biscuits were Jammy Dodgers, a staple of the cook house at any time.

"Where did you get the biscuits from, Dusty?" asked Bomber, thinking they tasted a bit musty.

"Oh, these are all out of date and were going to be thrown out by the cook Cpl, so I snaffled them boss. Okay, aren't they?" Dusty said stuffing two into his mouth at the same time.

Bomber nodded. '*Out of date or not, I'm going to eat them,*' Bomber thought '*and to hell with the consequences!*'

They were relieved just after the moon managed to break through the cloud cover. Cpl Jacob's section took over and Bomber briefed him on the layout of the land and houses below them. As Bomber and his section drove back to the school, he thought how good some hot food and the wobbly camp bed would feel.

He was just scraping the last piece of rice pudding from a corner of his mess tin when he was called to the Ops room. When Bomber entered, he could see Captain Bass and Chris studying a map and talking quietly.

He paused at the door not wishing to know what they were plotting but he couldn't just walk away, that wasn't in the game rules. '*Christ, what the hell are they cooking up now?*' he wondered.

"Don't just stand there C/Sgt, come and look at the map," ordered Bass. Bomber noticed Chris was not smiling but looked drawn and tense.

"What am I looking for, sir?" Bomber asked.

"The Ardoyne, you know it well and have an old contact who lives just on the edge on the Prods side," Bass answered.

"Paddy, our ex RE Cpl. I believe he is still there. He's best buddies with Armalite," Bomber answered, wondering where this was leading.

"Okay, I'll let Sgt Pickett brief you from here." With that, he handed over to Chris.

"As you know," said Chris, "the last time we spoke, my team was on stakeout for O'Brian and we believed we had him in a house near the Springfield. Well, we raided the house but he had flown the coop. How, without us spotting him, we don't know but we now believe he is in the Ardoyne."

"Why would he go there, especially if he knows you are on to him?" questioned Bomber.

"O'Brian has been doing the rounds of all the PIRA groups in every Cath enclave in Belfast. He may not be aware we are keeping tabs on him. Well, we were keeping tabs on him until now. We need help locating him and lifting him, the sooner the better."

Bomber responded, "I think the first thing we have to accept is that he knows you are on to him. So he's upped his game, hence giving you the slip. We know he's a bloody Houdini but he will slip up sooner or later. If he is in the Ardoyne and moves around then our recce lads, who know him by sight, will spot him."

"Unfortunately, the CO can't spare all the platoon, just your section to assist," Bass interrupted.

Bomber frowned, then said, "There's no way we can cover all the ins and outs of the Ardoyne with just six of us and the Sgt's team."

"I know," said Bass "but everyone is needed for another operation and we have to keep vehicles and feet on the ground in the areas we have cleared. If and when anyone becomes free, I will send them to you. That's the best I can do for now." Bass nodded to them both then turned his attention to a report of gunfire coming over the radio from one of the platoons.

Paddy had greeted them like long lost brothers and when Bomber handed him a bottle of malt whisky, he wanted to open it and have a party. Bomber explained the situation and Paddy was only too happy to let Armalite, Dusty and Cpl Wells use his front bedroom with its spy hole to watch into the Ardoyne.

Bomber had swapped Cpl Wells Ferret driver for Zika who, with his rifle and telescopic sight, was positioned on top of the Flax Street Mill with two of Chris's lads. From there, they could see all of one side of the Ardoyne.

This left Bomber, Harris, Chris and Lofty who, in two beat up cars, would do their best to cover the rest of the boundary.

Chris and Harris were resting in the Mill while Bomber and Lofty drove around the outside of the Ardoyne. They had one spare car stashed in the Mill which they could swap with in an attempt to be less conspicuous each time they went out on patrol.

At first, Lofty was withdrawn and refused to be drawn into conservation but then Bomber mentioned the names of a couple of old friends of his who were in two Para. Lofty looked at Bomber seemingly with less contempt than before and admitted he knew them and that in fact, he had served with one of them before joining the Brig's team, building up contacts prior to nineteen sixty-nine.

"So, you joined Chris from another team?" Bomber asked innocently, while watching a car being driven far too fast by a woman going into Berwick Road.

"Yes, good team too until things went pear-shaped," Lofty spoke with bitterness.

"What went pear-shaped?" Bomber prodded gently, still watching the woman's car, a small hatchback disappear down the street.

Lofty didn't speak for a minute, then sighed. "I was speaking with one of my contacts in an alley, my two man back up team was in the car about fifty yards away. I knew something wasn't right because the contact was very nervous and didn't want to speak."

"Suddenly, there was gunfire and I saw two men who must have come out of the house where the car was parked. They killed Roy and John and then they came for me." He stopped talking and looked down at his hands.

"You got away. What about the contact?" Bomber asked.

"No, I didn't get away. I went straight at the bastards, shooting. Killed one and wounded the other but I took a hit." He lifted his T-shirt and Bomber could see a thick, raised scar about nine inches long across his stomach.

"The wounded one managed to get away. I went to the car, put Roy on the back seat and drove to the hospital. Still not sure how I made it. The other two died before I got there."

"Shit, that's a real bastard to lose two of your team in a set up. What happened to your contact?"

Lofty again looked down at his hands which he was squeezing together. When he spoke, he had sadness in his voice. "The police found his body two days later with a bullet wound to the back of his head. According to the police, the IRA were holding his wife and two children hostage, they have now been relocated to somewhere in England."

Again, Lofty paused and sighed.

"Funnily enough, I liked the guy. He really did hate the IRA and what they stood for. Never asked for money, just if anything happened to him that we took care of his family."

"Could have been worse. They could have got you as well," Bomber said.

"Yep but I've got this scar to remind me constantly that I didn't make one of my team get out of the car and stand, ready for trouble. I was too casual. Now I have an ache for justice; no, for revenge. Call it what you want but I intend to get it, whatever it takes."

'Fucking hell,' thought Bomber, 'he blames himself for the death of his mates. Hope he's not going to go mental on me when I need him to be calm.'

"It's called hypertrophic scarring, before you ask," Lofty said, looking at Bomber.

"What?" Bomber was caught off balance by the statement and must have looked blank because Lofty went on to explain.

"Hypertrophic scarring is an abnormal healing response to a wound." Lofty sounded as if he was quoting some doctor.

"Oh yes, I see," mumbled Bomber, while watching a car with two men drive slowly past, the passenger eyeballing them as they passed. No recognition flared in Bomber's mind but he didn't like the look of either of them or being eyeballed.

"I think we should carefully follow that car." Bomber nudged Lofty as he said it.

Lofty eased the car into the road, the traffic was light and only one car was between them and the target vehicle. This turned off after a few hundred yards and Bomber could clearly see the passenger in the other car looking over his shoulder at them.

"They know we are following them," Lofty said, stating the obvious.

Suddenly the car accelerated away, turning towards Clifftonville and Lofty put his foot down to follow but Bomber put his hand on his arm and said, "No, I think they are a decoy, let's go back."

Lofty used the hand brake to turn the car on a sixpence, which jarred Bomber's neck and then sped back the way they had come. As they got close to Berwick Road, a car drove out not racing but faster than normal.

"That's it," said Bomber. "Let's go."

"How d'you know it's him?" Lofty barked as he raced through the gears.

"I don't for sure but first they use a decoy car to pull us off station, then a car makes a run for it. Must be someone up to no good." Bomber grabbed the handle above the door as Lofty dodged in and out of the traffic. He was now gaining on the speeding black Ford.

Bomber called it in, requesting help to stop the car. HQ acknowledged passing the information to all call signs in the area. They were now on the Falls road and up ahead Bomber could see an army road block so the black Ford had nowhere to go except to do a high-speed skidding turn and come straight back at them.

Lofty didn't slow down but aimed the car directly at the Ford, causing Bomber to have a vision of a full head-on collision with him going through the windscreen. Just as he thought that would happen, the Ford swerved away; the driver lost control, the car hit the kerb and flipped on its side, stopping at a lamppost that almost gracefully bent itself over the car.

Lofty brought their car to a tyre shredding halt, then reversed at high speed to the wreckage. Bomber was out before the car stopped. Bearcat in hand, he stooped and looked into the car. A teenage driver, his head now part of the windscreen, looked dead while the passenger was trying to crawl out of the shattered screen.

Bomber went round to the bonnet and dragged the boy out. He looked about sixteen. Bomber pushed him face first against the wall but the boy slumped semi-conscious to the pavement. Bomber quickly ran his hands over him to check for any weapons but found nothing.

Lofty came over saying, "Driver's dead, head's caved in and neck probably broken, no weapon."

The teenager against the wall started laughing but a fit of coughing stopped him and he clutched his chest. *'Broken ribs but why was he laughing?'* thought Bomber.

"What's so funny?" Lofty demanded, grabbing the boy by the shoulder and making him cry out in pain.

"You, you stupid bastards. He said you would do just what you did. Said you had no imagination." The boy laughed again but Lofty gripped him at the side and this time, the boy squealed in real pain.

"You with the gun, put it down and both of you put your hands in the air," It was said so politely Bomber had to hide a smile. Carefully placing the Bearcat on the floor while risking a glance at the speaker, Bomber saw a young Lieutenant in immaculate combats pointing a rifle at him. Spread out around him were half a dozen soldiers who, although young looked older than their platoon commander.

After being searched and their identity cards verified, they were released. Bomber got straight on the radio and told HQ they had been tricked. Then he turned to the boy who was being helped into an ambulance and asked, "Who said we had no imagination?"

"Fuck you!" The boy winced as the soldier who was guarding him told him to keep a civil tongue in his head.

"And fuck you too! I'm saying nothing," retorted the boy to his escort.

Lofty took a step forward towards the boy but the medic stepped in and shut the doors to the ambulance, giving Lofty a look that intimated 'Leave my patient alone'.

"Five minutes and I would have the bastard singing fit to bust," Lofty muttered.

"Yes but would it be the truth?" Bomber asked.

Bomber and Lofty sat in Paddy's kitchen drinking whisky laden tea.

"Trouble with drinking tea with whisky is it makes you want more," mused Bomber.

"There's more here," Paddy said, indicating the large tea pot and the half empty bottle of malt but Bomber declined, wishing to keep a clear head.

"He'll have gone to ground in Whiterock. From there, he can move through all the Cath areas with his own kind, unnoticed. In the Ardoyne, he was isolated as it's surrounded by Prod areas."

Everyone stopped drinking and turned to the speaker. Armalite stood in the doorway and with everyone looking at him, he shrugged and said, "What?"

Bomber put down his cup. "You're a bloody genius Armalite that's what, where's the map?"

Lofty produced the map and spread it on the table. "Look," Bomber said tracing a route on the map. "He can move through the Falls, Beechmount, Whiterock, Upper Springfield, Falls Park and all the way to Twinbrook more or less without leaving a Cath area."

Everyone studied the map. "He could be in any of them by now," Lofty grumbled.

"Unless," said Paddy, "this was his first stop of some sort of rallying PIRA teams in each area." Paddy paused and took a sip of tea. "He could be working his way through each area in turn geeing up the troops."

"I think you have the right of it Paddy, so let's assume he is in say the Falls. Now there's one bottle neck which is between Whiterock and Falls Park. He either has to take the Springfield road, this one," Bomber stabbed the map with his finger, "or go via Blackstaff or Windsor."

"Visitors," said Armalite. Bomber looked out of the window into the small backyard and saw Chris and Harris approaching.

Chapter 16
Stakeout

Bomber couldn't sit still in the back of the burnt-out van that had become their OP on the Upper Springfield Road. He was full of nerves and longed to be out on the road. The smell of burnt rubber and paint was still strong in the van, adding to his discomfort.

Harris was next to him, sipping warm tea from his flask, seemingly immune to the discomfort and doubts Bomber was suffering from. Armalite and Andy weren't too far away in a car parked out of sight but in touch by radio.

Bomber reflected on the briefing by Captain Bass. He had refined the plan and allocated another recce section complete with Ferret to cover the Musgrave area in case O'Brian took the long way round. They were basically spread out northwest to south east in three locations between Upper Springfield and Blackstaff.

Bomber knew it was a long shot spotting O'Brian and picking him up but couldn't think of any other way that would stand more of a chance of dealing with a key PIRA player who had vowed to kill him and Captain Bass. He wondered how many people had lost their lives because of O'Brian over the last two years.

Certainly, the PIRA would have benefitted from his knowledge of how the army worked. His weapons and explosives knowledge would make him a valuable trainer for new recruits.

Harris was just peeing into a bottle when Bomber saw the motorbike approaching. It was travelling well within the speed limit which made it suspicious for a start. No one travelled on this road at anything less than full pelt unless they wished to be a target for the yobs throwing rocks.

"Keep down!" Bomber told Harris pushing him closer to the floor.

The biker slowed and eyeballed the van, then sped up and rode past them.

"Shit!" exclaimed Harris, "when you pushed me, I pissed all over my hand."

"Sorry but your head was sticking up too much. He would have spotted you." Not waiting for an answer, Bomber called Andy telling him of the bike.

Two minutes later, the bike roared back past them and out of sight. "What do you think he's up to, boss?" asked Harris as he wiped his hands on his handkerchief.

"He could be a scout checking the route for someone following. If I'm right, we should see something in a moment or two."

Bomber watched the hands on his watch. Three minutes had passed when he heard the motorbike coming and by the sound of the engine, the rider was pushing it hard.

Bomber pressed the key on the radio and simply said, "Standby to block."

"We have him visual," replied Andy. As their position was more elevated than that of the van, they could see further along the road.

Then Bomber could see them. The bike gunning it in the lead was closely followed by a dark saloon car. As they passed Bomber, he had a glimpse of the driver and two others in the rear of the car. There was a squealing of brakes and a loud bang as Andy rammed into the side of the speeding car. A moment later, there was a second bang as the target car hit the wall on the opposite side of the road.

Bomber and Harris were out of the van running the fifty yards to the crash site; Andy was climbing out of the battered Austin Cambridge he had used as a ram. Steam was rising from the engine compartment and the Austin had collapsed at the front, giving the impression it had nosedived into the road.

Armalite came out of the trees to the side of the Austin, shouting a warning that the biker was coming back. The biker seemed really pissed off because he was firing at Andy with a semi-automatic pistol, not an easy thing to do accurately when gunning it on a motorbike.

Bomber could hear the crack of the shots going overhead as he ran towards Andy who stood in the middle of the road, legs slightly apart, arms extended in front of him. He stood like a statue as the nine-millimetre Browning pistol in his hand spat bullets at the biker.

The biker jerked once, then again as Andy's shots found their target. He crumpled over the handle bars and both bike and rider crashed to the tarmac. The bike slid into the kerb then somersaulted once before it came to a halt against the wall.

Bomber and Harris had reached the target car where they saw the driver was slumped against the wheel, blood seeping from a large wound to his forehead.

"For fuck's sake, look at this boss," said Harris. The two figures in the back looked dead, in fact they had never been alive. They were dummies. Their heads had come loose and were on the floor. Bomber noticed one had a beard and guessed it was supposed to be O'Brian.

"Boss over here, quick!" It was Armalite shouting.

"Take care of the driver, Harris." Then Bomber sprinted to the other side of the Austin car and saw Andy kneeling in the road, his head on his chest being supported by Armalite.

"He's been hit in the chest."

Bomber could see frothy bubbles coming from Andy's mouth. He pulled out a field dressing from his back pocket to plug Andy's chest wound where air was being sucked into his lungs.

Bomber plugged it tight and bound it even tighter. Armalite was already on the radio calling for back up, an ambulance and vehicle recovery for the two cars and the bike.

Bomber got Andy laying on the side that the wound was on and between gasps, Andy was trying to speak. Putting his ear close to Andy's mouth, Bomber could make out the words, "Did I get the bastard?"

"Yes, you got him, Andy. He's as dead as a door nail." Andy seemed to smile then lapsed into unconsciousness.

In less than ten minutes, the backup and ambulance had arrived and Andy was whisked away at high speed. During that ten minutes, Bomber could hear a report coming from six two alpha, the recce team watching the approach from Musgrave to the Falls Park area. They were under attack by a large 'rent a mob' with petrol and nail bombs.

'That's where O'Brian's going in,' thought Bomber. *'He's got us with the division in the northwest, now they are clearing the way for him in the southeast. The bastard's going to a lot of trouble to complete his mission, whatever it is and he is determined, even knowing we are on to him.'*

With the driver unconscious on his way to hospital and the biker dead, there was no one to question. So Bomber radioed Chris, who was the nearest with a car to ask her to pick up the three of them, while Lofty with Dusty were to move as close as possible to six two alpha's position and watch.

By the time they had all crammed into Chris's car and had travelled to where Lofty was on watch, B Company had dispersed 'rent a mob' and six two alpha had withdrawn.

They split up, the two cars acting as the ends of the line while Bomber, Harris and Armalite spread out between them trying to remain inconspicuous, which was not easy so they made sure they could see each other at all times in case of trouble. Everything had gone extremely quiet. The traffic had all but dried up. Two hours later, Bass called them in and they went to the briefing room.

Bass told them that Andy had been in surgery and was doing as well as could be expected. The driver was conscious and was being interviewed by the RUC. He was known as a PIRA supporter but was not talking. The dead biker was also known as an active PIRA operative and had been involved in the Springfield shootout.

Then Bass paused before saying the two who had been in the back of the car were more serious. They were known activists of the notorious Guy Fawkes mob. This brought about some laughter and lightened the mood for everyone.

Bass continued, "We are to stand down now, so get some rest. The search is to resume tomorrow. The Brigadier is coming to see us tomorrow afternoon after he has been to the hospital to see Andy."

Bomber went to bed feeling they had been fooled again by O'Brian and wondering where the slippery bastard was right now. He slept badly, all the time seeing Andy's face and the bloody bubbles coming from his mouth. Perhaps this was to be his new torment each night?

Bomber woke at six o'clock and felt like he had been drugged. He dragged himself to the showers next to the school gym and let the hot water soak away the effects of a poor night's sleep. After a quick breakfast, he went to the ops room to see if there was any news on Andy. The duty clerk gave Bomber a signal sheet which simply stated that surgery had gone well and Andy had had a good night.

"Where's Captain Bass?" Bomber asked the clerk.

"Asleep C/Sgt, he was on duty until three this morning." The clerk nodded to the room adjacent to the ops room that served as the ops officer's bedroom cum retreat. "I'm to wake him at nine o'clock and he said he would speak to you at nine thirty."

Bomber had an hour to kill so took his rifle to where his Lanny was parked, sat on the tail gate and stripped the rifle down to clean it. After that, he took out the Bearcat pistol and the Beretta and cleaned those.

By now, he had been joined by the rest of the team who busied themselves with getting ready for the day, not that any of them knew what they would be tasked with yet but it was essential to be ready for anything.

Harris was busy checking that they had the essential brew kit and Dusty had procured a new supply of biscuits which were in date.

At nine thirty, Bomber went to see Captain Bass who was in the ops room drinking strong, black coffee. Bomber was shocked to see how Bass was looking, haggard with dark bags under his eyes and the coffee seemed to be making him jumpy.

"Don't you think you should get a little more rest, sir?" Bomber asked quietly.

"Not a lot of hope of that C/Sgt. The CO and the second in command are both going flat out with everything coming down from Brigade and the Adjutant is even more the worse for wear than me. However, it should ease now the RSM is back and doing a stag here in the ops room, so once we know what we will be doing today, I intend to get a couple more hours sleep."

Bomber watched as he poured more coffee into both their cups and noticed his hands were shaking from fatigue. Bomber wondered how long he could keep going with so much sleep deprivation.

The door opened and Bomber looked up to see Paul and the Brig coming in.

"Good morning all!" the Brig said with enthusiasm and Bomber could see Paul was smiling.

"I bring good news on several fronts. Firstly, Andy is out of danger and barring any hiccups should be back in action in the not too distance future. The other points, we need to discuss in private. Is there somewhere we can use?"

Bass opened the door to his room where there was a small camp bed, several chairs and a small table with a notebook and pencil on it. Bass picked up the notebook. "My daily diary," he explained and put it on the camp bed. The Brig and Paul declined coffee and got right down to business.

"We are now officially known as the Special Intelligence Unit. I have been given more resources, including an SAS team which Bill will lead and I can handpick a dozen more operatives from wherever I wish." The Brig raised his eyebrows and looked at Bomber, then at Captain Bass.

Bass reacted first. "I'm not sure the CO would be happy releasing either of us Brigadier at this moment in time."

"No, he said as much but he did say that the Regiment was going back to Tidworth in one week and that I could keep you both here on loan for as long as was needed." Bomber noticed the Brig had the hint of a smile on his face when he had finished speaking.

"Oh David, I would like you to bring those two big lads who hang out with you as well. You know the ones I mean, Harris and the one with the weird name who's just been awarded the military medal for his action in that ambush."

Both Bomber and Bass said, "What!" at the same time.

"Have I let the cat out of the bag?" said the Brig with mock surprise. "Best not tell him or anyone else until your CO has informed him, eh!"

Paul had a grin on his face a mile wide and Bomber shook Bass by the hand and agreed to make sure they had drinks in for Armalite when the time came.

"Now, down to business," said the Brig indicating the table where Paul spread out a map. They all poured over it and the Brig pointed at one spot on the map.

Later, Bomber briefed Ian who would have the job of taking the platoon back to Tidworth. Bomber was not too sure how Amalite and Harris would react to being told they were staying but he needn't have worried. Both were keen as mustard and dashed off to pack their kit. The only unhappy man was Dusty who confronted Bomber as to why he was not included.

"You will need a good radio man, boss. You know those two are useless with anything technical."

"Sorry Dusty, the CO needs you here with the platoon," Bomber said, with a genuine regret that Dusty was not included.

"Is it because of my leg? It's fine. I can out run those two if needs be."

"No Dusty, it's not your leg, the MO has given you a clean bill of health. It's just numbers, three is all the CO can spare."

"Fuck it!" Dusty exclaimed. "Okay but if you need someone else, boss, promise me I'm first choice."

"You have my word Dusty, you will be first choice if anyone else is required."

Dusty nodded and started to walk away, then turned and said, "Stay safe, boss and keep an eye on those two for me." Then he was gone. Bomber went and packed his kit, feeling strangely deflated that the Recce Platoon was leaving without him.

Chapter 17
Lisburn-Thiepval Barracks

The car whisked Bomber, Armalite and Harris the eight miles south west to Lisburn and Thiepval Barracks, an unlikely sounding name for a barracks in Northern Ireland but it was named after a small village in France, close to where the battle of the Somme took place.

Built in the early nineteen forties from local red bricks, it looked typical of the wartime camps. However, the interior of the barracks was constantly changing as more troops began to swell the ranks of the units already stationed there. Bomber found the accommodation was not a great deal more comfortable than the school but at least he had a real bed in his own bunk.

Once they were settled in, they went to the Brig's private armoury to select pistols for Harris and Armalite. Waiting for them was Bill, who greeted Bomber like a long-lost brother. "Knew you couldn't keep away and you've brought these two to look after you, so that will save me a job!"

Bill showed no signs that his leg was bothering him and when Bomber asked him, he slapped it and said, "Good as new."

Harris and Armalite were wide eyed at the mass of weapons the Brig had collected. Harris was playing with a German Second World War Luger only to have it snatched from him by the ex-Scots Guardsman who acted as the weapons' custodian for the Brig.

"You'll be keeping your fingers off the guns until you have signed for them," he rasped in a high pitched, hoarse voice which was strangely at odds with his six-foot three frame.

"This is Robbie everybody, took a round through his throat; that's why he talks like a rasp on a brick. However, don't be fooled. He knows every weapon in here and can use all of them like he was born with them in his hands," Bill explained.

Putting two modern semi-automatics on the counter, Robbie rasped "Now these are for you two, Heckler Koch P9's. Weight just under two pounds without the ammunition in the nine-round mag. I've only just got them in, so make sure you look after them, right!"

He then plonked four mags per gun on the counter and four boxes of nine-millimetre rounds and said, "Sign here," thrusting a ten thirty-three form and a pen at each of them. He added, "Each round has to be accounted for when you use them and I expect the empty cases to be handed in."

Armalite and Harris looked at each other and shrugged as if to say, 'Is he for real!'

"We hand in the empty cases when possible as this prevents anyone claiming we fired more rounds than we did. Also stops anyone identifying what weapons we are using," said Bill. "Let's go to the range and see if you can hit what you are shooting at."

At the thirty-metre range, Bill took Harris and Armalite to one side and had them working hard with the pistols. While they were doing that, Bomber took the opportunity to sharpen up his shooting with the Bearcat. He found he could put a round into the centre of the head of the target both standing and kneeling and even when snap shooting at fifteen paces.

At twenty, he could still do it but not so accurately. The lightweight crack of the Bearcat was drowned out by the heavier bark of the P9s, which could put down a faster rate of fire thanks to their modern recoil system to reload a round into the chamber.

Bomber put the Bearcat away and took out the Beretta, cocked it and fired six shots at the head of the figure target at twenty paces. Bomber studied the target, five hits spread around as he had double tapped each time he fired. It meant he had hit the target each time but he wasn't happy that one shot had gone astray. *'Need to sharpen up, that miss could cost you your life!'* the voice in his head said.

Bomber knew the voice was right and that he needed more practice.

"Very impressive," a familiar voice said behind him. Unloading the Beretta, he turned and looked at the smiling face of Paul. Bomber thought he looked more like his old self again and hoped he was over the trauma of losing Mary and dealing with her killers.

Bomber and Paul sat at the side of the range and watched Bill coaching Armalite and Harris. Armalite was fluid and his movements almost looked lazy, very much like a cat stalking its prey. As he fired, he hit the target with an ease that Bomber felt envious of.

On the other hand, Harris was more solid. Once he locked onto the target, he didn't flinch or move but just hammered the shots home where ever Bill called. Head, chest, leg or arm, he hit every time.

Bomber didn't say anything but waited for Paul to talk, which after several more minutes he did.

"I can't get Mary out of my mind, the last day I spent with her just keeps replaying in my head and what she would think of me after what I did to her killers." He shook his head as if to clear it. "She hated violence of any sort. Said if we could just sit down and talk, putting the hatred behind us and start afresh, how good that would be. It would be year one as she called it." Again Paul lapsed into silence before saying, "Do you believe in an afterlife?"

Bomber was surprised by the question. He had never thought of Paul as religious but what did he know of Paul's private life? Was he Catholic, Protestant or atheist? "Well, yes sort of, not a physical one as we have now but I suppose in thought or spirit."

"And do you suppose whatever that might be, knows what we're doing here on Earth?"

'Christ,' thought Bomber, *'you need the padre not me Paul.'*

He responded, "No I don't, Paul and if that's what's eating at you, why don't you go and talk to the padre? He's a good guy who knows this stuff and will keep what you say to himself."

"Sorry, just getting a bit introspective and dealing with thoughts, that's all."

"No problem, I question myself all the time. Anytime you want to talk that's okay with me but I can't promise you any sensible answers about the beyond." Bomber laughed and Paul joined him, which Bomber thought was a good sign.

"So, what's the joke?" Bill asked as he walked over.

"Oh, nothing unless you know what's beyond this life," chuckled Paul.

"I never think that far ahead, it's not good for my brain. I just hope there is not a hell as depicted in those old paintings because as sure as eggs are eggs that's where I'm bound. I'm finished with these two, they are not bad, good grouping and consistent, which is more than I can say for you Bomber. I'm sure you missed your last shot with the Beretta."

'How the hell did he spot that!' thought Bomber. "Yes, I did miss the last shot but none with the Bearcat."

Bill picked up the Bearcat and studied it. "Nice, very accurate but slow rate of fire compared to the semi-automatics. I saw your grouping with this," he said as he waved the Bearcat in the air, "all in the head which is where you need to be with this lightweight. Time you used a Browning or better still one of those P9's the boys have. It will stop them dead no matter where it hits them."

Bomber looked over to where Armalite and Harris were cleaning their pistols. Both had a look of concentration on their faces as they cleaned and oiled their new toys.

"I know but I like the Beretta, it's reliable and easy to conceal. The Bearcat has the advantage of being extremely accurate so one shot at a time should be enough."

Bill nodded and said, "All that's true but when it comes to a close quarter fire fight, weight of fire is often the deciding factor."

"Maybe," replied Bomber, "but actually hitting what you are shooting at is just as important or there is no point in firing."

Suddenly Paul jumped up. "Bloody hell, I nearly forgot what I came here for!" exclaimed Paul. "We are off out this evening. The Brig is briefing us at seventeen hundred in the main briefing room, so don't be late." Paul stood, looked at Bomber and smiled. "Thanks," he said and strode off, looking like some warrior from Greek mythology.

"I'm glad he's back. I've not met anyone better to have along in a dodgy situation and he scares the shit out of the Paddies in a close fight. Like bloody Hercules and Enery Cooper all rolled into one," Bill said quietly.

"I know what you mean and he's clever too. Could have been anything he wanted I guess, not like us two thickos," Bomber said, feeling somewhat inferior to Paul at that moment.

"Speak for yourself. I'm so smart I could outsmart a box of Smarties," Bill said almost seriously.

Bomber looked at his watch. It was sixteen hundred. "Better get a move on. We have an hour to sort ourselves out and get a brew and a wad." Bomber called the others over, telling them to go and get something to eat and be at the briefing room for seventeen hundred.

Bomber and Bill made their way to the mess in silence. Bomber wondered what the briefing would throw up for them to do tonight. Odds on it would be something involving being wet, cold and sitting or lying still for hours on end.

Chapter 18
The Reckoning

Bomber felt vulnerable sitting in the car. Staying still in one place made an easy target for a gunman or a bomber. At least on foot and patrolling, you could move from cover to cover or hide in the shadows.

'*How many hours, no, days have I spent doing this?*' Bomber wondered. '*Most of the job is observing, probably ninety five percent of the time and just five percent is when all hell is let loose.*' Bomber had to admit he loved that five percent.

Paul and Armalite were concealed outside and Harris sat in the driving seat sipping more tea from his flask. Bomber wondered why their presence didn't make him feel any more comfortable.

'*It should do,*' he thought. '*They don't come any better than these guys at dealing with trouble.*'

Looking into the Lenadoon estate, he reflected on the failed attempts by the authorities to provide new mixed Cath and Prod estates with modern houses and facilities. Lenadoon and Twinbrook, relative new builds of modern housing, were classic examples of this.

They should have been fifty percent Cath and Prod with a strong housing trust and committee to ensure everyone could live in peace. However, through intimidation and violence of the worst kind, one or other of the religious groups had withdrawn into their own area or left completely.

Lenadoon was split with the Caths in the north part forming the majority. Twinbrook, the latest modern estate was virtually all Caths despite the housing trust's attempts to get Prod families to move there. The Prods felt just too vulnerable and isolated as they had to run the Falls road corridor to get to the city centre.

The Brig's briefing had been to surround the Lenadoon area with watchers as he believed O'Brian was there or would be there, coordinating the PIRA members to become the dominant force in both Lenadoon and Twinbrook. This could, of course, erupt into a power struggle between the IRA and the PIRA, which, with luck, would result in them killing each other off.

Bomber yawned. He wasn't tired, just bored; watching the same patch of houses could become tedious.

"Want a cuppa, boss, while it's still warm?" asked Harris, reaching for the flask on the floor near his feet.

"No thanks, it will just make me need a piss," Bomber replied.

"See the house with the yellow door, boss?"

"Yes, what of it?"

"Well, I think someone is watching us from the top right bedroom window. It's hard to tell with the reflection on the glass but I'm ninety percent sure." Harris was now staring intensely at the window.

Bomber focused his monocular on the window which was at the back of the house. "Yes, you could be right. I can see someone peering out just to one side of the curtain but not sure it's us they're looking at."

"The Dickers at the end of the street have just swopped over now." Harris nodded in the direction of two youths talking. Dickers were used to keep watch for any strangers in the area and Bomber knew they could have been fingered the minute they parked up but nothing had happened.

The youth with the long hair, who had been there as long as Bomber and Harris had been watching, walked away while his place was taken by a short, fat boy of about fifteen who stared down the street but not at them.

"Have you noticed boss that the street lighting is all intact?" Harris indicated with a wave of his hand at the pristine street lights. "Not what we are used to."

"No, it's not. I think it's time we made a position change. Let's reverse up into the road behind us, collect the other two and then go round to the top of the next street," Bomber instructed.

Harris did as he was told. Paul and Armalite jumped in after Harris had reversed the car into the side street. They drove out and took a circular route back to the next street. Pulling up a hundred yards short, Paul and Armalite got out, walking the short distance to their positions, while Harris moved the car, parking it with a van behind them and a car in front.

They now had a view along the street out of sight of the Dicker but could clearly see the front of the house where they had seen the watcher looking out of the back-bedroom window. Bomber looked up and down the street, trying to spot a Dicker but failed to do so. Glancing at his watch, he noted that they had another hour before they would be relieved to get some food and rest.

The Motorola radio came to life making Bomber jump. "Boss, car with three men coming from behind you." It was Armalite, stationed twenty yards away in the shadows.

Bomber and Harris ducked down below the level of the wind screen. Hearing the car go past, Bomber carefully peered over the top of the dashboard.

The car pulled up outside the house with the yellow door and the bedroom watcher. Two men got out, Harris already had the binoculars to his eyes and Bomber squinted through his monocular. They both reacted at the same time, "It's him, its O'Brian!"

Bomber switched channels so that all the call signs could hear him. "Target sighted, location—" Bomber paused as Harris held up a piece of paper with the house number and street name on and Bomber reeled it off.

"All teams, close in now!" ordered a voice over the radio which Bomber recognised as the Brig.

Just at that minute, Bomber saw O'Brian come out of the house and get back into the car.

"Quick Harris, let's go ram the bastard, don't let him get away, hurry, hurry!"

Harris already had the car moving as he raced through the gears and accelerated down the road. O'Brian's driver was just pulling out when Harris drove into the front left wheel arch of the car, smashing the car's wheel from its mountings.

The impact threw Bomber forward, even though he had both hands on the dashboard and his arms braced for the impact. *'Move, you tart!'* the voice in his head screamed at him. Bomber scrambled out of the battered car, Bearcat in hand, skirting around the two vehicles that were now locked together like a bent letter L.

O'Brian's driver was out of his car, pistol in hand and was firing at Harris who had to crawl over Bomber's seat as the door on the driver's side had jammed. Bomber fired back at the driver who ducked down beside his car and didn't come back up.

Bomber could hear Paul and Armalite shouting as they ran down the street, then the crack of Armalite firing his Heckler Koch P9. Bomber wasn't interested. He was totally focused on the running figure of O'Brian who had jumped over the small garden wall.

He then charged through the front door of the house next door that had been opened by an elderly man who must have heard the crash and had come to investigate.

More shots came from behind him, different weapons, thought Bomber, then he felt a searing, burning pain in his left calf, a shot or a ricochet had hit him a glancing blow but he kept running. He was close now. He jumped over the elderly man who was slumped in the doorway with blood coming from a head wound.

He could hear screaming from the kitchen. Kicking the door open he saw O'Brian, his left arm around the neck of a woman in her sixties, shielding himself from Bomber. In his right hand was a small semi-automatic pistol, the barrel pressed against her temple.

"Drop the gun, Brown, you fucking bastard or she—" O'Brian's voice grated on Bomber's ears. He already had the Bearcat aimed at O'Brian's head. The Bearcat had a very light trigger pressure, thanks to Cpl Johnson who had fixed it for him.

It was easy, a gentle squeeze and a copper jacketed, lead bullet entered O'Brian's right eye. Suddenly, it changed from an eyeball full of hatred and violence to a bloody pulp, as the bullet smashed through the eye socket and into the brain tearing through the grey mass that controlled all his functions, including that of pulling the trigger of his pistol. Then the bullet was out of the back of his head in a millisecond in a spray of blood and grey matter.

The pistol in the corpse's hand, which until a split second ago had been O'Brian's, fell to the floor and then his lifeless body crumpled on to the linoleum and ended up partly on top of the woman.

Bomber helped her up, pushing the corpse away. Standing up, the woman started shouting and beating at Bomber's chest with her clenched fists. "You bloody idiot! You could have killed me if you had missed!" Then she burst into tears.

Bomber held her, then set her onto a kitchen chair and whispered into her ear. "If I had missed or had put the gun down, he would have killed both of us."

The woman pushed him away. "He'd have killed you, soldier, but not me."

"No, he would have killed you too. You're like everyone else to him, expendable. He never liked leaving a witness behind."

The woman started crying again but Bomber wasn't sure if it was genuine grief or just the relief it was over.

The door burst open and the elderly man staggered in, supported by Harris and with a cry of relief, embraced his wife.

Time seemed to have stopped for Bomber. All that was going on outside was in another dimension. He knew that if O'Brian had been shooting when he came through the kitchen door, it would be him lying on the floor dead and not O'Brian.

Harris was talking to him, dragging him away from looking at the corpse of O'Brian who was once one of the men under his command, once one of the regiment's own. Bomber felt no remorse, no loss, just an emptiness. It was then he noticed that his leg hurt, a throbbing pain every time he moved.

"Boss, boss!" Harris was shaking Bomber by the arm. "We've got more trouble outside. The other man from the car started shooting at Paul and Armalite from the house next door. Paul went in and got him but now we have 'rent a mob' outside and they are after blood."

Bomber went out of the front door and sure enough, a large group of men and youths were shouting and crowding in on Paul and Harris, who had their backs to the wall as the mob tried to grab them, ignoring the pistols in their hands.

Bomber knew that in a second or two, they would be rushed and killed. "Give me your P9," Bomber ordered Harris who passed it to Bomber. Stepping forward, clear of the door, he fired four rapid shots into the air. The P9 was ten times as loud as the Bearcat. More like the roar of a tiger than the meow of the Bearcat.

The crowd split and ran but once they realised no one had been shot, they started to reform some fifty yards away. Now the other teams screeched up in their cars, parking in front of the house to form a barricade which they took cover behind, pointing their guns at the crowd who now seemed less inclined to rush the house.

Bomber handed the P9 back to Harris and said, "Go to the kitchen and lock the back door and stay on guard there. Armalite, go with him." Armalite acknowledged and went into the house.

Now there was the familiar sound of armoured Pigs arriving and a platoon of infantry pulled up in full riot gear. They deployed with practiced ease and started dispersing the crowd.

Bill left his car, came over to Bomber and asked, "Did you get the bastard?"

It was then Bomber realised that he had not sent in a contact report. "He's in the kitchen."

Pulling the radio out of his pocket, he sent a full contact report. Looking at his watch, he was shocked to see only six minutes had elapsed from the time they had sent the last contact report.

Bomber returned to the house, forgetting about the danger from 'rent a mob' as that task had now passed to the infantry platoon. The elderly couple were now in the lounge with the woman seeming to have made a remarkable recovery, as she was now swearing fit to burst.

The army, police, IRA and everyone in between were a target for her cursing. The man now had a field dressing on his head where O'Brian had hit him with the butt of his gun. He sat with his wife trying in vain to calm her down. *'He should be going for a scan on that head,'* thought Bomber. As he walked past the woman, she turned her anger on him. "You English bastard, you tried to get me killed!"

'Well, she has some vinegar in her veins that's for sure,' thought Bomber but he had had enough of her bile. He stopped, turned and stepped towards her, bending down saying quietly, "Keep opening your mouth and I will have you arrested and dragged off to the Crumlin for a little holiday."

The woman's eyes opened wide in shock, then her mouth started to move but something clicked in her head and she thought better of it.

"Good," Bomber said through clenched teeth, "now look after your husband. He needs to go to the hospital to get that head wound seen to."

Not wishing to engage more, Bomber went to the kitchen where he found Bill had just finished searching the corpse. "Nothing of interest," Bill said. "Good shot, where were you standing when you fired?"

"In the doorway," Bomber answered.

Bill paced it out. "Only eight paces, close but still a good shot."

Bomber nodded. "Don't look so glum," Bill chided. "O'Brian's out of the game now, plus two of his henchmen. Can't be bad. The Brig's going to be over the moon and you and Bass can live without the threat of O'Brian trying to shoot you from some dark corner."

Just at that moment, the commander of the platoon who had shifted 'rent a mob' from the street came in. "Any chance of anyone telling me what the devil happened here?" he asked.

"Yes, sir," Bomber answered automatically. Once he had briefed him, he found Paul and asked him what had happened at the other house.

"Oh, we were running after you and suddenly this twat was standing in the doorway firing at Armalite who was just ahead of me. So I stopped, gave him a couple of rounds, he turned and went back into the house. I followed and nailed him. One of the other teams got his body out ready for the meat wagon. They are also holding his wife who tried to stab me." Paul pointed to his arm. There was a tear in the sleeve and Bomber could see blood.

"What about the one who was driving and shot at Harris?" asked Bomber, now feeling a little tired from the throbbing in his leg. Looking for a chair but not seeing one close by, Bomber decided to sit on the bottom of the stairs.

"He packed in as soon as he saw Armalite pointing his pistol at him. He's now tucked away in one of the cars ready for the Brig to have a word with him."

"Any other in the house?"

"No one other than his wife but Chris is in there now giving the house a good search."

"Let's have a look at that leg," Paul ordered.

Bomber eased up his jeans and revealed a small but deep gash about two inches long in his upper left calf from which the blood ran freely.

Paul placed a small field dressing on it and bound it tight. "Best get the medics to see to that when we get back to Lisburn," Paul instructed.

"Are you okay?" It was Chris standing in the doorway looking at Bomber and Paul.

"Yes, I'm fine, just a scratch nothing to worry about but Paul needs his arm checking."

"Take the jacket off," ordered Chris.

Paul complied with a grin saying, "Yes, doctor."

Chris produced a small, very sharp looking knife from the back pocket of her jeans and expertly cut the shirt sleeve off and used it to bind Paul's bicep which had a puncture wound leaking blood.

"That will do until we get back."

"Thanks" said Paul putting his jacket back on. "What did you find next door?"

"Well, the woman's husband is the one Paul shot. O'Hallihan is his name. Listed as active PIRA possible quartermaster. She is going berserk but got her secured in one of the cars now. We are still searching the house but I suspect it will be clean."

"Okay, once the search is completed, let's get out of here because I expect 'rent a mob' will come back shortly with re-enforcements and I want to leave that to the infantry company and not get involved." Paul and Chris went off to the house to help with the search.

The search revealed nothing of interest which was not a surprise but still a little disappointing as it would have helped to have found a cache of weapons or explosives. However, Bomber knew no halfway competent IRA or PIRA quartermaster would keep that sort of thing at his own house. It would be stored somewhere which was safe but easy to get to.

Bomber let out a small gasp as he stood up. *'What a wimp!'* the voice in his head said. *'A little scratch and you act as if your leg's been blown off.'*

'Fuck off!' Bomber thought in reply.

Then he had an idea and called out, "Harris!" who came in and looked at Bomber, limping towards him.

"What's up, boss?" he said.

"Did we or did we not see a row of about twenty lock-up garages at the end of the street near where we turned the car round to come here?"

"Yes, we did, what of it?"

"If you were the PIRA quarter master living here, wouldn't you want your stash of weapons and explosives close by, where you could keep an eye on it all but not get incriminated if it was found?"

"Yep, the garages, right."

"Get Paul and Chris, we are going up there, all of us," ordered Bomber who then limped out to where the platoon commander was with his men, watching for trouble.

Bomber explained what he intended to do and that he should inform his company commander, as once the locals realised what they were doing, all hell would probably break loose.

Chapter 19
Boom Time

Bomber looked at the row of garages which were numbered one to twenty. Ten lock up garages facing across a wide strip of tarmac to an identical ten. The garages were built of red brick with corrugated roofs but no windows or door other than the steel up and over one at the front of each lock up.

He briefly wondered if the numbers were related to the houses but quickly dismissed that notion. These were rented through the council on a first come, first served basis, he guessed.

Paul, Chris and Lofty stood with Bomber looking at the garages. Eventually Lofty said, "Which one?"

Bomber sighed, "Let's get the woman out of the car. I want to see her face when she sees us breaking open the garages."

Harris held the woman by her arm. He had spittle running down his face where the woman had spat at him but he remained impassive, as if she was nothing more than a large stick for him to hold.

"Okay, let's start at that end and work this way," ordered Bomber. The lads got to work. The first two were completely empty. The third had a car in it which was subjected to a thorough going over, having had the driver's quarter light forced open to gain access. All the time Bomber watched the woman's face, having instructed Harris to nod to him if she tensed up.

The fourth garage was full of boxes, bikes and household junk which was all emptied out onto the tarmac and thoroughly searched but contained nothing other than old clothes and rubbish in the boxes. Bomber had noticed the woman had clenched her jaw as if something was amiss and Harris had nodded to him.

Limping over to Paul, Bomber said, "I think there must be something here. She is definitely agitated so let's have another look."

Indicating to Harris to bring the woman closer to the garage, he noticed she resisted and Harris had to force her forward.

'Now why is that?' he wondered.

After re-entering the empty garage, Bomber firstly studied the walls, which were single brick construction, no sign of any tampering that he could see. The roof was just some light steel supports to which the roofing was attached so couldn't hide anything there. The floor was dusty but otherwise clean, no sign of a trap door or anything.

"Looks clear, are you sure she reacted?" Paul asked.

"Pretty certain, don't look directly at her but she has a very slight smile on her face as if she is happy that we are missing something."

Paul glanced sideways, "I see what you mean, not the scowl of earlier."

Bomber shrugged his shoulders, leaned against the wall to ease his leg and Paul looked down.

"Now that's interesting," he said quietly.

Bomber looked down to see a small hole had appeared by the side of his right foot. Lifting his foot, he could see something was stuck to his shoe and pulling it off, he rolled it in his fingers. It was putty which was just beginning to harden but was still soft enough to stick to his shoe.

Paul knelt down and brushed away the dust, feeling the floor with his fingers. "What do we have here?" he cooed. He had cleared an area of about twenty inches and found two holes. Each had been covered over with putty and floor dust but there was a small metal hoop set in each hole.

"I've seen this set up before. Look for either some butchers' hooks or something similar," Bomber instructed Armalite and the others who had gathered to watch. Chris let out a cry of triumph! Just by the door on a tiny ledge, she had found two small metal bars about six inches long shaped like a shepherds crook.

Bomber looked at the woman who was now squirming in Harris's grip. Paul inserted the metal bars into the small metal hoops and pulled.

"No!" screamed the woman as she tried to get away from Harris.

A concrete block, roughly twenty inches square came out cleanly but as Paul lifted it, Chris shouted, "Stop! There's something attached to the block."

Paul froze. Attached to the underside of the block was a wire. Bomber got down on all fours, with difficulty because his leg had stiffened up and looked at the underside. A piece of wire was hooked in to a small ring bolt in the underside of the block.

Looking in to the hole he could see it was attached to something but was not sure what it was. However it wasn't worth the risk of trying to find out. Especially as the woman was now trying to do a runner.

"Okay," said Bomber to Paul, "gently lower the block back in place." Paul did so. Nothing happened and they all let out their breath at the same time.

"Let's get the bomb squad boys here to deal with this," instructed Bomber to no one directly but Chris was already on it.

Outside the garage the woman was kicking off, shouting and swearing vengeance on them all and spitting at anyone in range. Bomber ordered Harris to lock her in the car. Lofty called Bomber over and pointed at the ever-growing crowd gathering and facing the B Company platoon. Bomber went to the platoon commander who told him he had called for backup as another crowd was forming at the other end of the street.

"Trying to block us in, no doubt," he said casually, "but not to worry, we will keep them away so you can finish."

At that moment, two Land Rovers pulled up and out got the company commander of the platoon deployed there. A no-nonsense sort of man who didn't like things kicking off on his patch where he was not in command. Bomber briefed him on what was happening and he immediately got on the radio ordering another platoon to the area to deal with 'rent a mob', who were becoming increasingly aggressive.

The bomb squad with its escort arrived, braving a barrage of rocks and petrol bombs from the mob who were rewarded with a volley of baton rounds, which sent them scurrying for cover. The mob retreated out of range of the baton guns and the two platoons advanced to extend their cordon outwards.

Bomber briefed the young Captain and his Sgt from the bomb squad who asked a few questions, nodding at the answers. Then the Captain asked his Sgt to get the tool bag from the vehicle. While this was happening, the Captain went into the garage whistling, 'We all live in a yellow submarine.' The Sgt then asked Bomber to get everyone back a further fifty yards just in case and then followed his Captain into the garage.

"Jesus!" said Paul to Bomber and Chris, "those guys, a screw driver, a pair of pliers and that's it. Total madness."

Bomber had to agree it was not a job he would like to do. After about five minutes, the Sgt came out of the garage and walked over to Bomber. "My Captain thinks it's straightforward but if it isn't, we may have to blow it, so we will need to clear the area for another two hundred yards as we don't know what's down in the hole yet."

Not wanting to hang around to find out what was in the hole, Bomber asked the company commander for permission to return to Lisburn. The two bodies had been taken away earlier by the meat wagon so they only had the woman and O'Brian's driver to worry about. They would take them back to Lisburn for questioning.

The commander gave his okay so the teams piled into their cars and drove away at high speed to avoid any rocks from the mob.

The woman was in Chris's car. O'Brian's driver was squashed between Armalite and Harris. He was quiet and kept his head down as if he had decided that it was safer to be submissive than bolshie.

'Sitting between those two that was the right attitude to take,' thought Bomber, *'or maybe he was reflecting on living behind bars for the rest of his life?'*

Back in the relative safety of the barracks and with the prisoners handed to the RMPs, the Brig and Colonel Wilson greeted them like returning heroes. The whisky flowed in the briefing room and Colonel Wilson, who was just back from sitting in on an important government meeting in Darlington, even opened two bottles of champers as he called it.

Bomber and Paul were excused to get their wounds seen to. At the medical centre, a medic cleaned the wounds and then the MO had a look.

"They both look nice and clean so I'll stitch them up and give you both a shot of something to combat any infection," he said.

Later in the mess, Bomber asked Bill how Andy was. "Oh he's fine, sitting up in bed, chatting up the nurses and telling everyone he will be back in days but it's more like months if truth be told."

"Can we go and see him?" Bomber asked.

"Sure, finish your drink and we'll get a car and driver to take us," Bill said, slightly slurring his words.

"Are you sure they will let us in at this time of night?"

"Leave it to your uncle Bill, Bomber boy. Two minutes." Bill weaved his way to the mess phone next to the bar. A few minutes of chatting and smiles and he was back. "We are on!" he exclaimed.

"What's on?" said Chris who had just appeared with Lofty and Paul.

"We, that is the dynamic duo you see before you, are going to see Andy," Bill said, grinning like a Cheshire Cat.

"Not at this time of night, they won't let you in," stated Chris.

Bill just stood there, grinning.

"I think they will get in if a certain nurse or to be more accurate, Sister Noreen is on duty," laughed Paul. "Tell Andy we will come see him tomorrow and I haven't forgotten about the fruit and nut chocolate he wants."

As Bomber left the bar with Bill, he realised they had nothing to take in to Andy. "I have everything in hand, Bomber," Bill said, leading the way to his bunk. It was like a military supermarket, kit everywhere. Bomber picked up what looked like a homemade bomb.

"What's this?" Bomber asked.

"Ah, well you see, I get the bomb disposal boys to make those up. They are working bombs but with dummy explosives, then I try to disarm them. If the red light goes on, I'm dead but if the green goes on, I've succeeded," he said as he pointed to the small attachment at the side with the lights.

He then pointed to the bomb and said, "Not worked that one out yet. They are all based on real bombs that have been used around the world," he casually explained.

"How many have you done and been successful on?" Bomber asked.

Bill scratched his head, "Out of nine, so far I've managed to do four, so I'm hoping if I get this one that will be a fifty percent success rate."

"Or a fifty percent death rate," Bomber quipped.

Bill ignored the remark and said, holding up a carrier bag, "Okay, got everything? Let's go."

At the secure wing of the hospital, they showed their ID cards and submitted to a search. Their pistols were placed in a box with their names on and placed under the counter.

At the ward the sister, a stunning, dark haired woman in her late twenties, greeted Bill who hugged her. She pushed him away, blushing.

"Noreen, this is David. David, this is Noreen, the most beautiful girl in the whole world," Bill said and Bomber believed he meant it.

"Nice to meet you, David," she said in a soft Irish accent, totally different from the harder Belfast sound. "We will ignore this big lump. He's full of so much bull, he should have a ring through his nose!"

Bomber smiled and said, "Very nice to meet you, Noreen."

She smiled back and led the way to Andy's bed. "Okay, fifteen minutes and no noise or you are out, Bill and I mean it," Noreen said as she pulled the curtains round the bed, screening it from the other occupants of the ward who all seemed to be sleeping.

Andy was sitting up, reading. The small light above the bed made his pale face seem deathly white. Andy was anything but deathly. He whispered his greetings and shook hands with both of them. Bomber noticed the book he had been reading was a western entitled Ghost Riders.

Andy noticed Bomber looking at the book. "It's my way of escaping into another world. First chance I get, I'm taking a ranching holiday in Texas to ride the range," he said grinning.

"Good for you. How are you doing?" Bomber asked.

"Apart from my chest feeling as if it's been crushed and the pain when I breathe deeply, I feel pretty damn good considering." Andy put a hand to his chest and took several small breaths as if the sentence had left him short of breath.

Bill plonked the carrier bag on the bed. "That's the books and the other little thing you wanted."

Andy poked around in the bag and pulled out a half bottle of Jack Daniels whisky. Then he slid the bottle under the sheet, hiding it.

"Have to keep it hidden; one of the nurses found the other one but fortunately, I had drunk most of it." Bomber looked at Andy who quickly added, "It's the only thing that makes me sleep and those damn sleeping tablets are a complete waste."

"What about mixing whisky with your pain killers? A bit dodgy, don't you think?" Bomber said.

Andy revealed a handkerchief full of tablets. "They can stuff those as well. Nothing beats JD for easing the pain."

"Tell that to your liver," replied Bill and they all laughed quietly.

A few minutes later, Noreen came and ushered them out. "Still okay for Saturday evening?" Bill asked Noreen.

"Yes, I'll be there."

"Great, err bring that friend of yours, what's her name? You know the one I mean, blonde hair, long legs. We need to cheer up this miserable bugger," Bill said, poking Bomber in the chest.

"You mean Debbie. I'll ask her and if she says yes, you make sure you treat her like a lady," she said, punching Bill on the arm.

"Oh, I'll leave that to Bomber. He's the gentleman here."

As they walked to the car, Bomber asked, "What's all this about Saturday night and fixing me up with a date?"

"Mess party, live group, buffet and wait till you see Debbie. Stunning girl and intelligent. She won't fall for any of your chat up lines so you'd better polish up your dancing. That's your only hope!"

"I don't have any chat up lines and my dancing skills are bordering on a zombie on sleeping tablets," grumbled Bomber.

Bill started laughing and said, "Then all we have is your good looks, so God help us!"

The next morning started slowly with breakfast then everyone meeting for a work out in the gym. Bomber and Paul sat it out as they were both walking wounded. The APTC instructor put the rest of them through a gruelling circuit training session followed by a twenty-minute session of close quarter combat.

Bomber noticed Bill and his six SAS lads hardly seemed to break sweat. Armalite and Harris did well, especially at the unarmed combat. The others, a mix of Intelligence guys and various outfits, looked whacked but that was to be expected when they spent so much time sitting in cars or buildings, just watching. *'That's why these sessions are so important,'* thought Bomber, *'fit in body and fit in mind as the instructor liked to quote.'*

After lunch Bomber, Bill, Chris, Lofty, Paul plus two others from an intelligence unit attached to the Brig's unit, gathered in the Brig's smaller briefing room. Bomber hoped the Brig wouldn't produce any whisky as he had had enough yesterday. The Colonel was there and kicked off the briefing.

"The details of the find in the garage make interesting reading. Four remote control detonators complete with a radio transmitter. Very modern and lightweight but no explosives except the half pound attached to the wire booby trap which would have easily blown your heads off."

"Three pistols, nine-millimetre Browning's with ammunition. The Brigade Commander is over the moon with the success of our operation which has removed two major PIRA players from the scene. He wants to keep the momentum going and has ordered us to go flat out locating other IRA and PIRA members."

"You are each to lead a team to watch and report at the following locations; the main targets are in the enclosed envelopes. A rapid response team will be on standby to assist as needed."

The Colonel looked at the Brig who popped a mint in his mouth, crunched it then said. "We have to remain on the offensive. It's important that we don't let either faction regroup. Be vigilant, keep the information coming in and we will do the analysing. Car registrations, movement patterns anything. The bastards will have gone to ground for the moment but will want to hit back and you must stop them!" He finished the sentence with a thump of his fist on the table which made his packet of mints roll off and onto the floor.

As they left the briefing room, Bomber said to Bill, "So much for the party Saturday night."

"Oh, we will be back for that. I spoke to the Colonel who informed me we are only doing this for forty-eight hours, so we will be back sometime on Friday."

Chapter 20
Triumph and Disaster

Bomber woke Harris who had the next watch and he wriggled up to where Bomber was watching the farm not more than six hundred yards away. They had been given the countryside job because they were more accustomed to operating in the sticks, as the Colonel put it.

The farm was typical of those found in the murder triangle, a dairy herd and some arable land but Bomber guessed most of the income came from the herd. They had been in position for almost twenty-four hours and Bomber was conscious that if they had been spotted, they could be targeted by a PIRA or IRA team.

For that reason, one of the team was always watching the rear. This put additional strain on the four of them but it was necessary. They had been reinforced by a lad from Paul's team called Steve Barnes. He was an Intel Cpl but despite the general contempt the infantry boys had for the ability of the intel oiks to operate in the wild, he fitted in well with Harris and Armalite. They took great pains to teach him the ropes of living in a drainage ditch by a hedgerow.

They had inserted themselves late the previous night, walking in from half a mile away, which had tested Bomber's wounded leg. They had been dropped off by a mobile patrol and their gillie type suits made them almost invisible except from very close quarters.

What would give them away would be if the farmer moved the cows into either the field in front or behind them because cows are curious creatures who have a habit of gathering round anything strange. If the farmer saw that, he would come and investigate.

So far on their watch they had seen the milk collected, the dairy hand going in and out of the milking shed and the farmer ploughing a field to lie fallow for the winter. The farmer's wife had driven out late the first morning in a beat-up old Land Rover and returned two hours later, unloading carrier bags which she took in to the house.

Everything else had been a peaceful farming scene, yet the reports were that the farmer and his wife were hard line PIRA supporters actively engaged in actions against the security forces.

Dawn was just breaking and Bomber was talking quietly to Harris who was trying to come to terms with the lack of sleep. Suddenly, they could hear the barking of the farm dog who must have been let out which meant that the farmer was up.

"Which way's the wind blowing?" asked Harris, yawning as he said it.

"Still from the farm to us, so the dog won't pick us up," Bomber replied. He could hear Armalite and Barnes changing over behind him.

Soon after, they could see headlights from a car turning into the lane which led to the farm. "That should be the dairyman coming in to milk the cows," Bomber said to Harris. Sure enough, the car pulled up and a few seconds later, the lights went on in the milking shed, which made the image intensifier useless as the lights blurred the image in the scope.

Then they could hear the cows mooing as the herd slowly made its way to the shed.

"Hello, who's this then?" said Harris. Bomber used his monocular while Harris focused the binoculars onto a car which pulled up right outside the farm door rather than stopping near the milking shed. They both watched as a tall figure got out of the car.

The man stood for a full minute and studied the surroundings doing a three sixty. Once he had completed his scan he acknowledged, with a wave of his hand, the farmer who was now standing in the open doorway.

The man went to the boot of the car and took out a box which appeared heavy. This he carried to the farm and they both went in, closing the door behind them.

"We might be able to get the registration number when it leaves and turns at the junction," Harris said, almost to himself.

"Yes, you concentrate on that when he leaves. Get the binoculars focused on the junction beforehand. I'll write down the number as you read it out," Bomber spoke quietly to Harris as in the still air voices could carry a long way.

"Strange time to be delivering something, don't you think?" Harris mused.

"Yes, very strange time," agreed Bomber. "Let's call it in." The call was acknowledged and Bomber was told to let them know when the car left.

It was almost ten o'clock when the door opened and the man stepped out. Bomber could clearly see through the monocular that the man was dressed as a priest. He had a thin face and a nose that was beak shaped, grey hair which was longer than one would expect for a priest.

Along with his black clothes, it gave him the appearance of a vulture. He walked briskly to the car, got in, started the engine, turned the car around and drove along the lane, stopping at the road junction. Harris quickly read off the number plate and Bomber jotted it down, then called it in.

An hour later, a minivan arrived and this time they got the number as it turned into the lane. It pulled up at the farm door and a girl got out, going straight to the door which had been opened for her to enter. Bomber called it in and HQ gave the code word for a raid in progress on the farm.

Harris nudged Bomber and pointed to two Lannys and a Pig travelling at high speed on the road. With a squealing of brakes, they turned into the lane. In seconds, uniformed soldiers and an RUC man were at the front door breaking it down then entering the house. Bomber noticed movement beside the milking shed.

It was the girl and she ran for the gate leading into the field where they were hiding. She used the hedgerow to remain hidden from the farm and moved quickly towards them. Bomber alerted Armalite and Barnes to wait until she was on top of them, then to grab her.

Armalite acknowledge with a grunt. The girl was less than fifty yards away when she dropped to all fours gasping for breath. After a few moments, she crawled forward, stopping every few yards to look in the direction of the farm. Bomber could see her jeans were covered in mud and he could clearly hear her breathing in short, sharp gasps.

When she was less than ten yards away, Bomber tapped Armalite's boot with his own. Armalite didn't need any other instruction; he was up and grabbed her as quickly as a terrier on a rat. The girl shrieked in fear as Armalite lifted her off the ground and Barnes grabbed her legs.

Bomber called it in and was told to make their way down to the farm with the girl. On arrival at the farm, Bomber could see the farmer, his wife and the dairy man were already cuffed and in separate vehicles. The dog was running around barking at everyone. Bomber couldn't see what unit the soldiers were from as they had removed their cap badges.

The farmer called to one who was a Sgt and he listened to the farmer. The Sgt opened the Lanny door and the farmer called the dog which came whining to him, its tail tucked between its legs. Once the dog was there, the Sgt took it by the collar over to the barn, opened the door and put the dog in, shutting the door.

"Oh, well done! You got the girl." Bomber turned to the sound of the voice, which came from a young-looking officer walking beside a bomb disposal warrant officer who was carrying a box.

"Which vehicle do you want her in, sir?" asked Bomber.

"Pop her in the Pig with the dairyman and you chaps can travel in there with her. I'm to take everyone back to Lisburn once the search team arrives."

"What's in the box, sir?" Harris asked the warrant officer.

"About forty pounds of Semtex explosives rigged to go. Just needs the timer setting."

"Fucking hell," replied Harris, "that would make a big bang."

The RE search team arrived twenty minutes later ready to go over the farm with a fine-tooth comb. The RUC officer stayed with them.

As they all climbed into the back of the Pig, Bomber was aware they must look like mobile bushes to the others. "Oh no!" said Armalite as the warrant officer, complete with bomb, got in with them.

"Don't worry. It's perfectly safe as long as the driver steers clear of anything that will give us a big jolt," the warrant officer said with a grin.

"Oh, oh," replied Armalite.

Bomber eased his leg into a more comfortable position but it felt like it was bleeding. *'Must have popped a stitch,'* thought Bomber.

The two Lanny's led off at speed, the driver of the Pig swearing about fucking boy racers. "They know I can't keep up when they go flat out but will they slow down? Will they? Fuck!" He was swinging the heavy armoured personnel carrier around the bends with his foot to the floor but the Lanny's continued to pull away from him.

Bomber pulled his radio out and asked the driver what frequency they were on. "If it's a Motorola, its channel four but they won't answer. They'll just stop at some junction until I catch up." The driver was right, no one answered Bomber's call.

Bomber was looking over the driver's shoulder when he saw smoke and debris going up in the sky but because of the hedges and trees could not see anything else. Then they heard the roar of an explosion a second or two later.

"Shit!" said the warrant officer.

"Fucking hells bells!" the driver shouted and slowed down.

"No, don't stop! Get in visual then stop," ordered Bomber.

They rounded a bend and saw a hundred yards in front of them one Land Rover stationary in the road. Twenty yards in front of that was a large smoking crater.

Bomber ordered the driver to stop. "Barnes, stay here with the prisoners. Armalite, Harris, high ground on the left. You know what we're looking for. I'm going to get those dozy fuckers to get out of their Lanny." Stopping the warrant officer getting out, Bomber said, "Sir, I need you to call it in while we clear the area."

"You got it," he answered and picked up the mike of the vehicle radio.

Armalite and Harris had set off and Bomber sprinted to the Lanny. The passenger door had opened and the Sgt had stepped out but no one else had moved.

Bomber banged on the side of the Lanny and shouted, "Come on you stupid buggers, get out and take cover. There could be a second one."

This seemed to do the trick as three men jumped out and took cover either side of the road. The farmer, who was handcuffed in the back seat, started shouting about his wife and Bomber realised she had been in the lead vehicle.

The Sgt was now at the edge of the crater in the road, staring into it. Bomber caught him by the shoulder and said, "Get back to your team and take cover. Nothing you can do here."

The Sgt didn't move but just said, "All gone, nothing left. All gone."

Bomber, realising he was in shock grabbed him roughly by the shoulder and shook him. "I said, get back to your men and take cover, now MOVE."

The Sgt seemed to come out of his trance and looked at Bomber, then walked back to his team.

Bomber could see the crater was about twenty yards across and ten feet deep. On the left side, he could see the broken end of a culvert pipe. There was a smell of burning and another sulphur like smell. Of the Land Rover there was nothing, just a burning tyre, still attached to the wheel rim, smouldering in the bottom of the hole.

"IED made with fertiliser and such, judging by the smell. Must have been a monster. What's left of the Land Rover went through the hedge to the right."

Bomber looked, it was the warrant officer standing behind him. "Back up is on the way," he said.

Bomber suddenly heard two shots and reacted, running towards the sound of the shooting. Forcing his way through a gap in the roadside hedge, he ripped his gillie suit as he struggled over the three-strand barbed wire fence. Across the field, he could see Armalite kneeling down and taking aim.

Then he was aware of Harris running beside him. Harris looked like a hedge with legs in the ghillie suit and Bomber had an insane urge to laugh but hadn't got the breath to do so.

"Bastard was here, boss." Armalite pointed to the ends of wire wrapped round a stick which was stuck into the ground. "He was running when I got here but I managed to get a couple of shots off. I did think I'd hit him as he staggered but then kept going."

"Okay, well done, let's follow him and see if he has collapsed." They jogged as best they could in the ghillie suits. Then they heard it, a motorbike starting up beyond a stand of trees but by the time they got there, he was long gone.

"Look, boss." Armalite was down on his knees rubbing dark, stained soil between his fingers. "Blood."

"You did get him, well done, let's get back and call it in."

At the vehicles, the warrant officer had organised a search for survivors with two of the remaining crew but the explosion was so great that only unidentified body parts could be seen scattered around, mostly near the bent and twisted chassis of the Land Rover.

So powerful was the explosion that only the shattered roof section of the Makrolon armour was intact and that lay some fifty feet away from what was left of the twisted chassis. Of the rest, there was nothing but small pieces scattered over a wide area of the field.

Bomber looked up on hearing the distinctive sound of an Army Air Corp Scout helicopter. The four-blade rotor of the Scout had a song all of its own and Bomber had flown in that chopper enough to know its signature. Bomber watched it circle then land on the far side of the field away from the debris of the Land Rover.

Bomber made his way towards the two figures running towards the wreckage; MO and Combat Medic, guessed Bomber.

"Who's in charge?" the MO asked a little breathlessly.

"Guess that's me now, sir," replied Bomber as he introduced himself. "Sorry sir, I don't think there are any survivors and it could take some time to collect the body parts."

"My Cpl will make a start on that, C/Sgt. There's more backup on its way by road."

Bomber could see the medic placing small flags as he walked round the field.

"How many were in the vehicle, C/Sgt?" asked the MO.

Bomber counted it off. "The officer, driver, two escorts and the farmer's wife, sir, total five."

"Thank you, carry on with whatever you need to do."

"If you are both going to stay in the field, sir, I'll put a couple of men further out for cover," said Bomber.

"Oh yes, that would be appreciated."

The roar and downwash of the Scout rotor blades made them kneel down and wait until it had taken off. It gained height rapidly and then kept circling overhead at altitude keeping watch.

Bomber went back to the Pig and spoke to Harris. "Take two of the crew from the other Land Rover and go into the field and provide cover for the MO. I need to get on to HQ and update them."

Harris went over to the Land Rover where, despite Bomber's earlier order and the warrant officer's attempt with them to look for what remained of their mates, the crew had gathered back at their vehicle.

Bomber had just finished his update when he heard shouting. It was the Sgt who Bomber could now see was waving his arms at Harris.

Bomber strode over and stepped between the Sgt and Harris. Keeping his back to the Sgt and stepping backwards, he forced the Sgt to step backwards until he was backed against the Land Rover. Then he pointed at two of the men and said, "Names."

"I'm Crowley, this is Dunn, S/Sgt. (Staff Sergeant)," the taller of the two answered.

Bomber then knew they weren't infantry as they would have called him C/Sgt. "Okay, both of you will go with this man." Bomber pointed to Harris, "and do exactly as he tells you. Now move!"

The two looked shaken and tried to look at their Sgt. "Don't look at him. I have given you a direct order. Disobey it and I will put you under close arrest for disobeying my order and for cowardice." The last word seemed to galvanise the two and Harris led them away. Not that Bomber even knew if they could be charged with cowardice but it didn't matter. He just needed to sting them into action.

Bomber turned to the last remaining man, "You, over there and keep watch, see anything, call me." The man turned to leave when Bomber said, "Stop!" The man stopped and looked at Bomber, "You forget to say something?"

The man looked blank for a second then said, "Yes S/Sgt, will do."

"Good, what's your name?"

"Black, S/Sgt."

"Good man, keep a sharp eye out. That's the direction the bastard ignited the IED from."

"Will do, S/Sgt," he said and jogged over to the hedgerow.

Bomber felt the Sgt move behind him and he turned to face him. He looked pale and Bomber could see he was shaking. Shock was setting in but Bomber couldn't afford for him to collapse on him.

Taking him by the arm, he made him sit on the floor, knowing he had just seen his officer, three of his men and a woman blown to pieces a few yards ahead of him.

"Okay, this is the score," Bomber spoke quietly hoping to keep the Sgt calm. "We've lost five people to an IED. Now, we have to stay alert and make sure no one comes back for us before the backup arrives. I need you to take control of our left flank with your other man there."

Bomber nodded to where Black was hunkered down. "It's higher ground that side so it's the most likely place they would have a pop at us. Can you do that for me?"

"Yes, I can. Got to for the others. We were told travelling at high speed was the best way to avoid a road side bomb. Is that right?" The Sgt looked at Bomber almost pleading with him to say yes.

"Maybe if you were travelling at a hundred miles an hour but it's not the way I'd do it."

Bomber thought the Sgt was going to break down but he straightened his shoulders and nodded.

"Great," said Bomber, "I'm going to organise cover to our rear. Oh and by the way, my man who fired and winged the bastard. Found blood by where he stashed his motorbike."

The Sgt made his way to Black while Bomber went to the Pig. He was pleased to see Barnes was covering the rear with the driver backing him up from the back of the Pig.

As Bomber passed the open door, a voice called, "Soldier." Bomber looked in. It was the dairyman. The girl was sitting on the floor with her knees tucked up and her arms hooked over the top of them.

"What?" Bomber asked.

"Were they all killed, including John's wife?" The dairyman spoke softly with a catch in his voice.

"Yes," Bomber snapped back, guessing John was the farmer.

"Jesus!" He exclaimed shaking his head. "I told them not to get mixed up in this. That fucking priest twisted her round to his warped ways." He wrung his handcuffed hands and sobbed. "John would do anything she told him, the fucking witch."

"Was the priest the one who delivered the bomb this morning?"

"Aye, father fucking Doherty, said it was our duty to God to clear the land of heathens. Us against the evil of the nonbelievers of the Catholic Church. Nonbelievers, what the hell does that mean? Called it our holy duty, the bastard but there nothing holy about any of it. I don't believe in any of them, let alone God because if he existed, why all this?"

The man put his head in his hands and started sobbing. Bomber noticed the girl was now sitting up straight, looking at the dairyman, saying, "You keep your mouth shut, you gutless shit." Then she spat at him but the man didn't seem to notice. He just kept sobbing.

Bomber could see the girl had a wild look in her eyes as she transferred her stare to Bomber. Then she spat again, the spittle just missing Bomber. He just smiled at the girl who went back to lying on the floor, her handcuffed hands clutching her knees.

Bomber grabbed her by one of her ankles and pulled her out of the Pig. She thumped on to the tarmac, her backside taking the brunt of the impact, causing her to let out a cry of pain.

Turning to the driver, Bomber said, "Tie her feet and leave her on the road. If she spits again, gag her."

"Yes, sir," said the driver. "It will be a pleasure. She's been giving the dairyman a hard time and she likes spitting at me too."

Bomber walked over and spoke to Barnes who told him the girl had been giving the driver grief for some time. Bomber went to the Land Rover and used the radio to call in the information on Doherty and to confirm that the suspect IED man was probably wounded.

Bomber kept moving from position to position, checking everyone was alert and to help keep their minds off what had happened. The MO and Medic were still working the area, locating body parts. Bomber was truly grateful that he didn't have their job.

After an hour the backup arrived, a platoon of infantry who took over the perimeter. A team of RE began assisting the warrant officer who had been poking around the crater and wreckage looking for clues.

The Scout helicopter had left to refuel half an hour ago and was now back to pick up the MO, who waved a goodbye to Bomber as he left. The Combat Medic Cpl remained behind and spoke to Bomber, as an ambulance crew started putting the body parts into bags and labelling them.

"Never seen it this bad, C/Sgt. Normally there is a complete torso but not here. The explosion tore them apart and must have vaporised a good deal of them as they went up, incredible."

"Done much of this then?" Bomber asked.

"I've been here two years now. The worst was the Donegall Street bombing, total carnage."

"I know, I saw it too." Bomber didn't want to remember it but his mind started recalling the screams of the wounded and the stunned look in the eyes of others.

"Boss, you are wanted," it was Harris calling and pointing to an officer standing by the Pig.

Chapter 21
Lisburn-Thiepval Barracks

The mood was sombre at the briefing. The Sgt of the Int team was there and said very little except to answer the Brig's questions. Once the Brig had finished, he told the Sgt to go and report back to his unit.

When he had gone, the Brig looked at Bomber and said, "Tell me all about it David, exactly as it happened," Bomber related the events and he was surprised just how clearly he remembered it.

"Yes, when you called in about the priest, we intercepted him. Used the sniffer[1] on him and the car, which was a hundred percent positive for explosives, so I despatched the only group available at the HQ. They are one of the new intelligence groups coming out of Ashford. Well trained but lacking in experience here in Northern Ireland."

The Brig must have seen an expression on Bomber's face that he interpreted as 'Pull the other one' for he quickly said, "I assure you David, they are receiving the best training available and are much better than the ad hoc groups currently roaming around. I had a great deal to do with the formation of this unit and I intend that they become the very best."

"Oh, I wasn't doubting that sir, I was just thinking what shitty luck that the IED got them. It could, of course, have been any of the three vehicles that copped it."

"But not if you had been leading the group eh, David," the Colonel interrupted.

---

[1] Sniffer-device contains a combination of two inert gases that pass through a nozzle and can detect explosive residue on skin and fabrics.

Bomber wasn't sure if the Colonel was being sarcastic or not. "I would have adopted our normal country lane procedure. It takes time and it pays to have your list of likely IED sites for each road. It's not without its risks but less risky than just trying to drive flat out."

"Indeed," the Colonel agreed. "You are right and I will be passing this on to all concerned."

A knock on the door stopped the talk. An envelope came through the double letter box which was designed to allow a message to be put in but stopped anyone catching any of the conversation going on in the room.

Bomber collected the envelope and handed it to the Brig who opened it and read the contents. "Ah!" he exclaimed, "A combined army RUC patrol intercepted a motorcyclist near the border trying to ride one handed. He fell off when challenged. Left arm shattered by a gunshot. He's now in hospital, won't be long before we ID him. Your man did get the bastard, so let's have a drink to celebrate!"

Several whiskies later, Bomber made his unsteady way to the mess, stopping en route at Armalite and Harris's bunk to tell them the good news but they were both sound asleep.

'Bloody good idea that,' thought Bomber. 'Sleep, I could sleep for a week but six hours would also be great.'

The next few weeks were a constant round of watch and wait jobs but it seemed to Bomber their luck had deserted them. Paul's team pulled a couple of IRA minnows and Chris ran down a suspect car bomber but it turned out to be joy riders trying to dump the car they had stolen.

It was then that the Brigadier dropped a bombshell on them at one of the evening briefings.

The Colonel had conducted the briefing for the next day and then handed over to the Brig who toyed with his Polo mints before speaking. When he did so he spoke firmly, indicating that he was somewhat put out by what he was saying.

"The priest who was arrested by us with regard to the bomb at the farm has been released without charge."

There was a combined explosion of "What!" from everyone present.

The Brig held up his hand. "He has been interviewed by his Bishop and sent south to another parish."

Everyone was angry. Bill was especially so and asked if the Int unit Sgt knew of this. "I briefed his Commanding Officer half an hour ago and I told him the same as I am telling you. There will be no follow up by anyone. Have I made myself clear?" The Brig's voice had a hard edge to it and Bomber knew there must be a good reason for it.

Bomber coughed and raised his hand to attract the Brig's attention. "Yes David, what is it?"

"I assume there is a sound reason for letting him go, sir."

"The politicians, RUC and others are convinced if we arrest him and lock him up, there will be an escalation of violence to a level that will be totally uncontainable."

Bomber heard Bill mutter, 'bollocks' under his breath and Thorny let out a small laugh as if he couldn't believe that the authorities were so chicken livered.

The Brig continued, "I know it goes against everything we are fighting for but on this one we are doing nothing under the radar, nothing and it is not to be discussed outside of this room. We now know he was the quartermaster for this area's IRA and has been for some time. Now we need to find out who will succeed him. That's all for now." Everyone knew they were dismissed and left feeling let down by the system.

Outside Bill punched the air in frustration. "Fucking shits!" he said turning to Bomber, Paul and Chris, "Let's go get the bastard anyway. I'm sure the Brig wants us to."

"Are you crazy?" Chris almost shouted. "The Brig meant just what he said and he will have your balls if you so much put your foot over the border." Chris emphasised the point by punching Bill's arm.

"Alright, alright, I'll be a good boy but I can't be sure what's going on in Bomber's head."

They all stopped and looked at Bomber. Paul winked at Bomber and said, "Well, if you are going after him, I'm going with you."

"No, you are not!" said Chris and punched Paul hard in the chest. "Am I the only one here who obeys orders?"

"Oh, you are such a bully, woman," Paul said laughing, while rubbing his chest. "We are winding you up, can't you see?" Paul put a large arm over Chris's shoulder which she angrily shrugged off.

Bomber kept quiet and walked on. Chris quickly caught up with him. "You're not going to do anything stupid, are you Bomber?" she asked quietly.

Bomber stopped and looked at her. "No, not at the moment but why should we go south and take on the other scum and let him walk free. I don't see God punishing him in this life, do you?"

Chris shrugged her shoulders saying "Don't do anything, Bomber. It's not worth your life."

Bomber sighed. The others were now standing round him and he realised that if he said, "Let's go!" they would probably be with him but he wasn't prepared to drag them into any hare-brained scheme to dispense some sort of ill thought out justice. Instead he said, "The Brig is not a man to let this priest escape unpunished, so let's wait and trust him to do what's right."

"Okay," Bill said grudgingly, "let's go eat, then get a car and go see Andy."

"Good idea!" Paul said, "I'm starving and it will be good to see the lad."

They ate dinner with some light hearted banter being exchanged. Bill excused himself to phone the hospital to speak to Noreen to get the okay to call in on Andy. Bomber remembered that they would be seeing her and her friend Debbie tomorrow for the party in the mess.

A few minutes later, Bill walked in looking stunned. "What's up, Bill?" Bomber asked.

Bill stood still and looked at each of their faces in turn. "Andy died a little while ago. Some sort of problem with his lungs. They collapsed and his heart stopped, they couldn't revive him." Bill sat down heavily on a chair and said, "Fuck it, he was doing so well too."

All the diners stopped talking and looked at Bill. They had all known Andy as one of the Brig's key men. A warrant officer at the end of the table stood up and said, "I didn't know Andy as well as you all did but I liked him and I'll miss him cracking his corny jokes. So I'm going into the bar to buy drinks for anyone that would like to join me and drink to one of our own, Andy."

Everyone at the table stood and followed him to the bar. Glasses were filled, toasts were given, glasses drained, stories told and Andy was remembered.

One of the mess waiters came to Bomber and told him he was wanted on the phone. Picking up the phone he heard the Colonel speaking, telling him about Andy. Bomber told him they already knew and were holding a bit of a party to celebrate his life.

Bomber went back to the bar and held his glass up and made a silent toast, *'Here's to you Andy. I hope you are riding the range in Texas or somewhere.'*

That night, the dream was back. It played over and over again until eventually Bomber woke up, sweating and shaking. Looking at his watch, he discovered it was four o'clock in the morning. Unable to settle, he checked the stitches on his leg were okay then put some clothes on and went for a walk around the camp.

He walked slowly so as not to pop any of the new stitches that the medic had put in, after giving him a lecture saying he had better things to do than keep re-stitching his leg. Bomber was mulling things over in his mind when he was stopped by the guard who patrolled inside the camp.

After a brief explanation, he was allowed to proceed and his mind rewound what had happened. Andy had seemed well on the road to recovery when he last saw him but suddenly dying, that really was the shitty end of the stick. Events churned over in his head.

The fucking priest it seemed had got away with being a supplier of bombs and weapons to the worst terrorist mankind could spawn. The shooting of O'Brian probably wasn't the end of the PIRA having him and Bass on a hit list? But Bomber realised he no longer cared.

If someone as well trained and experienced as Andy could go just like that, a mere snap of the fingers, what hope was there for the rest of them. After two hours, he had had enough of weighting the ins and outs of life and limped back to the mess.

Back in the mess, he found the night kettle and made himself some tea which he took to his bunk where he stripped down the Bearcat pistol and cleaned it; then he did the same with the Beretta. With the walk, weapon cleaning, reloading them and a good cup of tea inside him, Bomber felt a lot better.

He shaved and showered, putting on combat kit rather than civilian clothes, of which he had a very limited supply and wanted to keep in as good order as possible. As far as he knew, they were in camp today and the party was scheduled for that evening but as much as he thought it would be nice to meet Debbie, he didn't feel he was in a party mood.

Breakfast was a quiet affair and there was a notice on the door saying the party was cancelled in respect of Andy's passing and the death of the intel boys in the IED.

"Jesus!" said Bill. "Andy would be the last person to want a party cancelling."

"I know but I don't think anyone in the mess is feeling like a party," Paul replied. "Remember that we lost the other four from that new Intelligence Company. I know there wasn't anyone from the mess included in that but its put a damper on everything at the moment."

"So what are we filling the day with then?" asked Chris.

"Listening to Bomber," Thorny said, walking into the dining room and plonking himself down next to Bomber. "Orders from the Colonel. Bomber, at ten hundred hours you, accompanied by us, are to lecture the new Intelligence Company, fourteen Company, I think they call themselves and we are to attend and put in our bit as needed."

"What am I talking to them about?" Bomber asked, somewhat taken back by the suddenness of it.

"Movement on country roads, IED's, what to look for and so on, according to the Colonel. Apparently they asked for you personally. I think that Sgt who lost his boss may have had something to do with it."

Bomber studied the faces of the thirty or more people sitting in front of him in the lecture room. They were mostly young with a few older heads scattered in the group but all were silent and sombre. Bomber thought that this could be difficult if they are looking for sure-fire answers as to why they lost four of their own.

"I would like to start by saying that all of us here are extremely sorry for the loss of your colleagues. We lost one of our own yesterday so we do understand how you feel."

Bomber looked at the faces and felt that went down like a lead balloon at a swim along.

"We," began Bomber as he indicated to the team who were sitting to one side, "have been asked to describe our own methods of vehicle movement on the country roads but I have to tell you nothing is fool proof and sometimes you do just have to put your foot down and go for it."

"On the other hand, you can stop at every site and dismount and check every likely ambush position. Ninety-nine times in a hundred you will find nothing but that's better than dying on the hundredth."

Bomber could see he now had some interest in the faces and went on to explain how they mapped all likely IED sites on a road and other possible ambush points. He also explained reaction drills to possible threats and actual incidents. Bomber went on until he thought it was time for some questions from the audience.

A dozen or more hands went up and Bomber passed most of the questions to the team to give himself a break. Bill, Chris and Thorny dealt with the questions in turn. Once the questions had died down, Bomber stood up again. "Before we finish, I would like to get two of the best spotters I know to tell you what they look for when out either patrolling or when in an OP." Bomber waved Armalite and Harris over from where they had been sitting and introduced them.

Bomber was surprised how well they carried it off, seeing how they had no warning that he would spring this on them. They told everyone how they scanned an area for trouble, what seemed out of place or a good ambush site.

Harris finished by saying, "Mostly it's your gut telling you to be careful, if it's not looking or feeling right. Don't worry if it turns out to be nothing, worry when it turns out to be something because then you have to know your drills and be slick and fast with your IAs." (Immediate action.)

Finally, Bomber finished by telling everyone, "You have to put yourself in the enemy's shoes and think about what you would do to kill the maximum number of security forces and how you would choose to do it without getting caught. Finally, keep adapting your tactics and never establish a routine."

Then it was all over and Bill said, "I think that went well. They seem brighter than your average squaddie. Now all they need is to get some on the ground experience."

As Bill finished speaking, a Major from the company joined them, thanking them for their time and indicating that they could be doing things together in the future. Then he left. Bomber thought he was young to be a Major but looked fit and sounded keen without being brash. *'Maybe, this new unit will make a difference after all,'* he thought.

They all turned as Paul strode into the room and headed directly for them. "Main briefing room in ten minutes. The Brig wants to talk to everyone, including you two," Paul said, pointing at Armalite and Harris.

"What's it about?" Bill asked.

"Can't say but if you thought you had the evening off, think again!"

"He knows exactly what it is," Bill muttered. "He and the Brig are like that," he said, holding up his index and middle finger entwined. "I had better phone Noreen and tell her the evening's off. She is going to be so pissed off with me."

Chapter 22
Stakeout

The Brig had spent years building up his network of agents both north and south of the border. Then he, the Colonel, Paul and others spent hours analysing the information.

Now, Bomber and his team were acting on some of that intelligence gathered. He shifted his weight in the hard, upright chair. It was set back from the first-floor window where he could watch the street and the front of house number seven opposite.

On his right was a Cpl by the name of Spencer, from the new Intelligence Company, manning a camera with a zoom lens the length of a rifle barrel. Anyone going in or out of the house was photographed in minute detail. The street was typical of the Victorian houses of Belfast which had seen various alterations over the years.

Armalite was sitting by the door, weapon in his lap, ready to blast any would be attackers if their position was compromised. Harris was making tea and counting out Jammy Dodger biscuits on to a plate. It went something like 'one for you, two for me'. Bomber wasn't sure between him and Dusty who was the most addicted to them.

Bomber tensed as a car drew up outside the house. He could hear the Cpl clicking away on the camera while Bomber trained his monocular onto the car. He could make out the driver clearly, young, thin faced and with long dark hair.

"Now he's a player!" Spencer said referring to the driver and clicked off a few more shots.

Bomber was more interested in the passenger getting out of the car dressed in a rain coat with a head scarf and flat shoes, a large pair of glasses obscuring her eyes. She reached back into the car and pulled out a large, heavy shopping bag, then walked the few paces to the front door which was opened by someone inside.

Harris was watching and said what Bomber was thinking, "If that's a woman, I'm the fairy queen."

"I think you are dead right, too big and walks like a man," Bomber replied.

"She needs a shave as well," Spencer chipped in. "The scarf and glasses can't hide that from this baby," he said, patting the zoom lens.

"Must be a transvestite's party. Are you sure we are at the right address, boss?" Harris asked.

Bomber flicked through the ID book, looking at photographs and the details of known terrorists. "How tall do you think she/he is?"

"At least six two I'd say and broad. Wouldn't want to meet her or him on a dark night, that's for sure," Spencer said without any humour in his voice.

Bomber turned the pages, ignoring anyone under six foot. Harris suddenly poked a finger into the book, spilling tea over Bomber's shoulder. "That one, I'm sure," he said with the same force that had he had used to jab at the photograph.

Spencer and Bomber studied the details, while Harris mumbled apologies about the spilt tea and tried to dry it with a tea towel before passing out the mugs and biscuits.

"It's a possibility, right build and weight but what would a Londonderry IRA quartermaster be doing here in Belfast?" Spencer asked.

"Whoever it is and whatever he is up to, we are calling it in." Bomber used the Motorola radio and passed the details to HQ for which he received an acknowledgement.

Two minutes later, they received the code word that the house was to be hit.

They watched and waited. Bomber found this was the hardest thing to endure as he wanted to be part of the action, charging in and taking down the bad guys. *'There's always the possibility the bad guys will take you down first,'* the voice in his head countered.

The daily routine of normal life, such as it was in that part of Belfast right on the divide of a Cath and Prod area could be heard. Beneath them was a small shop selling everything from newspapers to baked beans. When they entered the flat, they had avoided meeting any customers by arriving in the small hours of the morning from the rear alleyway and that was the way they would leave in the dark when told to do so.

"Here they are," muttered Spencer. Bomber watched as an army Land Rover followed by a RUC vehicle pulled up at the front door. There was no ringing the door bell and waiting for an answer! A large squaddie swung a battering ram at the door, shattering the lock. The door collapsed inwards under the impact. Soldiers charged in through the open doorway followed by two burly RUC officers.

The two drivers stood guard outside, using the vehicles as cover from any would be gunman. Bomber knew that a similar group would be at the back of the house cutting off any escape by the occupants.

They all flinched as they heard the two gun shots from within the house. Bomber and Harris picked up their rifles and aimed at the shattered door of number seven. Spencer moved to the side of the window and pushed the bottom half of the sash window up, giving them a clear field of fire. Anyone other than the army or RUC boys coming out was probably going to die.

Spencer had flicked channels on the Motorola until he found the right one and got the tail end of a contact report. Listening in, it appeared one occupant of the house had been wounded and an ambulance was on its way.

"Just like watching TV," Harris said as the medics carried out a stretcher with a body on it. The badly disguised man in his female clothing was brought out handcuffed between two RUC officers. They were followed by another man, handcuffed and bent forward by a soldier who had him in an arm lock.

Struggling when he got to the Lanny, he put his foot up against the door post in an effort to prevent himself from being put inside. His foot was instantly knocked down and the man was roughly bundled inside the vehicle.

A small crowd had gathered from the Cath side of the divide but seemed disinclined to interfere, contenting themselves with verbal abuse at the soldiers and RUC as they departed.

Once the vehicles had left, Spencer carefully closed the window. Bomber and Harris put down their weapons and Bomber walked the few paces to the kitchenette where he put the kettle back on as his tea had gone cold. Armalite and Harris swapped places.

Even though the action was over, Bomber had no intention of being caught napping by someone coming up the stairs and spraying them with bullets.

Sipping a fresh mug of tea while munching a stale cheese sandwich, Bomber reflected on the briefing by the Brig.

"This is Major Carson who is in charge of fourteen company," the Brig said to Bomber. "In future, all our operations will be a joint venture with them." As the Brigadier spoke, he looked at Bomber and the expression on his face said, 'Perhaps not quite all operations'.

The Colonel, who was sitting at his desk, then told of his trip to Darlington where he had been witness to discussions on power sharing in Northern Ireland. Then he dropped the bombshell. Clearing his throat with a harrumph, he then said, "From January, when both countries will be members of the EU, the border is to be treated as an open border, without any customs or identity checks."

Everyone in the room gaped in amazement. Bomber thought that it was ironic as currently the army was blowing up many of the unmanned road crossings to restrict movement! Only the Brits could be involved in a bloody war on its doorstep and agree to an open border for the terrorists while not allowing its own security people to cross in hot pursuit. Crazy or what!

Time dragged by slowly while they took turns watching the street and guarding the entrance to the flat. A gang of workmen had turned up with a large sheet of heavy-duty plywood, which they nailed over the doorway of number seven to make it secure.

The men worked crudely and quickly, securing the doorway. It was clear they didn't want to be there any longer than necessary.

'Aren't you forgetting something?' the voice in his head chimed. 'There's something you haven't done which we would normally do as second nature.' Bomber was sure the voice sniggered when it spoke.

'Christ, they have boarded the place up and there hasn't been a search team in!' Bomber thought.

"Cpl Spencer, wasn't there a search team tasked to go into the house after the snatch?" Bomber asked.

"Nothing came over the radio about one so perhaps there isn't one spare at the moment," replied Spencer.

"Shit, if there's anything worth finding in there, someone will be in and remove it shortly and we have no one covering the back."

"There's nowhere to watch from the back without the locals knowing about it and that will bring 'rent a mob' or a gunman on us," Spencer replied.

"We need to be inside the house waiting, then we can get the bastards when they come to collect whatever is in there," Harris spoke quietly, looking at Bomber for agreement.

"You took the thoughts right out of my head. Must be all those Jammy Dodgers you eat, making your brain work over time."

"I'm just naturally gifted, boss," joked Harris.

Armalite laughed and said, "Gifted at eating more than your share of the food you mean."

Bomber cut the banter short by telling Spencer to get on to HQ and tell them that if a search team wasn't on its way, they intended to go in. Within a minute, they received the go ahead.

In the small rucksacks, they had used to carry in what was needed for the OP were some basic civvies. Bomber put on a scruffy pair of jeans, tee shirt, trainers and a zip jacket under which he hid his Beretta. Armalite was similarly dressed and had brought his P9 semi-automatic with him.

Bomber waited until the shop was empty, then he went in from the stairway where a side door gave them access to the interior of the shop. He and Armalite bought a few snacks in the shop, putting them into a carrier bag as camouflage before leaving by the main entrance.

Bomber strolled casually along the street to the far end turning right and up the alleyway behind number seven. Armalite did the same from the other direction. They had studied the street for twenty minutes before venturing out. They had not seen any dickers or anyone else taking an interest in the house. The shopkeeper, a prod, with a son in the UDR (Ulster Defence Regiment) was only too happy to cooperate.

Bomber had to count off the houses as he went along the alley as they were not numbered at the rear. The yard at the back of the house was roughly twelve by ten with an outside toilet positioned in one corner and a single storey scullery jutting out at a ninety degree to the house. A large, galvanised, tin bath hung from a hook on the wall by the toilet.

Bomber waited for Armalite to arrive before trying the handle to the door leading into the scullery. It was open and Bomber stepped inside and listened. Nothing was disturbing the silence of the house, Armalite edged past, pushing into the next room and between them, they did a sweep of the ground floor's two rooms and then the two bedrooms upstairs.

Satisfied that all was as it should be, they discussed where to wait and agreed that the front downstairs room was the best bet as the door to the street was sealed by the plywood sheeting on the outside.

They adjusted the door from the front room to the back room, so that it was half open and they could see through into the rear room and through the window into the yard. Now, all they had to do was wait.

Bomber studied the room which was typical of a Victorian worker's house. A small cast iron fireplace was central on one wall. The remains of a fire in the grate gave the room an air of sadness and a smell of coal smoke. Above the grate on a mantelpiece, stood a small, wooden casement clock which had stopped at a quarter to four.

This was flanked by framed black and white family photographs of what Bomber thought were holiday snaps by the sea. The two adults and three children were smiling for the camera. *'Happy days,'* thought Bomber, *'but where have those days gone?'*

An old sofa took up all of the wall space opposite the window, which was hung with heavy net curtains that blocked out a lot of the daylight. Dark green drapes hung on either side of the net curtains.

Two hard upright chairs, a coffee table and to the left of the fireplace on a small side table stood a television of the type that was supposed to be really trendy and futuristic with its white oval plastic shell and twelve-inch screen.

'Well, it's home for someone,' thought Bomber, *'but we haven't seen hide nor hair of a woman or kids.'* Bomber looked around the room again. *'No woman's touch here or in the other room with its dining table, two chairs and used mugs and plates sitting there waiting to be washed,'* he thought.

He had to work hard not to doze off as the shadows lengthened through the window until eventually it was dark. Checking his watch, he saw it was nearly ten o'clock at night. *'Perhaps I got it wrong,'* he thought, *'maybe there's nothing here. God, I could do with a cup of tea and a good hot meal.'*

It was a little after eleven thirty when they heard the gate to the yard open. Then the back-door handle was turned and the door creaked open. The sound of whispering reached them as they waited. Bomber could see the shadows of two people. One he could tell was a girl by her slight figure and the sound of her voice, constantly whispering to the other figure, who looked like a teenage boy.

Armalite had moved to the side of the door, the P9 ready. Bomber had the Beretta in his hand as he waited and watched. After some more whispering, the boy switched on the light in the room. In the light, Bomber could see he was about fifteen years old and the girl was skinny, of a similar age.

Both were dressed in jeans and sweaters. The girl moved swiftly to the cupboard door which was situated under the incline of the stairs. A hard tug and the door opened. Inside, Bomber could clearly see an electric meter mounted on a board that was fixed to the rear wall.

The girl fiddled around with the meter for a moment, then let out a cry of triumph as the board that the meter was fixed to pivoted open like a door away from the wall.

Bomber gave the signal to Armalite who sprang into the room. Bomber was close behind, shouldering the boy onto the floor while Armalite locked the girl in a bear hug from behind, pinning both her arms. A bundle about the size of a shoe box clattered to the floor from her hands.

She started screaming but Armalite squeezed her hard and told her to shut up. She stopped while the boy lay on the floor not making a sound, with Bomber's foot and weight on his back.

Bomber had Armalite sit them on the two upright chairs with their hands secured behind their backs while he checked the bundle. Unwrapping it, he discovered two army issue Browning semi-automatic pistols. Ejecting the mags, he saw that they were fully loaded.

With the pistols was a box of fifty, nine-millimetre rounds and a cleaning kit. Placing them on the table, he went to the cupboard and checked the hiding place. His hand closed over a small rolled up wad of money held by an elastic band, probably about three hundred pounds, he guessed.

Reaching in further, Bomber extracted a small cardboard box and opened it. Wrapped in waxed paper were two modern looking timers complete with detonators wrapped separately. *'Hmmm, these would have gone well with the explosives recovered earlier.'*

Bomber placed the items on the table and looked at the boy. He was avoiding eye contact and kept his head down.

"What's your name, son?" Bomber asked gently.

"Don't say anything!" the girl shouted and lashed out with her foot at Bomber. "You leave my brother alone, you fucking English bastard."

"Your brother eh, so what's your name or are you the boss and saying nothing is going to be your line all night?"

"I'll tell yers nothing, so fuck off!"

Just then Bomber's ear piece crackled. It was Spencer telling him there were two men standing at the end of the street watching the house.

Bomber briefed him on the find, asking that backup be sent to pick up the two men and another vehicle for them plus the boy and girl.

While they waited, Bomber had a look at the hiding place. Very clever design, no one would think that it was a door that could be opened by sliding a finger down each side of the board to two very small catches, which could be pressed down at the same time to release it.

So the men outside had sent the kids in to collect the gear, rather than risk doing it themselves and the kids weren't talking. Bomber's ear piece went live again. "The men are moving towards you."

Bomber acknowledged, turned off the light and said in a low voice "Not one word out of either of you or else," he knew he wouldn't do anything but he needed to prevent the kids from calling out and hoped, despite her bravado the girl would stay silent.

There was a gentle tap on the plywood followed by another and a forced whisper, "Riane, Brian, get a fucking move on!"

Then Bomber could hear the distinctive sound that army Land Rover tyres make on tarmac. That unmistakable whirring as the heavy-duty cross-country tread grips the road surface.

Shouts from the men and soldiers punctured the night and Bomber guessed that the patrol had come in from both ends of the street trapping the two men.

Within less than a minute, the patrol had bundled the men into the vehicles and were away before the locals even knew it had happened.

Turning the light back on, Bomber saw Armalite removing his hand from the girl's mouth and shaking his fingers. Specks of blood flew left and right.

"The little shit almost bit through my finger, boss." In response to Bomber's raised eyebrows, he added, "I could hear her taking a deep breath to shout out so I clamped my hand over her mouth. Then she started biting."

"Another minute I'd have had your fucking finger off, you bastard!" The girl said with spittle and blood running down her chin. Despite everything, Bomber found himself admiring her courage.

Spencer's voice crackled in Bomber's ear again telling him they were in the pickup vehicle, a Pig and it would meet them at the end of the alleyway.

Leaving the house by the back door, they moved quickly along the dark alley, praying not to bump into a gang of locals.

Once in the Pig, the journey back to Lisburn was quick and without incident. Once there, they handed over the two would-be terrorists and the items found at the house to the RUC and RMP on duty who patiently took their statements.

Then they made for the Brig's briefing room where Paul greeted them and ushered them in. The smell of fresh coffee assailed Bomber's senses and he helped himself to a mug and a biscuit off a plate loaded with an assortment of the type that came from a shop bought selection. No Jammy Dodgers on this plate, he mused.

Sitting down, Bomber noticed the Brig and Colonel were not present but Major Carson was flanked by one of his warrant officers and Paul.

The Major started by saying the Brigadier and Colonel were in London for an important meeting and that he would be looking after the shop until they returned.

"Now," he said firmly, "the operation was a complete success. The arrest of the IRA Londonderry QM delivering twenty-five pounds of PE (Plastic Explosives) to the IRA cell here has dealt a strong blow to them."

"The follow-up by your team and finding the guns and more importantly the timers and detonators was excellent. The two teenagers are known to us as gophers for the local IRA while the two men are local IRA thugs, employed mostly as enforcers. So all in all, a very good job. Well done!"

He paused and looked at the four of them smiling. "I know it's a tradition that the Brigadier likes to toast success as he believes it brings good luck and I'm not one to break with tradition." With that he nodded to Paul, who like a magician, lifted a cloth and produced a tray with seven glasses of amber liquid and passed them round.

Once they all had a glass, the Major raised his and said, "To success, confusion to the enemy and peace." Then he threw back the generous slug of whisky in one.

Everyone followed suit except Bomber who sipped at his slowly, savouring the warm glow as it made its way to his empty stomach.

The Major indicated for everyone to sit down. He looked at Bomber then said, "I'm not sure if you will consider this good or bad news C/Sgt but you and your two lads are being sent on two weeks' leave, then back to your regiment which I'm told is going for a two-year holiday in the sun."

Bomber heard the small gasp of surprise from Armalite and Harris and looking at the Major, he asked "Have we not been up to scratch, sir?" Bomber felt sure this was part of getting rid of irregulars like himself.

"Oh no C/Sgt, if I had my way the three of you would be permanently attached to my company. This has come via the Brigadier. Apparently, your CO insisted that he has you all back for the unit's new posting; can't say I blame him, with all the infantry regiments under strength at the moment."

Bomber didn't go to the mess but went to the NAAFI with Armalite and Harris where he treated them to steak, chips and three pints of real ale. Bomber raised his glass to the other two and said, "Here's to whatever the future holds and luck to the three of us!"

They clinked glasses and downed the pints which Bomber had refilled, knowing that this was probably the start of a boozy night.

Chapter 23
The Rock

Bomber studied the Gibraltar border fence with Spain. It stretched from one side of the isthmus to the other, a total of three quarters of a mile with locked gates more or less in the centre where the road led from the town over the airstrip, before stopping at the border gates.

No man's land was just a few hundred yards to the Spanish fence where the guard towers and sentries mirrored the watch towers on Bomber's side of the border, which was manned by the men from Bomber's new platoon. Bomber was concerned with the situation he was faced with.

In the unlikely event that the opposing armed forces decided to mount a surprise attack, he and his thirty men were the first line of defence but apart from his six sentries, one in each tower armed with a rifle and no ammunition, he had no ready positions that were defendable for the rest of the platoon.

He, as the Frontier Commander, was only answerable to the field duty officer, who in turn could go direct to the Governor if he needed to. The other thing that concerned Bomber was that the ready ammunition was sealed in boxes and locked in the frontier post store room.

Rifle, GPMG and the rounds for the 84-millimetre infantry anti-tank gun (Carl Gustav) would take time to get out and distribute. Time they would not have!

Bomber made his decision based on a paragraph in his orders that said the frontier commander was responsible at all times for the security of the border. He called his Sgt and three section commanders into the posts ops room. All were veterans of Northern Ireland and distrusted having weapons but no ammunition ready to hand.

It was as if the powers that be considered them amateurs and not professional soldiers. Bomber opened the ammunition store and looked at the pile of handover certificates for the ammunition, then showed them to Bob Trueman, his Sgt.

"Christ," he said, "none of these have been opened in three years."

"Time they were then," Bomber replied. After a few minutes, the three GPMGs had a belt of two hundred rounds draped over them ready, the rifles (SLR's) had five magazines each loaded and distributed to every man and six Carl Gustav rounds were removed from their extensive packing.

"Okay," said Bomber, "now we are beginning to look like soldiers. Bob, let's go and select the stand to position in case of an attack." In truth, Bomber thought that an attack was extremely unlikely but how many commanders had been caught out by a surprise attack throughout history?

Having already picked the best sites on his inspection of the border, he had discovered one problem with all of them. The RAF married quarters came within about twenty yards of the fence with just a narrow road separating them from the border fence, which they drove along when changing sentries.

So any positions involved using the sides of these buildings Bomber knew would piss off the blue jobs (RAF) and scare the families. Technically, his authority stopped at the Gibraltarian side of the road and didn't extend to the quarters.

Walking out with Bob and the section commanders, he pointed out the best positions for each section, telling them when they practiced deploying, they had to stay on the edge of the road. Come the real thing, they could use the buildings for cover.

The Carl Gustav he positioned on the right flank and that would deploy using the Land Rover. From the right, it could enfilade the approach from the Spanish side to their side of the border.

Back in the post, Bomber told the section commanders to brief their lads. Once it was dark, they would have a practice deployment, as he knew from the intelligence reports that the sentries on the Spanish side did not have night viewing aids. *'Come to think of it we don't, what a shambles! So it will be all down to the mark one eyeball day or night for both sides.'*

"The quartermaster's going to have a fit come the hand over when he sees that the ammunition boxes seals have been broken," Bob told Bomber.

"Well, it states in the orders that the frontier commander is only answerable to the duty field officer, nothing to do with the quartermaster, so let's see how true that is," replied Bomber.

Bob chuckled and said, "I was warned you liked to buck the trend and that there wouldn't be an easy life with you."

Bomber smiled and sipped the mug of tea that the platoon radio operator had placed on the table in front of him. Since he had been recalled from Northern Ireland with Armalite and Harris, the regiment's stay in Tidworth had been cut short with an overseas posting to Gibraltar.

Bomber had been ordered to hand over his job in the Recce Platoon to Ian, his Sgt, who was being promoted. Bomber was given temporary command of five platoon B Company in Gibraltar until an officer was available to take command when he would then be shunted into a stores job. Something he was not looking forward to.

Gibraltar with its towering rock, once called the Pillar of Hercules by ancient sailors, had been a British Overseas Territory for almost three hundred years, the ownership of which was disputed by the Spanish, despite their signing of the Utrecht treaty in 1713 which ceded the rock to England for all times.

The border had been closed since 1969 when Franco ordered it to be sealed, causing many workers from the Spanish side of the border to lose their job in the Gibraltar dock yards.

Between the soaring north face of the rock and the border was the small airstrip built on a flat isthmus which the local Gibraltarians would cross to stand at the locked gates and stare across no man's land.

Once they had spotted a relative, they would shout across the border exchanging news and Bomber wondered how they could understand what they were saying as there would be dozens of people almost every evening shouting back and forth with news about family and friends.

At two o'clock in the morning, it was all quiet at the border. The last of the Gibraltarians relaying messages had left at midnight. The lights were out in the RAF quarters and it was the time when his men and the Spanish sentries opposite would be the most lethargic.

Bomber called 'stand to' and timed the response as the sections deployed. The Land Rover sped away with the anti-tank team to the right flank and the radio operator next to Bomber scribbled down the time when each section said they were in position.

'Eight minutes,' pondered Bomber, *'far too long. An armoured fighting vehicle would be across no man's land in half that time.'*

Four more practices and they had got the time down to three minutes. To do this, Bomber had ordered that those resting must keep their boots on as putting them on took longer than anything else they had to do.

Satisfied that everyone now knew what they were doing, he stood the boys down to normal routine.

Bomber was discussing the drills with Bob when the duty field officer's vehicle pulled up outside the post.

"Good Morning C/Sgt, everything alright here, is it?" Major Thomas was new to the regiment and had taken over one of the rifle companies on posting. Bomber knew he had been the chief instructor at the School of Tactic for SNCO's (Senior non-commissioned officers) in Brecon, a make or break course for people like Bomber, who had completed course number three some years previously.

"Yes sir, everything is good."

"Well, it's just that there's been a complaint from an officer in one of the quarters here saying that your Land Rover has been racing up and down the border and keeping him awake," Major Thomas said casually.

"I'm very sorry to hear that sir but operational necessity and all that." Then Bomber explained what they had been doing.

Major Thomas was studying the floor as Bomber talked but when Bomber had finished, he said, "Right, show me the weapons and ammunition readiness and then the position you have chosen on the ground."

"Very good sir, shall we walk or use the Land Rover?"

"Oh, I think the vehicle will be fine," he answered with a slight smile on his face.

After the inspection, the Major joined Bomber for a cup of tea in the guard room. Bomber was feeling more relaxed now that he knew the Major supported his actions.

Bob coughed an interruption when Major Thomas was about to leave. "Sgt Trueman thinks we may have a problem with the quartermaster when we hand over to the next platoon due to opening the ammunition boxes," Bomber said.

"Oh, don't worry about that. Quartermasters think stores are for storing not issuing. If that was the case, they would be called issues and not stores. I'll square that one, so no problem there. Good work tonight. I'll see you later this morning."

Major Thomas marched out and jumped into his Land Rover which sped away across the airfield towards the massive north face of Gibraltar.

Daylight seemed to suddenly erupt from the east in a glorious burst of orange and yellow as the sun rose. As it did, Bomber suddenly realised it was Sunday. Normally, this would be of little consequence but Sunday meant that the RAF dinghy sailing club would be out on the sea and this could lead to border incursions on the water.

Dinghies, due to poor handling, a change in the wind or just not paying attention to the marker buoys, could stray too far north and west into Spanish waters. The Governor was very hot on not having incidents involving service personnel who could be arrested by the Spanish for crossing the watery line that formed the border, thus causing an international incident.

Bomber walked down to the last lookout tower at the west end of the fence. The fence extended out into the water for about twenty yards before disappearing under the sea. Bomber briefed the sentry and they checked the line of the frontier across the sea with a compass, the line of which was marked by buoys.

Leaving the sentry, Bomber walked the short distance to where several people were preparing dinghies for launching on the small beach in front of a club house. "Good morning gentleman," Bomber started in what he hoped was a friendly manner. "Can I just remind you to keep to our side of the orange buoy markers while you are out sailing today?"

"No, you can't. Now go away. This is RAF property." The speaker was a large, florid faced thirty something, dressed in a dirty tea shirt and baggy shorts.

'Wonderful,' thought Bomber, staring at the speaker who Bomber could see was going bald and running to fat. "Yes, this is RAF property but cross that line," Bomber pointed in the general direction of the buoys, "and get back without the Spanish arresting you, then I will arrest you. As you know, the Governor's standing orders imply an automatic court martial for the culprits. So please be careful."

Bomber turned and start to walk away when the florid face man shouted. "You, I'm an officer and you will salute me."

Bomber stopped and turned and the voice in his head goaded him, *'Tell the fat knacker to piss off!'*

Bomber took a deep breath and ignored the voice. "No, an officer would not speak to the frontier commander or anyone else as you have done and certainly not shouting. That's for NCOs." Florid Face's mouth opened but nothing but some spittle came out as he tried to speak.

Bomber went on, "No, you are some grease monkey mechanic or maybe one of the fire crew." As Bomber turned and marched away, he noticed a couple of the men behind Florid Face had big grins on their faces.

'Fucking arsehole,' the voice chanted in his head, *'but you can't resist having a go at people like him, can you?'* Bomber thought the voice was right and one day it would backfire on him big time.

Marching back to the tower he spoke to the sentry, pointing out Florid Face on the beach saying, "Keep an eye on that one, seems he thinks he is above the rules that apply to us mortals."

"Will do C/Sgt," said the sentry, a lad named Wilson from Brighton.

Back at the post, Bomber phoned the Navy Guard Ship and reported in to the duty officer that the sailing club was going out today. The duty officer sounded somewhat weary as if he had had a good night partying. "Thanks for reminding me. It will be another day of shooing them back into our own waters, I guess."

"Why don't you arrest a couple of them, sir? Then the rest will get the message."

"Couldn't possibly do that as the repercussions and the paperwork would go on forever!"

The phone clicked dead. The Navy were responsible for the line between the two countries' territorial waters which were in constant dispute. The Spanish kept some small fast patrol boats on their side and on ours was a fast patrol ship, smaller than a frigate but well equipped to deal with anything that the Spanish might put out in the bay.

Bomber was thinking about Monday when they would hand over the job of guarding the frontier to the next platoon when the phone rang, the light on the console indicating the sentry tower at the west end of the fence.

Bomber picked up the phone, knowing what the sentry was going to say and simply said, "Report."

"One dinghy sail number R 40 has crossed the line of the frontier buoys C/Sgt, three on board and the Spanish have launched one of their rigid raiders to intercept it."

"Okay, what's the dinghy doing and how far is the raider away?"

"The dinghy's sailing back. I think it will just make it, C/Sgt."

"Okay, on my way." Bomber turned to Bob. "Report it in to Major Thomas, then the Navy Duty Officer."

Bomber picked up a hand held Motorola radio, summoned the driver and two of the guard and set off for the sailing club with the voice in his head saying, *'Bet it's your florid faced friend,'* as he laughed hysterically.

As Bomber got to the club, he could see R40 just being dragged up on the sand by the crew. *'Told you so,'* the voice said. One of the three was Florid Face.

Bomber stopped a pace or two from the dinghy, the guard and driver moved to his left and right, rifles held across their bodies. "Who's the skipper of this dinghy?" Bomber asked firmly.

Florid Face turned and faced him. "I am, why?"

"You contravened standing orders by sailing into Spanish waters and were chased by a Spanish patrol boat."

"That's a lie. I turned at the buoy."

"Whatever," Bomber replied "but you are under arrest, so now you have to come with me to make a statement."

"Like hell I am! You don't have any authority here. This is RAF property!" Florid Face was getting agitated and because of his raised voice, a crowd was beginning to gather.

"I can quote the standing order paragraph if you like but you can come quietly to the post and make a statement or my men here will use force if necessary to arrest you," stated Bomber.

"What's going on here?" a voice from behind the spectators asked. The crowd parted and a tall, thin man appeared, dressed in white trousers, a smart white shirt and a cravat, the attire being spoilt by a cheap pair of plastic flip flops on his feet.

"I need the skipper of this dinghy to come to the frontier post and make a statement about crossing into Spanish waters but he is refusing, so I'm about to arrest him. You are, sir?" Bomber kept his voice even and calm.

The speaker turned to Bomber, "I'm the sailing club commodore and station second in command." Before he could say anything more, Florid Face interrupted.

"I never went past the buoy," he shouted, looking round for support but no one in the small crowd seemed inclined to voice any.

"You did, Gerald. I saw you, now go with them to the post and do whatever you have to. Please carry on, C/Sgt."

"Yes sir," Bomber replied and saluted.

Florid Face complained non-stop on the short drive back to the frontier post. Firstly he didn't like sitting in the back of the vehicle, then the escorts were squashing him. When everyone ignored him, he started making threats about how he was going to put in an official complaint regarding his treatment.

At the post, Bomber sat him in the room that the guard used to eat their meals. He placed a pen and some paper in front of him and said. "Please write down your rank and name, the date, time and what happened as you remember it, sir."

Bomber was filling in the post log book word for word about what had been said and what happened, so there was an accurate record. He had sent Bob to get statements from the two crew members without them having to come to the post. So one of the section commanders was on duty at the door.

The sound of voices made Bomber look up and a Snowdrop walked in (RAF Police). Bomber could see he was a Sgt and looked back at the log book and finished his report, making the Snowdrop wait.

"I'm here to collect Squadron Leader Pickering," said the Snowdrop.

Bomber did not look up but said, "For the log, your name is, Sgt? And you will address me as C/Sgt or sir, as I am the frontier commander. Up to you."

"I'm Sgt Wood. The Station Commander has ordered me to tell you to release Squadron Leader Pickering into my charge," There was a slight delay before he added, "C/Sgt."

"Unfortunately the only person who can authorise that, Sgt Wood, is the Governor himself through the duty field officer and until he arrives, the Squadron Leader stays here."

The Snowdrop seemed at a loss as to what to do when he heard the Squadron Leader's voice from the dining room and took a step forward.

"I wouldn't do that unless you want to be arrested as well, Sgt," cautioned Bomber. Sgt Wood stopped and shrugged his shoulders.

"Are you sure he's a Squadron Leader? He sounds like a grease monkey to me, Sgt," questioned Bomber.

"Can I be honest with you, without it going any further, C/Sgt?"

"Of course, why don't you have a chair while we wait for the field duty officer?"

"Squadron Leader Pickle is something of a nuisance to me. Always calling me night and day with some complaint or other, wanting somebody arrested and he's never polite. He has ignored the rules about sailing out of our waters many times and until now, he has got away with it."

"Well, it was made clear on my briefing that the Governor's orders were to be strictly enforced due to the strained relations between us and Spain."

"Duty officer," called Cpl Manse from just outside the door, "and he's got brass with him, C/Sgt."

Bomber and the Sgt both stood up and straightened their head wear. As the Duty Officer Major Thomas came in, Bomber and the Sgt saluted. Behind the Major came a full Colonel in his Sunday best uniform braid and lanyards, the full five yards. Bomber snapped up a second salute which the Colonel acknowledged.

Then the Colonel spoke, "Right C/Sgt, where's the culprit who's had me dragged out of church by no less than the Governor himself to deal with yet another potential international incident?"

"Cpl Manse, fetch the Squadron Leader here please," ordered Bomber.

"Yes, C/Sgt," said Manse, hurrying into the dining room and returning quickly with the now sheepish looking Squadron Leader.

The Colonel looked him up and down with a hint of disgust on his face, then said, "Well, Gerald, we meet again for the same reason I see."

Florid Face seemed to think the greeting was friendly so he tried to sound jolly. "Oh, it's all a misunderstanding and I think this man has over reacted and has been very rude to me," he said, indicating Bomber with a wave of his hand.

"I think not," the Colonel snapped, "we have had an official protest from the Spanish and from what I know of the C/Sgt, his idea of being rude would be to shoot you in the head." The Colonel didn't smile at the end of the statement and Florid Face frowned and glanced at Bomber with a look of puzzlement on his face.

'*Shit,*' thought Bomber, '*who's telling stories about me now?*'

"Sgt, is that your Land Rover parked outside?" The Colonel was looking at the Snowdrop.

"Yes, sir."

"Be good enough to put the Squadron Leader in and follow us to the Convent[2] where you will escort him to the Governor's Office. Once you have done that, you can fall out."

---

[2] (The Convent is the official residence and working offices of the Governor of Gibraltar.)

"That will be all, C/Sgt. Keep up the good work," The Colonel smiled when he spoke, which made Bomber suspect he was being sarcastic.

So Bomber just saluted and said, "Yes, sir."

When they had all gone, Cpl Manse said, "Well fuck me, I think the shit has hit the fan big time sending the aide to the General. That Squadron Leader is going to be super pissed off with you, C/Sgt."

"I've never been worried about people being pissed off with me before Cpl, so I'm not going to start now. They would have had to send someone pretty senior to deal with a Squadron Leader. Normally it has to be a rank above in these situations. Guess our man is for a real chewing out."

A short while later the Snowdrop returned, looking a little hassled. "Like a brew, Sgt?" Bomber asked.

"Love one, can I sit down?"

"Of course. They call me Bomber by the way. What do your friends call you?"

"Pete or Woody amongst other things."

"Well Pete, it's been a nice, quiet Sunday so far. Now what do you do here for entertainment?" Bomber asked.

Chapter 24
The Challenge

Bomber clung tightly to the rock and waited for the squall to pass before risking another move up the crack. In the dark, he had to feel for every hand hold and feel with his feet for purchase before he could move. Up until this point, he had been ascending fixed ropes that he and one of his Corporals, Joss Reagan, had fixed weeks before in secret.

Where the ropes finished, it was relatively easy climbing. Bomber had told Joss it was no harder than an easy scramble. He was now eating those words as the wind tore at him, driving the rain through his combat jacket and making him shiver violently. He was close now to the top and his objective, the three big nine-inch coastal guns which sat at the top of the ridge.

These guns were old but still operational and dominated the twenty odd miles of the Straits of Gibraltar. They could sink any hostile ship with one hit from their massive shells. Now, he was very close to their objective so Bomber stopped. Taking in some slack on the rope, he belayed to an old iron stanchion that had been set into the rock.

Bomber thought it had probably been there since the war but it still seemed strong and solid. Once he was satisfied that all was secure, he gave the signal of three tugs on the rope which he kept repeating until he felt the return tug from Joss. Bomber felt the rope go tight when the weight of Joss and Nick Price went onto it, as they used the Jumar clamps to ascend.

Joss arrived and sat next to Bomber. *'Hell,'* thought Bomber, *'he's shivering more than me! We'd better get a move on before we all go down with hypothermia.'*

Nick arrived seconds after Joss and gave Bomber the thumbs up. Unclipping from the belay, they crawled up the last few feet to the top. Bomber could see the silhouette of one of the giant guns to his left which was Joss's target. Further to the left was Nick's gun while Bomber had the one to the right, which was furthest away.

Bomber knew that it was unlikely that there would be guards at the guns. Any guards would be at the top of the Med Steps (Mediterranean Steps) and on the narrow approach road on the west side. No one would be looking down the steep cliffs of the east side of the rock on a stormy night like this.

However, they could not take any chances and each set off carefully towards their individual targets. Bomber began to feel a little warmer now he was moving and his teeth had stopped chattering. *'Careful now,'* the voice in his head cautioned. *'Don't get careless, there could be someone there.'*

Bomber took heed and lay a short distance away from the gun, watching and listening. He heard them rather than saw them, snatches of sentences on the wind. "Fucking weather."

"Need a piss."

'Where the hell are they?' wondered Bomber. Then he saw the movement of two shadows right by the gun casement. *'So they've been sheltering from the weather on the lee side,'* Bomber thought*, 'should have guessed.'*

"That's better, c'mon, let's go," one of the voices said and Bomber watched as two shadows detached themselves from the gun and walked along the road.

Breathing a sigh of relief, Bomber walked the last few paces to the gun. He removed the small rucksack from his back and taking out the bomb, placed it against the gun housing where he taped it securely to the side. It was a dummy charge made up by the unit's Pioneer Sergeant. It was designed to blow a hole through the casement and destroy anything inside, including the breech block of the gun.

Back at the belay, Bomber found Nick shivering but no Joss. "Bomb placed, boss, no guards. Fucking hell, I'm cold!"

"Soon get warm abseiling down the ropes once Joss gets here."

A scrambling sound made Bomber turn and grab at a shadow sliding towards him.

"Thanks! Thought I was off down the quick way. Had to wait for two dickhead sentries having a smoke to fuck off."

"Okay," whispered Bomber, "you know the drill. Joss, you abseil down first then Nick and I'll bring up the rear. Once we are down this section, head torches on and remember to check each other's equipment is correctly attached to the fixed ropes before we start each abseil."

The descent, even with the head torches was hairy and Bomber, for the hundredth time that night, wondered why he had decided to do such a crazy stunt.

It had all started several weeks ago when the new Commanding Officer (CO) and his Second in Command (2i/c) had turned up to watch him putting the lads through some abseiling practice. Once the platoon had been marched away by the platoon sergeant, the CO spoke to Bomber.

"Good to see you again C/Sgt, the 2i/c tells me you have been up to lots of tricks since you've been with the regiment."

The CO had been a company commander in Bomber's previous unit before being promoted and taking over as the Commanding Officer of this unit. He also knew Bomber from their time in Germany and Libya before both had been posted to Northern Ireland.

"Just keeping busy sir, you know how it is," replied Bomber, wondering what was coming next.

"Exercise Eagles Claw, know anything about it?" the CO asked as he appeared to study some speck out to sea.

"Nothing at all, Sir, should I know something?"

The CO ignored the question. "Eagles Claw is an exercise in which we are tasked to blow up the guns on the top of the rock. Not literally of course but in all the years it's been run, no one has succeeded."

The 2i/c took over. "The approaches from the west side, roads and slopes are all guarded as are the top of the Med Steps that you have your lads running up most days. So that only leaves the east side which is all sheer rock."

They both looked at Bomber and the CO had a smile on his face as he said, "Be a real feather in our cap if we could do what others have failed to do."

"How long have we got, sir?" asked Bomber.

"The exercise starts in three weeks and lasts five days. What do you think?" the CO asked, still staring out to sea.

Bomber had sworn Joss and Nick to secrecy, then over those three weeks had spent hours working out a route up the east face. They had followed the lower Med steps to a point below a wide crack rising above them to a cave about one hundred feet above the steps.

They chose the middle of the day when most people were having lunch or a siesta when it was most unlikely any hardy soul would be walking on the steps. The poor condition of the path kept the faint hearted away.

As far as anyone else was concerned, they were climbing near the lighthouse at Europa Point.

The crack to the cave was not as hard as Bomber had anticipated and the belay in the cave was very comfortable. Getting out of the cave to the left proved a little testing and the rest of the route had Bomber climbing at his best. At the end of each day, they left a fixed rope in place, secure to a couple of pitons.

The ropes, being white, blended in well with the white limestone rock and were just about impossible to spot from below. It was on these ropes that they had ascended in the night to the guns.

They made good time on the path back to the barracks where they split up. Following a quick shower that put some warmth back into his bones, Bomber put on his mess dress and hurried down to the mess. He should have been at a formal dinner the RSM was hosting for the ADC to the Governor. He arrived to find dinner was over and everyone was standing around with drinks in their hands.

"Where the hell have you been?" asked Bomber's CSM (Company Sergeant Major). "The RSM (Regimental Sergeant Major) went ballistic when he saw you were missing and had the Provo Sgt out looking for you."

"Been doing a little job for the CO. Hush, hush, so couldn't tell you, sir."

"Look out!" whispered the CSM, as Bomber saw an angry looking RSM bearing down on him.

Bomber took the glass from the CSM's hand without asking, swallowed the contents in one and gasped as he felt the fiery liquid burn its way to his stomach. Pushing the glass back into the CSM's hand, he said, "Thanks, needed that!"

"Don't mention it. Any time you need a drink, just have mine," the CSM replied sarcastically.

"You've got some explaining to do, C/Sgt. Missing a mess dinner with important guests is a serious offence. But it can wait. The CO wants to speak with you now. Just be at my office at O eight hundred tomorrow," the RSM said through gritted teeth.

Bomber walked to where the CO was talking to the ADC, the same full Colonel he had met at the border incident. The RSM stalked him as if he couldn't be trusted to cover the twenty feet of carpet without doing a runner.

"Ah, there you are, C/Sgt, the Colonel was just reminding me that we only have until dawn tomorrow to complete Eagles Claw." The CO stared at Bomber and raised one eyebrow so high Bomber thought it would disappear into his hairline.

"Sorry sir, I should have mentioned it earlier but the guns have been destroyed. Perhaps one of the umpires could go and check," Bomber spoke firmly and watched as the Colonel turned to a young Captain by his side saying in a calm voice.

"Charles, perhaps you could telephone control and have things checked."

The Captain acknowledged and asked the RSM where the nearest phone was. The RSM gave a look of puzzlement at Bomber, then turned and took the Captain to the mess office.

Bomber suddenly became aware that the mess had become very quiet and everyone was staring at them.

"Well C/Sgt, once the umpires confirm the bombs have been placed, not that I doubt you, the drinks will be on me," the CO said, smiling at the ADC.

"Let's not jump the gun, Roger," replied the Colonel smiling.

The Captain came back in at a pace a little undignified for an aide to a full Colonel with the RSM in hot pursuit. "It's confirmed Sir, all three guns destroyed and no one saw a thing!" he said with a broad grin on his face.

Bomber was caught by surprise when the CO slapped him on the back and he had to take a step forward to avoid falling over. "Well done C/Sgt. RSM, I am buying the drinks tonight. No arguments!"

"But you can't Sir, you are our guest. It's just not done," the RSM blustered.

"Nonsense! I insist, just this once RSM. It's a special occasion. We have done what no other regiment has done before. Thanks to the C/Sgt and his lads."

"Very well sir, if you say so."

The next morning, Bomber woke with a headache and reached for the glass of water that sat on the small locker by his bed and drank it greedily. Looking at his watch, he could see he had less than forty minutes to get to the RSM's office.

Knocking on the door of the office with about thirty seconds to spare, Bomber heard the gruff, 'Come in.'

Bomber marched in and slammed his feet, coming to an abrupt halt. He saw the RSM flinch. When the RSM looked up, his eyes looked like piss holes in the snow. *'Feeling a little rough are you, you fat knacker,'* Bomber thought.

"What do you want, C/Sgt?"

"You ordered me to report to you at O eight hundred, Sir."

"Yes I did but I cancelled the order. Did you not get the message?"

'Fuck sake, Dick Head! Would I be standing here if I got the message?' said the voice in Bomber's head.

"Not that I recall, Sir but a lot was happening last night," he replied to the question.

"Yes just so, now you are excused as I have to work out how to give the CO this very large bar bill from last night."

Bomber started to turn when the RSM shouted at him, "It's not on C/Sgt, all this secret stuff doing jobs for the CO on the side. Next time, you tell me what's going on. Understand." His voice had taken on a hard, menacing tone as he glared at Bomber.

"You may have been the blue-eyed boy with the previous RSM but not with me. Got it!"

'Where the fuck's this guy coming from?' the voice in Bomber's head asked. *'Tell him to get stuffed.'*

Bomber wanted to do just that but a new RSM was not someone you went out of your way to piss off. Especially as most of Bomber's old Northern Ireland allies were away posted to new appointments. Standing out in any way was bound to invoke envy and jealousy from those who felt threatened by someone's notoriety.

"Yes, RSM," responded Bomber, "but unfortunately, the CO had ordered me not to tell anyone what I was up to. However, on reflection I'm sure he didn't mean that to include you."

"Don't you fucking well patronise me, you short arsed cretin." He had raised his voice to parade ground volume. "I'm the RSM and you are nobody. Do you understand? Nobody! Now get out."

Bomber didn't move. He felt his temper rising. His fists were gripped tight at his side ready to smash them into the face of the man sitting at the desk but instead he took a deep breath before speaking, "I'll get out RSM but think on this, everyone on this floor, the CO, 2i/c and clerks will all have heard your little outburst and for your information, RSM, I was nobody long before you got promoted out of the quarter master's stores and became RSM."

At that, he turned and walked out, leaving the office door open. Bomber held the look on the RSM's face in his mind, a look that was pure hatred, the red bulging eyes, the ashen pallor of his skin and the realisation of the fact that others would have certainly heard his outburst.

'You've made a bad enemy there, just can't keep your mouth shut, can you?' the voice in his head said. Bomber ignored it.

As he walked away, he heard his name called. The voice came from the open door of the 2i/c office. 'You're in the shit now,' the voice in his head said and chuckled.

Bomber turned, marched into the office, banged his feet in and saluted.

"Close the door, C/Sgt and sit down."

'Well, sit down sounds hopeful,' the voice muttered, 'Don't count on it,' Bomber fired back.

"RSM not happy with you, C/Sgt?" Bomber studied the 2i/c's face but it was expressionless.

"Seems that way, sir."

"Would you like the good news first or the bad news?"

Bomber's mind was whirring. "Whichever way you want, sir."

"Good news is the CO is over the moon with your job on the guns. The bad news for you is you are to hand over your platoon on Monday and take up a stores job."

Bomber felt his shoulders slump. He knew it was coming but hoped it would not be for some months yet. And then he thought, 'Oh shit, the RSM and QM are old buddies and I can see they will make my life hell once I'm under the quarter master's authority.'

"Don't look so glum. You will be taking over as the Signals Platoon C/Sgt, answerable to Captain Race and the Technical Quarter Master."

"Really, sir?" Bomber felt light headed at the revelation.

"Yes really, you've not just the stores to account for but you are to get them fit. We are off to Kenya on exercise in two months and the signallers will be carrying twice as much as everyone else." The 2i/c paused and put a hand to his head. "I shouldn't have told you that, so don't spread that around. The CO will announce it to the Regiment next week."

Leaving the 2i/c's office slightly dazed, he headed for the armoury. His platoon was doing weapon training under the watchful eye of his Sgt, so Bomber went and signed out his Bearcat revolver and went to the range.

The training wing warrant officer was at the range sorting out targets and as Bomber got nearer, he could hear him swearing loudly, cursing the Navy and anyone who ever got onto a boat. He was a big man who had played rugby for the regiment and he was known for not putting up with idiots.

"Good morning sir, problem?"

"I've had to close the range because some prat in a yacht has anchored in the range danger area[3]. The useless shits manning the patrol boat say they are too busy to go and shift it."

"Maybe we could fire a few rounds in the general direction of the yacht and that will make them move on," Bomber said with a smile.

"Believe me, I'm tempted but it's in the log now so I can't say I haven't seen it. Anyway, what can I do for you?"

"Just wanted to do some practice with my pistol, feel I'm getting rusty."

He looked at the Bearcat in Bomber's hand and grunted. "That toy will just about reach the first target, so it's not a danger to anyone out to sea, so go ahead and fill your boots."

---

[3] (The range danger area went out to sea for several miles and was marked on nautical charts for yachts and ships to avoid.)

Chapter 25
Radios and Spinning Plates

Bomber studied the store room crammed with radios and all the equipment that went with them. His store man was a Cpl called Kelly, an appropriate name as he was Australian by birth, so everyone called him Ned. He was perched at the top of a ladder, ferreting through boxes stacked on the top shelf of the metal racks that occupied three sides of the stores.

Kelly swore as he banged his head against the roof. "They're not here, C/Sgt, just some spare connectors." Kelly expertly slid down the ladder not using the rungs but by placing his feet on either side of the ladder uprights.

They had spent all morning looking for two C42 radios that appeared to be missing. As they were registered items with a serial number, the loss could involve a court martial for someone. Namely the man Bomber was taking over from, who had been promoted out of the stores and was now the Signal Platoon Warrant Officer.

"Okay, Ned," Bomber said wearily, "bring me all the paperwork since the Regiment took over here."

"Will do but it's a hell of a lot!"

"I know, so make some tea to go with it, then join me in my office." Bomber could hear Kelly muttering and swearing as he put the kettle on.

Bomber was not happy that the man he was taking over from was skiving from the handover by hiding in his own office, claiming he had to complete returns by the end of the day for the Technical Quarter Master. So he walked the short distance from the stores to the WO office and without knocking went straight in.

"All finished, are we?" WO Moore was a bit too smooth for Bomber to like him and he had edged his way up the promotion ladder by jobs outside of the regiment.

Bomber pulled a chair up to the desk and said, "You are missing two C42 radios, so what are you going to do about it before I have to report it to Captain Race and Technical Quarter Master?"

Moore's face paled and he licked his lips before stuttering a reply.

"They can't be missing! It's that incompetent Aussie bastard getting back at me for the time I charged him for being drunk on duty."

"Maybe but the buck stops with you, so here's what I propose we do." Bomber explained he would check through all the paper work to find what had happened to the radios. "If I solve the problem, just remember you owe me big time. Oh and no skiving off the fitness training tomorrow."

Bomber neglected to finish with sir, stood up and left, returning to his own office in the stores where he found Kelly with piles of box files and two steaming mugs of tea.

Two hours and a tea refill later, Bomber thought he had discovered the source of the problem. Concentrating on the files marked workshop, he discovered a ten thirty-three form which had six C42 radios on but only four serial numbers. Bomber could tell from the hand writing that it wasn't Kelly who had filled it in as he had a scrawl like a demented spider.

Bomber crossed referenced it with returns from the workshop but found that half a dozen forms were missing, including the one referring to the radios on his form.

'So,' thought Bomber, '*it could be the missing radios with the two without serial numbers entered on the form. They went to the workshop for repair but got written off and someone has misfiled or lost the returns.*'

"Penny for them, C/Sgt?" Kelly asked in his southern hemisphere drawl.

"Who do we take the stuff to for repair in the work shop?"

"It's a REME (Royal Electrical and Mechanical Engineers) Cpl by the name of Nobby Clarke. Played football against him just last week."

"What's he like?" asked Bomber.

"Oh, he's okay, easy going, likes a whisky chaser with his beer. What are you thinking, C/Sgt?"

"Seems our radios may have been written off but we don't have any record of it."

Kelly drove the Land Rover into the Royal Navy dockyard and parked outside of the building with the REME work shop sign on the wall. The dockyard buildings reflected the century they were built in. Solid rock walls several feet thick with solid looking doors leading into narrow corridors that ran the length of the building.

Bomber walked into the room that smelt of soldering irons and burnt rubber. Sitting alone at a work bench was a stocky man, probably in his mid-twenties, wearing a brown protective coat over his uniform. Spread out on the bench were various radio parts, which he seemed to be studying in great detail.

"Cpl Clark?" Bomber asked.

"Yes C/Sgt, that's me, what's in the box?"

Bomber put the box on the bench and opened the top, exposing a bottle of malt whisky nestled in some cables.

"Not a bribe, is it C/Sgt? Who do you want me to kill?" Clark said laughing.

Bomber smiled back. "No one that I can think of at the moment but I do need some of your time to help me solve a mystery."

"Sounds interesting. What is it?" Clark asked.

Bomber showed him the ten thirty-three form with the six radios listed but with only four registered numbers on.

Producing another piece of paper, he said, "These, I believe, are the missing registered numbers but I can't find any supporting paperwork but you must have a spare copy of what was repaired and written off somewhere."

Clark turned and looked at a row of shelves on which stood row after row of box files. Reaching up, he removed one with the same year on the cover as that on Bomber's ten thirty-three form.

After a few minutes of thumbing through, he removed a similar ten thirty-three. "Think this is what we are after. Now let's look in here." With that, he opened a drawer and pulled out a large ledger.

"Here we go. Yep, three were write offs and destroyed, two of which were the ones you are missing. The others were repaired and returned but God knows why I bother with these old relics. We should have had the new Clansman radios ages ago."

"Thanks. That clears up what happened to them so now what I need is a copy of your paperwork to clear my books for the handover."

"Well, I'm not sure about that," Clark said dubiously. "I could get it in the neck from my boss."

Bomber edged the box with the whisky in a little closer and Clark licked his lips. "Well, maybe I can sweet talk the girl in the office to let me use the photocopier. Trouble is, all use of that has to be logged."

"It's not that we are doing anything illegal, just replacing missing paper work," Bomber said as he nudged the box even closer.

Half an hour later, Kelly was driving Bomber back to barracks. "I don't believe you pulled that off, C/Sgt. That has saved the moron's bacon, sorry WO Moore's bacon."

Bomber turned and stared hard at Kelly, who seemed to grip the Land Rover's steering wheel tighter as he stared hard at the road ahead.

"Firstly, don't let me hear you call him that again. Secondly, you will not tell anyone what I have done. Is that clear?"

"Er, yes C/Sgt, sorry."

"Don't be sorry, just be bloody careful. What we do in the store stays there. Got it!"

Kelly glanced sideways at Bomber and muttered, "Yes, boss."

The March and Shoot competition had started at first light when it was cool but the sun was now high in the sky and Bomber could feel the sweat running into his eyes. Reaching out, he took the GPMG (General Purpose Machine Gun) from the gunner carrying it and handed him his rifle in return.

As they jogged and sweated their way back towards the range at Europa Point, Bomber knew they were making good time and he figured they must be close to the fastest platoon so far. Bomber edged up alongside Captain Race, who was jogging easily and not showing any strain from the five miles circuit of steep roads they had travelled.

"What do you think sir, up the pace a bit or stay as we are and rely on our shooting to clinch it?"

"Well, it's one mile to go and I would rather put money on our fitness than our shooting," Race responded.

"Okay, sir, I'll step it up a bit," replied Bomber who then increased his pace until he was in line with the three front men setting the pace.

The right-hand man was a six-footer called Cheeseman who hailed from Lewes in Sussex.

"Right Cheesy, less than a mile to go, so let's stretch the pace a little more, keep pace with me." Bomber slowly increased the pace and he could hear Race encouraging the rest to keep up.

Once Bomber was sure Cheesy had the rhythm, he dropped back to the rear of the platoon, handing over the GPMG to the platoon gunner as the finish came in sight.

At the range, the clock was stopped and Bomber heard the time keeper say, "That's the fastest time yet. Well done, Signals Platoon!"

No one else was listening as they were already lined up on the firing point staring at the four half size target figures of enemy soldiers on the right and twenty small steel plates to the left. Everyone was trying to get their breathing under control before the range controller gave the order to engage.

When he did, they would run forward twenty yards, adopt the prone position and then wait for the GPMG to knock down the four figure targets. Once that was done, they could fire at the steel plates which had to be knocked down. Knocking them down in the shortest time and with as few shots as possible was the key to winning the competition.

"Engage!" shouted the range controller.

Bomber was impressed with the GPMG team. They had dashed forward, loaded and put down two short bursts which took out the four targets before he had even got himself comfortable and sighted on the steel plates.

Clang, clang the sound of rounds hitting the plates stopped when Captain Race ordered cease fire. Then he ordered Bomber alone to deal with the one remaining plate which had been hit left of centre turning it partly sideways, making it a difficult target.

Bomber breathed out gently, then squeezed the trigger and listened to the satisfying clang as the round struck the plate. A groan came from the lads as the hit on the plate turned it even more sideways without falling.

'Shit,' thought Bomber as he calmed his breathing once again, aiming at the base of the plate where the upright and base formed a T making it a bigger target side on. Squeezing the trigger, the clang brought a cheer from thirty voices as the plate spun end over end and finished lying flat on the sand.

Everyone was in high spirits as they sat outside the armoury cleaning their weapons. They were all confident that they had won but Bomber knew that there were several of the rifle platoons who would be in the running and of course, the Recce Platoon would be the last to go.

The next morning, the buoyant mood of the day before had been flattened by the results appearing on Battalion Orders. As Bomber suspected, the Recce Platoon had won the competition. Zika, Bomber suspected, had knocked down all the plates single-handedly without anyone else firing a shot.

One of the rifle platoons was second, beating the Signals Platoon on the shooting, although there was some satisfaction in the fact they had been thirty seconds slower on the march, so it had been lost on the shooting. *'That bloody plate spinning sideways cost us second place,'* thought Bomber. *'Oh well, if it had been a terrorist, the first hit would have killed him.'*

Bomber found time dragged working in the stores. Kelly did all the day to day counter work, signing stuff in and out while Bomber just kept a tally of what equipment was serviceable and what had to go for repair to the dockyard workshop.

Kelly stuck his head through the small hatch in the office wall, reminding Bomber of someone with their head in an old fashion stocks. "C/Sgt, you are wanted by the platoon commander." Bomber resisted the urge to throw something at him but instead he pushed his chair back, pausing just long enough to lock the file he had been working on in the desk drawer.

Captain Race didn't look too happy and indicated for Bomber to take a seat opposite his desk. "I've just been informed by the CO that you are to leave on an RAF flight at fifteen hundred hours today." Race paused and looked at Bomber. "Any idea why, C/Sgt?"

"Not a clue, sir. No one has spoken to me about it!" Bomber answered in surprise.

"Well, its dammed inconvenient! Off to Kenya in six weeks and we haven't even worked out the equipment deployment yet."

"Oh I've just finished that, sir. It's in a file locked in my desk. I thought we could do it a little differently than in the past to speed it all up."

"Tell me," Race ordered.

Bomber explained how the section commander deploying to each company would pack and sign for his equipment there in Gibraltar. It would then be boxed and banded to go with the company equipment, rather than travelling to wherever the headquarters base camp would be, which would require the company C/Sgt's to travel from wherever they were deployed to collect the equipment.

"It might work, I'll run it by the Tech Quarter Master. Now you better get a move on as the 2i/c (Second in Command) wants to see you in eight minutes," Race said, looking at his watch.

Bomber double paced it all the way to the 2i/c's office, knowing he had less than four hours before he had to be on the RAF plane.

Bomber marched into the office having received a curt, "Come", in answer to his knock. Having saluted, Bomber stood at attention, waiting for the 2i/c to finish writing on a file cover.

"At ease, C/Sgt." The 2i/c hunched forward in his chair and looked up at Bomber.

"Seems you can't escape your past, C/Sgt. Recognise this man?" He flicked a grainy, black and white photograph onto the desk in front of Bomber.

Picking up the photograph, Bomber studied the man dressed as a priest and felt his pulse quicken. The last time he had seen him was through a pair of binoculars in Northern Ireland.

"Yes sir, I do. He was a PIRA quartermaster and I last saw him delivering a bomb to a farm. He was arrested but was released to go to Southern Ireland carrying on as a priest." There were other things he wanted to say about the murdering bastard but thought better of it.

"Well, it appears he is no longer in the south but is on his way to Switzerland and you are to go there. Other than that, I don't know what your orders are. They are in this sealed envelope which you can open now."

Bomber took the offered envelope and recognised the Brig's neat hand writing in blue ink, probably written with his black and gold Mont Blanc fountain pen he always had on his desk.

The envelope was addressed to C/Sgt D Brown with CONFIDENTIAL stamped on it in red letters. Bomber removed the single sheet of paper and read the neat, hand written note carefully. It was not in the normal military jargon Bomber was used to. It began:

My dear David,

I am sorry to put on you once again but this is unfinished business that I believe you feel as aggrieved about as I do.

Our unholy priest has departed on a walking holiday to Switzerland with two minders. I would like you to meet with a fellow mountaineer, Sgt Fanshaw, at RAF Brize Norton who will update you on the priest's movements.

Your job is to apprehend him any way you can, without causing an international incident, something I have assured people you are very good at.

'*No pressure then,*' ran through Bomber's mind.

On no account are you or Fanshaw to put yourself at risk of being arrested by the local authorities, even if it means aborting the mission.

Good luck! I know you won't let me down.

Yours,

Bomber smiled at the totally unrecognisable signature, the politeness of the order and the use of the word '*apprehend*' which could have many connotations.

P.S. Destroy this before leaving.

"I take it by the way you are smiling, C/Sgt, that everything is alright?" questioned the 2i/c.

"Yes sir, all good." Bomber indicated the shredder next to the desk. "May I, sir?"

"Of course, go ahead."

Bomber shredded the letter, then said, "I had better get a move on if I am going to catch that plane, sir."

"Yes, I've told the MTO (motor transport officer) to have a vehicle and driver at the mess for you at thirteen thirty hours. If possible C/Sgt, I would appreciate it if you are back well before we deploy to Kenya."

"I'll do my very best, sir. I'm looking forward to going back there."

"What! You've been there before, when?" asked the 2i/c.

"End of nineteen sixty-five into sixty-six, sir," replied Bomber.

"Interesting, well, get moving. You might just have time for some lunch."

Chapter 26
Deception

The RAF Bristol Britannia banked to the left and lined up on the runway at RAF Brize Norton. Bomber felt his stomach lurch and wondered if he would ever like flying. *'Maybe I've hated it because I'm not in control,'* thought Bomber. *'Could be you are just a wimp,'* the voice in his head muttered.

When he had been doing parachuting he had felt in control, knowing he could jump from the aircraft at any time. However, sitting in a metal tube with a hundred others, unable to do anything except trust the pilot somewhere at the front of the aircraft made him feel vulnerable, rather like a naked man at a giant hedgehog convention. No matter what you did, you would get spiked.

Bomber stood in the passenger terminal. His rucksack had arrived but not the ice climbing tools which the RAF load master in Gibraltar had insisted were packed separately into a re-enforced cardboard box marked Sharp Objects.

"C/Sgt Brown?" a voice asked from behind Bomber.

Turning, Bomber craned his head upwards to see the face of a very tall Snowdrop, complete with side arm (holstered pistol) and with Bomber's box under one arm.

"That's me," replied Bomber.

"I have orders to take you straight through. There's a car and driver waiting for you at the front."

Bomber had to almost trot to keep up with the Snowdrop whom he guessed was at least six foot eight tall if an inch.

Outside the terminal was a red Ford Escort with the boot open, parked next to a sign that said Strictly No Parking. A dark-haired man in his late twenties, dressed in jeans and a turtle neck sweater, stood by the open boot and waved at Bomber, who thought there was something vaguely familiar about him.

"Sandy's the name, climbing's the game," he chanted at Bomber with a grin on his face a mile wide as he took the rucksack and tossed it into the boot of the car.

"I'm Bomber, what's the score?"

"Well, Lofty here is to escort us off the station just in case we stop to nick something, then its foot hard down to the mountains," replied Sandy.

At the main gate, Lofty unfolded himself from the back seat of the car, straightened his hat, walked over to the barrier and spoke to the guard who nodded and then raised the barrier. Sandy floored the accelerator and the escort shot forward like a bullet. Bomber found himself checking his seat belt was firmly locked.

"In the glove compartment, package for you," Sandy said as he weaved his way past slower vehicles.

Examining the contents, Bomber found two hundred pounds in sterling and about three hundred pounds in Swiss Francs plus an outward ferry ticket. There was also an Alpine Club guide book to the Pennine Alps Volume two plus two maps, one of Europe and one of the Pennine Alps, centred on a small village called Arolla, a place he was familiar with from climbing there a couple of years before. A note folded into a small square completed the contents.

Bomber read the note written in a bold scrawl.

Dave, you can trust the idiot assigned to help you. I have worked with him on several difficult jobs. He's a good mountaineer and handy in a fight.

Take care of him, he's my sister's lad.

Bill.

Bomber folded the note then tore it into small pieces.

"From Uncle Bill, was it?" Sandy said, glancing sideways at Bomber.

Bomber ignored the question while the voice in his head said, '*So now you're a baby sitter for Bill's nephew?*'

Ignoring the voice, he asked, "I understand you are to bring me up to date on things, Sandy?"

"Not much to tell. Our man is currently in Arolla, has done a few short walks but it appears his minders are more like prison guards restricting his roaming, according to our contact there," replied Sandy.

"Who's the contact?" Bomber interrupted.

"An ex WRAC (Women's Royal Army Corps) Sgt, name of Sally Brice, can't pronounce her married name but she's known to all as Sal. Married to the

Swiss postmaster in Arolla whom she met skiing some ten years ago. Apparently, she still keeps in contact with a lot of her old army buddies."

Bomber grabbed the side of the seat as Sandy accelerated hard past a lorry, just squeezing back in between two cars before becoming part of the radiator grill of an oncoming articulated truck.

"Jesus, Sandy! Do we have to go so fast?"

"Once we get beyond this useless excuse for a road and on to a dual carriageway, we can throttle back a bit but we can't afford to miss the ferry," answered Sandy.

Bomber lapsed into silence and thought about the job ahead. He knew things were not straight forward and he had little idea of what they would do once they got there. The only thing he was sure of was that kidnapping the target and getting him back was not an option. Sandy broke into his thoughts.

"Bill said you were a quiet one and I'm told you are in charge but you need to give me some idea of what we are going to do, Bomber."

"Was that all the briefing you had? Nothing else? Cover story or backup for instance?"

"Just that we were on our own and not to fuck up but I did get the impression that bringing him back was not a good idea. Our cover is we are instructors at the Aberdovey Outward Bound School in Wales and the staff there will back our story if anyone checks, thanks to Bill."

Bomber nodded. That made sense, no one wanted to be held accountable for any cock up.

"What have they told you about me?" asked Bomber.

"Bill told me you are very experienced and good at what you do. He also said I can trust you and that's all I needed to know. However, the Brig said I was to cover your back and that I was to follow your orders, no matter what. I got the impression he thinks you are some sort of a miracle worker."

"Miracles died with Christ," Bomber said without smiling. "What we need is good planning and a lot of luck to pull this off!"

"So, what's the plan then?"

Sandy was driving a little slower now so Bomber relaxed slightly and took a deep breath. "To be honest, I don't have one. We have been ordered to apprehend him. Like you, I believe that means to terminate the bastard but I haven't yet reached the stage of being an out and out murderer."

"So it sounds like it's all down to luck then," said Sandy. With that echoing in his head, Bomber lapsed into silence.

'You lie like a cheap NAAFI watch,' the voice in his head said with a chuckle.

'Seems that way but you can't afford to trust anyone in this game and it's always best to have an ace in the hole,' thought Bomber.

At Dover, they joined the queue to board the ferry. Once on board, they headed for the canteen where they joined the lorry drivers tucking into all day breakfasts. After eating, Bomber sat brooding about what he had put into motion. After leaving the 2 i/c office, he had stopped at the Recce Platoon and spoken to the new platoon commander who gave him a phone number and said, "I never gave you this, C/Sgt!"

Later, on his way to the airport he ordered the driver to stop the car and then made a long-distance phone call from a public phone box. He remembered how relieved he had been when the voice that answered was the Brig. When Bomber told him what he wanted, the Brig had simply said, "I agree. Give me the phone number and I will make the arrangements."

'No good worrying about it now. It's all set. You just have to play the game out to the end,' the voice in his head chanted.

'Some fucking game this is!' replied Bomber to the voice. *'I just pray it all works out.'* Bomber realised just how far he had sunk into the darkness that was enveloping his very being.

The French customs and passport control gave a glance at the offered passport and climbing kit in the car, then waved them through. Sharing the driving they made good time, only stopping for fuel, coffee and some food.

They arrived in Arolla where the tarmac road stopped at the small village situated at the head of the Val d'Herrens. At almost two thousand metres, it was a mecca for rock climbers and alpinists during the short summer season so Bomber knew they would blend in with all the other mountaineers.

They pulled into the small parking area just as the sun was dropping below the soaring mountain peaks and casting an alpine glow over the panorama of rock and snow.

They stood for a moment admiring the view, before setting off for the post office. They followed the direction on the wooden sign posts which pointed into the collection of alpine buildings, most of which looked the same with carved wooden exteriors and pretty flower boxes at each window.

The post office was closed but sitting outside it was an attractive woman, sun tanned and athletic looking, aged about thirty something. Bomber guessed this must be Sal.

As they approached, she stood and smiled, the sort of smile that immediately put you at ease. "Hello, you two! You've made good time," she said as she held out a hand to shake and offered a cheek to kiss.

"How do you know we are who you think we are?" Sandy asked, kissing her cheek a little too enthusiastically, thought Bomber.

"Well, this shy one here," she said, touching Bomber's arm, "I recognise from two or three summers ago. You were climbing with the Army Mountaineering Association as I recall. I was given a very good description of you both by fax anyway."

"So you were told to look out for one very handsome feller and one shy one!" Sandy reeled off.

Sal laughed and said, "No, a cheeky bugger and a serious one! Now I've booked you into the pension above the restaurant there," she said, pointing to the building below the post office. Bomber thought it had more flowers decorating the outside walls than could be found in a florist's shop.

She led them into the building, said a few words to the boy behind the desk who handed her a key and led the way upstairs. The room was large with furniture that look like it could have been made by the same carpenter as had done the rustic woodwork on the outside of the building.

Sal closed the window and sat on one of the twin beds.

"I'm sorry I couldn't get you a room each but everything is booked solid at this time of year. I had to get Jean Luc to cancel two people at the last minute to get you this."

Bomber would have been happy to have stayed in one of the two small campsites but he was guessing the target was in this pension.

"Your man is on the floor above, he's in room 210 and his guards are in 211. They spend most of the time either drinking in the bar or taking walks up to the glacier and back. He wants to go up to the huts but the other two are against it. I'm not surprised by that as they look unfit but he is tall and lean. According to Jean Luc, they argue a lot and a couple of times it almost came to blows in the bar."

"Thanks, that's very interesting," replied Bomber. "Do you know where they are now?"

"Jean Luc's son, that was him at the desk, said they were asleep in their rooms but they had booked a table for dinner at seven. I've taken the liberty of booking you both a table at the same time."

"Perfect," Sandy shot back, "I could eat a cart horse between two bread vans right now."

Bomber looked at his watch. They had forty-five minutes before dinner. Enough time to get all the kit in from the car and have a shower. Normally, Bomber would have spent time on a recce of the village but he could still remember the layout and the pathways that led to the different huts in the mountains.

"Thank you, Sal, that's been very helpful. We'd better get a move on and sort our kit out."

Sal stood up. Bomber couldn't help admiring her figure and wavy brown hair. He guessed he was staring as she laughed and blushed slightly, giving her tan a youthful glow.

"Okay, if you need me, I'm at the post office. We have a flat above so just ring the bell if the office is closed. Oh and I've told Jean Luc that you will pay cash in advance for the room and food just in case you have to leave in a hurry."

With that she left the room, leaving a faint smell of scent in her wake.

"Stone the crows!" Sandy said, laughing. "Now that's what I call a really glamorous contact."

Bomber agreed, saying, "You're right there. I'll get the kit in from the car. You take a walk around the place and familiarise yourself with the paths in and out. The gravel road by the river goes for a couple more miles and finishes at the glacier."

By the time Sandy returned, Bomber had carried all the kit to the room and paid the boy at the desk for a stay of six days. Then he showered before putting on jeans and a sports shirt ready for dinner, just as Sandy came into the room.

"No time for a shower, Sandy. It's time we went down for dinner and sussed out our people."

"Well if you can stand the smell, so can I," Sandy replied cheerfully.

The dining room had the same wooden, carved furniture as the rest of the place with red and white checked tablecloths. The boy from the desk directed them to a table in the corner. Bomber could feel the eyes of the target and his minders following them as they entered the dining room. They were sitting at a table near the door which led to the bar.

He had brought the map and the Alpine guidebook with him and made a show of spreading the map out on the table while Sandy gave the boy their order for drinks and food.

Sandy pored over the map and muttered to Bomber, "They don't look a happy trio and I'm sure the fat one has a black eye."

Bomber glanced at the target's table where the three of them were in some sort of hushed argument. A bottle of whisky stood on the table and each of them had a large beer stein at hand. The whisky bottle was half empty and Bomber could see they were all flushed from the drink.

Opening the guide book, Bomber pointed to a triangle shaped mountain face and said to Sandy, "This is the one I want to have a go at. Looked at last time I was here but no one in the group would partner me."

"Looks interesting but hard, judging by the Alpine grade. Let me read the description." Sandy took the book and studied the route of the climb. He was so engrossed, he didn't even glance up when the boy plonked two large beers on the table and said in good English that their food would be served in ten more minutes.

Being careful not to make it obvious, Bomber watched the trio. The drink was taking over and their voices were getting louder. The dining room was filling up and he noticed that everyone avoided the tables closest to the trio.

"Bloody hell, this is some route; it's only had about a dozen ascents since it was first climbed in nineteen thirty-eight and that took thirty hours!" Sandy exclaimed.

"Yes but they didn't have front point crampons and modern ice axes so they would have been cutting steps. We've got the gear, fitness and the knowledge that the route's been done before. Although I only know of two British ascents so far," replied Bomber.

"I like this bit," Sandy chirped. "A big competitive climb, probably the most important in the Western Pennine Alps. A must for any budding north face hard man. That must be us two!" Sandy said, smiling as he banged the guide book down on the table. The boy arrived with a large tray and Bomber swept the map from the table.

The steak, fried potatoes and side salad were quickly consumed as were the two beers but before they could order any more beers, a shadow fell over the table. Bomber looked up. Doherty was standing before them. Swaying slightly, he pointed to the spare chair and asked in an apologetic voice if he could join them.

"Sure," replied Bomber, pushing the chair out with his foot, while glancing at the two minders still sitting at the other table and noting that they were both staring intently at him and Sandy.

Doherty looked at Bomber then Sandy, then leaned forward, his head lowered in a conspiratorial way. "I'm Doherty, Seamus to my friends. I've a little bet on with my two friends over there that you two are real mountaineers and will be going up to one of the huts in a day or two."

Bomber noticed the slur had left his speech and his eyes bored into them.

"Well, we like to think of ourselves as such, although working at the Outward Bound School in Wales we don't have a lot of spare time to get to the Alps." Bomber smiled as he paused, before continuing, "I'm David and this is Sandy."

"The lord above, I knew I was right. I said to those lazy lumps over there you weren't here to stroll around. I've been wanting to go up to one of the huts, cross a glacier and stare at the mountains close up. Not wander around a valley and drink my life away but they won't hear of it, insist I go with someone who knows the mountains."

"Have you thought of hiring a local Mountain Guide?" Bomber asked, knowing full well that at this time of year they would all be booked solid.

"Oh yes but there isn't one to be had anywhere in the valley until the end of August!" Doherty said waving his arms around to indicate the whole valley.

"Well, we are going up to the Dix hut the day after tomorrow. We don't mind if you want to tag along, then the next day you could walk back down as you will know the way," said Bomber.

"Hang on a second, Dave! How do we know Seamus is up to a hike like that?" Sandy butted in.

"Well, we said we would take it real slow and steady on the walk to the hut and conserve our strength for the climb," answered Bomber.

"True," said Sandy who then turned to Doherty and asked, "What hiking have you done since you've been here?"

"Up to the glacier a couple of times and several tracks up to the moraine to get some real uphill work in."

"Sounds like you've been putting in some sound work. Okay, I don't mind you joining us. What about you, Sandy?" Bomber had pushed his foot hard against Sandy's under the table.

Sandy pursed his lips and looked thoughtful. "Yes, okay then," and he smiled.

Doherty stared at Bomber, then a thin smile creased his face as he nodded his head. "That would be wonderful if you really don't mind. I'm going crazy hanging around the valley with those two."

"Okay, we have to sort out our kit and take a walk tomorrow to iron out the kinks from our drive here. I'll leave a message at the desk to let you know what time we intend to leave the following day," Bomber said, offering his hand.

"Great!" Doherty said rising from his chair and shook the offered hand. "Can't wait to tell those two," he said jerking his head at the two stooges.

He turned to go then spun back looking at Bomber. "What Outward Bound School did you say you worked for in Wales?"

Bomber held the gaze. "I didn't but it's the Aberdovey one, lovely place. Have you been there?"

"Sadly no but I guess the work is most rewarding."

"Yes, it is and we both like it but it won't make us rich," laughed Bomber.

"Your reward will be in the next life, I'm sure," Doherty said, breaking his gaze and walking in a straight line back to his own table.

"Not as pissed as he would have us believe in the beginning," Sandy muttered.

"No and what's the betting one of them will be on the phone checking us out as soon as they leave the table," Bomber replied.

"So, what plan are you hatching in that head of yours?"

Chapter 27
The Devil Looks After His Own

"So, have you always been an outward-bound instructor?" The question was casually asked but Bomber could see Doherty's eyes were firmly fixed on Sandy's face.

They were sitting at the Pas de Chevres, the high point between Arolla and the Dix hut that was their objective for the day. The hike had taken some three hours of slow but steady walking up hill from Arolla. From this vantage point, they could look down onto the glacier that they had to cross to get to the hut.

"No," replied Sandy. "I was a plumber's mate in Manchester for a short while but it was as boring as hell, so I went to work for a scaffolding firm. Where I met this old man." Sandy nodded at Bomber who smiled. "He introduced me to mountaineering at weekends and that was it.

"I was hooked. Then one day we saw an advertisement in the paper, wanted instructors to work in a challenging and rewarding environment." Sandy spread his hands in the air as if conjuring up the words. "Apply to, well you get the idea. So we both applied, along with about a hundred others but we got offered the posts and that was, um, some three years ago. Never looked back. Can't say I want to do any other sort of work."

Bomber marvelled at how Sandy made it all sound so plausible without it being rehearsed.

"And you," Bomber asked Doherty, "What line are you in?"

Doherty looked into the distance as if trying to remember some long forgotten past life. "I'm a soldier for God." Doherty shifted his gaze to Bomber as if challenging him to deny his claim. Then he laughed and said, "I'm a priest but I'm not too sure if I still am. A little indiscretion and my Bishop has sent me to reflect on my past here in God's mountains," Doherty finished, lowering his head but then jerked it up as if realising he had said too much, glaring at Bomber and Sandy in turn.

Bomber ignored the glaring eyes. "Well, this is about the best place you could come to if you want to think. No hassle from people, the peace and majesty of the mountains. I find it the perfect place to find peace of mind."

Doherty replied cynically, "Hah, it's when I can get away from those two dummies who are supposed to help me come to terms with my life. They are useless as counsellors and even worse as walking companions. No guts you see to stand up against tyranny." For the first time, Bomber noticed the wildness and temper in Doherty's voice.

'And you think that blowing up men, women and children who have never done you any harm is standing up to tyranny!' thought Bomber.

"Well, I guess we need to get a move on if we are to get across the glacier before the sun warms up the snow bridges and makes them too soft to cross."

They descended the short iron ladder fixed to the rock that served as the easy way down from the Pas de Chevres to the glacier moraine. Bomber indicated to Sandy to slow up and Doherty started to pull ahead. He must have realised that he was getting ahead as he stopped and looked back at them. Both Sandy and Bomber had large packs with ropes and climbing gear while Doherty carried only a light day pack.

"I'll go on and get the beers in," he shouted, pointing to the hut standing proud, perched on its rocky outcrop on the other side of the glacier in the distance.

"Okay," Bomber shouted in reply. "Stay on the line of the footsteps."

The earlier traffic of climbers and walkers had beaten a path forming a shallow trench through the snow which lay on top of the ice and masked the crevasses of the glacier.

Bomber stood and watched silently, praying God or nature would dispense justice and send him to the bottom of a crevasse, thus relieving him of the task.

"Are you hoping what I'm thinking?" Sandy asked.

Bomber just nodded as he watched Doherty striding out over the glacier. "Come on. Let's follow."

Bomber could feel the snow getting softer with each step. Normally, he would have stopped to rope up but something made him reluctant to do so. Instead he told Sandy to drop back ten paces so that if he broke through the snow into a crevasse, Sandy wouldn't go with him.

"So much for that plan," Sandy said, just loud enough for Bomber to hear.

Bomber glanced up and could see Doherty had reached the rocks on which the hut stood.

'Maybe God is on his side,' chuckled the voice in his head. *'God doesn't take sides. He just watches and waits to see if good men are smarter than bad men,'* Bomber fired back.

'What makes you think you are a good man?' the voice snarled. *'You're just as bad as the rest of them!'*

Bomber stopped and looked firstly at his feet, then at the sky and felt a darkness close over him.

"You all right?" Sandy was shaking Bomber's arm.

"Yes, yes, just thinking," Bomber said, shaking his head to clear it.

"Okay but can we think after we've got off this fucking crevasse line. Another half hour and the snow won't hold our weight."

Once on the rocks of the outcrop, which served as the base for the Dix hut, Bomber told Sandy that they had to ensure Doherty didn't stay at the hut for more than an hour when the snow would then be at its softest from the sun's rays. After this, the sun would be dipping to the west behind the peaks and the glacier snow bridges would begin to harden as the temperature dropped.

At the hut, they found Doherty sitting at one of the outside tables on which stood three beers, the one in front of him already half empty.

"Come on. Beer's getting warm," he said laughing.

Bomber and Sandy dumped their rucksacks by the table and sat down. Bomber lifted the beer glass in salute, thinking he would rather have a jug of tea.

"That wasn't such a bad hike, I enjoyed that!" declared Doherty.

"Good," said Sandy, "but don't leave it too late going back. You don't want to be going down the track in the dark."

"Agreed but the warden told me to wait until the sun dips behind the peak over there. Then the snow bridges over the glacier will harden again. I've got a good torch if I run out of daylight."

'Shit, even the warden's on his side,' thought Bomber.

"I'm glad you enjoyed the hike but take it easy going back, you don't want to break a leg on that track. There's not going to be anyone coming back up this way until tomorrow morning and it will drop below freezing tonight," Bomber replied, wondering if plan B would fail the same way as plan A. He suspected it would.

Sandy was pointing out their intended route on the beautiful north face of Mont Blanc de Chelion that topped out at twelve thousand eight hundred feet which they would try if conditions were right the next day.

Bomber noticed an older Alpine guide, sitting at the next table with four clients, taking an interest in Sandy's explanation of the best route on the face.

"That's a very impressive looking mountain," Doherty replied, then leaned forward and lowered his voice. "You know, my colleagues had you marked down as something else last night but I told them you were real mountaineers and I guess this proves it," he said, waving his hand towards the steep north face.

"I think I have time for another beer before I set off." Doherty pushed his glass towards Sandy who took it and stood to go into the hut.

"Want another?" Sandy asked Bomber.

"Not for me but ask for a jug of tea, will you?"

Sandy nodded and went inside.

"So what did your colleagues think we were then?" Bomber asked, smiling. "Firemen or something?"

Doherty stared at Bomber, then a thin smile creased his face. "Oh no, they thought you were soldiers."

Bomber gave a choked guffaw on the last mouthful of his beer. "Jesus, that's the last thing I would ever want to be. All that marching up and down and people shouting at you. No thanks!"

Putting his empty glass down, he continued, "No, this is the life for me, out in the mountains or on the sea in a sailing boat. Trouble with the sailing boat is I do get a bit sea sick when it's rough." As he said it, he realised just how true those words were.

Doherty let out a laugh that almost sounded genuine.

"Bloody hell!" exclaimed Sandy, returning with two beers and a steaming jug with some tea bag strings and labels hanging over the edge. "The price of a beer here would keep me going for a month back home."

"Here," Doherty said and pushed a handful of notes onto the table. "Have it on the church. I'm on expenses."

"No, I've paid and you bought the last round," said Sandy.

"I insist; without you boys, I wouldn't be sitting here," Doherty replied.

The conversation waned as they watched the sun slowly dipping towards the peaks in the west and they felt the temperature dropping. Finally, Doherty stood up and picked up his day pack. "Better be on the way. Maybe I'll see you back in the valley once you have finished your climb."

"I'm sure you will," Bomber replied.

They both watched as he descended to the glacier but then their gaze was blocked by the guide who Bomber had noticed earlier. Standing next to him was the hut warden.

"I'm sorry to intrude," the guide said in guttural English, "But do I understand you intend to attempt the north face tomorrow?"

"Yes, I believe it's in good condition," said Bomber who watched as the two looked at each other. The warden then said something in a dialect of German which Bomber couldn't understand.

The guide nodded and looked at Bomber, saying, "The warden has just told me that two groups have tried it this season but didn't get very far. Are you sure you are up for the climb? The face is very unforgiving."

"Well, we think we are but we won't know for sure until we try it," answered Bomber.

The guide was nodding his head. "You are climbing the face left of centre, yes?"

"That's for sure to avoid the rocks that come from the right arête when the sun hits it," Sandy replied.

"Good, good, that is the way. Good luck then and start early," said the guide. He nodded to the warden who seemed to relax before going back inside the hut.

"Sorry, I didn't get your name," Bomber said, holding out his hand to the guide and introducing themselves.

"I'm Etienne, a very old guide," he said smiling and shaking their hands in turn.

"Etienne, wasn't it an Etienne who made the second ascent in fifty-one?" Sandy asked.

Etienne smiled and nodded his head once before saying, "I must return to my clients. Stay safe tomorrow."

Bomber turned his gaze back to the glacier and noticed that the far side and the short rock face that led to the Pas de Chevres was in deep shadow.

"Can you see him?" Bomber spoke quietly to Sandy.

"No, too much shadow now. So what's the plan now that A and probably B have failed?"

Bomber's head sank on his chest as he thought about the next move and was tempted to tell Sandy he had a plan C. Then he shivered as the last of the sun's rays disappeared behind a peak. "Let's go inside and get something to eat."

The voice in his head said, *'Smart move. You have to act this out to the end.'*

"I've had better Spag Bol," muttered Sandy. "However, it's filled the fuel tank. So what now?"

"The first thing is to maintain our cover, so tomorrow we climb and then back to the valley and hopefully, he will join us on a trip to another hut."

"Good, I'm really up for the climb. I've filled in the details in the hut log book and the warden is waking us at four with some hot water for tea."

Chapter 28
North Face and Death

They were in trouble. They had been on the face for three hours. Bomber was half hanging off two ice pitons hammered into the ice which was under the covering of hard snow. He was belaying Sandy who was fifty feet above with no protection between the two of them to arrest any fall.

That was when Bomber had spotted that Sandy's right crampon had come loose. As he had swung his right boot back to drive the front points of his crampon into the ice, it dangled free on the heel strap. At any moment, it could slide off his boot and plunge hundreds of feet to the glacier below. A lost crampon would be a nightmare.

"Stop Sandy! Your crampon's loose!" The shout echoed off the face of the glacier and Sandy seemed to freeze with his foot drawn back in mid-air.

He hung precariously off his two ice axe straps, the picks of which he had driven into the ice as he carefully refitted the crampon, knowing if he fell, he would go down a hundred feet before the rope came tight on Bomber, with all the force of the fall coming fully on the two flimsy ice pitons.

Bomber knew the pitons were unlikely to withstand the impact of a direct load and both of them could end up as a smear of red with broken bones on the glacier below.

He realised he had been holding his breath, when he suddenly gasped as Sandy successfully refitted the offending crampon and regained his front point stance on the ice.

"Onwards and upwards," Sandy shouted down and started climbing again.

'*Bloody hell!*' thought Bomber, '*that was a close shave.*'

They had left the hut some four and a half hours earlier. The young female assistant to the warden had given them extra water for their tea and seemed almost tearful when they set off across the glacier, as if she thought that would be the last time she would see them.

They were now at the half way point and he could see the sun just starting to appear on the north east ridge. He knew that once it warmed the rocks, being held there by the frozen snow, they would come loose and hurtle down, smashing anything in the way. Bomber wanted to be at least three more pitches up the face before that happened.

"On belay," Sandy's shout echoed off the glacier below.

Once Bomber was climbing up, he felt better, his crampon points biting into the hard snow and ice as he kicked his feet in. Then it was right axe pick in, then the left pick and move up. In less than a couple of minutes, he was next to Sandy who was grinning like a demented gargoyle.

"What's so funny?" asked Bomber.

"Your face when my crampon came loose. I could see you looking up and going blue in the face from holding your breath."

Bomber laughed. "I was holding my breath. Why I don't know. If you had come off, we would have both been goners."

Two pitches later, Bomber was back in the lead when he heard a whirring noise and a rock the size of a bucket flew past, twenty feet to his right. He was setting up a belay when they started coming down thicker and faster while getting closer.

"Shit! It's like being in a shooting gallery and we're the ducks," Sandy said with some force as he arrived at Bomber's stance.

"Once we are up the next pitch, we should be clear of the fall line. Then it's through the rock band and then on to the summit," Bomber countered, with more confidence than he really felt.

Two hours later, they were sitting on the summit enjoying a sandwich.

Suddenly, they were both laughing. "We did it, we did it!" Sandy exclaimed. (*see author's note)

"Too bloody right we did it. Great day, hairy and scary at times but a great climb." Bomber was elated, the problem of Doherty and Northern Ireland never having once intruded on his mind during the climb.

"All we have to do now is get down," said Sandy.

"Traverse the ridge and down the flank. Should be easy, just follow the tracks made by the climbers coming up the easy way. Then we cross the glacier and head back to the hut. Four hours or so should see us drinking tea."

'Four hours,' thought Bomber, *'that means we would have been on the go for fifteen hours and it will be dark soon.'*

Bomber could see a light in the window of the hut as they wearily crossed the glacier. He didn't want to admit how much the climb had drained him mentally. The legs were working fine but his brain had gone into neutral which was why he probably didn't see the crevasse fracture line in his head torch light.

One second his right leg was going forward expecting to feel hard snow, the next it was dangling in space over a narrow but deep crevasse. He felt the pain in his left leg as it stayed out behind him, his crampon biting into hard snow. His right hand holding his ice axe was out in front of him and the pick had dug into firm snow on the opposite lip of the crevasse.

Now he was suspended between the two edges of the crevasse which was less than a metre wide but like most crevasses, was shaped like an upside-down funnel getting wider as it plunged into the depths.

The light from his head torch shone upwards like a search light and then he felt the rope go very tight on his harness as Sandy, realising what had happened, walked backwards and belayed him.

"Can you get yourself out?" Sandy shouted.

"Give me a little slack in the rope and I'll see if I can crawl forward," replied Bomber, who felt the tension on the rope ease. As he swung his left arm over, he felt the pick of his ice hammer bite into solid ice.

Working his left foot free, the lower half of his body swung into the crevasse, his weight held solely by the two ice picks. Inch by inch, he managed to crawl free from the jaws of the ice-cold coffin, dragging himself forward using the axes until he could get some purchase with the crampons.

Once Sandy was safely across, they took stock. Bomber's left leg felt it had been stretched like a rubber band and his right shoulder hurt but apart from that there was no other damage.

An hour later, they were in the hut. Everyone except the young assistant warden had gone to bed. As they entered the hut, she hugged both of them, telling them she had prayed they would be safe and that she was sorry about their friend.

Bomber guessed she meant Doherty but without pressing her, he guessed she would say no more.

After serving them with several jugs of tea and some reheated Spag Bol, the girl went off to bed. Although they were both exhausted, sleep eluded them so they settled down to talk and doze.

"What do you think, plan B worked and he's at the bottom of a crevasse?" Sandy asked softly.

"I don't know and to be honest, I'm too bloody knackered to care," answered Bomber.

In his sleep, Bomber was dreaming of the climb but someone was attacking him and he couldn't respond.

He woke to find his attacker was Sandy who was shaking him by his shoulder. "Wake up, everyone is getting ready for breakfast."

People were shuffling around the hut half asleep and the warden was handing out steaming jugs of hot water for tea. Some of the people came and congratulated them on climbing the north face. One group of Americans also gave them some brand new karabiners and ice screws, claiming they had brought too many with them.

After all the people left the hut and the warden had finished his work, he came to their table with the girl. He looked down at the table top as if trying to decide whether to clean it or not. Bomber was slowly gaining his senses after two mugs of tea and some biscuits that Sandy had produced and was ready to get off back to Arolla but before he could move, the warden spoke.

In broken English, prompted by the girl when he struggled for an unfamiliar word, he said, "He's dead, your friend. The police want to talk to you."

'So the devil can't protect his own,' thought Bomber and looked at Sandy before saying, "How? What happened?"

"I know nothing else. The police radioed the hut in the evening. You must go to Arolla as the police want to talk to you."

Bomber nodded and said, "Yes, of course, we will go down at first light."

The warden left them and a minute later, they could hear him using the radio, probably informing the police that he had delivered their message.

They were less than thirty minutes from Arolla when they spotted the police and the screened off area further down the narrow track.

"Look up to your left," Sandy said to Bomber.

Spread out high up on the steep side of the mountain amongst the boulders and bushes, uniformed men were carefully searching. "I've seen them," Bomber replied.

As they arrived at the screened off area, they were halted by an armed police officer. Once he had ascertained who they were, they were escorted by another officer armed with a rifle fitted with telescopic sights to Arolla and the car park.

In the car park was a large truck with Polizei on the side in white letters. A set of steps led up into an open door at the back of the vehicle and they were told to wait. One of the officers ascended the steps and Bomber could hear him talking to someone inside.

The officer reappeared and waved Bomber and Sandy to go up. Inside the vehicle was a desk at which a man was sitting. Bomber judged him to be about forty something and dressed in an immaculate uniform. Behind him was a bank of radios at which another officer sat scribbling notes on a message pad.

The forty something stood, smiled and said in perfect English, "Please sit down," and indicated to the two camp chairs opposite him.

"I'm Inspector Bischoff, in charge of the investigation into the death of Herr Doherty."

Bomber watched as Bischoff produced his and Sandy's passports from the desk drawer and opened them. He knew they had left the passports in the pension safe before heading up to the Dix hut.

"I see from your passports that you are David Manners," Bischoff said, looking at Bomber, "and you are Samuel Brooks?"

"That's correct," Bomber replied. "Would you mind telling us what this is about and why we are here?"

The inspector ignored the question, which Bomber interpreted as not a good sign.

"Herr Doherty was found dead on the path that leads to the Dix hut, a short distance above Arolla. I understand that he accompanied you to the Dix hut the day before yesterday. Is that correct?"

"That is correct," Bomber replied. "He did not wish to go up to the hut on his own."

The inspector paused and made a show of looking at some notes. "He then came down the same day and you stayed at the hut. Is that also correct?"

"Yes," both replied to confirm it was so.

"You did not leave the hut at all for the rest of that day. Is that also correct?"

'*Bloody hell!*' thought Bomber. '*He knows all this from the warden so why is he trying to catch us out.*'

Sandy butted in and confirmed that they had not left the hut until the following day when they climbed the north face of Mont Blanc de Chelion.

"I understand that is a very demanding climb?"

"It's one of the best in this part of the Alps," Sandy said forcefully. "Now why are we being questioned?"

The inspector looked at Sandy, then at Bomber before speaking. "You should know serious accusations have been made against you by Herr Doherty's colleagues."

"What sort of accusations?" Bomber asked in a surprised tone.

"Firstly, you are not what you pretend to be and secondly, you are responsible for his death."

"That's ridiculous!" Sandy almost shouted the words.

"May I ask at what time he was killed and how?" Bomber said quietly.

"I am still waiting for an exact time but he was shot late afternoon or early evening."

'*Great,*' the voice in Bomber's head said, '*so much for making it look like an accident.*'

Bomber ignored the voice and said, "Let me guess. He was shot with an eight-millimetre round from a hunting rifle, just like the ones I've seen being carried around by the locals."

Inspector Bischoff stared at Bomber, then said "You seem to know a lot about weapons which would be in keeping with what you are suspected of being by Herr Doherty's colleagues."

"I know about the hunting here because the last time I was here, one of the hunters showed me his rifle. Can't remember the make but I do remember him saying that the standard bullets were eight millimetre."

Bischoff nodded. "Yes, that is normal and once I get the report, I am sure it will confirm that it is an eight-millimetre round that killed Herr Doherty."

Bomber interrupted, "If it was evening time, the light would have been failing when he was at that point on the track. Could it have been a tragic accident? He could have walked into the line of fire of some hunter." Bomber spread his hands to emphasis the point.

"Yes, that had occurred to me," Bischoff said with some sarcasm. "My officers are checking all the licensed hunters in the area. However, that does not explain why these accusations have been made against you. I am having your identity checked very carefully, gentlemen. Do not attempt to leave Arolla. I have your passports and," he produced a set of keys from the desk drawer, "your car keys. Now, for the moment you can go to the pension."

"Thank you," Bomber stood and turned to leave when the inspector said "When did you say you were here last, Herr Manners?"

'Shit,' thought Bomber, *'that was a mistake saying that, especially when he checks and can't find any one called David Manners.'*

"Two years ago but I was wild camping. Couldn't afford to stay in a pension or anything like that."

The inspector smiled and nodded, knowing there would not be any record of someone wild camping.

'But there would be at the huts if he decides to check back that far,' thought Bomber.

As they headed back to the pension, Sandy said, "I don't like any of this. Who the hell shot Doherty?"

"Maybe we were here just to draw him out but I think I know who to ask," Bomber replied.

'You lie too easily, old son,' the voice said.

Bomber went into the post office and looked at the postcards on display. Behind the counter was a tall, athletic looking man, probably late thirties who Bomber guessed was Sal's husband. Bomber laid the cards he had selected on the counter and asked for stamps for England.

"That will be six francs," the man said. Bomber handed over the money and as he did so, the man said, "Sal is at the back of the building with the dogs."

"Thanks," Bomber replied and made his way round the side of the building where he found Sal brushing a large dog that looked more like a bear. Another dog, which resembled a Border Collie but with longer legs and large shoulders, growled as Bomber approached.

"Beggar, here!" Sal commanded. Beggar stopped growling and went and sat beside Sal. "Okay Huggy that's all you are getting today." The large dog flopped on its side and without a pause started snoring.

"Beggar and Huggy, one alert and dangerous, the other lazy and sleepy," Bomber said without any humour in his voice.

"Oh, don't let Huggy fool you. He backs up Beggar all the way and he's like a tank once he gets moving."

Sal paused, studying Bomber for a second. "By the look on your face, you've spoken to the inspector."

"Yes, he said the two stooges are making accusations against us. The inspector is not a fool and will have us checked out. Now tell me, were we here just to get Doherty into the open for you to knock him off?"

To Bomber's surprise, Sal laughed. "No, we did as we were told which was to leave everything to you."

"We?" Bomber asked.

"I forgot to mention my husband, Kobi was a member of the Swiss Special Forces and did an exchange tour with the SAS. That's where I first met him but he had to leave the service after a bad parachuting accident."

"So tell me, do either of you own an eight-millimetre hunting rifle?"

"Yes, we do but they are both clean and I can assure you it wasn't us."

"Well, if not you or the two stooges, there must be another team here. I don't think it could have been an accident, do you?"

"No, not an accident and I've already sent a code message to the Brig updating him."

"Okay, I'm going back to the pension and as soon as the police give us the all clear, we will head back to England."

Sal nodded and gave a wave as Bomber walked to the pension, escorted by Beggar and Huggy who stopped at the front door and sat on the pension steps.

In the room, Bomber found Sandy sitting on the bed. He was holding his fingers to his lips and pointing at the ceiling light where Bomber could just make out a small hole that looked to have been freshly made. He knew that the room above was occupied by the two stooges.

Standing, Sandy said in a normal voice, "Room's been searched by the police apparently and the car. I've hung all the gear back up in the cupboard."

"Well, I don't know about you but I could do with a beer, so let's go to the bar," Bomber suggested, looking up at the hole.

"Lead the way, lead the way!" Sandy slapped Bomber on the shoulder as he spoke.

They took the beers outside and sat on the steps next to the two dogs. Huggy took a shine to Sandy and when Sandy put his beer down, Huggy upended the stein and lapped up the spillage.

"Fucking great, mugged by a woolly rug with legs!" exclaimed Sandy.

Once Bomber had stopped laughing, he briefed Sandy on the conversation with Sal before asking, "The hole next to the ceiling light, any ideas?"

"Old trick, just make a very small hole in the ceiling or the floor if you are in the room above, then place a funnel or better still a stethoscope to the hole and you can hear most things. It's cheap and no fancy gadgets required," Sandy muttered curses at Huggy as he tried to wrestle his now empty beer stein from the dog.

Having lost the fight, Sandy continued, "Any idea who the competition might be?"

"No," Bomber answered, getting up to go for refills.

Carefully guarding his new beer from Huggy, Sandy spoke quietly, "I do have a spare set of keys to the car if we need to leg it."

"No, we need to bluff this out," replied Bomber. "Trouble is, our inspector Bischoff is not a fool and in time, he will work everything out."

They had almost finished the second beer when Beggar started growling. Bomber looked up. Doherty's two stooges were approaching the steps to the pension. Now, Beggar was standing and Bomber could see that the fur along his spine was erect, signalling trouble.

"Steady Beggar, sit." Surprising Bomber, Beggar sat but looked as if he would spring into action at any hostile move.

Both men stopped some ten yards from them and stared at Bomber and Sandy. Fatso spoke, his Irish accent more pronounced than before. "We know who you are, you murdering English scum. You're from the army and we've told the police." It was then Fatso made the mistake of taking a step forward.

Before Bomber could stop him, the dog leaped forward down the steps snarling with his teeth bared. Huggy, his attention torn away from Sandy's beer, lumbered after Beggar causing Sandy to spill his drink.

A voice suddenly cut through the air, "Beggar, Huggy, heel!"

Beggar, an inch from sinking his teeth into Fatso's arm, swerved and raced to Sal who stood at the side of the pension.

Huggy, who had now reached terminal velocity for a hairy rug, tried the same swerve but failed to make it. Instead, he crashed sideways into both men, sending them sprawling onto their backs.

Sal ran to the men, apologising for the dog's behaviour.

"Bloody things need putting down. They are dangerous. I'll report them to the police," Fatso shouted to the small crowd that had now gathered to see what was going on.

"I wouldn't advise that and I want you out of my pension by tomorrow." It was Jean Luc, the owner of the pension, standing at the top of the steps by the pension door. "You have been nothing but trouble since you arrived and it's not just the dogs that don't like you, so you will leave."

Jean Luc was a big man, heavy set with bulldog features but it was Sal's husband, Kobi who intimidated the proceedings. He was a head taller than Jean Luc, broad in the shoulder and he moved like lightning, leaping down the steps and grabbing Fatso by his jacket and lifting him to his feet with ease. Bomber could hear the words spoken even though Kobi's face was only inches from Fatso's.

"Do anything to harm my dogs and I will beat the shit out of you!" With that he pushed Fatso backwards, causing him to stumble and fall flat onto his backside.

"I bet he learnt that well-known phrase when he was with the regiment," Bomber muttered to Sandy.

"Yep and I think he could beat the hell out of the pair of them with one hand," Sandy said quietly.

"What's going on here?" a voice demanded. It was the police officer who had escorted them earlier to the inspector.

The small group of onlookers edged closer, eager to see what would happen next. "These two," Jean Luc said, indicating the stooges with a wave of his arm, "I want them out of my pension now and they don't like it!"

"They can't leave Arolla until the inspector says so," the officer countered.

"They can stay in Arolla but not in my place. If that's a problem for the inspector, I don't care," Jean Luc was shouting and Kobi placed his hand on his shoulder to calm him.

"I will speak to the inspector but for now, they are to stay here where we can find them," said the officer.

Jean Luc didn't seem happy with that but Kobi took him off back into the pension, talking quietly to him.

Bomber saw Sal looking at him and indicating that he should come and talk to her but before he could move, the police officer called him and told him the inspector wanted to see both of them right away.

They followed the officer to the car park and the police incident truck. Sitting outside of the truck on a camp chair was the inspector, his head thrown back, eyes closed, enjoying the sunshine.

As they approached, he sat up, looked at them and smiled. Bomber couldn't help thinking it was the sort of smile a spider, if it could smile, might make when two flies flew into its web.

They stood in front of the inspector like naughty school boys. The smile had gone from his face now and as he stood, he simply said "Come," and led off, climbing the steps into the incident truck.

"Please sit," he said, indicating the same two camp chairs they had used before, while he made himself comfortable in his swivel chair behind the desk.

The silence that followed was meant to make them uncomfortable and it was working. Finally, Bischoff spoke. His voice was neutral and unhurried. "My enquiries through our police intelligence unit regarding both of you is, how shall I say, a little vague. However, as your alibis make it impossible for either of you to have shot Herr Doherty, I have no option but to let you go." Bomber noticed that Bischoff clenched his hands on the table as if letting them both go was painful to him. "Letting you leave doesn't mean I have dismissed the possibility that you had an accomplice who might have done the shooting."

Bomber interrupted, "I assure you, inspector, we had nothing to do with Doherty's death."

Bischoff's demeanour changed as he sat forward in his chair, glaring at both of them in turn. "I am fully aware of Herr Doherty's relationship with the terrorist organisation in Ireland and I am not happy that you bring your squalid little war to my country."

His voice had now risen and Bomber could imagine how criminals would cringe under his verbal assault. Bomber braced himself so as not to be intimidated. He glanced at Sandy who seemed to be totally relaxed in his chair.

Bischoff continued in a clipped voice, "You will leave Switzerland within the next twenty-four hours or I will have you arrested and deported. That is all. You may go!"

"Thank you, inspector," Bomber replied as he stood but the inspector was already looking down and writing in a buff coloured folder. Without looking up the inspector gave a wave of his hand, dismissing them.

Sandy was driving and Bomber sat silently in the passenger seat, watching the mountains rising above the valley floor and wishing he could stay and just wander among the peaks and glaciers.

After about an hour, Sandy spoke, "So, who do you think did it or is there something you forgot to tell me?"

Bomber sighed before answering. "Well, a number of possibilities have passed through my mind. At first, I thought it could have been Sal or Kobi, then I dismissed that after Sal assured me they had nothing to do with it. Then I had the thought it could be that the Brig had sent a second team to do it once we had flushed out Doherty but I've binned that idea."

"There's also the outside chance that the two stooges did it, then tried to shift the blame to us. Somehow, I don't see the church sanctioning that but PIRA would. Lastly, it could have been the UVF (Ulster Volunteer Force) or one of the other splinter groups. They have the knowhow and the weapons. So take your pick!"

"Fucking hell mate, that's the most you have spoken since we started this job!" Sandy exclaimed "So, who's your money on?"

"My thinking is that he was an embarrassment to the church and the PIRA, so that's my first choice followed by UVF."

"Not us? The Brits, I mean," asked Sandy.

"Unlikely, the Brig was very firm that it shouldn't become an international incident."

"Well that's literally been shot to hell. Guess we will not be flavour of the month when we get back."

"I asked Sal to send a report in whatever secure system she had. Apparently, she sends a fax in jargon to her mother who forwards it on. It appears the Brig's world is larger than we think and more devious than the strands in a spider's web."

It was twenty-four hours later when Bomber was sitting in a small, windowless room in RAF Brize Norton with the Brig, Bill and Major Carson. Sandy remained silent next to Bomber while he gave the detailed report of events to the Brig, including his thoughts on who could have been responsible.

As he did, he watched the Brig's face for any sign that indicated he had touched a nerve but he might just as well have been looking at a poster for all the reaction he got."

Bill, on the other hand had a smile that grew bigger, the longer Bomber went on.

After Bomber had finished, the Brig waited as if processing all the information in his head, then finally he took a Polo mint out of the packet that lay on the table and popped it into his mouth.

"Very interesting, David. Anything to add, Sandy?" the Brig asked casually.

Sandy shook his head and said, "No sir."

The Brig then summed up. "It is clear a third party had a hand in Doherty's death. Absolutely nothing to do with us, of course and you both handled the situation perfectly. So that's another tick in the box of things getting done, regardless of how it was achieved. So it's back to normal duties for you both. There's a flight back to Gibraltar tomorrow, David. A seat has been booked for you. Enjoy Kenya and thank you both for your efforts."

The Brig shook hands with both of them as they left and Bomber thought he gave him a hint of a smile but he could have been just crunching a Polo mint.

Outside the room, Bill ushered them to the mess where the barman was just opening up. "Right you two, I'm buying. What are you drinking?"

Once they had a beer each, Bill sat smiling at them. "Come on then," he demanded, "how did you do it?"

"What do you mean?" Sandy asked, looking at Bill over his beer glass.

Bill looked at Bomber. "You crafty buggers, sticking to the story but I know you Bomber, you never leave a job unfinished and that little package I had to have delivered to that lad of yours, was that part of it?"

"For fuck's sake Bill, we never did it!" Sandy hissed at Bill.

"Did the Brig say it was us?" Bomber asked quietly, not looking at Bill when he spoke.

"Oh, you know him, he only tells you what he thinks you need to know."

"Maybe it was divine intervention, nothing to do with us," Bomber said as he took a gulp of his beer but it tasted sour in his mouth.

Bill stared at Bomber for a second, then he spoke, "You mean an angel with a gun?"

Bomber and Sandy both nodded.

"Well, I guess I'm not meant to know." Bill downed the rest of his beer, plonking the mug on the table. The grin was reappearing on his face as if to say, *'You are not fooling me.'*

Bomber looked out of the RAF Britannia's small window where he could see the narrow passage that was the Straits of Gibraltar with numerous ships either leaving or entering through the Straits. It was easy to see why Gibraltar was key to the security of the Mediterranean.

Towering over the ships passing through its gateway, the massive rock appeared as the guardian between the two great bodies of water. Perched high on the rock were its big naval guns that could fire clean across the Straits, if the need arose, adding to the impression of a fortress.

As the plane continued to bank, ready to land, he looked at the still form of Zika, sleeping peacefully in the next seat, and reflected on how special a man had to be in order to be a good sniper, an ace in the hole. Devil or angel, who cared!

Author's Note

The North Face of Mont Blanc de Chelion was climbed by the author and Sandy Sanderson in the summer of 1978.